W9-AZK-561

The Busy Body

The Busy Body

Kemper Donovan

JOHN SCOGNAMIGLIO BOOKS
KENSINGTON BOOKS
www.kensingtonbooks.com

In memory of Catherine Brobeck, my partner in crime.

JOHN SCOGNAMIGLIO BOOKS are published by

Kensington Publishing Corp.
119 West 40th Street
New York, NY 10018

All Kensington titles, imprints and distributed lines are available at special quantity discounts for bulk purchases for sales promotion, premiums, fund-raising, educational or institutional use.

Special book excerpts or customized printings can also be created to fit specific needs. For details, write or phone the office of the Kensington Special Sales Manager: Kensington Publishing Corp., 119 West 40th Street, New York, NY, 10018. Attn. Special Sales Department. Phone: 1-800-221-2647.

Library of Congress Control Number: 2023944262

ISBN: 978-1-4967-4453-1
First Kensington Hardcover Edition: February 2024

ISBN:978-1-4967-5219-2
First Kensington Trade Edition: February 2024

ISBN: 978-1-4967-4459-3 (e-book)

10 9 8 7 6 5 4 3 2 1

Printed in the United States of America

Part One
The Client

CHAPTER 1

I tell other people's stories for a living.

You can call me a ghostwriter, though usually I just say I "freelance," which is vague and boring enough to put an end to strangers' polite inquiries. Among friends I call myself a "lady Cyrano," which is meant to be self-deprecating. (I have an unusually large nose.)

That's a lie, actually. Not about my unusually large nose, but about my supposed friends. I have lots of acquaintances, and colleagues, and associates—an assortment of people who pepper my existence so that if you saw me from the outside, you'd think my life was perfectly full. There are times it seems full even to me. But the truth is I don't have any friends. Not the kind I always pictured having: friends so close, they're family.

Oh—I don't have a family, either. We decided years ago it would be best if we stopped talking. I'm not telling you this to make you feel sorry for me. I'm telling you because I want—I *have*—to be honest. It's the only way this is going to work.

Ghostwriting is not about honesty. It's about strategy. A good ghostwriter will manipulate a story for purposes of maximum engagement. And I am a very good ghostwriter. My specialty is memoir. I tell the inspirational life stories of outrageously successful people: actors, athletes, politicians. Assholes, in other words (though I guess that's just one word). I make the assholes likeable *and* interesting. Like a sculptor, I carve out something beautiful from the rough-hewn block of their existence, and then polish it till it sparkles. You may think of me as a professional bullshit artist, but I love what I do. Ghostwriting has been around since there were stories to tell. I've always been a snoop where other people are concerned, and I discovered in my late twenties I have a knack for spinning tales about them, and for making these tales sing.

But I refuse to strategize or manipulate here. This isn't about some celebrity overcoming the odds, and there's no need for me to sell you anything. Because somehow, I managed to get myself wrapped up in an honest-to-goodness murder mystery. And for once?

The story's all mine.

CHAPTER 2

It started with a phone call.

This wasn't the way things usually started. My agent, Rhonda, almost always e-mails me, knowing I prefer to keep my interactions limited to the written sphere whenever possible. (If I could send her handwritten notes on creamy stationery sealed with wax, I would, though at this point e-mail is pretty much the equivalent of a feather quill and ink pot, anyway.) If a phone call were absolutely necessary, she'd schedule it ahead of time. And yet here she was, calling me unannounced.

One of the few happy outcomes of the so-called Digital Revolution is that no one is expected to answer their phone anymore. So I stared at her name on my screen, allowing the vibrations to run up my arm while noting how smudged the glass was—almost greasy. Apparently I needed to wash my face more. I was still waiting for a voice mail when her text came through.

Call me back ASAP.

Uh-oh. The cortisol began chugging its way through my midsection like Drano through that U-shaped pipe in one of those animated commercials. But then, because she knows me so well, Rhonda sent a follow-up.

Good news, not bad.

Her assistant patched me through immediately.

"Well, well, well," she began. I could hear a whipping sound, which meant she was doing squats or lunges or something equally horrifying behind her standing desk. Rhonda is one of those overachievers who doesn't know when to quit. "Look who the cat dragged in."

"Why is it that I'm being forced to hear the sound of your voice right now?" Rhonda likes to spar—probably because it burns more calories than regular talking. "You know how I hate that."

She laughed—a throaty, rasping sound that would make you think she smoked if you didn't know she ran several marathons a year. Rhonda's laugh is what sealed the deal when she was courting me as a client. I've always maintained you can tell a lot about people by the way they laugh. Someone should create a dating app where all you have to do is upload an audio feed of yourself laughing, none of this "I like to take long walks on the beach" crap.

"Apparently that winning personality of yours has been doing you favors about town," she said.

"Which town? *This* town?"

I was in D.C. at the moment, finishing up a heartwarming bildungsroman à la *Mr. Smith Goes to Washington*. My client was a senator who wanted to be president someday—a family man who'd made no fewer than three passes at me during our time together. I'd managed not to stab or shiv or otherwise maim him, so I suppose my personality *had* been rather winning.

"In a way. Not that you need to stay in D.C. for this one, I know you're crushed."

I've never much liked D.C., a city provincial enough to be subsumed by a single preoccupation—much like its soul sister on the opposite coast, L.A. It was my great misfortune that so many of my projects tended to take me to either "metropolis," and yes, those are air quotes I'm using. My heart will always remain in New York City, along with my permanent address.

"Where to this time?"

"North," she said.

"North?"

"Way north."

"Is it *Santa*?" I asked breathlessly.

"The thing is"—she was getting out of breath herself—"we need to move fast."

"Who is this person?" I asked.

"Are you sitting down?"

"What do you think?"

I was in fact *lying* down in a king-size bed at the Four Seasons, with three fluffy pillows behind my back. I moved my laptop from off my bare thighs, where the battery heat was beginning to burn them. Often I get a good hour or two of work done this way, while still in bed. Hey, it worked for Edith Wharton. Why not me?

The whipping noise stopped, which meant Rhonda had gone stationary—her version of a drumroll.

"It's Dorothy Gibson."

If my life were a movie trailer, this is where the needle would have scratched the record.

Dorothy. Freaking. Gibson.

Her middle name is Chase, of course, not Freaking. Actually, Chase is her maiden name. But you already knew that.

This was a big get, a far cry from the first memoir I worked on—practically for free—about the CEO of a golf ball manufacturing company who overcame a number of addictions. (Title: *Whole, in One*. I tried to talk him out of it. I really did.)

"Hello? Did you just have a stroke?"

When I spoke, my voice echoed because I was already in the bathroom turning on the shower.

"Tell me everything."

Rhonda let loose another of her fantastic laughs.

CHAPTER 3

Three hours later, I was in the air, doing my best not to brain the teenager YouTubing his little heart out next to me, sans headphones. I was headed to Maine, scheduled in the afternoon for what Rhonda liked to call "the official sniffing of the butts." Since writing a memoir is such a personal endeavor, most clients like to feel out their collaborator before committing. It goes both ways, of course, and I'd gotten to the point in my career where I had no problem walking away when my gut advised me to abandon ship. You know how sometimes when you go on a first date and you see the person across the room, and you just *know* before you even reach the table that it's not going to work? I'd had similar experiences with clients, though I had no intention of feeling this way about Dorothy Gibson. As Rhonda put it:

"Her butt will smell like roses. And you better make sure yours does too."

"I am not throwing away my shot," I promised her.

Dorothy's people had offered to fly me on a private jet, but I declined. While I'd like to pretend this had everything to do with the environment, mainly it was due to my fear of irony. A private plane is two hundred times more likely to crash than a commercial one, and if that's the way I'm going to go, I'd like my fiery death to be an unmitigated tragedy rather than one of those situations where people say I had it coming to me, you know?

A book sat open in my lap: a bestselling novel everyone seemed to love except me, which is often how these things go. Usually I'd be doing some light research on my potential client—enough so that I didn't embarrass myself, not so much that I'd begin forming any major biases. But in this case there was no research necessary, no hope of avoiding preconceived notions. Better to be upfront about whatever bias I was bringing to the project, I decided, and review what I knew about Dorothy Gibson—or at least, what I thought I knew.

She'd been famous for so long, her fame came in phases. There was Early Dorothy, the modest homemaker from Small Town, USA (technically Skowhegan, Maine), who married her high school sweetheart, the handsome and charismatic Edward Gibson. With great reluctance, Dorothy allowed him to drag her and their newborn son to Washington in 1981, where Edward became the youngest member of the 97th Congress, not so much a rising as a shooting star—which made his death a few months into his second term all the more shocking. The official cause was—and still is—a heart attack, but there were whispers about a drug overdose, and the suggestion that good ol' Eddie Gibson wasn't as squeaky clean as his image led people to believe. Whether or not his wife was one of those believers was a question pondered behind many a closed door (this was pre-Internet, remember), but Dorothy never said a word against him. She finished out his term, a latter-day instance of the political tradition of "widow's succession" or "widow's mandate," in which a surviving wife is used as a placeholder while the party machine lands on a suitable (ahem, male) replacement to run in the next election. (I jotted down "Widow's Succession" as a possible title in the Notes app on my phone.)

There's an iconic photo of her from this time—you've seen

it, trust me—where she's squatting on the front steps of the Capitol in a billowy black blouse and high-waisted slacks, feeding her toddler son orange slices out of a brown paper sack. Everyone loved her back then, as hard as that is to imagine now. She wasn't a threat, wasn't really part of the game. But then like many of the widows who refused to leave once they got a foothold, Dorothy flourished in Washington, despite—or as she would argue for the rest of her career, because of—her initial distaste for it. She served several of her own terms in the House before pivoting to the Senate, where she built a reputation as a centrist willing to cross the aisle to get the job done. For my money, Early Dorothy lasted all the way through her Congressional years, from the eighties into the nineties and the first half of the aughts. Middle Dorothy came into her own when she was tapped to run as vice president with the war veteran John Murphy, a man who badly needed the bump in publicity a female veep brought him. Her credentials were impeccable, but the scrutiny of her appearance was both nasty and nonstop: whole articles were written about the cost of her designer outfits, the time spent styling her hair. Some even took issue with her reading glasses, which were made in South Korea rather than the U.S. All in all, it was a disastrous campaign that ended in a walloping at the polls. Plus, she'd been forced to relinquish her post as senator. But this turned out to be a blessing; it freed up her time for frequent television appearances as a talking head, and speaking engagements for which she charged a hefty fee. For the first time in her life, she began to make money—a *lot* of it. Dorothy Gibson became a fixture in the political firmament, an elder stateswoman whose opinion on pretty much everything was solicited regularly.

And then, about two years ago, she officially entered her Late Period, becoming even more famous (or do I mean notorious?) by drawing on her personal fortune and running for president. As an Independent, mind you. If anyone was going to pull this off, it was Dorothy; she had always been hard to pin down on any issue, and there were countless votes in the Senate in which she was the only member of her party to join the other side. And, of course, she nearly *did* pull it off, garnering a third of the popular vote in one of the most fractured and bruising elections in history. As I sat there on the plane, the election had taken place just three weeks earlier and the country was still reeling from the shock. Dorothy's participation had thrown the usual two-party proceedings into chaos, and one of the few things everyone seemed to be able to agree on while the smoke cleared was that she was at least partially responsible for the unlikely election of . . . well, you-know-who.

My loathing of politics had kept me from regarding Dorothy Gibson with either the adulation or the aversion she inspired in so many. But there was no question she had a story to tell, especially at this point in time. After her concession speech, she'd fled back to Maine, holing herself up in the mansion she'd bought a few years earlier. Up till now the only books she'd published were policy oriented and dry. Talk of a memoir had started circulating in the book world almost immediately. People were angry at her, but they also wanted to hear from her. She'd tried to be the bridge between two warring sides, and that bridge had collapsed. Spectacularly. Now we all wanted to gawk at the destruction, and who better to gawk alongside than the one at the center of it all?

We're all rubberneckers at heart, as much as we'd like to pretend otherwise.

Chapter 4

The flight from D.C. took less than two hours. The sky was perfectly clear, which was a shame because I like flying above a thick cloud cover and feeling smug about the sunshine I wouldn't be enjoying if I were still on the face of the earth. But it meant I got a bird's-eye view of the greater Portland area as we made our descent.

The inky waters off the coastline looked cold and forbidding, as no doubt they were. It was late November, after all. The land was thick with trees, and if it had been a few weeks earlier, there's no question I'd have been blown away by the fall foliage. Except for a healthy smattering of evergreens, the trees were all naked now, their bare branches blending into a dusty gray that led unbroken to the edges of man-made clearings and small bodies of water—black lakes that looked like Swiss cheese holes from up here, rivers flashing at me like dental floss made of metal.

Dorothy's house was in Sacobago, an upscale suburb of Portland. (That's Sock-o-BAGE-oh, with a hard *g*, emphasis on the third syllable. Wouldn't want you mispronouncing our setting the whole way through like I would have—mispronunciation being a common hazard among avid readers as opposed to avid talkers. I still haven't gotten over the fact that "vague" is one syllable and "chaos" is two.) There were some Mainers who grumbled that she'd betrayed her roots by settling in the south, having been raised in the rustic north. Technically, her hometown of Skowhegan was in the middle of the state, but there was no denying it was culturally closer to the north than tony Sacobago. The north/south divide was a whole thing in Maine, as I'd learned earlier via some furious googling.

We landed and deplaned without incident. I wheeled my suitcase through the passenger terminal of the Portland International Jetport, which was definitely protesting too much with that "International." I actually love small airports; they're a throwback to a time when flying was streamlined and exciting, not the soulless logistical nightmare it is today. This one had a lot of character: the ceiling was made of exposed wood stained a rich, honeyed brown. I felt like I was in a massive log cabin, which was as good a start to a stint in Maine as any I could imagine.

I suppose I could pretend it was *such* a drag having to hurry from one gig to another like this with no time in between. But the truth is I prefer working to not. I also love taking public transportation—love killing time in public spaces, love everything about traveling because it affords me the opportunity of observing others, but never at the expense of having to interact with them. Sometimes I think if there's a Heaven, it looks exactly like an airport terminal: a vast room in which everyone gets to exist "together alone," always on the brink of something new, forever luxuriating in a blissful state of anticipation. . . .

I put on the flimsy windbreaker I'd shed on the plane. Even inside the terminal, it was noticeably colder here than in D.C. I'd been told someone would be waiting for me, and I scanned the small crowd gathered near the baggage claim, disappointed that none of them was holding a piece of paper with my name on it, because I always get a kick out of that. Figuring someone would approach me sooner or later, I began hunting for a coffee shop, which was when I caught sight of a woman I recognized.

It wasn't Dorothy Gibson. Pfft, you think Dorothy Gibson fetches ghostwriters from airports? I knew this woman by sight because Dorothy Gibson was so famous, even her personal aide had become a news fixture by then.

Leila Mansour had a sophisticated appeal that was a product of style rather than beauty. I've always preferred this brand of attractiveness, which relies on qualities acquired rather than inherited: an accomplishment, as opposed to an accident of nature. This meant I could apply any tricks I picked up from such people to myself (#dontstopbelievin). I watched as Leila clip-clopped her way toward me in tan calf-length boots—the focal point of her otherwise low-key, black ensemble. She seemed to be wearing no makeup other than a pop of bright red lipstick, though I suspected she was simply good at applying makeup. Her parents had emigrated from Egypt, and though she'd been born and raised in New Jersey, her first language was Arabic—a fact that hadn't gone unobserved by fringe conspiracy theorists who once objected to her security clearance, claiming baselessly she had ties to terrorist organizations. She did not. What she did have was long, silky hair that was truly black. She wore it loose, flowing over one shoulder.

I was surprised Leila and not some underling had come for me, because even though she was an aide, she was more of a policy wonk, a "right-hand man" factotum as opposed to a proper assistant. I was reasonably sure that if Dorothy had won the election, Leila Mansour would have had a senior advisory role in the administration. But now here she was on airport pickup duty.

She was also carrying two coffees to go. These cups were so

gigantic, they looked more like thermoses. Or fire extinguishers. She stopped in front of me, grinning as if we were old friends reuniting at last.

"I promise I was five minutes early, but then I decided we could both probably use one of these."

I was struck by the brightness of her pointy teeth, and realized I'd never seen her open her mouth before. At press conferences she played the "good wife" role, standing silently by Dorothy's side. If she ever needed to tell her boss anything, she'd lean in and whisper it in her ear.

"Please don't feel like you have to drink it. I know afternoon coffee isn't for everyone. I could easily have both of these."

I assured her I was all about the p.m. caffeine, relieving her of one of the cookie jars. When I took a sip, I was pleased to note it was exactly the way I liked it—a tablespoon-size dollop of cream (yes, I've measured it), no sugar.

"How did you know how I take my coffee?" I asked, playing up the wonder in my voice. I was no stranger to the extraordinary—sometimes alarming—lengths the assistants of famous people will go to make a good impression. But I didn't want to seem ungrateful.

"I have my ways," she replied, wiggling her shapely eyebrows. (I'd learn later she simply texted Senator Handsy's assistant.) She eyed my jacket. "You have anything heavier than that?"

I shook my head. "I came here straight from D.C."

She sucked in through her teeth. "We'll have to remedy that. Motto up here isn't so much 'Winter is coming' as 'Winter never left.' But then I'm a total wimp when it comes to the cold. Let's walk fast, I'm not parked far."

I hurried after her, forcing myself not to react when the coffee slopped out of the little hole in the lid and scalded the side of my index finger.

* * *

Leila drove a nice yet nondescript sedan: a Honda Accord, or maybe a Toyota Corolla, something like that. I wouldn't know because I take pride in not caring about cars. She set her coffee on the roof, fishing for her keys with long fingers that tapered like candlesticks.

"So how's she doing?" I asked.

She looked up at me. "You mean, is she in her sweats binging TV shows between walks in the woods?"

"Something like that."

I'd of course seen the famous photo of Dorothy Gibson in the woods near her house, posing with an adorable dad hiking with his adorable baby. Like everyone, I'd wondered what she'd been up to in those first few days after the election, when most people would have curled into a ball and cowered under the covers.

"Nah, she's already back at it." Leila held up her keys, pressing a button. The car chirped back at us. "That's why you're here."

CHAPTER 5

I made a point of sitting in the front passenger seat. There are some professional drivers (especially older, male ones) who interpret this as a belittlement of their livelihood and take offense. But Leila wasn't a professional driver, and she was making a big show of being friendly. Whether the friendliness was real or not didn't matter; it was in my best interests to reciprocate.

"Just so you know"—she turned to me, one hand slung over the steering wheel—"I'm the one who recommended you for this job. I'm a *big* fan. I *love* what you did with Daisy's story. So powerful."

I thanked her profusely, which is the only way I can think to get out of these situations without ducking my head or otherwise acting like an insecure teenager. Daisy Lester was a fifty-something actress whose memoir of extraordinary personal and professional struggle had come out two years earlier. It hadn't been a massive bestseller or anything, but it had gotten noticed in the right circles, and I'd been working steadily ever since. I'd had no idea while I was writing it what a boon it would be to my career, but then that's often the way of these things. It definitely boosted my profile. As Rhonda put it: "You're in the big leagues now, slugger."

"So feel free to ask me anything you want." Leila lifted her paper-towel roll of coffee from the well between us, taking a generous swig. "It's in both our interests for this interview to go well."

I appreciated her directness. It's rarer than you'd think.

"What should I call her?"

"Dorothy is fine. No need to be formal, she knows that's what everyone calls her. On a good day."

"Am I right in thinking this is going to be much more of a personal book than anything she's written before?"

"Yep, full-on memoir. No one would shut up during the campaign about how she's not open enough. So let's give the people what they want. Jerks."

"Are we talking exposé slash tell-all level? Dorothy lets us know what she *really* thinks about her two opponents, et cetera? Or more of a retrospective, lie-down-and-let-mommy-tell-you-what-it-was-like-when-she-was-younger sort of thing?"

She rotated her head toward me on her sylph-like neck, regarding me with an astonished expression. For a second I thought I'd gone too far, but then her red lips parted and to my relief, I saw she was smiling.

"Up to you. Between us I'd prefer it to be more of the former, but she'll almost definitely nudge it in the latter direction."

"Timeline?"

"Yesterday?" She tossed her head, flicking her hair from off her shoulder the way an animated pony might have. "That's pretty much the deadline for everything in Dorothyland. She's the hardest worker I know, and I'm including myself when I say that."

She let out a self-conscious laugh to let me know she didn't *actually* think that highly of herself (incontrovertible proof that she did).

"It's why we want you to live in the house, which I realize is an imposition."

It was one of my hard-and-fast rules never to embed with a client. There had been an unfortunate incident involving a record executive who clearly thought my acceptance of his invitation to stay in his home—along with his grown daughter, I might add—meant I wanted to have sex with him. After disabusing him of this notion, the deal fell through.

"It's fine," I assured her. Because rules are made to be broken (didn't you know?), and even if it wasn't fine, I could always renege later, whereas any reservations up front might sour relations from the get-go. "*More* than fine. I realize what an amazing opportunity this is."

One of the revelations of my adult life has been the discovery that more often than not, playing it "cool" or "hard to get" does you no favors. Most people want enthusiasm, and validation; they crave warmth, especially from a woman. And due to the systemic nature of the problem, this double standard is never truer than when another woman is the one doing the craving.

Playing it cool is for teenagers. I was more than happy to play it nice and balmy.

We exited the airport, taking a series of windy, two-lane highways that cut through the abundance of bare trees I'd seen from above. One of the roads had a river running beside it, affording a view of its grassy banks and the dense woodland bordering its far side. That's Maine for you: even the highways are scenic routes. The ground was shot through with the yellows, oranges, and reds that had fallen there—so recently, they hadn't dried up yet. They looked soft, and I would have loved to walk or even to lie on them.

I'd decided a long time ago I was a city mouse through and through. And yet, confronted with this sylvan landscape, I couldn't help feeling an animal exhilaration. The sky looked higher out here than it did through my hotel window in D.C.: bigger, and lighter, despite the clouds that were beginning to gather. I leaned back in my seat, breathing more deeply than I had in a long time.

We passed a yellow sign with what looked like the springing silhouette of one of Santa's reindeer on it.

"What's that?" I asked.

"The deer crossing?" said Leila incredulously. "Oh, you'll get used to them. They're everywhere here. As are the deer. Total nuisance. I wrecked a car of mine a few years back. Thing came out of nowhere. This poor state trooper had to shoot it in the head to put it out of its misery, it was awful. Basically I killed Bambi."

She took the curves much faster than I would have, or maybe I was feeling nervous after her charming anecdote. The clouds were taking over the sky now: flat and low with a grayish underbelly, nothing puffy or wispy about them. I realize any cloud type can appear in any season, but if there were such a thing as "winter clouds," these would be it.

"I'll take you through the town, it's the fastest way," said Leila. "Not that we have any plans to leave the house anytime soon. She's lying low for the foreseeable future."

"Of course," I replied.

I'm pretty sure Sacobago looked the same as it did in the '80s, or '50s, with its wide sidewalks and boutique-y storefronts—though the three yoga/Pilates studios I counted had to be recent additions, as did the "Mindfulness Retreat." It was the kind of town where white-collar professionals raised their families, and it had all the flourishes that came with a healthy tax base: top-rated public schools, a bustling farmers' market every Saturday, an independent movie theater that played all the latest artsy movies. We passed a number of respectably ramshackle Victorians before turning onto yet another windy road carved through the woodland. Leila slowed down a few minutes later, cranking the wheel to the right and by all appearances plunging into the forest. There was no sign marking the narrow road we turned onto, nothing other than a warning that read: PRIVATE—KEEP OUT. It was little more than a hiking trail, really, branching off about a half mile later into two paths—all very Robert Frost. We took the right one, which was barely wide enough for our vehicle, the trees' naked branches meeting like curved claws overhead.

The car slowed to a crawl as the tires began spitting dirt and pebbles. I wondered what happened if another car was coming in the opposite direction before guessing that Dorothy's security team coordinated such operations. I knew from years spent with Very Important People on their Very Important Compounds that the mark of a superior security system was its invisibility. For all I knew, a robot camera was trained on my face that very instant, scanning my left iris. It was when something out of the ordinary happened that the security measures revealed themselves: bollards rising out of the ground, long-range rifles at the ready, poisonous gases siphoned in from valves buried deep in the earth (not so much that last one, but a girl can dream). It's similar to how people say a hostess is like a duck, except in this case the duck is concealing razor blades and explosives in addition to paddling feet.

I think it would be impossible for any building that sits in the middle of the wilderness not to appear a little fairy tale-adjacent. Dorothy Gibson's house was no grandmother's cottage or oversize shoe, nor was it a witch's lair made of gingerbread. But it had the look and feel of an *oasis*: the kind of place where you could retreat while the world raged on outside its walls. It was a Dutch Colonial with two wings, each featuring a roof that came to a barn-like peak. The house was big (seven bedrooms, I'd learn) but without being grand—no columns, no balconies, not even much landscaping. Just a whole lot of windows amid white clapboard panels that were so discolored, especially closer to the ground, they were more brown than white. No fuss, but a healthy amount of muss.

I liked it immediately.

"Please don't think it's lost on any of us that it's a white house with an east and a west wing," remarked Leila before exiting the vehicle.

I got out, glancing upward. The sun had officially disappeared, along with most of the sky. *It's going to snow*, I realized with a thrill—which is one of the small ways I bely my Southwestern roots. Snow will always be exotic to a kid who grew up in the sunbaked suburbs of Phoenix.

And that is the last you'll hear about my childhood in these pages. I don't mean to be coy, it's just that my backstory bores me. Suffice to say, I wasn't the victim of anything—not of abuse, or trauma, or misfortune of any kind. My parents were white and comfortably middle-class. They were even in love with each other—still are, though I can't say for sure. It would take a miracle for me to speak to them again, and I do not believe in miracles. (I spit on miracles.) I had one older sister, who always let me play with her toys. She and my parents were perfectly nice, and I couldn't wait to be rid of them. I can't even fault them for not understanding me, because back then I didn't understand myself.

I do now, which is why I have the power to move on. To move forward with my story rather than backward, as I stand in front of Dorothy Gibson's house, on the precipice of the biggest break of my career.

Leila was waiting for me at the front door. I hurried toward her.

CHAPTER 6

You might think an interview with a prospective client would be an ordeal for a crabby and introverted writer such as I. But I don't mind interviews at all. They have a clear purpose, plus there's a script to them. Ninety-nine percent of the anxiety of social interactions is the uncertainty they engender: an uncertainty that's compounded each time you add another person to the mix, which is why parties are such a disaster. But a one-on-one chat for a clearly established business purpose? Doable.

Leila showed me into a room to the left of the rather gloomy front hall, promising it wouldn't be long. As she retreated, her boots rang out on the wooden slats of the charmingly uneven floor I suspected was well over a hundred years old. I sipped my coffee, taking stock of the space. It was definitely a traditional "morning room," what with its east-facing windows and antique writing desk. And what with my Victorian novel–addled brain, I couldn't help picturing the mistress of the house sitting at it with her topknot and braid loops, frilly cuffs brushing against the letters she wrote each day with a serene and steady hand, nary a cancelation party or TikTok meme among the responses she'd receive days, even weeks later. (Those were the days; who needs central heating or the ability to vote/own property, amirite?) The burgundy-colored sofa I was sitting on was a hard, unforgiving little affair, the upholstery tight as a sausage casing. But I sank into it anyway, giving my lower back a few minutes' reprieve. No question I'd be clenching once more, the moment my interview with Dorothy began.

It was a nice room, and even though I didn't know it yet, representative of Dorothy's taste. The focal point was the fireplace, with an original map of Maine from the early eighteenth century hanging over it. On either side of the hearth were built-in bookcases filled to bursting with a motley assortment of hardcovers and paperbacks arranged in no discernible order. But for me the key element was the lighting scheme, which relied not on overhead lighting but on a series of tableside lamps. (The lateness of the day combined with the cloud cover had made interior lighting necessary.) It was a warm, buttery light that went perfectly with the battered coffee table, the threadbare rug, the jolly blackened mess I spied inside the fireplace. After weeks of living in the sterile confines of a hotel, it was nice to be inside a place where people actually lived—i.e., a home.

I was just beginning to feel at ease when an unreasonably beautiful man entered the room.

He was too tall and too broad—in the same way you might judge a pastry to be "too sweet" while you're inhaling it. I don't mean to sound like some oversexed teenager, but it made me dizzy to look at him, and not just because I had to crane my neck so far upward. He was wearing blue jeans and a black T-shirt, and I found myself wondering why any man wore anything else. The jeans were ripped an inch or two above one knee, and I couldn't help focusing on the way his meaty quads bulged through the hole. (In my defense, said meaty quads were at my eye level.) A surprisingly dark thatch of hair covered the exposed skin—surprising, given he was a blond.

His face was so stupidly, stereotypically pretty I find it hard to describe even now—even after everything that's happened. It was an angular face, which would have been easily reproduced using stone or even metal. I suppose that's why the Greek gods were always depicted with such chiseled features; these features were literally chiseled, after all. His only curves were in the hollows of his cheeks and an indentation in his chin—a veritable chin butt à la Cary Grant or Tom Brady. In fact, he didn't look unlike that most irritatingly attractive of athletes, except that whereas Brady's eyelashes are trash, this man's were long and luxurious. Also, he had a much smaller, almost feminine mouth, which was a point in his favor as I saw no trace of the trademark Brady sneer.

Did I mention he was an infant? His skin was glowing—not with the ruddiness of exertion but with the satiny sheen of youth, a proof of fine craftsmanship that deserts our bodies by middle age. No question he was in his twenties, closer to twenty than thirty if I had to guess—which I *didn't*, but already had before he'd come to a stop on the rug in the middle of the room.

I figured he was one of Peter's friends. Peter Gibson is Dorothy's only child, of course, who caused such a stir when he came out all the way back in 2001. Or as the *New York Post* put it in one of their puntastic headlines: NOT JUST A SON BUT A FRIEND OF DOROTHY TOO! (Oh, 2001: you were so homophobic and you had no idea.) Practically overnight he became the gay version of JFK Jr., the most eligible bachelor in the country. The paparazzi loved snapping photos of him with his parade of gorgeous exes, and I could easily see this man gracing a glossy tabloid or two. He exuded good health, and it was obvious by the way his otherwise taut skin crinkled around that little mouth of his that he was used to smiling.

"Heya!"

He actually said this. I'm not exaggerating. *Heya.*

Good Lord.

"I'm Denny Peters, one of Senator Gibson's personal protection officers. Feel free to call me Officer Peters, even though I'm not a cop. Or, you could call me The Bodyguard if you want, which makes me sound pretty exciting. But you should know about ninety percent of my job is logistics. Denny works just fine."

This introduction had a practiced ring to it. I suspected it was what he said to everyone he met in an effort to disarm them—an effort I imagined was successful approximately 99.99% of the time. I resolved to be among the 0.01%.

It was stupid of me not to realize he was in security. We're conditioned to picture such people wearing suits and sunglasses, but they wear whatever helps them blend into their surroundings, and as I was about to find out, no one got all that dressed up in Dorothyland. I think it was the hair that threw me off; it was downright shaggy—the kind of luxurious, tawny mop you might see on a surfer or a musician. You just don't expect anyone in a law enforcement–adjacent job to have hair like that. But also? It was his attitude. He was just way too . . . *friendly*. More oversize puppy than Doberman.

I raised an eyebrow.

"Heya, Bodyguard."

The puppy barked at me: a single syllable, the way I imagine Spot or Fido does when you come home and he's just *so* excited to see you. I wouldn't know. I loathe dogs.

He opened his eyes wide, those ridiculous lashes framing them like daisy petals. Cows are usually depicted as having brown eyes, but these were the first blue ones that struck me in their immense and friendly aspect as bovine.

"Oh, so it's like that? All right, I can see I'm going to have to keep my eye on you. So this is a total pain, but I have to take a look through your bag, do a quick pat-down."

I know what you're thinking, but the pat-down was notable for nothing other than its efficiency.

The Bodyguard led me down a cool, dark hallway. (I did my best not to stare at his backside, but sometimes our best just isn't good enough.) We stopped at a closed door. He pointed his thumb at it sideways—the way people do when they say: *this guy!*

"Knock 'em dead."

"Thanks."

He moved aside. I turned my back on him, rapping the door with my knuckles.

A hand fell on my shoulder. What the hell?

"Sorry. Your tag is just—"

He was so close now, I could smell his sandalwood cologne mixed with the scent of fresh laundry. When he tucked in my tag, his fingers brushed against my skin and I shivered, silently willing the little hairs on the back of my neck to stand down. He gave my shoulder a pat.

"Now you're perfect."

Good God, did this really have to be happening now?

It came as a relief when someone yelled from the other side of the door: "It's open!"

CHAPTER 7

The light was blinding compared to the darkness of the hallway. There was a bay window with a built-in seat on the opposite side of the room, and the sky had taken on that harsh glow it often does sometimes when it's snowing—which it was by this point, steadily. I turned toward the inside of the room, squinting.

This was obviously the library. Built-in shelves lined every inch of available wall space, just as overstuffed as the shelves I'd seen before, making the room cozy in spite of its size. There were two bay windows, I saw now, each with their own cushioned bench, and for the briefest of moments I imagined Jane Eyre sitting in one of them and perusing a picture book about birds. . . . Opposite them was a fireplace big enough for me to fit into if I crouched a little, an ancient, pockmarked mirror hanging above its ornate mantel.

"We're down here."

I walked in the direction of the voice, past a grand piano with a lace tablecloth draped over it, a good foot of creamy fringe dripping toward the floor. There were at least two dozen photos propped up on the tablecloth, and I knew instinctively they were of world leaders and other celebrities (I focused on one at random; yep, that would be Malala). If I ever found myself alone in this room, there was no question I'd pore over each of these photos, one by one. But I wasn't alone, so I kept walking, past a leather armchair lined with brass studs and a mahogany magazine rack with the latest *New Yorker* peeking out of it, toward the fuzzy glow of two tasseled floor lamps on either side of an oversize couch.

The couch was the massive, pillowy kind with three tiers of cushions sewn into the back of it—a dull, brownish affair that belonged in a den or family room, or maybe a basement where teenagers could play video games on it in addition to doing God knows what else. It definitely didn't belong in a formal room like this, and I had to admire the spirit in which it had been placed here—for comfort, hence focus. Dorothy Gibson certainly looked comfortable enough, perched on the middle cushion with her legs drawn up under her.

I don't have to describe her to you, because you already know what Dorothy Gibson looks like. I always thought she was more attractive than people gave her credit for. She's got amazing cheekbones—more round than sharp, giving her that rosy, "apple-cheeked" look whenever she smiles wide, which she so often does. Her nose is handsome rather than pretty, with its wide bridge and protruding nostrils—the perfect staging ground for those South Korean eyeglasses she likes so much, and over which she's made many a cogent point while in session. Most people wish their eyes could sparkle as much as hers do, their sea-green color popping so easily on camera—and in person, as it turned out. Already her mouth was open in that trademark *I'm just so gosh-darn happy to see you!* way she had about her, which so often comes across as overcompensating, and can be so easily manipulated via editing to make her look like a crazy lady.

"Hi there!" she exclaimed, the phrase descending with a playful lilt I recognized immediately.

It was unmistakably her, and yet it was so *odd* seeing her here in this domestic setting—a little like seeing your elementary school teacher shopping in the supermarket. I was used to seeing Dorothy Gibson on a legislative panel or behind a lectern, maybe in one of those awkward, low-slung chairs people insist on using for staged interviews. She should have been wearing a brightly colored monochrome pantsuit. Her dark, short(ish) hair should have been moussed to perfection and at least two inches high. But here she was in black leggings and a white, long-sleeved shirt made of a stretchy material that hung loosely from her shoulders in a boatneck line, her hair plastered to her head via a series of bobby pins.

At Dorothy's feet sat Leila like the world's hippest handmaiden, her back against the couch's leg rest. "Take a seat," she said. "If you can find one."

She had a point. File folders were scattered here, there, and everywhere like throw pillows, loose papers in the spaces in between. I hadn't seen so many of those heavy-duty, black metal paper clips since I was little and used to hoard them, pretending they were butterflies. (This wasn't as sad as it sounds, I promise.) I found a few inches of free space and sat down gingerly, so as not to cause any debris to tumble my way.

"Well, Leila just thinks the world of you," began Dorothy. "And I can't tell you how excited I am to—"

"Yeah yeah yeah." Leila tossed aside her laptop, tucking a lock of silky hair behind her ear. "Plenty of time for that later. So what was it like getting frisked by that slab of gorgeous man out there?"

Dorothy put her head on a diagonal, opening her eyes wide and pressing her lips together.

"Leilaaaaaaa."

"Oh, please." She swatted the air in front of her. "You know you were thinking it too."

They were performing for my benefit. But they were also enjoying themselves. It was endearing—which was exactly how it was intended.

"I'm not normally this immature," explained Leila. "But cut me a break, he's a ten out of ten and it's only been a couple of days."

"Is he new here?" I inquired politely.

Leila nodded. "All of them are. We didn't have much security before the election."

"The good old days," said Dorothy dryly.

"And then we had the Secret Service." Leila's eyes darted in Dorothy's direction without getting all the way there. "Till a few weeks ago."

There was an awkward pause. Dorothy Gibson had of course enjoyed a Secret Service detail as a candidate for president. But that privilege had ended when she lost the election.

"Unfortunately, the death threats haven't stopped coming," continued Leila airily. "If anything, there are more of them. Hence the hottie bodyguard."

"Are we done being inappropriate?"

"Sorry, boss."

"Your apology is accepted." Dorothy turned to me. "Now! Let's talk about you."

CHAPTER 8

Surprise surprise, but I'm invoking my authorial privilege and skipping over the first part of our interview, during which I talked about myself, and Dorothy—wonder of wonders—listened.

Often when people find out I worked with Dorothy Gibson, they ask me what the "real" Dorothy is like compared to her public persona—what it was about her that surprised me the most. I have two answers to this, neither of which is juicy enough to satisfy the craving for dirt that invariably lies behind the question. But they're both true, so I may as well share them now.

The first, more superficial answer is that she's a lot shorter, and smaller, than you'd expect—practically petite. It's hard to gauge a person's physical stature when she's alone on a stage. Also, the confidence a politician is expected to project in front of a camera makes it easy to mistake her for being bigger than she is. Dorothy Gibson is neither an inch above 5' 3" nor a pound over 115—noticeably, though not freakishly, small. The second answer is that Dorothy Gibson is an *excellent* listener. This too is not something the public gets to see, though now that I know to look for it, I can't help noticing the way she concentrates whenever anyone asks her a question in an interview—how she nods along, interjecting every now and then with her trademark murmur, an "mm-hm" in which the "mm" is drawn out, pitched lower than the afterthought of a "hm."

MMMM-hm.

It was both a benediction and an encouragement, and often she'd do it two times in a row for good measure:

MMMM-hm, MMMM-hm.

She listened to me in this way for a good twenty minutes, while I gave her the quickie (and rather bowdlerized) version of my life story.

This was not the way such interviews normally went. I've had more than one client who never asked me a single question about myself. There were some I'm fairly certain never knew my name, placing me in the same category as the people who cooked their food and drove their cars, i.e., "the help." Which isn't to say I felt insulted by the comparison—what else is a ghostwriter if not a literary drudge? But these experiences gave me an appreciation for what it's like to be disregarded.

Spoiler alert, but it sucks.

Dorothy Gibson didn't disregard a thing. It soon became clear she hadn't just taken Leila's word as to my writerly abilities but had read practically every sentence I'd written. She didn't start reeling off quotes or anything, but the way she referred to minute aspects of the different memoirs I'd worked on—the connections she made so nimbly between them—I could tell she'd absorbed them all, and then sat back and thought about them.

In other words: girlfriend had done her homework. This was no surprise, as Dorothy Gibson has a reputation for being a workhorse. Plus, everyone who's successful is in fact a workhorse, even if they go out of their way to hide it (lookin' at you, Kim Kardashian). No one likes to talk about this too much because it's boring, and depressing, but working closely with such people has taught me that hard work is a necessary—though by no means sufficient—element of success. There are plenty of people who work their tails off and don't achieve their dreams, but among those who do, hard work is *always* a component. Often, I'll downplay this aspect of a client's story (see above re: boring and depressing), but in Dorothy's case, I'd already decided I was going to highlight it, hard work was such a core part of who she was. Even now, in the first half hour of meeting her, I could see the way it animated her, drove her: the love she felt not for whatever the end product happened to be, but for the process itself. It wasn't the work she loved; it was *doing* the work, and I felt a kinship with her because it's the exact same procedural fascination that keeps me going as a writer.

If this were a first date, I hadn't just gotten to the table and eaten dinner. I was lingering over dessert and coffee. But was I willing to spend the night?

"I'd love to move forward," she said after we'd been talking for well over an hour. "What do you say? Are you ready to make this official?"

"Do—I understand you'd like me to stay here?"

She nodded briskly. "I want this book to be different. I . . ." She hesitated, placing her hand in the space between us, and even though she wasn't anywhere close to touching me, it felt like an intimate gesture. "I don't open up all that easily." She looked at me, the flesh at the corners of her mouth wrinkling upward into those prominent cheekbones of hers, making her look like a mischievous chipmunk. "Shocking, right? Maybe if I did, I wouldn't have lost."

"Or maybe you wouldn't have done as well as you did," I replied. I'd meant this as a compliment. She'd almost won, after all. But I realized as soon as I said it how easily it could be interpreted as a dig—as though I were suggesting that the more people knew about her, the worse she would have performed.

She burst into laughter, and I almost jumped in my seat before catching myself. That cackle of hers is so infamous, it's been spoofed by multiple A-list comedians on *Saturday Night Live*. And yet it took me by surprise.

"You may be right!"

"I didn't mean—"

She waved me off. "I know what you meant. Look, I want you to tell my story, and I believe the only way you're going to be able to do that is if you stay here with me. For however long it takes. So what do you say?"

I looked over her shoulder—out the nearest bay window, onto the front of the house. The light was fading, and the snow had begun sticking to the grass on either side of the flagstone path, highlighting the unevenness of the ground. It's not like the snow influenced my decision in any practical way: Leila's car, or an Uber, could have easily navigated it. But I have an aversion to exposing myself to any form of precipitation, and this aversion lined up nicely with the decision I'd made hours earlier—when Rhonda first said the name "Dorothy Gibson."

I stuck out my hand.

Leila beamed at us from her seat on the floor, watching as we shook.

It was official.

I was living with Dorothy Gibson.

CHAPTER 9

A few hours later, I found myself sitting on the edge of a full-size bed with a log-cabin quilt thrown across it that I suspected may have been sewn by the real-life Laura Ingalls Wilder. On the nightstand was a vintage dish featuring the colonial ship *Susan Constant*, its sails unfurled on the open sea. (According to Google, the *Susan Constant* was one of the first ships to reach Jamestown, Virginia, in 1607, thereby out Mayflower'ing the *Mayflower*. The more you know.)

There was a small desk—so small I suspected it was a child's—pushed against the room's single, square-shaped window, outside of which the snowflakes were dancing. Opposite the bed was a small fireplace that had actually been lit by someone before I came up from dinner. Maybe Anna, the maid from *Downton Abbey*? Which would make me Lady Mary.

Who was I kidding? I was Lady Edith all the way.

I'd just gotten off a FaceTime with Rhonda, most of which was spent contemplating the original Andrew Wyeth above the fireplace. It featured a gauzy curtain billowing before an open window, one of his famous fields rippling off into the distance. By "contemplating," I of course mean "wondering how much it was worth." Rhonda, who owns a few pieces herself, guessed mid-six figures.

Dinner with Dorothy had been a simple affair: pasta, fresh vegetables, a sauvignon blanc so dry, it made my mouth twist when I first tasted it. Leila, who also had a room in the house, had gone out for the evening. I hadn't seen her since the interview in the afternoon, and I suspected this was on purpose so that Dorothy and I could bond. Mostly we talked about books and television. (We both loved *I Capture the Castle* and *The Good Wife*, which boded well for our partnership.) The older woman who served our food was named Trudy, and she was one of the smallest people I'd ever seen—several inches below five feet. Dorothy had stood behind her while introducing us, putting her hands on Trudy's nonexistent shoulders while saying, "Trudy is my everything, I'd be lost without her." (Trudy was probably the one who'd lit my fire.) For dessert I was served a nondisclosure agreement that stipulated I tell no one what I was doing until the book came out, and even then, only industry professionals. If I ever talked to the press, I'd have to give back every cent I earned on the project.

I knew Rhonda would be annoyed with me for signing this without showing it to her, but I did so anyway as a gesture of good will. Annoying Rhonda was a bonus. These NDAs are meant to function as deterrents and are almost never enforced. (Or at least that's what I keep telling myself as I write these very words. . . .) Not quite twelve hours had passed since that phone call in my hotel room in D.C. And now I was shacking up with Dorothy Freaking Gibson. My stomach curled in on itself like the delicate flower it is. This was craziness. Insanity. But for once, in a good way.

And maybe the best thing about it was that I could pretend to myself, sitting there on the edge of my bed, that there were lots of people I would have called to share my news, if only I were allowed to do so.

Wow, talk about a sad sack. I don't want you to get the wrong idea about my friendless, singleton state here, so I'll go ahead and say the thing you're not supposed to say. I'm *proud* of my refusal to partake of mediocre brunches with mediocre friends, or to settle for a partner who's less than perfect for me. My high standards are proof not only of my self-worth, but of the fact that despite appearances, I haven't given up yet.

Not by a long shot.

Part Two
The Victim

Chapter 10

I'm an early bird by nature, but my career as a writer has reinforced this tendency to the point where more often than not, I wake up when it's still dark out. This might sound miserable, but the fact is there are fewer distractions at that time of day (or is it night?)—both in the greater world and inside my head. It's as if I wake up empty, but in the best sense of the word: not depleted, but fresh, full of potential. Available, if that makes sense, whereas by nighttime I'm full of the thousand little indignities that befall us each day. I mean, the Internet alone is enough to ruin me; I check my e-mail, poke around Twitter a little, and suddenly I've lost the ability to hold on to a thought for more than two seconds at a time. I can wrestle myself back into lucidity if I have to (a looming deadline helps), but there's nothing like those first few hours of the day.

I could see stars through the window as I leaned out of the bed, hauling my laptop up from the floor, where it had been charging all night. I brought it into my lap like a child who's had a nightmare and needs a cuddle. It wasn't snowing anymore, but I stopped myself from getting up and looking through the window, deciding a look outside would be my "treat" for a good hour's worth—maybe two?—of concentrated writing. Besides, the room was cold, and my bed was deliciously warm.

I'm nearsighted and can only see about three inches in front of my face without glasses, which is why I've gotten into the habit of lying down with at least one pillow under my head and my laptop resting on my chest—so close to my face, it's practically tucked under my chin. This puts my keyboard on a slight incline, and even though I have to stick out my elbows like chicken wings to position my hands correctly, I find the whole setup extremely comfortable.

I did a little journaling to start, which quickly turned into a brainstorming session as to the best approach for Dorothy's book. Already an idea was forming in my head about casting her story in the mold of the typical hero's journey, the whole Joseph Campbell shebang: the adventurer heeding the call to explore the unknown and returning from his ordeal a changed man. And I do mean "man," because this was unquestionably a masculine tradition. But what if I applied it to Dorothy's life? The "unknown" would be the world of politics itself, this man's world into which she'd journeyed—winning some, losing some, returning with scars, but perhaps some spoils too, slipping into the quieter existence she'd left behind decades earlier. . . .

By the time I looked up from my screen my forearms were aching and daylight had flooded the room. I slid the laptop to one side, threw off the covers, and rolled my wrists in circles while approaching the window. Even though I knew what to expect, I felt that little jolt of surprise that comes from seeing the world coated in white for the first time—an awe that diminishes with each successive snowfall of the season.

Judging by the accumulation on the ledge at the base of my window, we'd gotten a good five or six inches. My room looked out on the back of the house, where a large concrete patio had been cleared of furniture for the winter. Beyond that was a modest yard, and beyond that a great expanse of trees—

as far as I could see. These must have been the famous woods Dorothy Gibson liked to go walking in.

The cloudless sky was such a pale shade of blue, it looked like a watercolor painting in need of more pigment, the blue fading to white at the edges. It was still early enough that I was able to experience the trippy hush that falls over the world when it's been blanketed by snow. I threw up the lower sash to luxuriate in this silence more directly, the cold air prickling the skin up and down my arms.

Five minutes later, I slammed the window shut, retreating into the man-made warmth. I began gathering my things for a nice, hot, morning shower. Fingers crossed Dorothy had good water pressure.

The water pressure wasn't good; it was excellent.

My hair was still air-drying when I descended the main staircase, which was the kind that folded back on itself with a landing between the two halves. This landing had its own picture window looking onto the back of the house, and was roomy enough to hold two antique benches resembling church pews with a coffee table between them. On one of these benches sat the Bodyguard, absorbed in a book.

He was wearing khakis today and a short-sleeved, collared shirt made out of a shimmery, synthetic material that was pearl gray in color. His sleeves were so tight on his arms they looked like they might leave a mark, and his nipples were poking through the shirt's front panel. Except for the tan construction boots he was resting (rather rudely) on the coffee table, he looked like a golfer who moonlighted as a bodybuilder. Or vice versa.

I froze, staring at him, but not for the reason you think. (Okay, not *only* for the reason you think.) The book he was reading was *my* book. And not one of my memoirs, either.

I neglected to mention this because it isn't important, but once upon a time I published a book under my own name. It was at the very beginning of my career, and it was a novel. It was also a colossal failure. I can't even look at this stupid book without cringing, and I do mean that literally because it's what I did now as I stood there on the stairs, looking down on him.

"You caught me." He'd been holding the book in one hand, and he raised it now as though it were a dumbbell and he was performing a bicep curl. The cover stared back at me, on which the title—which I will *not* be sharing with you—was arranged in the shape of a heart. (Kill me now.)

"What are you doing?"

"What's it look like I'm doing?"

He grinned at me, which involved all sorts of crinkling and dimpling, his whole face getting in on the action. Today, however, I found his pulchritude oppressive. It wasn't even eight o'clock—much too early to enjoy the stomach-churning pull of sexual attraction. I required several ounces of both caffeine and protein before I could begin to process such emotions.

"Where did you get that?" I asked—demanded, if I'm being honest.

"Saw it lying around." He shrugged. "Figured I'd take a peek."

Dorothy must have read it, then. She hadn't mentioned it in our chat.

"It's really good," he said.

"It's really not."

I watched as he unfolded the slipcover's back flap and used it as a bookmark. He looked up at me and then back down at my author photo, which was nearly fifteen years old. He looked up again.

"Almost didn't recognize you."

"Yeah, well. I'm a lot older now."

"Nah, I meant without your glasses."

I'd worn contacts for the photo, worried my black glasses would come across as clichéd, or trying too hard to look like a serious writer even though I wear them all the time. Esmé—one of my favorite editors to work with, she always makes me laugh—calls them my "smart glasses."

"You don't like them?" I asked coolly, resettling the frames on my nose.

"Oh, no, I think you're beautiful either way."

I laughed before I could stop myself—not a girlish giggle, but a disbelieving snort. Was he for real?

He raised his eyebrows, wrinkling his smooth, lovely forehead.

"Is that so funny? That I think you're beautiful?"

It *was* funny, actually—not to mention inappropriate. But I wasn't about to be drawn into a conversation about my personal appearance with a man who'd be a regular presence in my place of work. No matter how attractive he was.

"You're sweet," I said, the fact that I was standing many steps above him making it easy to adopt a condescending tone. "And I'm starving. Know where I can get some grub?"

He held up his hands in surrender (even though one of them was still holding my book). "Kitchen's downstairs to the left."

He pointed, showcasing a sizable wet stain underneath his arm. I wondered if this was due to our interaction, and felt a pang of pity for him, which is not something I often feel for men—especially beautiful ones.

"I'm on break a while longer, so I'm gonna head outside now, stick my face in the snow and use it to muffle my screams of humiliation."

"Don't worry about it," I said, hoping this came across as generous rather than dismissive. I trotted down the few steps that were left, crossing the landing to the lower half of the staircase. "We can just pretend it never happened, if you want."

"I don't want that at all," he said, forcibly establishing eye contact in that way men do when they're making it clear they're interested.

His eyes were gray, I realized, not blue as I'd thought they were the day before.

I nodded—at what I have no idea—and hurried away before either of us could say anything else.

CHAPTER 11

I found the kitchen by way of Dorothy's distinctive cackle, which rang out in response to the deeper tones of someone I didn't recognize. At the end of a short hallway, just past a grandfather clock I stopped to admire, was a sitting room with French windows leading to the back patio I'd seen from above. A woman stood alone in the room. She had a ponytail that came to a point between her shoulder blades, and I guessed from her posture and the wire running behind her ear that she was a colleague of the Bodyguard's. When I nodded at her, she nodded back, but without smiling.

I was no stranger to the presence of security. I'd once worked on a series of personal essays about disordered eating with a teenage pop star who had no fewer than eight bodyguards covering her at any time. In my experience there was an invisible yet unmistakable layer of reserve that separated these people from their employers—and from anyone, like me, in their employers' orbit—no matter how friendly you were. For them it was a working relationship, which was why the Bodyguard's behavior was so unusual. Was he just an inappropriate sort of person? Or maybe it was because he was so young? (Just how young *was* he, anyway?) Or—this was the silliest question of all—did he simply find me *that* irresistible?

Fortunately, I was prevented from pursuing this perilous line of inquiry by the appearance of a figure in the doorway to my right.

"There you are! We were about to send out a search party. This is an early-bird household, I hope you know."

Peter Gibson, the most eligible gay bachelor in all the land, puckered his lips at me before taking a swig of coffee from a giant mug.

Peter was not handsome like his father. He had a fleshy nose, and his eyes were too close together. But he *did* have his father's charisma, and his mother's intelligence, and there were rumors he was gearing up for a political run of his own. His co-operation would be crucial to the success of the book, and I knew I had to match wits—or at least audacity—with him now, or else run the risk of losing his respect.

"Oh, I've been up for hours," I replied, sailing past him.

The kitchen was surprisingly small, but then it often is in old houses. I saw an antiquated gas stove and a more modern, chrome-faced refrigerator. Against the back wall in a built-in nook sat Dorothy and Leila. I nodded at them, finding the coffeemaker easily and plucking an empty mug from the cluster of hooks above it. I poured myself a hefty cup while looking at Peter.

"Some early birds don't feel the need to gorge on worms immediately, you know?"

I took a sip for effect, though I hadn't gotten a chance to add my tablespoon of cream yet.

"You'll do nicely." He turned to Leila. "Well done, sis."

Leila shook her head at me in an ostensibly private moment of commiseration that was (obviously) meant to be witnessed by everyone.

"I call Lay sis cuz she's the daughter my mother *thought* she never had. Till I started being real with her," explained Peter.

He spoke with a twang, acquired from his childhood in Virginia—and not the northern part, which might as well still be Washington. After her husband's death, Dorothy had settled as far from D.C. as she could while still commuting there every day. The result was that this no-nonsense New Englander had raised a Southern boy. They were a funny mother/son pair. But somehow, they worked.

"Yup, I figured that one out for myself." I leaned my hip against the island in the center of the room, moving aside a newspaper so as not to crease it. "Thanks, though."

"Well, aren't *you* a sassy one!" he marveled. "I can see I'll have to be on my best behavior while you're around."

"I'm *very* glad to hear that," said Dorothy. "Did you sleep well?" she asked me.

I assured her I had.

"We usually fend for ourselves in the morning," she said. "So help yourself to anything you'd like."

"Junky cereal's in the cabinet behind you," Leila offered.

"My son has been entertaining us with dramatic readings from the paper," Dorothy explained as I retrieved a box of Cracklin' Oat Bran (though what I really wanted was the box of Cocoa Krispies next to it).

"Ragging on journalism's sort of a family tradition," said Peter, leaning over the paper and clearing his throat. "Okay! Police blotter time! This should be good, let's see. . . . Ooh, gotta drunk and disorderly in downtown on Friday night. The mean streets of Sacobago, keepin' it real, I like it. Oh wow, an as yet unidentified homeless man found dead, apparently of exposure. To the elements, that is. Wasn't a flasher. Though who knows? Coulda been." He tsked, clicking his tongue in quick succession. "Thought the Chamber of Commerce made sure all the bums got carted elsewhere. Or else incinerated 'em on the spot."

"Peter, stop," Dorothy admonished him.

"Ooh, apparently there's a local woman gone missing. Paula

Fitzgerald, forty-two. Swim instructor. And as *fit* as you'd imagine a swim instructor to be by the looks of her. Where'd you go, Paula, you naughty girl you? No one's seen hide nor hair of her for two days now."

"Join the club, Paula," remarked Dorothy.

I saw Peter and Leila exchange a look. They really did seem like siblings: a brother and sister checking in on mom's mental state, silently registering their concern. I got the feeling Peter had come over to boost his mother's spirits. He lived in New York, but popped up to Maine frequently—or so I'd read. They were said to be extremely close, and from what I could see, this was one thing the tabloids had gotten right.

Those two tidbits of mystery Peter had read out from the paper interested me more than I cared to admit, by the way. I'm a true crime junkie, though these days that's almost as basic as noting how good TV has gotten, or saying you can't stand the word *moist*. I'd been reading Ann Rule back in the '90s—decades before countless podcasts and Netflix documentaries took the genre mainstream. I made a mental note to look into both these mysteries on my own time.

Peter looked down at the paper again.

"Hmm, let's see. Someone's been making a whole bunch of prank calls to the mayor's office. I didn't think prank calls were a thing anymore, but okay, I can respect that. Gotta give the mayor something to do." He looked up at his mother. "It was more fun reading the Richmond rag, huh? I remember you'd be crying sometimes, you were laughing so hard."

"Yes, well, I think keeping the tears at bay is a good strategy for the time being."

Dorothy got up abruptly, dumping her plate in the sink with a crash.

"Otherwise there's a good chance I might never stop."

Chapter 12

We spent eight hours on the fluffy couch in the library. Lord, but that woman could work. Not that we weren't interrupted regularly: usually in short, apologetic bursts by Leila for what seemed to be important business, occasionally by Peter, who'd barge in with some inane (yet amusing) observation or request. And yet after each interruption Dorothy would dive back in without missing a beat. I have an arsenal of tricks I use with clients—little mental exercises to get them to concentrate, to calm down, to stop looking at their damn phone every two seconds. But I knew within the first hour of that first day I'd never have to use any of these tricks on Dorothy. That to do so would be an insult.

By four o'clock *I* was the one in danger of flagging. I'd been up for almost twelve hours by then, but she showed no signs of stopping, and I refused on principle to call it quits before she did. So it was with more than a little relief that I saw Peter saunter into the room, hands in his pockets.

"Howdy."

Dorothy didn't look up from her laptop. We had the same Google doc open, and I watched as the red cursor labeled "DCG" danced about the screen, zapping words into oblivion and spitting out replacements just as quickly.

"It's four o'clock," he announced.

"I always knew you'd learn to tell time one day," she said without looking up.

Peter sighed. "How the American public ever thought you were humorless is beyond me."

She jerked her head up and so did I, curious to see how she'd take this. Her eyes were dancing; I suspected Peter was one of the only people who could get away with saying things like this to her.

"Whatever do you want, child of mine?"

"Well, now that it's four o'clock, that means it's socially acceptable to start drinking. Or so my mother taught me, anyway."

"Wise woman. Why aren't you mixing yourself a drink then?"

"Because I don't want a mixed drink," he pouted. "I want a big ol' glass of red wine. Doesn't that sound nice? With all this snow? First proper red wine weather we've had all year."

I'd never heard the term "red wine weather" before, but I knew exactly what he meant. Apparently, Dorothy did too.

"Hmm." She stuck out her bottom lip. "That *does* sound pretty nice. Well, we must have a few bottles lying around."

"Nope. Aussies cleared us out, remember?"

"Oh, *God*, how could I forget?"

I made a note in a separate document to ask about these wine-guzzling Australians.

"Well then, why don't you go out and get some more?" she asked him patiently.

"Because you'll complain what I got is *trash* and then make me go out again, so I'd rather we just went together," he replied just as patiently. "Isn't it time you stopped working, anyway? I know this is a crazy idea, but maybe you could for once, y'know, not overdo it?"

Dorothy stared at him a long moment and then snapped her laptop shut.

"You're right. Let's go get some wine." She looked across at me. "Do you want to come?"

What I wanted was to retreat to my room and solve half a dozen *NY Times* crosswords on my phone while lying flat on my stomach. But it was part of my job to respond in kind to overtures like this—especially in the beginning, when we were still getting to know each other. I nodded brightly, running upstairs to fetch the flimsy windbreaker I knew would be no match for the North Atlantic cold.

Chapter 13

Betty's Liquor Mart was a run-down building I would have assumed was an old barn or an abandoned warehouse if it hadn't been for the sign, situated at the end of a country lane a few minutes' drive away. Since Dorothy went there regularly, the building had been vetted by her security detail already, which meant we had to wait only a few minutes while Officer Choi (the ponytailed woman) did a quick walk-through. She'd gone ahead in a separate vehicle, while another guard drove us in a black Lincoln Town Car. This man was older, with a grizzled crewcut more in line with my clichéd expectations of what a person who works in security should look like. His name was Officer Donnelly, and I sat with him up front rather than squeezing in the back with Dorothy and Peter. Neither of us said a word on the way over.

"We're clear," he announced suddenly. (I assumed that Officer Choi had spoken into his earpiece.)

"You mind going in without me?" asked Peter.

I turned in my seat; he was holding his phone up with an apologetic air.

"Got a business call I have to make."

Dorothy served him a generous helping of side eye before getting out of the car. Peter winked at me.

"Have fun."

I scrambled after her.

"What exactly does Peter do?" I asked her as we approached the building.

"Excellent question, you should ask him."

Dorothy opened the door: a gust of warm, humid air I found by no means unpleasant blew over us.

"If he gives you a straight answer, let me know. I'm curious myself."

From the inside, Betty's Liquor Mart reminded me of the stacks in my college library, or the cramped spaces to be found in some of my favorite used bookstores. It was a dark labyrinth of narrow aisles, the shelves towering over us and filled to bursting with alcohol. Booze was a downgrade from books, of course. But only a slight one.

After exchanging a nod with the lantern-jawed crone manning the register (Betty herself?), Dorothy led the way with confidence. The rows of shelves were organized by varietal, and I had to swallow a few times to keep the saliva from pooling as we wormed our way into the bowels of the store.

"How do you feel about Cabs?" asked Dorothy, pointing to a big CABERNET SAUVIGNON sign that dominated one part of the store.

It was impossible to know which answer she wanted, so I decided to be honest.

"I'm not a fan," I said. "I think they're a little boring."

She froze in place. "*Thank* you! If I have to listen to one more person go on and on about their favorite Napa Cab . . . *Been* there, *done* that, right?"

"Right!" I exclaimed.

We were in the Malbec zone, doing that head-tilted-to-one-side thing you do in the face of endless choices presented in a compact manner, when the sound of footsteps made us both turn.

The woman was holding one of those plastic carriers, its metal handle slipped over her forearm à la Dorothy's wicker contraption (the other Dorothy, that is, of Oz fame). She looked like she'd just been exercising, but then that's how everyone looks these days—in yoga pants and a tight-fitting hoodie (Lululemon by the looks of it, or something equally pricey). She was in that indeterminate zone of middle age that can extend into a person's fifties or even sixties with a good diet, regular exercise, and lots of sunscreen—especially if that person is rich enough to upgrade this holy trinity by way of a nutritionist, a personal trainer, and a plastic surgeon.

Her hair wasn't blond so much as "honeyed," a delicate hue that gave away nothing about its natural color. It was styled so perfectly in a layered pixie cut, I wondered if she'd come straight from the salon. In other words: she looked good, which in the dim and flickering fluorescent light of Betty's Liquor Mart was saying something. But she also looked like all the other thousands of wealthy white women who live in southern Maine, which is why I didn't look at her very closely—didn't bother to take in much more than a vague impression of a trim body and well-moisturized skin.

It wouldn't be long before I'd come to regret my failure of observation.

"Dorothy!"

The way she said it, I thought maybe they knew each other.

Dorothy tilted her head back, lowering her jaw and showing off the whites of her eyes. It was a gesture of delighted surprise I'd seen her make countless times before—at rallies, or while mingling with audience members after a debate. Now that I'd spent some time with her, I realized how exaggerated this expression was. She was overcompensating, the same way one does with a toothy smile when the cameraman says *cheese!* Because when you're an introvert and dialing it up whatsoever is a chore, it's hard not to go straight to an eleven.

"Hi there!" Dorothy boomed, her voice doing that downward lilt thing again.

"I can't believe you lost!" the woman cried. "I'm so heartbroken!" She grabbed a bottle from a nearby shelf, dropping it into her basket without looking.

"Thank you, that means a lot," said Dorothy. "I'm sorry I couldn't get it done for you."

"Oh, I don't blame *you*, I blame the idiot who won. I blame the people who'd actually *vote* for him!"

"What's your name?" asked Dorothy, rerouting the conversation with practiced ease.

"Ugh, how rude of me. Vivian Davis, it's so nice to finally meet you! We're neighbors, actually?"

"We are?"

"My husband and I have a house off Orchard Ridge, near the Baptist church?"

The upspeak was strong with this one. Dorothy's eyes lit up in recognition.

"But for the last few weeks we've been staying at the Crystal Palace?"

The Crystal Palace? This sounded as weird to me as it does to you, but Dorothy indicated by a series of nods that it made perfect sense to her.

"It's *so* beautiful, we just *love* it. Walter—that's my husband—needed a space that would inspire him? He's a doctor—well, he's really an *inventor*. He's in the final stages of this invention he's been working on? But I shouldn't say more than that."

She pressed her plump lips together, waiting to be begged to say more. Dorothy just waited politely for her to continue, which was when a cell phone started up, playing "Cheap Thrills" by Sia. The woman turned her head sideways, digging in a tiny shoulder purse that probably cost thousands of dollars. (Behind her, Officer Choi edged closer, ever so slightly.) I caught a glimpse of her screen as she lifted it to her ear; the person calling was "Bitch Sister," whose photo was a cat screeching in close-up.

Interesting.

"I can't talk right—What?" She paused. "Ugh, gimme a second, I'll be right there." She ended the call, looking up apologetically. "My sister. She's coming to stay with us tomorrow. Because we don't have enough guests already. Talk about a drama queen." She looked down, fiddling with her phone while she continued talking. "Anyway, I've actually been doing a little project of my own? It's stupid really, just a little fun." She held out her screen triumphantly. "I thought we could all use a laugh so I did a Kickstarter? You know, the crowdfunding thing?"

"Sure, sure," said Dorothy.

"For five bucks I'll send a video of me yelling at our future president on my TV screen to go—well, you know. Eff himself."

"Ah, I see," said Dorothy.

How long was this nightmare going to continue? Now the woman was reading off her screen.

"For *ten* bucks I'll slowly cut up one of those dumb signs of his with a pair of kitchen scissors. For a *hundred* I'll throw a glass of red wine at a cardboard cutout of him." She looked up, gesturing around her. "Figure I better stock up, right? Because it's kind of catching on? I mean, just friends, and friends of friends. And whatever I make I'll donate to charity, obviously."

"That's wonderful!" crowed Dorothy, "I'm glad to hear it."

Vivian held up her phone.

"Would you mind taking a picture with me?"

I expected her to say no, or at least to insist on going outside for a backdrop more neutral than a wall of liquor, but Dorothy didn't hesitate.

"I'd love to!"

She took the phone out of her hand, which was a trick I knew from previous clients: when a selfie is inevitable, take control of the situation by holding the phone yourself, which makes you seem warm and generous but secretly ensures you take just *one* photo, at the angle and distance *you* prefer, and that it happens with zero delay. She sidled up to the woman, placing her face next to hers without touching it, or any part of her body. She was as much of a pro at this as anyone I'd seen.

Click.

When she handed the phone back, Vivian grabbed on to her hand.

Officer Choi stepped forward, but Dorothy shook her head gently.

"He'll be gone by summer, right?" she said pleadingly. "That's what everyone's saying."

"Well, I don't know about *that*"—

"He will," she said. "He *has* to be."

Maybe it was because she'd moved a little closer, but I could feel the anxiety vibrating off her—could see it in the way her lower lip was trembling. . . .

"Well"—she cast a quick glance at me, which was the first and only time she exhibited any awareness of my existence—"I'm sorry to have bothered you, I just *had* to say hi."

"I'm so glad you did," said Dorothy.

She turned, disappearing around the corner. Dorothy rolled her eyes at me.

"We should probably get one of those baskets. So we can carry more."

CHAPTER 14

We worked steadily for the next three days—Wednesday, Thursday, and Friday. Each morning I'd wake up at four thirty or five and go over my notes from the day before. The sun rose at seven, and as soon as the darkness had loosened its hold on the sky, I'd bundle myself up and go out for an early-morning walk in the woods: a bracing constitutional à la Elizabeth Bennet, though it was so cold and forbidding out there, à la Fanny Robin was more like it. Fortunately, Dorothy had lent me one of her enormous coats—this fabulous tented number that went well past my knees, made of thick, kiwi-green wool in a raised zigzag pattern, pink and purple hyacinths embroidered on the lapels. It was every bit as hideous as it sounds, the sort of muumuu overcoat you could imagine another Dorothy, Dorothy Zbornak, wearing whenever she traveled north of Miami. But the ugliness was so audacious, so unapologetic, you couldn't help admiring it. Also, it was wonderfully warm. (On Wednesday, one of Leila's minions had taken my apartment key and flown to New York, packing a whole suitcase's worth of extra clothes for me over FaceTime. This included the black winter coat I'd been wearing for years. But I kept using Dorothy's anyway.)

After my outdoor exercise I'd shower, ladle some sugary cereal down my throat, and settle in for three hours of steady work, an endlessly refillable mug of coffee by my side. At noon, Trudy would serve us one of her plain yet delicious meals, and then we were back at it from one until five. There were no interruptions, Peter having gone back to New York on Wednesday morning and taken all the hubbub with him. Even those two little mysteries he'd ferreted out in the local paper had fizzled. The dead homeless man turned out to be a veteran who'd done a tour in Afghanistan. The paper had run a fairly devastating follow-up, detailing his downward trajectory over the last five years or so, ending in what appeared to be an accidental overdose. (His sister would be collecting his body and bringing it back to their Ohio hometown for a proper soldier's burial.) As for the missing woman, I learned via the Nextdoor app on my phone—a great tool for snooping—that she was very much around, and in the process of filing a temporary restraining order on her husband, having informed him (via text no less) that she was leaving him. Apparently he was a jerk, and everyone who had anything to say about the matter was glad she'd gotten out.

So we two were free to hunker down on either end of the fluffy brown couch—Dorothy tending to talk, while I tended to type.

Given the steely façade she presented to the world, I worried she'd be unwilling or, worse, unable to share with me in a meaningful way. But on Wednesday she cried twice, talking about her mother. What I came to realize was that Dorothy Gibson lacked that quality so many male politicians are celebrated for: the ability to connect with people en masse, to bring a personal touch to the public sphere. But how many of us women have that ability? Haven't we been conditioned across umpteen generations to keep the public and private spheres separate? Is it fair to condemn Dorothy Gibson for being "stiff" and "robotic" when the dangers lurking on the other end of the spectrum ("loose," "desperate," "easy") are ones that have been haunting women, oh, pretty much since the dawn of civilization?

Yeah, I don't totally buy this argument, either. It's not like "women" are a homogeneous mass. There are plenty of "cool girls" out there, especially in the political sphere—women who could out-slick the slickest of men. But there was enough in this theory to provide a decent through line for the first part of the book, which is often the hardest part to write in a memoir (and perhaps also in a mystery!).

In other words, we were making real progress, which was why I was annoyed when Leila clip-clopped her way into the room on Friday afternoon, holding out an iPad screen.

"Do you remember taking a picture with this woman?"

It was the photo from the liquor store. And even though I'd been there when it was taken, I was surprised by how Dorothy's busybody neighbor—what was her name again?—had managed to make her eyes pop and her lips contort into a surprised O at just the right moment, something vaguely pornographic about her expression. She'd obviously added a filter, too, which made her skin appear dewier than it was. Even the black wine bottles surrounding them looked brighter, sexier.

"Yes," said Dorothy without hesitating. "Vivian Davis. Lives on Orchard Ridge, but she's currently staying at the Crystal Palace. We met her at Betty's."

By this point I'd stopped marveling at her bear trap of a memory, since it had been on full display for several days.

"Oh." Leila retracted the iPad. "Okay then. Just wanted to make sure."

I realized there were probably as many fake or photoshopped images of Dorothy Gibson out in the world as real ones.

She sighed, looking up at Leila. "I suppose I could have said no, or forced us to go outside. But why bother? What, are people saying I'm an alcoholic? It wouldn't be the first time."

"No-o-o, the booze isn't the problem. I mean, people *have* been commenting on it, but it's not like I'd bother you about *that*."

"Then what *is* it you're bothering me about?" she snapped.

Leila and I glanced at each other. I raised my eyebrows in what I hoped came across as a commiserating gesture. Somehow, within five days, I'd become another sibling to confer with about mom.

"Oh, nothing big," said Leila airily. "Just that this woman is dead now."

She took a step back, surveying the wreckage from the bomb she'd just dropped.

Dorothy made her eyes big. "*Real*-ly?"

Leila nodded. "Suicide. Husband found her in the bathtub yesterday with an empty bottle of sleeping pills."

"Wow," I said.

"Yep." Dorothy nodded slowly. "Wow is right."

"It's getting picked up by a lot of the majors." Leila's index finger was doing a little jig across her tablet. "Apparently she had a Kickstarter?"

"She mentioned that," said Dorothy. "Seemed like a joke more than anything."

"Yeah, I see what you mean. . . ." Leila let out a snort. "Did you see what she'd do for a thousand dollars?"

"No, what?"

"Dress up as Wonder Woman and lasso herself to the fence outside the White House. But then there's an asterisk that says, 'or at the very least, the fence outside *my* house.' Cute." She scrolled a little more. "Their target goal is one *meeeellion* dollars, spelled with like eight *e*'s. I guess that's an *Austin Pow*—oh. Wow." She looked up. "Do you know how much this thing has raised?"

"Ten thousand?" I guessed, imagining it may have gotten some traction in the wake of Vivian's death.

"Try a *hundred* thousand. And counting. It's literally gone up by at least one or two thousand since I've been looking at it." Leila shook her head. "I hate the Internet." She stuck the tablet under her arm, where a diner waitress would have stowed a laminated menu. "I think we can just let it play out, then."

Dorothy nodded.

Leila walked to the doorway while I began scanning my notes to see where we'd left off.

"Does she have any children?" asked Dorothy.

Leila stopped. "No, I checked."

"Well, at least there's that."

Leila turned to go, but then she paused, setting her sights on me.

The trapdoor that nearly four decades of neuroses have carved into the bottom of my stomach flew open, incapacitating the lower half of my body with its acidic contents—like boiling oil poured over a hapless army. Yes, I realize this simile is a bit much, but what I'm trying to convey here is that I felt extremely anxious because I knew with the unerring instinct of an ex-teenage loser that Leila was about to taunt or tease me in some way.

"So I hear Hot Bodyguard has a thing for you."

"Oh for goodness' sake," said Dorothy.

And yet she was looking at me with interest. They both were.

"Where did you hear that?" I asked.

Leila shrugged. "Around. But you're not denying it, I see. Interesting."

"There's nothing to deny," I protested. And there wasn't. Ever since our interaction on the stairs, I'd gone out of my way to avoid the Bodyguard, icing him out whenever necessary—

which is a particular skill of mine. (Not to brag or anything, but let's just say the cold never bothered me anyway.)

"Okay, okay. Hey, don't mind me." Leila winked, making it that much easier to hate her. "I'm just being an asshole."

She made a triumphant exit, closing the door behind her.

The bullet points of my outline branded themselves into my field of vision on the screen in front of me. It was several minutes before I dared to look up, and when I did, Dorothy was staring at me.

"Did Vivian Davis seem like a woman on the brink of suicide to you?"

"Not really," I admitted.

"I didn't think so, either. The way she was asking me how long you-know-who would be around, for instance. Didn't sound like someone who was planning to do away with herself a few days later."

"She *did* seem anxious, though," I pointed out. "Or even manic. Maybe she was bipolar."

"Or maybe she had good reason to be depressed right about now."

We weren't nearly close enough for me to tell her how ridiculous—and egotistical—it was for her to blame herself for a stranger's suicide.

Leila poked her head into the room again. I looked down, pretending to be absorbed in my work.

"So apparently someone from the Crystal Palace called, and they're holding a memorial tomorrow for that woman. They want you to come. They say it's going to be *intimate*."

Dorothy considered a moment.

"I think I should," she said. "But I'd also like you to come, if that's all right?"

"Of course," said Leila.

"No, no."

I looked up. Once more, Dorothy's eyes were trained on me.

"I meant *you.* Since you were there when we met. Unless you'd rather not?"

Behind her, I could see Leila struggling not to look hurt or annoyed. I had no wish to antagonize her, so I made a point of looking at Dorothy alone when I answered the only way I felt I could.

"I'm happy to."

It also happened to be the truth.

Part Three
The Autopsy

Chapter 15

I've always liked funerals. That sounds ghoulish, I realize. But like interviews, there's a script to them: we all know more or less what we're supposed to say at a funeral. Or not say. They're the rare public gathering where it's okay to be antisocial. No one is going to chide you for failing to "mingle" at a funeral. Add to this the fact that compared to other rites of passage (weddings, graduations) they're short *and* easy to dress for (well over half my wardrobe is black; you're shocked, I'm sure), and you have my ideal ceremony.

Technically there wasn't going to be a funeral for Vivian Davis. There would be a memorial service—a small gathering of friends and family at the place where she and her husband had been staying, the so-called Crystal Palace. To my surprise, this building was actually next door to Dorothy's house, though there was so much space between the two—so many acres of wooded land on both pieces of property—you'd never know it.

Early on Saturday afternoon we took the Lincoln Town Car down the narrow path through the woods, doubling back to that fork in the road and then taking the left path. (So apparently you *can* take both roads. Suck it, Frost.) This one was just as narrow and winding, but with a lot more evergreens than on

Dorothy's property—so many, I suspected they'd been put there by a landscape architect. These trees made the woods feel darker, their bristly branches throwing heavier shadows on us than any deciduous plant could hope to do this time of year. The snow enhanced the effect, filling in the spaces between the needles, fattening the branches with its powdery padding. (It had snowed two more times that week, though not as heavily as the first time.) It was one of those intensely sunny days you get sometimes during a cold snap, but here, the sun barely reached us. It almost felt as if we were inside a cave, and maybe it was because we were headed to such a somber occasion, but I didn't like how quiet it was.

Just two days earlier, Vivian Davis had succumbed to this silence . . .

But why? What could have caused her to take her own life? Because Dorothy was right. She hadn't seemed suicidal when we'd met her. She'd seemed angry, and opportunistic: full of a grasping sort of energy I find galling because deep down I share it, as much as I pretend not to. I hadn't seen any of the flat despair that seems required for a person to end her life. That's what happened to the one person I knew who'd killed herself: her personality went comatose, all the fizz and sparkle stamped out.

But what did I know? Maybe that Kickstarter was Vivian Davis's peculiar cry for help. Maybe she was more fragile than she looked, and the prospect of the next four, if not eight, years was enough to send her over the edge. If there's one thing I've learned, it's how very little I know about anything—especially when it comes to the inner lives of other people.

In the back seat, Dorothy turned to Leila. (I was sitting up front with the grim-faced Officer Donnelly again.)

"Tell me about these people. The husband is some sort of an inventor?"

Leila nodded, her glossy mane falling forward as she looked at some notes on her phone. Or maybe she knew all this by heart and she was looking at her phone because she was always looking at a screen of some sort.

"Walter Vogel. He was born in Poland, actually, though he came over here for college and never left."

"Where'd he go?"

"Harvard. Same for med school. Specialized in dermatology. Set up shop here in Portland, which you might think was an odd choice except he made a name for himself as the go-to guy for cosmetic procedures for all the ag-ed ladies up and down the coast of Maine. The vapid ag-ed ones, anyway."

"Hey, now. Wait till *you're* pushing seventy, see how you feel. This ag-ed Mainer lady wouldn't say no to a little lift right about now."

"Oh, stop. You don't look a day over sixty-eight."

She'd just turned sixty-nine the month before. Dorothy threw her head back and let loose one of her crazed cackles.

"He and Vivian Davis got married three years ago. And get this: she was one of his patients. That's how they met."

"Talk about a meet-*cut*."

I'd said it before I had a chance to wonder whether it was in poor taste—or rather, whether the poor taste in which it was undoubtedly made might be inappropriate. But Dorothy chuckled, and Leila held up her hand for a high five I gamely returned.

"Nice one," said Leila. "Leave it to the writer. I think you might have even made Joe crack a smile."

We all turned to Officer Donnelly, whose thin red line of a mouth *did* seem to have gone slightly diagonal.

"I like puns," he said solemnly, setting us all off again.

Looking back, I'm a little embarrassed. We were on our way to memorialize a woman who had *killed herself*. But isn't that often the way of these things? Death makes us nervous, hence punchy. Sometimes laughing at bad jokes is the best we can do.

As the car crept deeper among the evergreens, Leila informed us that this hadn't been Vivian Davis's first marriage, either. A runner-up for Miss Virginia, she'd rattled around New York awhile doing off-Broadway plays and a little local TV anchor work before marrying a much older investment banker. A few years later, the i-banker died, leaving Vivian a well-off widow with a vacation home in Maine who apparently wasn't opposed to a nip here and a tuck there while vacationing.

"Now he's developing some sort of 'dermal regeneration' thing? It's all pretty vague. From the little I could find online the idea is you take a few skin cells and make whole sheets out of them. It's supposed to use the same technology that powers 3D printers. Or something."

I imagined a skin suit slowly sliding up the tray of an HP inkjet. . . .

"They don't have any funding yet, but someone from one of the big Silicon Valley VC firms is out here," she continued. "Vogel's been putting on a whole dog and pony show, which makes sense. You don't really rent the Crystal Palace unless you want to impress somebody." She looked up, flipping her hair out of her face. "Ugh, you remember when those solar energy assholes were staying there? That whole Musk-adjacent crowd?"

Dorothy's eyes widened comically. "How could I forget?"

Musk-adjacent crowd? What sort of a place was this?

And then, as so rarely happens, my question was answered as soon as I asked it.

Like a bevy of grinning chorus girls ushering in the final act of the show, the evergreens fell away, revealing the Crystal Palace in all its glory.

* * *

Well, I wouldn't have to ask anybody how it got its name. The entire façade was made of windows—or window, I should say, because it appeared to be a single pane of glass. It was three stories high and exactly as wide as it was tall—a perfect cube, and so blindingly bright, I couldn't even look straight at it as it sat there glittering in the harsh December sun.

I made a visor with my hand, wishing I'd thought to bring sunglasses like Dorothy and Leila had. (Leila had rose-colored aviators, standard-issue, but Dorothy's were black tinted and enormous, à la Anna Wintour.) There wasn't anything leading up to the house—no path, no stairs, nothing even to indicate where the front door was. Just that sheer glass structure plopped in the middle of a clearing. It looked more like a neolithic monument or alien spaceship than a building inside of which humans went about their daily lives. Did people really heat up soup inside such a place? Clean out their ears?

We pulled up to a black valet stand, the kind I was used to seeing outside restaurants and other places of business. Towering over it—and over the valet as well—was the Bodyguard, who'd come ahead of us for security purposes. I looked away from him, which took some effort, as he was living up to his name this afternoon. The best way to blend in at a fancy memorial service is with a black suit and tie, of course, and there was no question he was rocking his *Men in Black* variation on this theme.

We'd gotten out of the car by then, and stood for a moment staring up at that fever-dream of an architectural monstrosity. Now that we were closer, I could see a door-sized rectangle etched in the exact horizontal center of the smooth glass wall, a security camera above it protruding an inch or two, angled downward.

"It's even weirder on the inside," murmured Leila as the door-sized rectangle swung inward.

A young woman in a form-fitting cocktail dress appeared in the frame, her box braids piled high atop her head. She beckoned, stepping aside to let us through.

The Bodyguard led the way, his Minotaur back straining against his suit jacket.

The door closed behind us, sealing us inside the Crystal Palace.

Chapter 16

Excuse the history lesson, but the original Crystal Palace was an exhibition hall made of cast iron and plate glass built in London's Hyde Park in 1851—a showcase for the many wonders of the Industrial Revolution up to that point. The building itself was one of these wonders, the mass production of large sheets of glass being an innovation at the time. Even the ceiling was made of glass. In fact, the Crystal Palace had the highest proportion of glass to non-glass of any structure in existence, and I have to imagine that if the builders could have left out the iron frame, they would have. In this way, the "Crystal Palace" buried deep inside the woods of Sacobago, Maine, was true to its namesake. It was a hybrid residence/event space that could be rented out for weeks or months at a time at outrageous expense, and it had been built for this express purpose at the height of the dot-com bubble, about twenty years ago. Fortune 500 companies held intimate, senior-level retreats there, while individuals for whom money was no object considered it a point of pride to vacation there for a week or two. Its cachet had only risen when Dorothy Gibson moved in next door, and apparently the waiting list for reservations was almost as long as the one to get a Birkin bag. The fact that Walter Vogel and Vivian Davis had been staying there spoke to their status as a local power couple.

We entered a long and narrow hall that afforded an unobstructed view both horizontally and vertically, proving what I'd already suspected—that the rear of the building was also made of glass, as well as the roof. It was tinted glass, the sky overhead appearing a shade or two darker than it really was: blueberry instead of robin's egg. I felt sure the exterior walls to the left and right were also see-through, though I'd have to wait for confirmation because the hall had been partitioned on either side by great sheets of plaster. In front of these interior walls was a series of columns that ran in a U shape down either side of the room and along the rear. These columns reached two-thirds of the way toward the ceiling and were bisected by a balcony marking out the second story, with another balcony on top of them constituting the third story. In this way, the two balconies created a horseshoe-shaped arcade on the first and second floors—much like the gallery in a church, where the choir sings from on high. It felt a lot like stepping into a church, actually: one of those grand European cathedrals with its narrow, soaring dimensions.

As I usually do when confronted with great heights, I imagined what a catastrophe it would be to fall from either balcony onto the floor—a black-and-white chessboard made of marble. In addition to a church, it could have been a museum lobby, or maybe the atrium of a ritzy hotel. Large potted ferns had been placed between the columns, enhancing the arcade effect. A staircase would have helped make the space feel more like a house, but there was none in sight.

"Welcome," said the woman who had ushered us in—quietly enough that it failed to make an echo. She gave us a smile perfectly attuned to the occasion: friendly, but muted, as though to say, *How wonderful it is to meet you despite these unfortunate circumstances.* I was already envious of her figure, which was on display in that form-fitting cocktail dress: full, but fit, clearly the product of intense exercise at regular intervals. The dress itself was the darkest of grays; in fact, the only way I could tell it wasn't black was by the black houndstooth pattern printed on it. It struck me as a sensible yet stylish choice for a memorial service.

"I'm Eve Turner, Mr. Vogel's personal assistant."

She was extremely young, and self-possessed—less of a contradiction than you might think. I swear the older I get, the more energy it takes to hide the unseemly aspects of my personality. I remember a time when such outward serenity came more easily (but by no means naturally) to me. Now that I'm careening toward forty, I find I don't have as many fucks to give, whereas Eve Turner was clearly still chock-full of them. If she'd been my kindergarten teacher, I would have thought she was the prettiest lady in all the world. But now that I was older, I knew better than to mistake poise for beauty.

"Paul will take your coats."

A man wearing a double-breasted chef's jacket and those checkered pants you see on kitchen staff appeared from behind her, giving us an embarrassed wave. He was portly, with a sizable stomach and an excess of flesh spilling over the jacket's mandarin collar. His sunken, squinty eyes reminded me of a pig's—but a friendly one, more *Babe* than *Animal Farm*. The hair at his temples was slick with sweat, and I got the feeling that if he decided to shake his frizzy mop at us, we'd get soaked.

"Let me show you to the Reception Room," said Eve once we'd peeled off our things and deposited them in Paul's arms. "That's where everyone is assembling."

It had been a while since I'd heard the verb *assemble* used in conversation. We followed her down the arcade running along the righthand wall.

"Hey, boss," Leila stage-whispered.

"Yeah?" Dorothy stage-whispered back.

Leila jammed her index finger upward. "There's another glass ceiling you won't be breaking anytime soon."

Dorothy let loose a whopper of an eye roll. "Good one."

* * *

We followed Eve through the second door to the right, down a short hallway where I clocked a powder room (always good to keep track of these things), before entering what was without question the Reception Room.

Square footage is meaningless to me, but you could have fit at least four, if not six, of my studio apartments in there—putting it somewhere between two and three thousand square feet. We're talking airplane hangar size. The floor was cement with chunky, angular furniture dotting the space like little islands in a concrete sea: two leather armchairs with a cube of a coffee table between them; a high console where you could rest an elbow while admiring the pretentious bonsai tree placed on top of it; four stainless-steel benches that made a square, with a well in the floor for your feet.

Several car lengths lay between each of these tableaux. Their placement seemed calculated to show off how much space there was, rather than to fill it. Leila was right. This place was weird. Now that I was inside I found it harder than ever to picture normal people going about their normal lives—the soup eating and the ear cleaning. It was a house made for posing: for the conveying of grand statements rather than the puttering about required in the course of a person's day-to-day existence. I suppose it helped that it was meant only for short-term stays, but personally, I would have been miserable living in a place like this for any amount of time.

Apparently, Vivian Davis had felt the same way.

The room was bounded not only by the rear exterior wall, but by one of the side exterior walls—which, wouldn't you know, was also made of glass. In this way it was a little like entering a fishbowl: an effect amplified by the fact that when we came into the room, everyone turned to us and stopped talking.

There were twenty or so people dispersed in knots of three

or four. I could tell by the luster of their dark clothes and the way their skin glowed in the tinted sunlight that they were rich. Very rich. Almost all of them were middle-aged—by which I mean somewhere in their fifties. (The older I get, the farther I push the boundaries of "middle age." If I ever get to seventy, I'm sure I'll assume anyone shy of 100 has decades ahead of them.) Normally twenty people indoors would have felt like a crowd, but not in that room. Eve navigated confidently among them, toward a man who slipped out now from one of the knots, and turned to greet us.

Walter Vogel was completely bald, though you could see it was only the top of his head that had stopped producing hair: the sides and back had a layer of stubble that contrasted with the eggshell-smooth crown. And yet it was an appealing head. There's a confidence to male baldness—or there can be if it's worn right—and this was one of the more successful versions of "bald is beautiful" I'd seen on a white man.

The absence of hair drew focus to his features, all of which stood out in high, sculptured relief. He could have been a Rodin statue except for the fact that Rodins don't have much to speak of in the way of eyes, and Walter's eyes were his most prominent feature. Even from halfway across that vast room I could see them—icy blue, so light they were practically transparent. Cold eyes: the eyes of a huckster or quite possibly a maniac, and from the start, before we'd reached him, before we'd even exchanged a word, I knew he wasn't to be trusted.

Or maybe that's just hindsight.

"Dorothy." He held out a hand as we drew near. "Welcome."

It was weird how everyone felt they were on a first-name basis with her. But then, they kind of were.

Eve turned, stepping sideways at the same time in a graceful, balletic motion. "Here's Walter," she said simply, gesturing for us to close the gap. I watched her walk back to the door we'd come through. The Bodyguard was standing there now, looking conspicuous despite his suit and tie. He had to be a good twenty, thirty years below the median age of this gathering, and at least as many pounds above the median weight (muscle weighs more than fat). A frisson of jealousy lashed at my insides as Eve passed him and they registered each other, but how could I blame them? They were easily the most attractive people in the room.

Walter Vogel wasn't far behind, however. Even with his bulky sweater and heavy woolen pants, I could tell he had barely any body fat on him. Dorothy stepped forward. He grasped her hand in both of his. He wasn't a big man; in fact, he was almost short. But there was an energy to him, an intensity to his movements—and to those Rasputin eyes of his—that conveyed a bigger presence.

"I am so glad you can be here," he said. "I am honored that you and your friends"—he paused to nod at me and Leila—"could join us for this occasion."

He had no accent, but his formal word choice and the way he failed to use contractions betrayed the fact that English wasn't his first language. Like many non-native speakers, he spoke as if he'd written out what he was going to say and then committed it to memory.

"Walter, it's a pleasure, though I wish we weren't meeting this way," Dorothy said after introducing me and Leila. "Let me just say how sorry I am for your loss."

"Thank you. We are all very sad today. But it warms my heart to see you here because I know how very pleased Vivian would have been to see you. I cannot tell you how"—he paused, searching for the idiom—"*over the moon* she was when she met you. She showed me your photograph one hundred times."

Dorothy smiled politely. "She was very kind. Very supportive."

"It was the only time since this election for president that she was bright and sunny. Like her usual self." He sighed. "I hoped the change of scenery would help her, but it did not. We live nearby," he explained. "We have been staying here for two weeks now."

"Yes," said Dorothy. "Vivian mentioned that."

"I am presenting an innovation of mine in the biotextile space," he said. "To a former colleague. We are hosting him, and his wife, and their son. My assistant, Eve, who you just met, has been staying with us because we have been so busy. And Paul, I think you met him when you entered?"

We nodded.

"He too is staying here. It is a full house, and I fear it did not distract, but rather overwhelmed her. My Vivian was such a sensitive soul."

I couldn't help thinking that "sensitive soul" was not how I would have described the woman we'd met at the liquor store four days earlier. But it was worth repeating: what did I know? No one deserves to be judged on five minutes' worth of conversation.

"Her sister is here too, isn't she?" asked Dorothy. "Vivian mentioned she was coming. I'd like to pay my respects to her as well."

A cloud passed over his eyes, the brightness dimming for just a moment before he recovered. "Laura is staying upstairs," he said. "She is too . . . emotional to come down."

"Of course. That's understandable."

There was a pause that lasted a beat too long.

"How much longer will you be staying here?" asked Dorothy.

"A few days," he replied. "Then I will return home." He shook his head. "Though I cannot imagine being there without her. Here Paul comes now, with refreshment. You will excuse me?"

We excused him, relieving Paul of three of the wineglasses balanced on his tray. It was a Gewürztraminer, which is one of my favorites—though Gewürzes can so easily go wrong.

Happily, this one did not: so lush and flavorful, it was like drinking a lychee. No one came up to us, which you might find surprising, but this was a phenomenon I'd noticed before with famous clients, especially whenever I found myself in an upper-crusty milieu such as this one. Rather than besieging celebrities, many people will go out of their way to ignore them, eager to prove they're a member of the cultured elite who couldn't care less about fame. The fewer pretensions a gathering has, the more likely it is that people will engage directly with a famous person. In fact, it's a good litmus test as to the socioeconomic status of a group: the more the celebrity gets ignored, the higher the status.

Apparently, we were at an *extremely* hoity-toity gathering, free to drift unmolested toward the view through the rear of the building.

I hadn't realized it till now, but the Crystal Palace was built on top of a hill. The snow-covered ground sloped away dramatically, something smaller than a river yet larger than a brook running along the base of the hill, the stream's clear water glinting in the sunlight as it rushed along with purpose. Maine is filled with such bodies of water—in and among the woods that pervade the state's interior. Beyond the water were more trees, the white-coated woods stretching as far into the distance as we could see.

"Kick-ass view, isn't it?" observed Leila.

I nodded.

"Much nicer than mine," said Dorothy. "They built this place on the highest spot in the area." She pointed at the running water. "That's Crystal River. It runs through most of the town and empties out into Crystal Lake a little to the north. Also on the property. We can't see it from here because the hill's blocking us."

"Oh yeah," said Leila. "*Everything* runs into that thing. Remember the whole hullabaloo about polluted runoff? That actress was staying here then. God, she was here forever, what was her name? She was in *Orange Is the New Black*, you know who I mean, right?"

I didn't, but I nodded anyway.

"What a pain in the ass she was. She wanted everyone with water rights to sign a pledge saying they wouldn't dump anything into the river."

"Careful, Leila," muttered Dorothy above the rim of her glass.

"Sorry," Leila muttered back.

We were in someone else's space; no telling who might be listening. It's moments like this that keep me from feeling jealous when it comes to my clients' supposedly fabulous lifestyles. Because it's really true, what they say.

Nothing comes for free.

Chapter 17

I ducked out of the festivities to visit the powder room we'd passed on our way in.

I love snooping in other peoples' bathrooms, don't you? It's the only place where you can be reasonably sure no one's hidden a surveillance camera. And some bathrooms have a great deal to tell.

This wasn't one of them, unfortunately. It was your typical half bath for guests: a pedestal sink and a toilet (a bidet too—fancy!), no medicine cabinet to rifle through for prescription drugs, no way of gleaning hygiene rituals as there would be in the bathrooms upstairs. I couldn't even find a place to put my wineglass, so I chugged it while staring myself down in the mirror.

I looked tired. The skin around my nostrils was flaking, which it has a tendency to do in winter when the heated indoor air is so dry. I set my empty glass on the floor and gave myself a squirt of the moisturizer that had been set out on a stand beside the fancy hand towels—the terry-cloth kind that come rolled up like dinner napkins. It was hand moisturizer, of course, but when you're competing with the likes of dewy-skinned twenty-something secretaries, you take what you can get.

Competing? Competing for what? The Bodyguard? *That's*

never going to happen, I reminded myself, placing an index finger between my mouth and nose. This is a tic of mine that started when I was twelve and despaired regularly at how my face resembled those eyeglasses that come with the big nose and mustache—the vaguely Marx Brothers–like ones. I'm honestly not sure whether I still do this as a statement of how far I've come since then, or if it's every bit as self-loathing now as it was a quarter-century ago. Either way, I still do it whenever I look at myself in a mirror.

I switched off the light, exiting the bathroom.

"This is unacceptable."

I stopped short in the doorway. The voice had come from my right, the sharpness of its tone rendering it perfectly clear. There was no question it was Eve Turner who'd spoken, she of the unattainable youth. No one else was around, so I lingered shamelessly, waiting for more.

"I understand what a backlog is, Dr. Islington, which is why I'm asking you, for the *third* time, what we need to do to get to the head of the line."

This didn't seem to go over well on the other end, judging by the way she kept trying to interject "Doctor" into what must have been a long tirade. About a minute later, she let out an agonized "Aaugh!"—very Charlie Brown deprived of his football—and came hurrying into the hallway.

"Oh! Hello."

"Hello," I said serenely.

"I apologize if you just heard my primal scream."

"I'd hardly call it a primal scream," I said. "More like what an eye roll sounds like."

She smiled, but it was nothing like the gentle parenthetical curve she'd bestowed on us when we entered the building. This was a goofy, lopsided grin. Suddenly I could picture her in pigtails, food smeared across her face with grass stains on her knees. It hadn't been so long since she was a little girl, after all.

She was tired, I realized—exhausted.

"What's the matter?" I asked. "Is there anything I can help you with?"

Full disclosure: that glass of wine I'd chugged was having its effect on me. I don't usually make overtures like this, and when she drew her shoulders back I felt sure she was going to rebuff me. But then, she paused.

I watched her think it over.

"You know what? Maybe there is. But only if you promise to tell me if I'm overstepping."

"I've never had a problem telling people that," I replied.

She smiled again, gesturing for me to follow her into the room she'd just exited. I marveled—as I tend to do whenever I'm under the influence of alcohol—at how easy it is to connect with others. Apparently, all you have to do is be . . . nice? Friendly? Why didn't I do this more often?

We entered a giant larder. The wall to my left was lined with bins containing various roots and bulbs—half a dozen kinds of potatoes, tiny and misshapen onions I suspected were shallots, a rainbow's worth of carrots tied together by their green tops. In one corner was an assortment of dried pasta and grains, and on the right were shelves made from rough planks of wood holding hundreds upon hundreds of tinned cans. The light was dim and the temperature was low—for purposes of preserving the food as long as possible, I guessed. A cement staircase in the middle of the room led down to what must have been a wine cellar, and on the wall opposite was a door that led into the kitchen proper, the light seeping through on all four sides.

"I'm not trying to creep you out," said Eve. "It's just, this is one of the only rooms that feels private."

"I'm more than happy here," I said. After the exposed

brightness of the rest of the building, it was a lovely space. "That Reception Room is . . . something else."

"I hate this place. I can't wait to get out of here." Eve shivered, drawing her lightly muscled arms across her chest. "This has all been such a nightmare."

"I'm sure," I said. "I can't even imagine."

"I don't know how Walter is functioning right now. He was already so stressed about his funding. And it's *so* important, what he's doing. Have you heard about it?"

"It's . . . skin regeneration, right?"

She nodded. "It's going to change so many peoples' lives. Babies born with facial disfigurements, burn victims, skin cancer survivors—I don't think people understand, he's going to change the *world*. And I'm supposed to make sure everything goes smoothly for him. But right now? It's all a mess."

I could hear the dedication in her voice, could feel her passion. She was obviously an excellent assistant. But was that *all* she was to him? It's such a cliché: the devoted assistant falling in love with her boss. But like most clichés, it's a cliché for a reason.

"So what do you know about medical examiners in Maine?"

I must have looked startled, because she let loose her goofy grin before continuing.

"About as much as I do, apparently. Don't worry about it, I thought you might have had to deal with them at some point. Maybe when your boss was still senator. Although I guess that was a while ago, you couldn't have been working for her then, right?"

She thought I was another assistant of Dorothy's, and for two reasons I failed to correct her: (1) the nondisclosure agreement I'd signed prevented me from telling her, or anyone else, what I was actually doing; and (2) I had a much better chance of extracting whatever information I could if she continued believing we shared a profession. Suddenly the backdrop for our chat made a lot more sense: two "downstairs" lackeys huddling in the pantry to talk about their "upstairs" employers.

"I only started working for her recently," I said. "How about you?"

"I've been here almost ten months. Well, not *here*, thank God. I've got a place in Portland. That's where Walter's office is."

"Are you from Maine originally?"

She gave me a knowing look. Maine is not exactly renowned for its racial diversity. As a person of color, she stood out among the snow-white populace.

"I grew up in Michigan, but I went to Bowdoin for undergrad. I started working for Walter when I was still a senior."

That meant she was twenty-two, or thereabouts. I'd known she was young, but I hadn't realized she was practically still a teenager.

"I actually like Portland a lot." She glanced around the room. "I can't wait to get back there, honestly. This house is beautiful, I guess, but it's soulless."

"I know what you mean," I said. "So what's the deal with the medical examiner? Is that who you were just on the phone with?"

She nodded. "Nathan Islington, MD. Which in his case stands for Major Dick. He came and picked up the body on—" She stopped herself. "I don't really have to tell you all this if you don't want. It's pretty boring. And gruesome."

"Are you kidding? I spend an embarrassing amount of my free time inhaling true crime. Boring and gruesome's my bread and butter."

"Okay, well, he came and picked up Vivian's body on Thursday afternoon, and since she didn't die of natural causes he had to do an autopsy, which he did by Friday morning."

"Yesterday," I clarified.

"Yesterday," she confirmed. "And technically? She drowned. She must've passed out after taking all those sleeping pills and then slipped under the water."

"Really?" I remarked with somewhat callous relish. "I hadn't realized that."

Eve nodded. "When Walter found her, her head was under the water. But we all know it was the pills that did it, which is why I'm trying to get him to do the toxicology report as soon as possible. I—people have been saying some nasty things online, and I just want everything squared away for Walter so he isn't distracted any more than he has to be. This is all hard enough as it is."

I nodded, even as I wondered whether Eve Turner was desperate to move on from Vivian's death for her boss's sake, or for her own.

"You know, toxicology reports usually take a lot more time than they do on *CSI* and *Law & Order*," I said.

"That's what I'm learning. Especially when the morgues are full of opioid overdoses." Eve grimaced. "Apparently there's a backlog."

"How were you even able to get in touch with him?"

"That's the most frustrating thing," said Eve. "Walter *knows* him. He *requested* this guy. But now it's working against us because he was a total jerk to me on the phone just now, and it's not like I can register a complaint or anything."

"How long did he say it would take?"

"Up to *two months*."

I winced in sympathy. And yet two months was by no means outrageous. We're all used to such instant gratification these days, but there are a lot of moving parts required for the completion of a forensic toxicology report. I've looked this up since then, and one month is pretty much the minimum.

She lowered her chin, regarding me shyly. "I guess I was hoping Senator Gibson might have some sway?"

"You can just call her Dorothy," I said. "Everyone else does."

"I voted for her, you know," said Eve. "I'm really sorry she lost."

This was getting pathetic. "I'll ask her," I said. "But I think it's a long shot."

"Thank you. So much." She let out a big sigh. "This really couldn't have happened at a worse time. I realize that sounds terrible, but it's true."

"You didn't like Vivian, did you?"

"What makes you say that?" she asked sharply.

I shrugged. The real answer was that sometimes I liked to stir up trouble. As a younger sibling, I harbor the propensity to poke, to goad, deep in my bones.

"Just a hunch," I said. "I met her, you know. When she ran into Dorothy a few days ago. She seemed like she could be a . . . challenging person."

"You could say that," replied Eve cautiously.

"I obviously don't want to speak ill of the dead, it's just . . . were you surprised when this happened?"

"You mean when she killed herself?"

I nodded.

Eve hesitated, and I waited. There's no better way to get a person to talk than presenting her with an awkward silence. We're all desperate to fill such voids.

She sighed, giving in. "Vivian was one of the most selfish people I've ever met. I was honestly shocked when I found out she'd killed herself. I would have thought it was much more likely—" She hesitated again.

I waited again.

"I guess what I'm trying to say is that it would have made a lot more sense if she'd been murdered. That's also why I want the cause of death put down in writing. Maybe it's the real reason. Because until an official document says that Vivian committed suicide? People are going to wonder."

Chapter 18

Eve got a text immediately after this that forced her to hurry away. Or maybe she regretted what she'd said and was looking for an excuse to leave. I wandered back, purposely going in the wrong direction so as to get another look at the Great Hall. I have no idea if other people called it that, but it's what I called it because there was no question the space had earned the adjective "Great." Now that I was alone, I wanted to gaze upward and properly gawk.

But as it turned out, I never so much as lifted my chin, so arrested was I by what I saw in the middle of that grandiose space. At first, I thought it was a statue I'd missed the first time—of a woman dressed in what I can only describe as widows' weeds: a long, poofy black dress that Scarlett O'Hara might have donned during one of her (many) mourning periods. A black veil covered her head, running the full length of the dress—the funereal version of a bridal veil. One of her arms was curved upward, the other downward, forming an S bisected by her torso. It was the arms that made me think of a statue, because there was no question she was posing.

But then the arms came down and the statue began moving in my direction. I could just make out the tip of her nose through the veil's netting as she drew closer, her gown brushing gently against the floor with a rustling sound that must have been a regular part of life a hundred and fifty years ago. I was standing next to one of the columns on the right-hand side of the hall, and when she drew next to me, several palm fronds poked into her skirt.

"Hello, sugar."

"Hi?" I said—or asked, I suppose. No one had ever called me sugar before.

"I'm Laura. Vivian's sister."

Now that she was closer, I could make out her features a little better. There was definitely a resemblance, though Laura's hair was dark brown, and her nose was much longer—and larger—than her sister's. (I guessed Vivian had gotten a nose job at some point.) It's often difficult to identify what it is about siblings that makes them so alike, especially when their basic features don't match up. Was it coloring? Head shape? Body type? A similarity in gesture or tone of voice? Or something more ineffable? Even though my older sister was a redhead and I dyed my brown hair black starting in middle school, people were constantly asking if I was "Cassie's sister." Usually in a tone of disbelief given how outgoing, athletic, and good at math she was.

"I'm so sorry for your loss," I said.

"Thank you, darlin'."

I hadn't extended my hand, but she found it anyway, sandwiching it between both of hers and squeezing tight. The spicy-sweet scent of liquor—brandy, I guessed—traveled the short distance between us. Not that I was one to judge; I probably had wine breath myself. But I wondered how much she'd had, and whether she was the kind of person who took a nip or two (or ten) during daylight hours. I suspected she was.

"And who might you be?"

"I'm here with Dorothy Gibson," I said.

"And who is Dorothy Gibson?"

I waited for the punchline, but she wasn't joking. Allow me

to remind you it was barely three weeks after the presidential election. Was it really possible for any adult—especially any adult *female*—not to know who Dorothy Gibson was?

"She's a neighbor," I said. "Lives next door, actually. I'm staying with her for a while."

"A neighbor, how lovely! Well, thank you fuh yuh condolences."

Her voice had a husky quality to it; I wondered if she was a smoker. I could easily imagine her with a cigarette holder poised dramatically between her index and middle fingers.

"Did you come up here from Virginia?" I asked her.

"Why yes I did!"

The way she said "did," she gave the word two syllables: *dee-id*.

"Now how'd you know that?" she asked. "Aside from the accent, I s'pose."

"I heard that Vivian was from Virginia," I explained.

"Well, that's right, sugar. We grew up jus' over the border from Kentucky. Real, *real* deep in the country. Not that you'd ever know it to hear *heh* speak. But Veevo—that's what I always called her growin' up, closest I could get to Vivian when we weh little—she cast off huh South-uhn roots a *long* time ago."

"Were you close?" I asked her, the "Bitch Sister" label in Vivian's phone presenting itself to my mind's eye.

"Well." She paused for effect. "When we weh little? Nothin' could part us. But times change. Hadn't seen her for *years* when she called me out of the blue, practically begged me to come up 'n' visit her. Wouldn't take no for an answer."

Well, this was interesting; Vivian had made it seem like her sister's visit was an imposition. I waited for her to say more, knowing I wouldn't have to wait long.

"I knew somethin' was wrong the moment I saw her. A sister always does, no matter how much time you've spent apart."

She nodded at this—so vigorously the folds of her veil

bounced along with her. Sisterhood was not as durable a bond in my experience, but I let this go.

"She was . . . *nervous*, I guess you'd say. Almost jittery-like. Which wasn't like Veevo a-tall. Growin' up she was always *cucumbuh* cool. I was the one who wouldn't shut up! Yappy li'l sister. But when I got here Wednesday she just kept babblin' away."

That was the day after we'd seen Vivian at Betty's, when she *had* seemed a little nervous.

"What was she babbling about?" I asked.

Laura slapped the air between us. "Nothin' in particular. The election, blah blah blah. Veevo was always very . . . civic minded. I never gave a fig about all that. Republican, Democrat. They're all the same, aren't they? Bunch a crooks."

"You . . . you don't think that was the reason she did it, do you?"

"What, politics?" I saw her eyebrows draw together behind her veil. They were much darker, and thicker, than her sister's sculpted brows. "It's a thought. I know it might sound silly, Lord knows it does ta *me*. But she really did cay-uh about it, you know? She really did."

I decided that if I ever had a reason to tell Dorothy about this conversation, I'd excise this portion of it.

"If I had just *one more* day with her, one full day, I'm sure I would a' coaxed it outta her. But of course when I woke up . . ." She let out a long sigh, shaking her head. "She was gone."

"Walter was the one who found her, wasn't he?"

"That's right. And it wadn't like in the movies or those crime books you read, where someone screams and ever-one comes runnin'. He's got too much sense for that." She drew closer. The brandy smell was overpowering. "He's a good one. Veevo did well when she married him. Came to my room before the authorities did, asked if I wanted to see her before they took her away."

"Did you?"

"Course I did. That was my sistuh in there. Our parents are both dead now, I was the only family she had left."

Through the veil, I could see her eyes glaze over, taking on a faraway look.

"It was awful. Poo-ah thing. Jus' lyin' there in her bath like she was takin' a nap. He'd pulled her outta the water by then, you see. She looked peaceful, face all relaxed. . . . Exactly like the Veevo I used ta know. 'Specially with her hair all wet cuz that made it dark for once. Like mine." She put a hand up to the back of her head. "The way God made the both a' us."

"What are you doing downstairs, Laura?"

I whipped my head around. Walter Vogel was standing in the doorway I'd just come through, his blue eyes blazing with displeasure. He was looking at Laura, not me, but when he saw me staring he smiled, all the anger in his face banished instantly.

"You should be lying down," he said in a concerned voice, walking over to us. "You were not feeling well just a little while ago, is not that true?"

"I'm tired of lyin' down," Laura pouted. "Lyin' down is all my poo-ah sistuh can do. I may as well be upright for the both a' us."

"Come with me." He cupped her elbow with one hand.

"Ouch! All right, all right. No need to pinch, honeybunch." She batted her eyes at him. "You were always such a good husband to heh, I hope you don't blame yourself."

"I do not," he replied, leading her across the hall.

"Bye, doll!" she called out.

Walter turned to me while they were still in motion, putting the thumb of his free hand to his mouth and wiggling his other fingers in the universal sign to indicate when someone's been drinking.

"Sorry," he mouthed.

I averted my eyes, resisting the urge to mouth "that's okay" or placate him with a gesture, as he clearly wanted me to do. It takes immense willpower to violate such small yet significant social niceties. But it's a power I've built up over the years.

"Bye, Laura," I said, watching the gauzy train of her dress sweep along the checkered floor. "Good chatting with you. Maybe we can chat again sometime."

Chapter 19

When I reentered the Reception Room, Paul happened to be standing nearby with a fresh set of wineglasses. Against my better judgment—and in a pointless gesture of solidarity with the woman currently being hustled up to her bedroom—I grabbed one, taking a moment to survey the scene.

In the time I'd been gone, five or six of the shiny wealthy people had approached Dorothy. She and Leila were holding court with them now. (I saw Dorothy spread out her hands and Leila lean forward, a ripple of laughter running through the crowd.) So apparently they weren't *that* hoity-toity—though there's nothing like a splash of alcohol to render a celebrity more approachable.

The Bodyguard had moved over to their side of the room, no doubt to keep a closer eye on the proceedings. I felt a contrarian's unwillingness to join the group, so after a lengthy pull on the liquid courage curled in my right hand, I drifted in the opposite direction.

I was off to do the unthinkable.

I was going to mingle.

Remember the four metal benches arranged in a square? When I first saw them, they were empty. But now three out of four were occupied by a man, a woman, and a teenager. I assumed not only by the fact that the boy was a perfect blend of the two adults but by how bored they all looked with one another that they were a family, and I gravitated toward them now—I suppose out of some Tolstoyan impulse that every unhappy family has a unique story to tell. Or maybe it was just because they were the closest island in that glittering sea, and the fourth bench was begging to be filled. Or—here comes the real reason—I realized they were the ones Walter had mentioned earlier, the family who had been staying here when Vivian died. I was curious what they had to say about the whole thing. Have I mentioned I'm nosy?

I was also drunk.

I plopped down on the unoccupied fourth bench.

"Hello!"

The father was sitting opposite me. He looked up from his phone, flashing me a perfunctory smile. His body type was the stringy sort of skinny you can't cultivate, and wouldn't want to anyway: elongated chicken legs, an enlarged Adam's apple bobbing up and down what I'm reluctant to describe as a "pencil neck" because it's a term bullies use, except that's exactly what it was—the perfect neck for the dress shirt and tie he was wearing. His fingers were freakishly long, like a cartoon villain's—Ebenezer Scrooge, or better yet, Mr. Burns.

The son sat to my right. He had headphones in his ears, and either hadn't heard me or was pretending I didn't exist. He looked about twelve, which meant he was probably sixteen, with the round, fatty face of a baby. An Orion's Belt of pimples dotted his greasy forehead, and a Martian desert of red, bumpy skin was spreading out from one corner of his mouth. I have a knee-jerk horror of teenagers—first instilled in me when I was one myself—and looked away from him immediately. Judging by experience, most people that age are so uncomfortable with their appearance, the kindest thing you can do is not look at them too closely.

The wife scooted down the bench to my left, holding out her hand.

"I'm Anne, how d'you do?"

Her ponytail was several inches too high for a grown woman—unless she was about to compete in an adult cheerleading competition later that day. She had at least ten years on her husband; I could see the whitish-gray streaks in her blond hair, the rings around her neck that made it look like a turkey's wattle, though she was by no means overweight. She was in fact extremely well put-together, an attractive, fiftysomething WASP in a dark Chanel suit with the obligatory pearl necklace and matching stud earrings.

I'd have bet cash she had her son via IVF when she was forty or thereabouts.

"I do okay I guess," I replied. "You?"

She smiled—a small one, a sad smile if anything. I decided I liked her.

"I guess I do okay too," she said. "Given the circumstances."

"You're from the Bay Area, aren't you?"

She nodded. "I see our reputation precedes us."

From the opposite bench, her husband let out a snort.

"Walter told us you were staying here," I explained.

"I'll bet he did." The man still hadn't lowered his phone, but he was looking at me now. "I'm gonna give you some advice. Don't trust a word that comes out of Walter Vogel's mouth."

"So you're not here to check out his skin invention thingie?" I demanded—a bit artlessly, I admit, though in my defense I'd had a glass-and-a-half of white wine by then, with nothing to dilute it other than a long-gone bowl of Grape-Nuts and a tiny piece of lobster for lunch.

"Nah, that's true. I'm the skin invention thingie checker, all right."

"This is Samir," said Anne. "Say hi, Samir."

"Hi, Samir." He was already back to his phone.

Anne shook her head like a put-upon housewife in a sitcom,

scooting closer to me. I did the same, meeting her at the corner. We settled in for a nice gossip sesh. All we were missing were the hair curlers and the tube of raw cookie dough.

"My husband and Walter went to medical school together," she explained.

"And he was as much of a fraud then as he is now," added her husband—not all that quietly.

I scanned the room. Walter hadn't come back yet; presumably, he was putting Laura to bed. There was no way he could have heard, and yet it seemed a tacky, if not cruel, move to savage a man's reputation at his wife's memorial service.

"That's enough," Anne scolded him, before turning back to me. "Samir works at one of the big venture capital firms in Silicon Valley. He's the entrepreneur-in-residence."

I actually know a little about the venture capital world, having ghostwritten a memoir for one of the early titans of the industry. Let me rephrase that: I know much more about the venture capital world than I ever wanted to, which was why I knew that "entrepreneur-in-residence" positions were held by people who'd already had some success with ventures of their own. The firm employed them to vet proposals in their area of expertise, to see if they were worth taking on.

"*I* actually came up with a skin invention thingie."

He put his phone aside, springing up as though his bench had a hidden ejector button. He had to be several inches north of six feet, and he loomed over us now, rolling on the balls of his feet. There was a wiry, vibrating energy to him that couldn't have been more different from his wife's old-fashioned composure. She folded her hands in her lap and stared up at him indulgently.

"You wouldn't have heard of it, but it's used in labs all over the world."

I hadn't asked, I thought.

"Samir was doing him a favor by coming out here," said Anne.

He snorted again. "See how that turned out." He swooped down, landing beside his wife. "Hadn't talked to the guy in almost twenty years when he called me up, but I figured why not? Always help out an old friend if I can. Not that I had high hopes."

"Why was that?" I asked.

"Walt was one of the worst performers back in school, and from what I heard he didn't get much better once he went into practice. Botched a few procedures, got sued more than once. But I figured what the hell, who doesn't want to see New York around the holidays, right? Take in a few shows, blah blah blah."

"You make it sound so magical," I said.

He made that snuffly noise you do in the back of your nose—the one that tickles your upper palate. I usually hate arrogant men, but this one at least had a sense of humor.

"Pretty obvious in about twenty minutes he didn't know *squat* about biotextiles," he said. "Total waste of a trip, business-wise. And I had to put my neck out to get them to sponsor it, they're not gonna be happy."

"You'll be *fine*," said Anne. "Everything you've done for them?"

"So neither of you met Vivian before a few days ago?"

Something changed at the mention of her name. They did their best to hide it, but I could feel the tension ratchet up—could *see* it, even, in the way Anne's hand crept up to her necklace and Samir's leg began to shake. We all have our tells, no matter how hard we try to hide them.

"That's right," she said. "It's *such* a tragedy. My heart goes out to the family. I know these things happen all the time, but it's a shock all the same."

Samir cleared his throat uncomfortably. "Horrible thing."

"I know this is a weird question, but did you see it coming at all?"

"*Definitely* not." Anne was rolling one of the pearls between the pads of her thumb and forefinger now like a worry stone. "She was very lively. Very amusing."

I felt confident Anne Shah had never once found Vivian Davis amusing.

"She certainly never seemed depressed," she added.

"No clue till it happened," her husband agreed.

"Nothing about her that seemed . . . off in any way?" I persisted.

They both shook their heads.

They were lying. Even before what happened next, it was obvious they were holding something back.

What happened next is that the peripheral vision my humanoid ancestors relied on to avoid predators sensed movement. I turned my head to the right. The teenage son was standing up now, headphones slung around his neck, a glare of loathing on his face so intense, it was scrunching up all his babyish features. He looked like a toddler gearing up for a meltdown.

"You are such *fucking* hypocrites."

"Alex!" barked his father.

Alex stormed away, practically running out of the room.

I busied myself taking sips of wine. Somehow, my glass was almost empty.

"I'm sorry about that," said Anne eventually.

Her cheeks had caught fire, along with her neck. Flushed skin is often the purview of younger people, but the redness made her look older, somehow. More vulnerable.

"He's taken all this very hard, he's only"—she gulped, and I could see she was on the verge of tears—"he's only sixteen."

Her husband put an arm around her, and she nestled into it. It was the sort of unthinking, understated intimacy that gut-punches me as a single person much more effectively than the performative gestures. The only thing more mysterious than the inner lives of other people is the relationships these people form among themselves. I had no idea how or why Anne and Samir Shah worked as a couple, but I could see they *did* work, and I felt what I usually did when confronted with the irrefutable evidence of a functional relationship: irritation and—I'll admit it to you, and you only—jealousy.

I can prop myself up all I want, talking about what high standards I have. But what if my standards are higher than I deserve? What if "settling" is simply coming to terms with who, and what, I really am? It can't be the world's fault I haven't been in a serious relationship since—well, ever.

(Just a little sneak peek at my Friday and Saturday night affirmations for you. Good times.)

I was already searching for an exit line when Leila came up behind the Shahs, widening her eyes at me while jerking her head toward the door. Her message couldn't have been clearer: *Let's get the hell out of here. ASAP.*

She didn't have to tell me twice.

CHAPTER 20

"Well, *that* was a shit show."

I turned around in the front seat. Leila and Dorothy were both wearing their sunglasses again, which along with their grim expressions made them look like they came in a set—the female version of Statler and Waldorf, or Marge's two older sisters (I swear I'm not even that big of a *Simpsons* fan).

"What a creepster," continued Leila.

"Walter Vogel?" I asked.

She nodded. "He actually wanted to take a picture. That's when I called it."

"It was . . . unfortunate," said Dorothy.

"It was gross," retorted Leila. "And don't get me started on the cringers."

"Cringers?" I asked.

"Ever since the election, when people see me they tend to cringe," explained Dorothy. "Apparently the sight of me is painful to them. One woman said just now she couldn't bear to look at me, it reminded her too much of what could have been."

"*So* rude," said Leila. "It's like they forget you're a human being."

Dorothy took off her sunglasses. "You'd think *I* was the one who died."

Leila made a noise that did double duty as mocking and supportive.

"What did you think about it all?" Dorothy asked me.

"Me?" I asked, stalling for time.

She nodded.

"About the memorial?"

She nodded again.

"I thought it was . . . sad," I said, not realizing this was how I felt till I said it.

"Really?" Leila was on her phone again. "No one seemed too broken up she was gone."

"That's why it was sad," I said.

Dorothy and I made eye contact, and I'm probably making a bigger deal out of it than it was at the time, but it felt as if an understanding passed between us—about how many women there were like Vivian Davis. Women no one liked very much. Or cared much about.

Leila looked up from her phone. "You took your sweet time in the bathroom. Not that I blame you."

I told them about my run-in with Vivian's sister, and also about my conversation with Eve Turner, including her frustration over the medical examiner.

"Wow," said Leila. "Remind me to take you to my next cocktail party, you get the *dirt*."

Dorothy turned to her. "Do you have Andy Blair's number in your phone?"

I didn't know it then, but Andy Blair was the mayor of Sacobago.

"Course. Want me to dial him?"

"Please."

About two minutes later, Dorothy had the mayor on the line. We still hadn't exited the Crystal Palace grounds.

"Andy, hello. Well, that's very kind of you, I do appreciate that. Andy, listen, I have a favor to ask. I've just come from a memorial service. For Vivian Davis? Yes. Yes, I know, I agree. So sad, yes." Our eyes met; we exchanged a smirk. "Well, I hear there's some holdup with the toxicology follow-up and I'm wondering if we can do something about that. Yes. Yes. Well, I understand that, but I would appreciate anything you can—uh-huh. Uh-huh. *Ab*-solutely. Okay, well thanks, Andy. Yes, yes. Of course. Oh, I'd love that, I really would. Bye now."

She clicked off, mic-dropping the phone onto the middle seat.

"Well, *he's* useless." She looked out at the wall of evergreens surrounding us, eyes narrowed in concentration. "The Office of the Medical Examiner works on a county level, is that right?"

"I think so," said Leila cautiously.

"Can you get me a name? Whoever the chief medical examiner is?"

"On it."

We were at the fork in the road, making the hairpin turn onto Dorothy's property, when Leila dialed a Dr. Theo Barton. It was late afternoon by then, and nearly sunset. In the middle of a ditch by the side of the road I saw a lonely patch of crabgrass crusted over with muddy road slush. One of my favorite things about winter on the East Coast is how inviting it makes the artificial world, the one we humans have created for ourselves. I adjusted the heating vent in front of me so that it blew straight onto my forehead.

"Hello, Dr. Barton! Oh, well, Theo then. And you'll have to call me Dorothy, everyone else does." She let out her deranged cackle before giving a concise rundown of the situation, ending by wondering aloud whether there was anything that could be done to speed up the process. There was a long pause afterward.

"That's *great*, Theo, I really appreciate that."

She hung up, letting the phone fall to her side and closing her eyes, leaning back in her seat as though this interaction had drained her, which I supposed it had.

But a few seconds later, her eyes popped open again.

"Leila, what was the name of that local donor, the one who's a forensic pathologist and lives in Standish, I think?"

Leila stared at her, at a loss.

"He'd always get *way* too drunk at our fundraising dinners?"

"Oh! You mean Jeff Lombard."

Dorothy pointed at her triumphantly. "Yes! Jeff Lombard. That's *exactly* who I mean. I seem to remember him droning on and on about postmortems once?"

Leila shrugged her shoulders helplessly.

"It's worth a shot. Can you get him on the line?"

By this time we'd parked at the house. Leila and Dorothy hurried off to the living room, while I went upstairs to retrieve my laptop. By the time I rejoined them, they'd moved on to other things. It wouldn't be till late the next day, on Sunday, that I learned Dorothy *did* get in touch with Dr. Lombard, who said he'd put a call into the Department of Labs and Research to make sure Vivian Davis's "tox screen" was being handled as quickly as possible. And it was early that same Sunday evening, a little more than twenty-four hours after the memorial, that Leila burst into the library holding her iPad in both hands, its screen facing outward.

Dorothy and I were reviewing some notes together on the puffy couch.

"Have you seen this?"

"Seen what?" asked Dorothy wearily.

Leila handed her the tablet. "Just read it."

She took it with a sigh . . . but when she saw what was on the screen she sat up straight, bringing it closer to her face.

"What's going on?" I asked.

She didn't answer me.

"Your friend over at the Crystal Palace should be happy," said Leila. "The secretary, I mean. What was her name?"

"Eve Turner?" I asked.

"Right. Well, you can let Eve Turner know the toxicology report's in. Actually, I'm sure she knows by now."

"It's done already?"

Leila nodded as if to say *of course*; she was used to things happening at warp speed upon request. This was the world she and Dorothy lived in, and they had imposed their exacting standards on the Office of the Medical Examiner for Cumberland County.

"It's not the full report from what I can tell, but a big enough chunk of it was just leaked to the press. Story broke a few minutes ago."

"Why?" I asked again—more impatiently this time. "What does it say?"

Dorothy looked up. "Vivian Davis didn't have a single drug in her body."

"What?"

Dorothy looked down and began reading aloud: " 'The victim, who had no external signs of trauma, exhibited significant lung distention and alveolar edema. This plus the presence of abnormal amounts of water in the respiratory system indicate she died by drowning. Given that she was found in a bathtub full of water with an empty bottle of Lunesta at her side, the working theory was that she overdosed, drowning while in a stupor. This theory has been shattered by the toxicology report rushed through and delivered this evening, stating the victim had no eszopiclone or for that matter any other drug in her body at the time of her death.' "

Dorothy looked up again.

We all stared at one another.

"I guess you can't drown *yourself*, right?" asked Leila.

"Not in a bathtub you can't," replied Dorothy.

"But it still doesn't make any sense." Leila popped a squat in front of the couch, her curtain of hair nearly reaching the floor. "If someone held her down, she'd have bruises all over her body, *some* sort of mark. Even if she bumped her head and it was just an accident, you'd see the bump. You said there were no external signs of trauma, right?"

"Right," said Dorothy.

"So it couldn't have been an accident. But then how the hell did it happen?"

We fell quiet, thinking it over.

"Brides in the Bath!" I shouted, piercing the silence.

Leila turned her head sideways: a birdlike, quizzical movement. "Excuse me?"

"Brides in the Bath. It was this famous case from the early twentieth century. This psychopath George Joseph Smith married women all over England. Usually he'd just clear out their savings and disappear, but three of them ended up dead in the exact same way. They were all found drowned in a bathtub with no marks on their body. No signs of violence."

"MMMM-hm." Dorothy was nodding her head. "This is ringing a bell."

"The reason the case is so famous is that there was this pathologist Bernard Spilsbury who figured out how Smith did it. He actually hired female divers and tested his theory by putting them in a bath. When he pulled on their feet really quickly, the water flooding their nose and mouth would cause them to lose consciousness, and they'd drown. One of them almost *did* drown, actually, during the test. It was easier than anyone thought. And there were no signs of violence."

"MMMM-hm, MMMM-hm."

"Smith was put on trial for the third murder, but the prosecution used the pattern established in the first two as evidence that he must have done the third one, too. That was the first time that was ever done. All on the basis of Spilsbury's experiments. He's sort of a forensics hero for that reason even though he started buying into his own hype and became kind of awful."

I paused for breath. They were both looking at me with admiration . . . and maybe a little fear?

"Seems like you're a good person to have around when something like this happens," observed Dorothy.

Is it possible to be flattered and insulted at the same time? (Apparently so!)

"This doesn't look so good for Walter Vogel then," said Leila.

"No," I agreed. "In Smith's case, only a husband or a maid would have had the access required to pull off a murder like that. And a lot of the women he married didn't have their own maids."

"Well, I suppose there's an argument to be made that other people may have had access to Vivian while she was taking a bath," said Dorothy, reasoning it out in her lawyerly way.

I nodded. "Her sister at the very least. But who knows?"

"MMMM-hm. Modesty quotients have changed a lot since a hundred years ago."

"And she didn't seem like the most modest person in the world," I added—somewhat uncharitably, which was why I followed this up with a question. "Does it say anything about the time of death in there?"

"Based on temperature readings taken at the scene"—Dorothy was reading again—"the time of death is estimated to have been anywhere between nine p.m. last Wednesday night, the thirtieth of November, and three a.m. the next morning, the first of December."

"Oh shit, TMZ just picked it up." Leila was looking at her

phone now. "This is going to be everywhere in about two seconds. And I mean *everywhere.*"

"The cause of death is not conclusive," Dorothy read on. "But the police are currently operating on the assumption of death by foul play."

It slipped so easily out of her mouth. *The police. Death by foul play.* And yet with these words, everything changed.

We sat there gaping at one another . . . till Leila's phone began ringing. Followed by Dorothy's.

And then, things did what in my experience they seldom do.

They began to happen.

Fast.

Part Four
The Investigation

Chapter 21

The interwebs were aflame and aflutter over the news of Vivian Davis's "shock tox report" (people really called it that). It was the selfie with Dorothy that did it. Who could resist sharing such titillating news when there was photographic evidence of the almost-president standing cheek to cheek with a murder victim? Before we went to bed that night, every major news outlet had contacted Dorothy's spokesperson for a comment, and both the president-elect and her other former opponent had tweeted their "concern" about the situation.

Dorothy and Leila had a tense conference call that included at least six other people and went late into the night, during which a written statement was crafted—word by painstaking word. I can't say the result reflected all the time that went into it.

> *My thoughts go out to the loved ones of my late neighbor, Vivian Davis, a woman who like so many these days was struggling to make sense of the times we find ourselves in. As the investigation into Ms. Davis's untimely death is ongoing, I have no further comment at this time.*

The statement was sent to a small conservative paper in Minnesota whose editor had written an influential endorsement during the general election that helped Dorothy win the state—by a hair. Once they published it on their website, it was populated everywhere within minutes.

No one had asked me to leave the room during any of this, but if they had, I would have insisted on staying. My pretext would have been that it was all background for the book, but in truth I wasn't about to pass up a juicy mystery dropped in my lap via a serendipity that up till then had always seemed reserved for other people. I refused to miss out on my chance to play a role—to put my skill at spinning a story and my love (yes, love) of writing to good use.

I wasn't going anywhere.

The next morning, Monday morning, the police came bright and early.

Dorothy and I were outlining on the fluffy couch, which isn't to say they caught us unawares. When I'd come down to breakfast, there were two suits sitting with her in the breakfast nook. One was pearl gray and rumpled, his jacket double-breasted. The other was navy blue and tailored, his pants riding well above the ankle to expose pink-and-white argyle socks. Pearl gray was a senior lawyer among Dorothy's vast team of legal representatives—one of those bespectacled white-haired men who so often inhabit positions of authority. Navy blue was younger, a hotshot at the firm that handled Dorothy's PR business, and while he wasn't chewing gum (it was seven in the morning), he may as well have been.

Dorothy was in a suit herself: one of her signature pantsuits, a pale-lavender number with white piping on the lapels and up the seam of each leg. Her hair had been styled, straightened, and hair-sprayed into the chunkily fashionable mullet she'd been sporting for years. It was the first time in my experience of her that she looked like "Dorothy Gibson," and I found it hard to concentrate on the task at hand as we sat together on the fluffy couch. True, we were reconstructing a granular timeline of her long tenure as senator, not the most scintillating of tasks. But do you know who wasn't having trouble concentrating? The lady in the pantsuit, who looked up sharply as her lawyer and publicist entered the room.

"Are they here?"

They nodded.

"Good." She put her laptop to one side, smoothing out her trousers. "Let's get this over with."

Technically, Sacobago was a hamlet inside the township of High Castle, which was why Detective Sergeant Daniel Brooks had a windbreaker with HCPD stamped over his heart. He was at least a few years younger than I was, with a bright/boyish energy I found attractive, despite the fact that he wasn't good-looking. His complexion was greasy, his glasses, unfashionable. Unusually for a police officer, he had one of those puffy hipster beards so many men insist on wearing these days. (I swear that when people look back on the prevailing trends of male facial hair from our current age, it's going to look as ludicrous as all those Victorian mutton chops.) He was also extremely short. I'm five foot six and had a good inch or two on him.

I find that extremely short men tend to fall in one of two categories: (1) those who are resentful of their stature, hence awful; or (2) those who learned to push past their physical limits early on in life, making them some of the nicer, more enlightened men around. From the way he gave my hand a friendly squeeze and inquired as to the year the grand piano was built (1937, in case you were wondering), I was pleased to note that DS Brooks had every appearance of falling in the latter category.

I wish I could say the same about Special Investigator Locust.

From what I gather, the Maine State Police don't get involved in homicide investigations too often, but the powers that be had decided the township of High Castle needed some help with this one, and Stephen Locust from the Major Crimes Unit South was the man sent in for the job. Unlike Brooks, he was clean-shaven, with sandy-colored hair in the process of making a getaway. His hair was receding in a straight line, leaving a massive forehead in its wake. It wasn't that he was outrageously tall, but with his stern demeanor and the height differential between him and his partner, he enjoyed a towering presence—if SI Locust was capable of enjoying anything, that is.

My third-grade teacher, Mrs. Carney, used to say the best punishment for bad-tempered people was being stuck with themselves, and I believe this adage applies to no one more than SI Locust. He was a *magnificently* disgruntled man, which is why when I picture him, it's his great beak of a nose that comes to mind more than anything else. I swear that schnozz could have done Shakespeare, it was so expressive—always up to something, whether scrunching in disgust, flaring in annoyance, or quivering impatiently. Like a product hawked on television late at night, the possibilities were endless.

On this morning, one of his nostrils was higher than the other: the nascent stages of a snarl. He wore a no-frills, off-the-rack suit, and I could tell instantly he was the sort of man who'd never be caught dead wearing shorts. (DS Brooks, on the other hand, probably threw off his khakis and shimmied into Umbros the moment he got home.) I should note that the titles I'm using for them, "DS" and "SI," are not what they used themselves, or what anyone else called them. They were called "Detective" if they were called anything other than their last names. The reason I started saying "DS Brooks" and "SI Locust" to myself was that it made them sound more like my favorite members of the fake British police: DCI Morse, DCS Alleyn, etc. And now I find I can't think of them any other way.

Leila did the introductions. What with the publicist and the lawyer, there were seven of us in the library, quite the crowd. The two officers sat on spindly chairs that wouldn't have looked out of place in a Jane Austen adaptation. They'd been placed opposite the fluffy couch, where Dorothy was flanked by her lawyer and publicist, with Leila and me perched on either end. Some people may have found this double layer of protection intimidating, or at least off-putting. SI Locust was not one of these people.

He held up his phone. "I assume no one minds if we record this? It makes our lives a lot easier."

"Actually . . ." The publicist scratched a sideburn apologetically. "We kinda do. Sorry."

Locust's nostrils swelled to their fullest, glorious extent.

"That's cool, I always take notes." DS Brooks slipped a black Moleskine notebook from the inside pocket of his windbreaker, clipping open a pen. "Helps with my process."

Locust glared at him. *"Fine."* He turned to Dorothy. "How are you feeling today, Mrs. Gibson?"

"All right," she said. "And you?"

"Not so all right, actually. I'm confused. And I don't like to be confused."

There was a pause. I saw DS Brooks raise his eyebrows while keeping his eyes trained on the notebook in which he hadn't yet written a word.

"The reason for my confusion is as follows. You spoke with three different officials on Saturday afternoon requesting that a toxicology report for Vivian Davis be processed as soon as possible. Imploring them, I should say. That's the word one of them used. They said you 'implored' them, Mrs. Gibson. And even though toxicology reports routinely take a few weeks, at least, even though there are dozens of other cases that should have been processed before this one, because *you* asked, the people delivered. And now that your wish has been carried out . . ."

He spread his hands wide, making the universal sound for a bomb exploding.

"Was there a question in there somewhere?" asked the publicist.

"Why were you so desperate for this toxicology report, Mrs. Gibson? There's a question for you. Because that's what I don't understand. I can't fathom why this was in any way your business. Hence my confusion."

"I'm not sure—" Dorothy's lawyer paused to clear his throat: a long pause, as there was a lot of wet matter in there to get through. When he spoke again, it was with the plodding precision of one who's used to taking his time—one who expects others to wait for him while he follows through his every thought. "I'm not sure that I like, all that much, the cut of your jib, young man."

SI Locust's nose recoiled. "The *cut* of my *jib*?"

"It's a nautical term," said Leila. "For being a jerk."

"*I* was the reason."

They turned to me as one.

Before my nerves had a chance to tie up my tongue, I plunged into as concise a recitation of my conversation with Eve Turner as possible, taking comfort in the companionable scratch of DS Brooks's pen on paper.

"Have you spoken with this secretary since Saturday?" demanded Locust when I'd finished.

I shook my head. "No."

He was scowling at me. Honestly, if he'd bared his teeth or let out a growl, I wouldn't have been surprised. Scared, yes. But unsurprised.

"I'll be confirming all this within the hour."

He made it sound like a warning. I bobbed my head at him like a housemaid. He turned, setting his sights on Dorothy again.

"So we're to believe you made all these calls out of the kindness of your heart? Is that your position?"

Dorothy's lawyer stuck out his hand like a traffic guard.

"My understanding was that this would be a routine question-and-answer session. For clarification purposes. Not an inquisition."

"I'm just trying to understand how all this happened," said Locust. "Because the only thing I'm sure of at this point is that none of it happened the way it was supposed to."

"*Lots* of ruffled feathers," put in DS Brooks cheerfully.

"I hardly see how that's the senator's fault," the lawyer said. "If anything, you should be thanking her."

A close-lipped smile spread slowly across Locust's face, his nose flattening the way a snake does before it strikes.

"Now why doesn't it surprise me you feel that way?" He took a moment to survey the crowd before him. "You all probably think we policemen are bad at our jobs. Too dumb, or bigoted, or corrupt to find our way to the end of a case the right way. Well, let me be the first to tell you that on this matter, the one we're investigating today, you're going to be proven wrong about that."

DS Brooks had sought refuge in his notebook, where he seemed to be taking notes on Locust's tirade—or pretending to.

"Now, does anyone else have any other information?" Locust looked from one to the other of us, stopping at me. "*Anything* at all?"

I could have told him about my interaction with Laura. Or the way Anne and Samir Shah had gotten weird when I mentioned Vivian's name. But as he'd already pointed out, they were about to interview these people for themselves. When I woke up that morning I had every intention of telling someone in an official capacity about Bernard Spilsbury, and my pet theory as to how Vivian Davis could have been drowned in a bathtub with no marks on her. . . . But the sooner SI Locust was off the premises, the better for us all.

"Fine." He put both hands on his knees and heaved himself upward, the chair protesting noisily. "I'll go ahead and make a wild guess no one has *any* idea how the toxicology results were leaked to the press?"

"You think *we* did that?!" exclaimed Leila. "Are you joking?"

"You're way out of line there, buddy," said the publicist.

SI Locust nodded, grimly satisfied. "I'm also sure I don't have to tell you we'd prefer if you didn't go anywhere without telling us. Just in case we need to have another chat. Since this one has been so productive."

"That won't be an issue," said Dorothy's lawyer.

Locust turned to leave, but then he turned back, advancing on the publicist.

"And if you ever have to address me again? You'll say 'Officer' or 'Detective.' Not 'buddy.' Understood?"

The publicist stared at him, frozen. But eventually, he nodded. There wasn't much else for him to do.

Before he left the room, Detective Brooks made eye contact with me. He gave me a shrug, and I gave him one in return.

"Wow," said Dorothy once the front door had closed.

"What a prick," pronounced the publicist.

"I have to agree," the lawyer said. "Mainly bark, of course. Though I for one have no desire to see how his bite measures up." He turned to Dorothy, patting her hand. "You'd do best to stay put for the time being, my dear."

Dorothy snatched her hand away from him. "What the hell do you think I've been doing, Larry? That memorial service was the first time I left this place for days."

The suits didn't stay for lunch. Dorothy wanted to be alone the rest of the morning, and when we met up at noon in the dining room, she was still out of sorts. Trudy had prepared a frisée salad with a bacon vinaigrette topped by a poached egg: scrumptious, and yet Dorothy wasn't touching hers, which was unlike her. (Despite her small size, she had a big appetite.) She was back in one of her typical at-home outfits: dark leggings and a heavy, loose-fitting sweater—this one goldenrod in color—that hung almost to her knees. She'd flattened her hair with a headband. (What else? Early Dorothy had been known to rock a headband or two, though this one was stretchy/sporty.)

"I'd like to take a little ride," she announced. "Who'd like to come with me?"

Leila and I both indicated we'd be delighted to join her.

"And if that ride should just so happen to take us near the Crystal Palace, and if we should just so happen to drop in and ask a few people a few questions, so be it."

"Do you really think that's a good idea?" asked Leila.

"Yes," said Dorothy. "I do."

"Those cops might still be there. What if you run into them?"

"What if I do? They said not to leave the area without telling them, they didn't say anything about visiting my neighbors. Or talking to people. I'm not an actual prisoner, last time I checked. As much as some folks might want me to be."

"But Larry and Todd—"

"I know what Larry and Todd would say. I'm tired of listening to Larry and Todd. And Vanessa. And Leslie. And Phillippe. And Geraldine. And Seth. And Magda. What's the *fucking point*?" she shouted.

The stories of Dorothy's temper are legendary, of course—as they are for every woman who's managed to achieve a modicum of success. How she has a potty mouth, how she verbally abuses her subordinates, hurling obscenities at them left and right. How sometimes she gets physical, throwing whatever might be close at hand (a phone, a stapler, etc.). Everyone's heard about the time an assistant forgot to pack a fork with the salad she was eating on a plane. Dorothy insisted on eating the salad with a nail file she produced from her bag, which she then made the assistant clean.

Now that I've spent so much time with her, I doubt that most, if any, of these stories are true. But I have to admit it was scary to see how quickly—and easily—her anger had risen to the surface. The fury was there all the time: poised, ready to lash out at a moment's notice.

"I hear you," said Leila. "Believe me, no one hears you more than I do. But that doesn't mean—"

"Do you know how many words I said during that train wreck of an interview this morning? I'll give you a hint. You can count them on one hand. *Every* single one of you said more than I did. *Every* single one."

I glanced at Leila, watching as she lay her fork by the side of her plate. She looked tired—haggard, even, despite her glossy glamor. For the first time I wondered how hard the last two years had been on her.

"My *goodness*," continued Dorothy, "If I haven't earned the right to do what I want to by *now*, when will I ever? It's not like I have anything else to lose!"

"You know that's not true," said Leila quietly. "There are so many people who look up to you, who rely on you—"

"All I want to do is talk to some people. Maybe help figure out why a woman was murdered in the house next to mine. Clear my name in the process, since apparently I've been deemed a person of interest for making a few phone calls!"

She picked up her water glass, chugging it angrily.

"Not to mention the fact that whoever did this tried to make it look like a suicide brought on by *my* loss."

"You can obviously do whatever you want," said Leila slowly. "But it's my job to give you my honest opinion, and I think it's a bad idea. Like really bad. The senior policeman was obviously vindictive. I'll bet you anything he voted for—"

"We're not talking about the election! This has nothing to *do* with the goddamned election!"

She slammed the flat of her hand on the table—hard enough that her (untouched) glass of wine fell over.

We stared in shock as she righted the glass, throwing a cloth napkin over the rapidly spreading stain. She rubbed at it uselessly. She must have done this for a good minute before looking up.

"I'm sorry," she said.

Leila shook her head. "You have nothing—"

She held up a hand. "I have a lot to be sorry for, actually. And I'm not looking for a pity party, or fishing for compliments, so please. Let me say this." She folded the damp napkin, setting it aside. "I am *so tired* of rule by committee, and focus groups, and the way we agonize over every little decision. Because no matter how many people's opinions I take into account, I'm still the one on the hook. *I'm* still the one who lost, the one who shoulders the blame for that man winning when it should have been that *woman*—" She poked herself in the chest. "Me. It should have been *me*, and I only have myself to blame. So I'm not asking for anyone's opinion"—she caught Leila's eye—"as much as I might respect it. I'm going, and that's final."

Dorothy picked up her fork. She took a heaping bite of salad.

"I'll still go, if you want me to." Leila's voice was softer than I'd ever heard it before.

Dorothy shook her head. We waited for her to swallow.

"That won't be necessary. You're probably right, you know. And I'd never forgive myself if you got into trouble on my account."

"Well, I definitely want to go," I said.

I tried not to look at Leila, but the pull of her gaze was too powerful. I met her eyes, encountering a look best summed up as: *Really, Brute? Really?*

"All right."

Dorothy sounded amused—like I was a pet or a small child who'd surprised her by piping up from its corner, asserting its overlooked presence.

"Who knows?" she said. "Maybe this whole episode can work its way into the book somehow."

Oh lady, I thought, shoving a glob of runny egg past my lips before it had a chance to drip down my shirt, *you have no idea.*

CHAPTER 22

The security detail were as horrified as Leila was at Dorothy's insistence on going to the Crystal Palace, so much so that Officer Donnelly flat out refused to drive her. She took this refusal in stride—literally, setting out for the woods behind her house with nary a backward glance. I hurried after her, relieved to see it was Officer Choi hurrying alongside me, and not the Bodyguard.

Before long we were power-walking our way through a maze of trees, sinking every now and then into the snowbanks that had built up beside the larger trunks. (Luckily, I'd had the presence of mind to ask the assistant who packed for me to bring my winter boots.) No one spoke for a while. I've always preferred the silence of winter to the cacophony of summer—not because it's a perfect silence, but because it makes you that much more aware of whatever sounds intrude upon it: the delicate crunch of footsteps, the odd chirp from small birds hopping along the naked branches above, the scamper of what I hoped were just squirrels and chipmunks on the forest floor. Every now and then, Officer Choi's earpiece would squawk at her, and she'd murmur something in return.

"So what if the police really *are* still there?" I asked, breaking the silence.

She stopped without warning, Officer Choi and I stopping with her. We were all breathing much harder than I'd realized while we were in motion, great clouds of breath massing in front of our faces.

"They can tell us to leave. Which we will, of course."

I nodded.

"If you're uncomfortable with this, we can turn back," she said.

"Uncomfortable with *sleuthing*? Are you joking?"

Dorothy squinted at me, puckering her lips. What with the cold, the apples of her cheeks had never looked more rosy-hued and apple-ish than now.

"That's what I thought."

We began walking again.

"Did you know what I wanted to be when I grew up?" she asked after a while.

I shook my head.

"A writer. I was coached a long time ago never to tell people that, because it isn't relatable. It doesn't fit very well into the story of how I became a politician." She paused. "If you think about it, a writer is pretty much the *opposite* of a politician."

"Well, that's the nicest compliment I've ever gotten."

It was a cheap shot but she laughed anyway, her hoot uprooting a cardinal from the tree above us.

"I'll bet it is! I just have so much respect for a person who can sit down and create something out of nothing. And I've always loved books, of course. It sounds a little depressing to say, but more than any person, they've been my best friends over the years."

I nodded. "Mine too."

She stepped into a snowdrift, her right foot sinking almost to her knee. I was sure some snow must have gotten in her boot, though she didn't react other than to wave me around it.

"I learned pretty quickly I'm not very good at working alone," she said.

"I learned pretty quickly I'm *only* good at working alone," I replied, before realizing this was a rather damning admission for a ghostwriter to make—and to her star client no less. Fortunately, I was saved by the rustling sound of someone approaching.

"Who's there!" barked Officer Choi—not a question but a command, her hand slipping inside her jacket.

A figure appeared from behind the wide trunk of a tree. He was wearing puffy shorts over leggings and a sleek hoodie made of some silky, synthetic material that looked expensive. His eyes were trained on the ground and he was kicking the snow as he moved through it—kicking it with a brutal, almost savage violence that matched the deep scowl on his face. It was Alex Shah, and he looked exactly as he had when he'd run out of the Reception Room during the memorial—as though he hadn't stopped grimacing for two days straight.

"Hey!" yelled Officer Choi.

He looked up, his gloved hands shooting out of his pockets.

"What the—?" He slipped off a glove, removing a wireless headphone. The sound of music with a heavy bass beat came leaking through the air. "What are you doing here?"

"We could ask you the same question," said Dorothy cheerfully.

"My dad told me I had to go exercise," he said. "So this is me exercising."

"Aha. Well, we're doing the same!" She inserted a laugh in the middle of "Well," making it two syllables long: "weh-hell." She did this sort of thing a lot, especially when she was in Official Dorothy mode.

"They want me out of the house while the police are there," he said glumly. "They've been there all morning."

"We figured as much," said Dorothy. "They paid us a visit first."

"Yeah?" He didn't sound very interested, though. "They tell you you can't go anywhere?"

"They did."

"We were supposed to be in New York by now." He kicked an exposed root. "We were gonna see *Hamilton* tonight. But now we can't."

"Well, that's a shame," said Dorothy.

"Yeah," I added. "What do they think you're going to do, disappear into the night? It's like they're cosplaying at being gumshoe detectives or something." I lowered my voice, making it gravelly. *"'No one leaves the premises!'"*

He trained his grimace on me. "It's not a joke, you know. Someone actually *killed* her."

His fatty chin was jiggling like one of those individually packaged cups of Jell-O. Was he going to cry?

This is why I don't talk to children.

"Are you all right?" asked Dorothy—not gently, but with a directness that was much kinder, because it was obvious she was interested in the answer.

"'Mfine," he mumbled, looking at the ground.

"Well, *I* wouldn't be," she replied. "If I were you."

He jerked his head up. "What do you mean?"

He was practically snarling, and to my alarm he focused his ire on me again.

"What did my parents tell you? After I left?"

"They didn't tell me anything," I answered truthfully.

"Alex." Dorothy paused, waiting for him to turn back to her. "It *is* Alex, isn't it?"

He nodded.

"All I meant was that if I were your age and someone had died in the house where I was staying, it would have upset me. A lot. To be honest, I'm upset about it *now*, and I'm *much* older than you are. I also wasn't on the property at the time."

"When did the police say it happened?" he asked quietly.

"Well, the police didn't tell me anything. But according to the autopsy report, it took place sometime between nine on Wednesday night and three the next morning. Why? Did you hear something? Or see something?"

He shook his head. "I wish I did," he said wistfully.

"Are you sure there wasn't anything you wanted to talk about? Having to do with Ms. Davis, or . . . anything else?"

The ground had resumed its fascination.

"No." He shook his head a few times, underlining the point.

"Okay. Okay. But just in case there *is* something, I hope you have people you feel you can talk to. Like your parents?"

No response.

"Well, at the very least, maybe Leila can help you trade in your *Hamilton* tickets for another date," said Dorothy. "She's a wonder at that sort of thing—"

"Don't bother, I already sold them on StubHub."

"Oh. Well. I hope you get to see it sometime. It really is a fabulous show."

"I know that," he said. "I'm not an idiot."

And with that he shot past us, running deeper into the woods and getting the aerobic exercise he'd been so determined not to.

Dorothy turned to me, her eyebrows nearly at her hairline. "Do you have any idea what that was all about?"

I shook my head. "Probably has nothing to do with anything."

As soon as I said it, I realized how wrong it sounded, how dismissive. I could see the doubt cross Dorothy's face—doubt, and maybe a little disappointment?

"If there's one thing I've learned over the years," she said. "It's never to discount children. In any way."

We started walking again. I couldn't help feeling like I'd failed a test, or at least a quiz, and I was annoyed: both with myself and her. The truth is that spending time with highly successful people is exciting but it's also exhausting, and for the same reason. There's just so much *stimulation*, so many expectations placed on every little interaction. Also, it's hard to feel smart when you're not the one defining the terms—when you've been relegated to the sidekick role. There's a reason Watson and Hastings come across as idiots, and Miss Marple tends to work alone.

If I was going to be a part of this, I was going to have to up my game.

We'd almost reached the Crystal Palace when Dorothy's phone began ringing. She fished it out of her coat pocket, grunting when she saw who it was.

"I was wondering when I'd hear from you."

I had no idea who it was, but my suspense didn't last long. A minute or two later, she took the phone away from her ear and put it on speaker.

"Can you both hear me?" the caller asked. But I already knew who it was; the accent was unmistakable.

"Yes, Peter, we can both hear you," said Dorothy wearily.

"Good. Cuz you both need to know this is a bad, *bad* idea. Cuckoo."

"Thank you, child of mine, for your—"

"Com'on, Mom! Why do you want to get mixed up with these weirdos? I saw that woman rush out of Betty's while you were still in there, y'know. The one who died?"

"Vivian Davis," said Dorothy. "What about her?"

"That's the one. Her sister was there too—"

"How did you know she has a sister?" I asked.

"Lay told me."

Dorothy and I exchanged a look: of course Leila did. This phone call was obviously a coordinated attempt between the two of them.

"You know what that woman did? Laura or whatever? Got

outta the car before Vivian could get there, took one a' those wine bottles off her, and uncorked it *right there in the parking lot*. Had her own corkscrew on her and everything. She was swiggin' straight from the bottle! Till Vivian hustled her back in the car. I mean, takes one to know one I guess, but the woman's a drunk."

I thought back to when Vivian had taken her sister's call in Betty's, on Tuesday. "I'll be right there," she'd said before hanging up. That wasn't something you said to a person calling from hundreds of miles away. So why had Vivian pretended Laura wasn't there yet? And why had Laura herself claimed not to arrive till the *next* day, on Wednesday? Something wasn't adding up.

"Well, thank you for that," said Dorothy. "It might actually prove helpful."

"No, I didn't mean"—

"Bye now."

She ended the call. When he tried her back she switched off the phone, slipping it in her pocket.

"You don't have children, do you?" she asked.

I shook my head—nowhere near as vigorous a gesture as the *hell no* this question invariably inspired in me.

"Then you have no idea how satisfying it is to ignore your offspring without personal guilt, or fear of sociolegal retribution," she said cheerfully. "It really *does* get better. Just keep that in mind, in case you ever do."

CHAPTER 23

We had to use a little footbridge to cross Crystal River. This bridge had a high arch—so high it was practically a semicircle, the sort of thing you'd expect to see in a Japanese tea garden—and at the top I caught a glimpse of the pond we hadn't been able to see from the house. It was larger than I expected; in fact, I was tempted to call it a lake, but I've never been clear on where the boundary lies between the two. There must have been a shallow waterfall where the river ran into this body of water, because I couldn't quite see where the two connected, but I could hear the telltale burble.

The Crystal Palace looked as stark and imposing from the rear as it had from the front—more so, because this time we approached it from the bottom of the hill on top of which it sat. Fortunately, there was a staircase built into the hill, or else we would have had to scrabble our way up it in all that snow. Doubly fortunate, the staircase had been shoveled, each step sanded and salted. I didn't have to guess who'd done all this grunt work because when we reached the top, Paul was standing there with gardening gloves on and one arm wrapped around a sack of salt pressed against his side like a football. With his free hand he was shaking crystals onto the patio flagstones.

He still had those checkered pants on, but with a blue nylon jacket that had rainbow stripes across its chest and shoulders. He'd smashed down his clown's wig of hair with an orange knit cap, and his curls were making a run for it, springing out around the edges.

"Hello, Paul!" Dorothy stuck out her hand.

In his eagerness to remove his glove, he dropped the sack of salt, spilling it on the ground.

"Shit!" The ungloved hand flew to his mouth. "I'm so sorry, Madam—I mean Senator, no—"

"Dorothy is fine." She grasped his hand, pumping it warmly. "And don't worry about the cursing. I hear it all the time. Usually from myself!"

His piggy eyes grew wider. "Haha. Okay."

He had a nervous habit of injecting these little "hahas" into his speech every few sentences. I'm not going to reproduce them here for the most part, because they were annoying enough the first time.

"I hear the police have made an appearance?" asked Dorothy.

"Yeah, yeah. They already talked to me. Not that I had anything to tell them! I'm as clueless as anyone. Although I gotta admit it was kind of a thrill to be asked to"—he did finger quotes—"account for my whereabouts on"—he did them again—"the night in question. I still can't really believe it. You don't expect a murder to happen right under your nose, you know?"

Had he been this nervous on Saturday? But we'd never spoken to him. He'd just been the silent manservant who took our coats and brought us our drinks. Also, it was hard to judge anyone for being nervous when Dorothy Gibson was addressing them directly.

"I do know, Paul. Believe me, we're all shocked. And I hope you're taking the time and space you need to process all this.

It's a lot. So tell me, did you work for Walter and Vivian in their permanent house too, here in town?"

Apparently we were jumping in—striking while the proverbial iron was hot, though *nothing* was hot on this cold December day. When Officer Choi placed her back against the wall of the house, I wondered longingly if the glass was warm. The three of us stood at the edge of the hill, looking down at the river below.

"Oh, no-no-no, I live in the city, actually. New York, I mean. Brooklyn. Windsor Terrace? I'm just here for the few weeks *they're* here, in this place. I'm not like a domestic worker or anything. Not that there's anything wrong with that obviously! It's just that I'm an actor, so I do odd jobs on the side from time to time. Gotta pay the bills, right? Mainly I do TaskRabbit."

"Is that how you got this job?" I asked. "Through TaskRabbit?"

"Oh, no-no-no, Viv and I knew each other, back in the day? Waaaaay back. That's why I took the job, no way I would've traveled so far otherwise. Fun fact, actually, but when we first met she was still going by her real name. Joycelyn."

"Jocelyn?" I asked.

"Nuh-uh." He shook his head, grinning. "*Joyce*lyn. Can't really blame her for changing it, right? We did our first show together, actually. Back in New York. I remember it like it was yesterday, even though it was a loooooong time ago, way longer than yesterday. Haha. Shakespeare. *Richard III.*" He gave a self-conscious little shrug with his rainbow shoulders. "Viv was pretty good, actually. She was always super good at impersonations, used to crack me up imitating our director, who was the *worst*. But so was she. Total troublemaker. Made a habit of not returning her costumes, which is such a dumb way to get on people's bad side. No surprise she didn't stay in the business long. *I* kept slogging away, dummy that I am. I'm actually doing Shakespeare right now, *Much Ado About Nothing. Lot* more fun than *Richard III.*"

"I adore *Much Ado*!" exclaimed Dorothy. "Who are you playing?"

He knelt down and began scooping the salt back into the bag. "Antonio? Not one of my bigger roles, admittedly."

I too love *Much Ado About Nothing*. (There are few Shakespeare films more perfect than the Branagh/Thompson version, in my opinion.) But even I couldn't remember who Antonio was, the role is so small. No wonder Paul had to supplement his income by partaking in the gig economy.

Looking at him in the unfiltered sunlight, I could see he was older than I'd realized. Though puffy, there was a roughness to his skin that comes with age—the same way a rock's surface takes on pits and crags over time. He even had the beginnings of those doleful parentheses some people get on either side of their face, from nose to mouth. He must have been a struggling actor for at least twenty years.

I have a lot of respect for people who refuse to give up on their dreams: even—or perhaps especially—when they don't achieve great success. But it couldn't have been easy to perform such menial work for a former castmate. I wondered if his whole goofy schtick was a way to mitigate the awkwardness of these situations. The so-called fool in Shakespeare is often the wiliest character in the show, after all.

"Well, break a leg!" cried Dorothy.

He stood up, having rescued as much of the salt as he could. "Haha. Thank you."

"So what *were* you doing?" I asked. "On the night in question?"

"I cooked dinner, of course. All the meals are buffet-style here. I put them out on this big sideboard in the dining room. With those little Sterno heaters under them? People can serve themselves whenever they want, which means they don't have to gather at a set time if they don't want to. Also means I don't have to serve them, thank God. I'm sure I'd pour sauce in someone's lap or spill ice down their neck or something."

"So you were in the kitchen all night?"

"Oh no-no-no, after I put the food out I made the coffee and set it up in the lounge. It stays hot there for hours. Then I went up to my room and binged *The Crown*. Have you seen it? *Soooo* good. Must've watched, like, four episodes? And then sometime after ten I went down to put away whatever hadn't been eaten, clean everything up. Went back to my room a little after midnight. Should've gone to bed, but I only had two more episodes in the season, couldn't *not* finish it, obviously."

"And you didn't see anything out of the ordinary in all your comings and goings that night?" asked Dorothy.

He shook his head. "Nope. Unfortunately. Didn't see anyone, but that was pretty much by design. House guests catch sight of the guy who cooks and cleans for them, they start having all sorts of requests for stuff they can easily get themselves."

"What about the next morning?" asked Dorothy. "On Thursday?"

He shook his head again. "Mornings are quiet here. That morning was like all the others. I got up at six to do breakfast and coffee. People could go to the dining room anytime between seven and noon. Viv was always the last one up, she's always been a night owl. Seeing her in the a.m. is like a rare cameo appearance. That's why I always left the cleaning till the afternoon. So I didn't disturb her beauty sleep with the vacuum cleaner. Perish the thought, right? I spent the rest of the morning doing all my food prep for the day . . . and *maybe* a little googling of Elizabeth the Second. Anyway, I was just about to head upstairs to scrub some toilets when I saw the ambulance pull up. Crazy."

"Do you have any idea why someone would have wanted to murder Vivian?" I asked.

"Not really," he said—which was as artful a way of making a "yes" sound like a "no" as I'd ever heard.

"Because she was such a nice person and you can't imagine anyone wanting to do her harm?" I asked impishly.

"Well." His grin matched my tone. I imagine an impish grin comes in handy when doing Shakespeare. "I wouldn't say *that*. 'Nice' usually means 'boring,' right? Viv definitely wasn't boring."

He paused, struggling to find the words.

"We were both so young when we met, you know? It's hard to have any perspective on people you knew from when you were that young. It's like . . . they're more a part of you than people you meet later on."

Dorothy was nodding. "MMMM-hm."

"Like, she was always in a fight with someone or other. Viv had a really bad temper, zero to sixty in the blink of an eye. And she was one of those people who didn't mind confrontation. She actually liked it. I always wished I was more like her in that way. Probably would've gotten further. Squeaky wheel and all that."

"So you kept in touch over the years?" I asked.

"Off and on. She made a point of going to my shows, which I always appreciated. She was a good friend that way."

"What about her marriage to Walter?" I asked. "Do you think they were happy?"

"Well, to be honest, I'm not the best judge of whether a marriage is going okay or not. I'm in the middle of a divorce of my own," he explained.

Dorothy made a noncommittal sound of sympathy.

"Yup yup, we're real trailblazers, me and my hubby. One of the first to exercise our constitutional right to same-sex divorce. Thing is, I never really saw Walter and Viv together. Barely met the guy before now. They were always up here, and whenever Viv came down to New York, she came alone. Viv and I always used to hang out just the two of us, anyway. One of the perks of being the gay friend, right? Will to her Grace. Haha."

I forced a chuckle from my throat.

"I'll tell you this. Her first marriage was a shit show. Even *I* could see that."

His eyes flitted apologetically in Dorothy's direction.

"Oh please. *Shit show* is a term I've been using a lot these days," she observed dryly.

"Well, she'd never admit it, but she obviously married that dude for his money. Viv didn't care about him *at all*, not even a little. Least they never had a kid together, that's when things get *real* messy, take it from me." He rolled his eyes dramatically. "But Walter? She was obsessed with him. I have no idea how he felt about her, but I can promise you she was a hundred percent in love. Viv could never fake it that well." He smirked, hugging the sack of salt against his chest again. "Guess that's why she quit acting. But seriously, she wouldn't shut up about him, it was so boring. And she really threw herself into the whole 'society wife' role. Became a mover and shaker so she could help him out with his career. That was *not* the way she was when she was younger. Back then she was one of those people who had a ton of potential, who was, like, super-talented, but too lazy to ever do all that much with it, you know? I was actually kinda glad for her that she'd found something to be passionate about. Even if it's pretty basic for your passion to be your husband. Whatever works, right?"

He reached his hand into the sack, scattering crystals on the ground.

"I didn't say anything at the time because what the hell do I know, but it never made much sense to me that she would've killed herself. Not now. Not when she had all this"—he waved his hand at the behemoth structure behind us, a salt crystal flying in that direction—"going on. Not that it makes *sense* she was murdered, but it definitely makes more sense than Viv killing herself."

He turned to me.

"So I guess I'd say that even though *I* have no idea why anyone'd want to kill her, I'm not surprised *someone* did. Or at least, I'm less surprised where she was concerned than someone else. You know what I mean?"

I did. I knew exactly what he meant.

CHAPTER 24

Paul told us he'd seen Walter in the kitchen earlier, so we headed there now, passing through a back door etched—just like the front door—in the building's smooth glass wall. It was easy to miss if you didn't know to look for it, or to press where you would have expected to find a doorknob.

"I've spent some time here," explained Dorothy as she led the way through the Great Hall, Officer Choi bringing up the rear in her unobtrusive way. We entered the corridor where two days earlier I'd eavesdropped on Eve Turner. "At conferences mainly. It's as much an event space as it is a residence. Most of the bedrooms on the second floor are set up as offices or meeting rooms."

We went around the larder and down another hallway to the right, which ran along one of the side exterior walls. This meant it was all glass on one side, looking onto a garden gone hard and frosty. But even in December, its geometrically precise walkways and perfectly spaced flower beds were impressive—if scary, in a *Mommie Dearest* kind of way. Like a miniature Versailles. We stopped a moment at another rectangular doorway etched into the wall to stare at it.

I pointed to an unassuming, boxy little building on the far side of the space.

"Guess that's the gardening shed where they keep the arsenic."

Dorothy smirked. "*Hard*-ly. It's a hyperbaric oxygen chamber. I once attended an OPEC summit here, and we all got a turn in it. You breathe in pure oxygen for an hour with music or whatever piped in. It's extremely refreshing."

Rich people are so weird.

"Before we see Walter, I just wanted to suggest . . ."

She hesitated. My stomach, always looking for an excuse to flip out, began to do so quite literally, flipping round and round my midsection.

"How about I ask the questions during this interview. Would that be all right?"

"Of course, I'm sorry if I—"

"You have nothing to be sorry about," she assured me. "I just think this might be a . . . delicate conversation, and my sense is that it would work best if one person were steering it."

"I totally understand."

She patted me on the shoulder, and it was this pat more than what she said that made it clear I'd been rebuked. I was to shut my trap for the time being, and I suppose I should have been annoyed, but mainly I felt relieved that she was taking control. Also, I got the feeling that Dorothy respected me for having to rein me in.

More proof that we were more alike than perhaps either of us had realized.

Farther down the hall was a door through which we entered the largest kitchen I'd ever seen. Unlike the Reception Room, there were no windows here. The space was internal to the building, suffused with the honeyed glow of artificial track lighting. This landlocked state was actually the room's best feature, as it meant nothing was on display.

You probably already know that the "drawing room" in

grand old houses refers to "withdrawing," as opposed to any artistic endeavors that may have gone on inside its walls. In this way, I believe the kitchen was the Crystal Palace's true drawing room—a place where you could retire and simply *be*. As a bonus, you could also sneak a snack out of its industrial-size refrigerator. Or heat up that can of soup I apparently couldn't stop thinking about, on any of the massive range's dozen or so burners. Or sit on one among the motley collection of chairs ringing the table, which was nothing more than a rough slab of wood placed in the center of the room, copper-bottomed pots dangling above it like wind chimes.

Walter Vogel and Eve Turner were seated on either end of one corner of that table—the way young couples do when they can't get enough of each other and have to be physically close all the time (or so I'm told). It wasn't that we'd come upon them while they were kissing or anything, but when we entered they were in the act of springing apart, and there was a vibration to their bodies—to the very air around them—that made it clear we'd intruded on an intimate moment. The kitchen was a noisy place, what with the refrigerator humming, a vent in the ceiling through which hot air was blowing, and a kettle in the early stages of boiling. Without meaning to, we'd surprised them, and even though Walter's face was turned away from us, his fury was obvious in the way his jaw was clenched. But then he turned, and when he saw who it was his mouth sprang open, his lips producing a muted version of that smacking sound people make when air-kissing.

"Dorothy! You have returned."

"I have! Tell me, Walter, are the police still here?"

"They have just left."

"Well, that makes things a little less awkward."

Did it, though?

"I wanted to see if there was anything I could do to help," she added.

"That is very kind of you."

"I'll go send those e-mails now." Eve rose gracefully. Today she was wearing a dove-gray pencil skirt with a crisp white blouse rolled past her wrists. She nodded coolly at the two of us, exiting before anyone could say anything about it.

"Please." Walter patted the table. Now that he'd gotten over his surprise, he looked as though hosting Dorothy Gibson and her weirdo mute sidekick was the one activity he'd been hoping to accomplish today. "Sit."

Officer Choi remained standing just inside the door, while Dorothy and I sat opposite him, on the same side of the table. His slacks were khaki, and I felt sure his sweater would have been called "oatmeal" in a mail-order catalogue. All those neutral colors made his eyes even bluer—obscenely blue, as though a child had colored them in with marker.

"You can tell us to buzz off if you'd like," said Dorothy. "I really mean that. I have no intention of interfering with the police, and I'm not even sure *how* I can help. Just that I want to."

"I am glad you came. Both of you," he amended, with a glance in my direction. "From what Eve has told me, I understand we have you to thank for this quick turnaround from the medical examiner's office."

"It was nothing," I said, before remembering I wasn't supposed to talk. "All I did was tell Dorothy about it."

"And all *Dorothy* did," said Dorothy, "was make a few phone calls. I have no idea what happened after that."

"From what I am brought to understand," said Walter in his plodding way, "the chief medical examiner took over the case and conducted all the drug screens himself, without delay. This is not something that usually happens. Usually it takes weeks, at least."

"Well," said Dorothy, "I'm glad I was able to goose things along. So then it's true, I take it? That there were no drugs in her system, meaning she must have been forcibly"—he winced, and she broke off. "I'm sorry, if this is too difficult—"

"No, I must be able to talk about these things. The police are not as considerate as you. This morning they made me go over everything, and at the end they warned me they will do so again. Many times. It will help me to talk through everything with a . . . sympathetic audience." He ran one hand down his face: a gesture of manly fatigue I'm pretty sure I've seen Jimmy Stewart do in more than one old movie. "Someone must have drowned her, it is true. And even though they do not say it, I know they suspect me. I am not a fool. Everyone looks to the husband because, often, it is him. I realize this. But I promise you."

He looked from one to the other of us. If I could have dived into those eyes of his, I would have.

"I did *not* kill my wife."

Either he was telling us the truth or he was an epic liar—a true sociopath. They were two equally robust possibilities, and despite the distaste and distrust I felt for him, I had no idea which was the valid alternative.

"I wonder if you could take us through last Wednesday night then. The last time you saw Vivian, till you discovered her body the next day. It *was* you who found her, is that right?"

He nodded. "On Wednesday I dined with the Shahs. In the dining room, which is just past this room." He gestured in the general area.

"All three of them?" asked Dorothy.

"Yes, including their son." He paused, the ghost of a smile hovering on his lips. "Alex, he spent most of the dinner demanding a glass of wine and being refused."

"Vivian wasn't there?" asked Dorothy.

Walter shook his head. "Her sister had just arrived."

"So Laura came here last Wednesday, from Virginia?"

He nodded.

"She didn't come up any earlier? Even by just a day?"

He drew his eyebrows together, a line appearing between them. "No, I am sure of this. Have you heard otherwise?"

"No," lied Dorothy. "I'm just trying to get the timeline straight. I haven't gotten a chance to speak to Laura as of yet."

He turned to me. "I believe you spoke with her, the day of the memorial service?"

I nodded.

"She is an alcoholic," he said bluntly. "I am sure you noticed she had been drinking. Her life has not been easy. Vivian left home when she turned eighteen, but her sister never did. She was left to nurse their mother through a long illness. It was not easy and there was much guilt on Vivian's side. As for Laura, I am sure she resents Vivian. How could she not?" He sighed. "They did not see each other often."

"What brought Laura here, then?" asked Dorothy.

Walter shrugged. "I think that she was lonely."

"So then it was Laura who proposed the idea of a visit?"

"Yes," said Walter. "She insisted. Even though Vivian told her it was not a convenient time. We were here in this place, hosting many guests. Vivian tried to delay her arrival until the end of the month, when we would be back in our home. But Laura came anyway."

Laura had said the opposite, of course—that it was *Vivian* who begged her to come. Dorothy and I exchanged the briefest of glances. I could tell she was thinking the same thing. It seemed we had a few questions for Laura.

"And what about your assistant, Ms. Turner?" asked Dorothy. "Was she at dinner?"

"No," said Walter. "She was invited, of course, but she chose to work in her office. I believe she made a sandwich for herself later. She often does this. In my opinion she works too much. And eats too little. But then"—he smiled broadly, a dimple appearing in each cheek—"she is American."

"I understand Paul cooked the meal, though he didn't serve it?"

Walter nodded. "That is correct, we serve ourselves. You have accounted for everyone who was on the premises that evening, I congratulate you. After dinner, the Shahs and I went across the hall to the lounge, where Paul left us coffee. It was a dull evening. Already I could see that my former classmate, who showed such promise in medical school, did not have the vision needed to comprehend the full scope of my innovation. He will probably tell you it is worthless, but do not believe him. He does not understand. I found his wife and son to be equally narrow of mind and"—he paused, searching for the word—"provincial."

The kettle grew louder, the water beating steadily against its sides.

"They went up for the night before I did. There is a reading area in the lounge where at the end of the day I read a number of newspapers. This is something I have done for many years. After this, a little after ten, I went upstairs. First, I went to my wife's room to say good night."

"You slept in separate rooms?" asked Dorothy.

"Yes," he said. "Vivian was a light sleeper, and every day I would get up early to focus on my work."

I couldn't help feeling this explanation would have carried more weight if we hadn't just caught him canoodling with his secretary.

"She and Laura were sitting on her bed with wineglasses in their hands. Vivian did not often drink alcohol, but it was obvious this was not her sister's first glass. I remember how happy Vivian looked. I hoped her sister's presence would ease the anxiety she was feeling. I think I already mentioned how much the election had upset her. She tried to make light of it, perhaps you have seen her Kickstarter account?"

"We've seen it," said Dorothy. "It seems to be doing a brisk business. Not that that's any consolation to you," she added.

"It is, though," he insisted. "All these donations, these so kind messages, they are a testament to her spirit. I look forward to putting the money to a good cause."

"I'm glad to hear that," said Dorothy.

"I went to bed before eleven and woke up at five. This is my habit. It was very quiet in the morning. No one entered the property other than a flower delivery at eight, and the flowers were left outside. I spent many hours on the presentation I was to make to Dr. Shah. This was to be my final effort with him. It should have happened on Friday, though it never did."

"When did your wife usually wake up?" asked Dorothy.

"Late," he said. "Vivian stayed awake late, and slept late too. I used to joke with her she was like an Italian. Or a Greek. But I always loved this about her. She would spend her first hour or two in bed, on her phone. It was not until a little after eleven that I thought it strange I had not heard from her yet. So I went up to her room."

"Do you remember the exact time?"

"Yes, I do. It was 11:17," he said. "I remember looking at this"—he held up his wrist, his sleeve falling away to reveal a chunky gold watch. "I knew at once something was wrong because her bed was not slept in." He drew his hand over his face again, but this time he left it there, as though hiding from what came next. "She owned a silk robe I gave her for our first anniversary," he said through his fingers. "She liked to wear this after her nighttime bath. This robe was lying across the foot of the bed, where she left it while bathing. The bathroom was en suite like all the bathrooms here, so I went in at once."

He paused, dropping his hand, taking a few seconds to gather himself.

"Would you like to stop for a bit?" asked Dorothy. "Have some tea? It sounds like that water is almost ready."

The kettle was rattling now.

He shook his head. "I would like to finish. The tub was at the end of the room, perpendicular to the door. It has its own little space. *Alcove*. That is the word. There was no one in it, and I was relieved. But then I saw something bobbing on the surface. I realized it was quite full with water, so I drew closer. The bobbing object was a wireless headphone, and by then I could see there was something . . . something large beneath it—"

The kettle began to whistle. Walter hurried over to turn it down, the whistle dying away. He remained at the stove, standing with his back to us.

"The other headphone was on the floor beside the tub. She had a white-noise app on her phone she liked to listen to while bathing. This helped her relax. And since they were wireless headphones, there was no danger. Later I found her phone in the bedroom, nowhere near the water."

What this meant, of course, was that she wouldn't have been able to hear a thing. Assuming she had her eyes closed, anyone could have snuck up on her and yanked her by the ankles à la Bernard Spilsbury. Hey, presto: drowned lady.

Walter Vogel had to know the headphones helped him, in that they widened the circle of suspects to everyone in the house. He could have added them to the crime scene. It would have been so easy to do.

"I lifted her out of the water. I had an idea I would perform CPR. But there was no question. She was gone." He laid both hands flat on either side of the range, as though for support. "The bottle of sleeping pills was on the side of the tub. It was empty, and I knew she had filled the prescription recently. There were no marks on her, not one. I knew right away what had happened. Or so I thought." He turned to us, releasing a long sigh. "I called a colleague of mine who works as a medical examiner. I wanted—I thought it would be better if a friend took her."

"So you didn't call for an ambulance?" I asked.

Dorothy put a hand on my wrist, and even though she didn't look my way the message was clear: *Shut. Up.*

Walter gave me a pitying smile. "I am a medical doctor," he said. "An ambulance was not necessary, I knew this. I wanted the process to move forward as quickly and as quietly as possible."

"I can understand that," said Dorothy.

"While I waited, I went down the hall to Laura's room. It seemed right that she should know about this."

"How did she take the news?" asked Dorothy.

"Calmly," he said. "This surprised me. She asked to see—the body. She spent some minutes alone in there, while I waited in the bedroom until the medical examiner arrived." He dug his thumbs in his eyelids. "It does not seem real. It is like I am remembering a television show, or a story someone else told to me. But this is what happened."

"I'm so sorry, Walter," said Dorothy softly.

He insisted we have tea with him, and as he puttered about the kitchen retrieving various accoutrements, I admired the floor, which consisted of large terra-cotta tiles—about the size of the bases on a baseball field. There was a good half inch of grouting between them that had attracted all sorts of dirt/dust/random debris: a toothpick, an unused staple, a surprising amount of glitter. I've always been partial to kitchens. When I was a kid it was my favorite place to read, usually lying across one of the two hard wooden benches we kept on either side of our table. My parents could never fathom why I didn't lie on our couch or in my bed like a normal person. I wouldn't have been able to put it into words then, but I think I preferred the kitchen precisely *because* it wasn't a space for relaxing. The kitchen is for creating, and engaging, and I was always at my most creative and engaged with a book in front of me. I still am.

"You must forgive my fussiness."

He'd laid an individual mesh strainer across each of our cups and was spooning loose tea leaves into them. He picked up the kettle, pouring a steady stream through each metal well with an expert hand. "We brought these with us when we came to stay here. Vivian and I are very particular about our tea." The kettle jerked in his hand, a little of the water dribbling into Dorothy's saucer. "Forgive me. Would you like milk? Sugar? Lemon?"

Dorothy took her tea with a splash of milk while I opted for nothing. Walter took his with lemon, and if you're wondering whether I waited for him to take the first sip, wonder no more because I one hundred percent did. Unless he was secretly the Dread Pirate Roberts and had laced our cups with iocane powder, I was good to go.

We sipped in silence for a while.

"So tell me." Dorothy put her cup down. "How long have you been sleeping with your secretary?"

This time *I* was the one who spilled. But interestingly, Walter didn't seem too perturbed by the question. If anything, he was relieved.

"Ah." He stirred his tea unnecessarily. "I was wondering how much you saw just now. Thank you for being forthright, it will allow me to explain. Vivian and I met later in life, you see. I was her doctor, although—you probably know all this."

"I know a little," admitted Dorothy. "But I'd like to hear it from you."

He nodded, picking up his steaming cup again and wrapping both hands around it as though he were in a commercial for herbal tea, or maybe a commercial for antidepressants in which people drink herbal tea.

"Up to one year ago I had a practice in Portland. Before I

devoted myself to research and innovation. Mainly, I performed cosmetic procedures. Vivian was one of my patients. She came in . . . it must be a little over three years ago now. I will not say what procedures I did for her. A doctor never tells. Nor a husband."

We smiled weakly.

"I cannot believe it has only been three years since I first met her. It feels like we were together much longer. You must understand, I do not make a habit of getting involved with my patients. It is unprofessional. But from the moment I met her, there was an energy. A passion." He looked down, pausing a moment before looking up again. "It is easy to feel less alive as one gets older. But around Vivian I felt more . . . *vital* than I had in a long time. She was wonderful."

When were we getting to the part where he started screwing his twentysomething secretary?

"I was married once before. When I was very young. We were not a good match. But this is no surprise because I did not know myself then. It is one of many benefits of marrying later. That you know who you are. And what you need."

"MMMM-hm." Dorothy's head was on the move. "MMMM-hm."

"We were both in our forties when we married. We had already learned not to mind the expectations or approval of others. We chose our own moral code by which to live."

Here we go, I thought.

"We have what many would call an open marriage," he explained. "We are not religious in any way, which is hard for so many in this country to understand. Americans are so religious." He lifted his cup to his lips. "Even though I have lived here many years, this still surprises me."

He swallowed noisily.

"I loved her very much. Please make no mistake about this."

"So Vivian was aware of your relationship with Ms. Turner?"

For the first time he looked unsure of himself. He turned his head aside, contemplating the shiny peaked hood above the stovetop. I watched him purse his lips and squint, as though the answer to her question required some working out.

"We did not throw these outside relationships in each other's faces. The awareness was more general than that."

"I understand," said Dorothy, in as neutral a tone as (I imagine) she could muster.

"I hope you do," he said. "I would hate to feel you are judging us. I know Vivian would have been very upset by this."

Dorothy added another splash of milk to her tea. "Buh-*lieve* me, Walter, I stopped judging people a long time ago for any personal decisions they make. Especially along those lines. Would've been pretty hypocritical of me if I hadn't."

I stared at my cup, not knowing where else to look. Dorothy had her own complicated history with her late husband, of course. In addition to the rumors of drug use, it had come to light soon after his death that he had been cheating on her with multiple women. And yet no one, not even her fiercest opponents, dared question her grief or the enduring love she felt for him. Both emotions had been palpable in the wake of her loss.

Dorothy rattled her spoon against the inside of her cup. "So was Vivian involved with anyone?"

"No." His response was quick, but then he smiled, as though he'd caught himself. "At least, not of which I am aware."

"Do you know of anyone who might have wanted to harm her?"

"I can think of no one."

"What about the possibility of an outside intruder?"

"I cannot say for certain," he said, "but I think it is unlikely. There was no window in the bathroom, as is the case for all the bathrooms in this house. They are internal rooms, otherwise the glass walls would present a problem."

Fair enough, I thought.

"There is an alarm system on all the doors and windows that I turned on when I went upstairs for the night. This would have sounded if anyone had entered the building in the middle of the night."

"And I assume there are security cameras?"

He nodded. "All entry points are under twenty-four-hour surveillance. This is one of the many benefits of staying here, where people bring so many valuable items. The cameras are easy to see, and would have deterred an outside intruder."

He was right about that; I'd noticed the camera over the front door the first time I saw the place.

"The police are right now retrieving these records from the off-site location where they are stored. If anyone did come onto the property, we will know."

"Yes, I see," said Dorothy thoughtfully. "And how about inside? Any interior cameras?"

He shook his head. "No. Privacy is greatly valued by those who stay here." He leaned forward, those blue eyes of his boring into us. "This is why it must have been someone inside the building. *And yet it could have been anyone.* She never locked her bedroom door. She would not have heard this person's approach. Sometimes, she would lie in her bath with her eyes closed for hours." He leaned back in his chair, arms sagging at his sides. "I have been researching it this morning. Online. It is easy to drown a person when you have the element of surprise. It does not take much." He picked up his cup, draining it of its contents. "It must have been quick, otherwise there would have been marks from where this monster held her down. Also, if she had screamed, I would have heard. Everyone would have. All the bedrooms are on the second floor, on the same side of the building."

"Can you think of why anyone would want to kill your wife?" asked Dorothy. "In particular, any of the people staying here?"

He shook his head. "Of course I have been thinking very much about this. But I cannot find a reason. She did not have any money of her own. Her few possessions go to her sister, but they are not worth much. And I cannot imagine Laura doing anything like this. Paul is an old friend. The Shahs—"

He hesitated.

"What about the Shahs?" pursued Dorothy.

"I am uncomfortable saying it," he said. "But I have promised to tell you everything."

He lifted the teapot, offering us a top-off. Dorothy declined, as did I. He gave himself a second cup, taking his time. It was obvious he was stalling.

"Samir and Anne are good enough people, even though they are boring. But their son. Alex. He is at the age when boys develop infatuations so easily. . . ." He trailed off, sipping thoughtfully. "Earlier that day, on Wednesday, Vivian told me he had made . . . a *pass*, I believe it is called, though it sounds strange to my ears. She laughed about it. But I can still remember what it is like to be a boy of sixteen years. It is not so funny, then."

He took a bigger draught, staring at the two of us over the rim of his cup.

"Are you suggesting Alex Shah killed your wife because he had some sort of fascination with her?"

He shrugged his shoulders. "I do not know. But it is a possibility. Especially when so little makes sense."

"What about Ms. Turner?" asked Dorothy.

"Eve? Oh, no. Eve is not a possessive person. From the beginning I have been clear with her that our relationship will not lead anywhere. She understands this."

Did she, though? I wondered.

"The fact is that everyone who knew Vivian loved her."

Well, we knew enough about Vivian Davis by then to know this was a big, fat lie. Maybe Walter Vogel was just a loving, grieving husband who had no perspective where his late wife was concerned. Or maybe he was lying to protect himself—or someone else. Either way, there was no question in my mind that there was at least one person in the world—inside that very house—who hadn't loved her.

One person who had meant her a great deal of harm.

CHAPTER 25

There were no stairs in the Crystal Palace, I learned that day, which was another quirk of its quirky design. Instead, there were four triangular elevators—isosceles right triangles, if we're being specific about it—one in each corner of the building, with the sliding doors located on the triangles' hypotenuses. These corners corresponded exactly with the four points of the compass, which was why the elevators were labeled "N," "S," "E," and "W."

Walter escorted us to the "W" elevator and then gave us directions for where we could find Eve Turner, who was the next person Dorothy asked to see. I could tell he wanted to go with us, but knew better than to try or even suggest it. As the elevator doors closed, I could feel my shoulders sink, the upper muscles of my back relaxing as soon as he was gone from view.

"So what did you—"

Dorothy shook her head, raising her eyes upward. The implication was clear: she was worried someone might be listening to us. I was reminded of the way she'd shushed Leila in the Reception Room downstairs (or I suppose I should say down-elevator) two days earlier, during the memorial service. It had seemed paranoid then, but I wasn't so sure now.

"What happens if the power goes out?" I asked instead, as

the metal box holding us lumbered upward. "Are you trapped till it comes back on?"

"Oh, I'm sure they have a backup generator. Actually, I'll bet they have a backup for the backup." She turned to Officer Choi, who had assumed a guard-like stance even in this tiny space. "How are you doing, Sarah? Today's going to involve a lot of standing, so I think I'll request a chair for you for the next interview."

"Thank you, ma'am."

Dorothy turned to me. "Sarah here has a five-month-old at home. Benjamin. He's adorable. She hasn't yet regained the luxury of sleeping through the night, though."

I learned later that when Dorothy had needed to hire a private detail after the election, she'd requested that any female security officers with children who were looking for active duty be assigned to her.

Officer Choi and I exchanged an uneasy glance. I searched my brain for a follow-up question or at least a pleasantry, coming up blank as I often do when people's children are the subject of conversation. Though to be fair to her, I could see the relief in her eyes when it became obvious I wasn't going to say anything.

We lapsed into silence, during which I tried reviewing everything Walter Vogel had told us. The problem was that he'd told us *a lot*, and I felt sure some of it wasn't true. Did he and Vivian really have an open relationship, for instance? That was an easy lie to maintain now that Vivian wasn't around to contradict him—especially if he'd been telling the same lie to Eve Turner for months. And what about Alex Shah? Could that awkward kid really have murdered someone in cold blood? My mind flashed to the way he'd been kicking the snow outside, the rage he clearly harbored. . . . Not that rage in a teenager was proof of much.

The elevator doors slid open without a sound. We stepped

into a hallway exactly like the one below it, the glass side looking onto the garden we'd already seen (hello, creepy little hyperbaric oxygen chamber). The view from up here was much better. The ceilings in the Crystal Palace were unusually high, which made for a more elevated second story than usual. Beyond the garden, the ground fell away like it did in the back of the building, though the slope was gentler here, and covered in trees.

People spend a lot of time swooning over leaves: be they spring buds, the verdant canopies of summer, or the piebald foliage that autumn brings. But I'd like to take a moment to shout out the strange beauty of bare trees in winter. By this point, most of the recent snow had fallen to the ground, rendering the trees' branches naked and exposed, like the ends of nerve cells—which, as any high schooler can tell you, branch out in a starburst pattern when viewed under a microscope. (They're called *dendrites*, which is Greek for . . . wait for it . . . "trees.") Stripped of their leaves and blossoms, they look more like the root systems we can't see—the mirror image that every one of them harbors underground. For this reason, it's easier in winter than at any other time to remember that each tree has as much going on hidden from view as it does in plain sight. I guess trees and humans are similar that way.

Beyond them, in the far distance, I could see downtown Sacobago (spindly spire of a church, squat cylinder of a water tower, petite cupola perched atop a rectangular edifice I guessed was the high school). Given our height, as well as our distance, the electrical wires crisscrossing the densely populated area were particularly noticeable. I'd been brought up to think of nature as messy and chaotic, but contrasting this expanse of forest with the commercial district beyond, I couldn't help feeling the chaos and messiness were all man-made. Or maybe that was just my—

"What are you doing?"

I turned. Dorothy was staring at me from farther down the hallway, her arms crossed over her bulky coat. She huffed impatiently, doubling back past Officer Choi.

"I don't want to give him a chance to warn her," she whispered. "Or coordinate what she's going to say. I don't trust either of them. Do you?"

"Oh!" I said. "Totally. I mean—of course not. Sorry, let's—"

She hurried away again.

I followed meekly (yet swiftly!) behind.

Chapter 26

We heard Eve Turner before we saw her: tapping away at a keyboard, the delicate tattoo of fingerpad on plastic so steady and rapid, the subject matter under consideration had to be either insipid or inspired, nothing in between. My guess was that her task fell on the "insipid" end of the spectrum, but maybe that was snobbish of me. There are plenty of people who have a passion for administration, and if I'm being honest with myself, I'm one of them. There's a unique satisfaction to the clarity of administrative tasks—the precision they require, the finality their completion affords. I find they scratch the persistent itch my neurotic personality generates on a regular basis.

Eve's office overlooked the patio, including the steep drop beyond it. In the distance I caught a glimpse of Crystal River flowing with enough speed to produce the occasional streak of foam among its whorls and eddies. She was sitting with her back to this splendid view, which meant she was facing us when we entered. Her desk was little more than a table: a fashionably minimalist, stainless-steel affair. Personally, I think half the point of a desk is to hide the lower portion of one's body. I would have hated working at this one, which put its occupant on full display. Eve Turner was making the most of that display, her pencil skirt showing off her stupendous legs, crossed elegantly at the ankle.

She looked up at us, her hands continuing to type. I was reminded of those old ladies who can knit while carrying on a conversation—as if their fingers harbor a separate brain.

"Hello," she said coolly. "Can I help you with anything?"

"You can!" Dorothy took a jovial, hopping sort of step inside. "Would you mind if we asked you a few questions?"

"Not at all. I'm finishing up one thing, if you don't mind. Please. Take a seat."

Dorothy made a joke about taking this statement literally, securing a chair for Officer Choi and placing it outside the room, in the hallway.

We sat, waiting for Eve to finish typing. On her desk lay a letter opener with the lustrous gleam of real silver. Its handle was mother-of-pearl, and it was propped up on a smooth wooden block with a notch that fit its sharp point perfectly—the way you see chopsticks arranged to the side of a plate in fancy restaurants. Did anyone get enough physical mail anymore to justify such a thing? I guessed it was more ornamental than functional.

She was all business today, practically officious. Not that I expected her to be as familiar with Dorothy as she'd been with me. But if we hadn't come upon her in the kitchen earlier, I wondered if she'd be more open now. Maybe Walter really *had* texted her a warning in the time it took us to reach her office. Or maybe, like Paul, she was just feeling nervous around Dorothy Gibson.

While Paul's nerves had expressed themselves in unwarranted laughter and a propensity to babble, I felt certain Eve's would take her in the opposite direction, her native reserve hardening. It was exactly what I would have done, and it happens more often than you'd think where the rich and famous are concerned. In the same way people don't like approaching celebrities for fear of seeming smarmy, they also act coldly toward them—even after the approach has been made. I've heard countless celebrities complain about how awkward their conversations with "normies" can be, how they have to pretend not to notice the cold shoulders they get, and overcompensate with warmth and good cheer on their end.

"So sorry about that." She closed her laptop, folding her hands and resting them on top of the computer's burnished silver surface.

"I imagine you were as upset as we were to hear the details of Vivian Davis's death," began Dorothy.

"It's shocking," said Eve, not sounding shocked whatsoever. "And scary to think how long it might have taken to get that information if it hadn't been for your intervention. I have to thank you both for honoring my request as quickly as you did."

"Oh, it was the least we could do."

"With all due respect, ma'am, I disagree. The least you could have done was nothing. It's what most people would have done."

Dorothy let out a throaty chuckle. "Plea-hease don't call me ma'am! Dorothy will do just fine."

"I knew you'd move things along," Eve continued smoothly. (She was warming up already, I was happy to see.) "That's why I'm so sorry you lost. Well, *one* of the reasons I'm so sorry you lost."

"Why thank you!" exclaimed Dorothy heartily. "Hearing that from a capable young woman such as yourself really helps soothe the sting of defeat. I mean that."

"I'm also glad you came back today. I know you can't say it yourself, but the police didn't inspire much confidence. I think Walter can use all the help he can get. We all can."

She raised one hand and then lowered it. I felt sure she'd been about to touch her face and had made the conscious effort not to. I wrote a self-help book once for this cheesy high-profile trial lawyer, and by far the most useful piece of information in it was that jurors hate when a witness touches her face. It's gross, and indicates discomfort, hence untrustworthiness. I wondered if some life coach or etiquette instructor had taught

Eve Turner about this. She was so polished, she seemed like she'd attended some sort of "finishing school" at some point in her young life.

Dorothy scooted forward.

"Let's just get the awkward part out of the way, shall we? Walter told us about your relationship."

Eve nodded once, briskly. She was trying so hard to keep up the business-like façade, but the emotion was rippling right underneath it, practically visible. All we had to do was wait for it to erupt.

"I don't want you to think that's how I conduct myself in a work environment. Up till now we've been careful to keep everything professional during business hours. Not because we're hiding anything, but because that's the way it should be." She hesitated delicately. "But since Vivian died, and especially since last night . . . everything's gone a little crazy."

"Well, of course it has," said Dorothy.

"I assume Walter explained how the two of them . . . ?" She hesitated again. "How they had an understanding? There was no sense that we were . . . What I mean is, I wasn't . . ."

"A homewrecker?" I offered.

I'd meant it to be funny, but I could tell by the way they both jerked their heads toward me that it hadn't been received that way.

"Yes," said Eve sharply. "Thank you."

She glanced at a photo on the corner of her desk. It was a picture of her with an older man, streaks of gray at his temples. He was dressed in a tuxedo, and she had on a poofy white dress I would have called bridal if she weren't so young. She looked exactly as she did now, except that her face still had the smooth, almost liquid quality of a child's: an elasticity we trade in for character upon making our acquaintance with the world. They were grasping each other by both hands and their mouths were open—this dignified father/daughter pair (he was obviously her father, there was no question about it) captured in the act of dancing and laughing together. It was Joy personified, and to my surprise, I found my eyes prickling while I looked at it.

I'm by no means a daddy's girl (can we officially retire that phrase?). But I can still remember what it felt like to be thrown in the air by my father when I was little—the exhilaration of it, and never at the expense of security. . . . I should have appreciated this more when it was happening. But I had no idea how special, or fleeting, it was. Children never do.

Eve angled the photo away from me. "I wasn't raised to be someone's mistress. I was very clear with Walter about that from the start."

It made perfect sense that she'd been a debutante; there were those finishing lessons I'd been wondering about. But she'd been in the Crystal Palace for only a week or two, which meant this photo traveled with her wherever she went. I'd bet my livelihood that her father had given her that letter opener. Clearly Eve Turner *was* a daddy's girl, which made her the perfect candidate to fall in love with a domineering older man like Walter Vogel. It was depressingly predictable.

"Yes, Walter told us about that, too," said Dorothy. "The unconventional nature of his marriage. Tell me, did you ever discuss it with Vivian?"

Eve shook her head. "That would have been awkward, even with the most evolved of wives." She paused, clearly unhappy with the implication that this "open marriage" business was a sham. "He's brilliant, you know. I hope you realize that. I don't think Vivian ever did. He's not the sort of person to be confined by convention."

Ugh.

"He mentioned something along those lines," said Dorothy. "But the way I heard it, he seemed to be suggesting a disregard for convention was something he and *Vivian* shared." Dorothy turned to me. "Did it seem that way to you?"

"Definitely."

Eve glared at me (so much for our being gal pals), before turning back to Dorothy.

"He was being kind. He always is where Vivian's concerned. Especially now. But I don't mind being honest about her. She never supported him the way he needed. Vivian had to be the star of the show. She was always overshadowing his work with her latest scheme, sucking all the air out of the room so the rest of us couldn't breathe. For a while it was the election"—she looked apologetically at Dorothy—"not that we all weren't caught up in it. But she managed to make it about her, as usual. And then after—well, after you—"

"After I lost, yes."

"Right. Then it was this ridiculous Kickstarter thing. Have you heard about that?"

"We're aware," said Dorothy drily.

"And now this. And I know it sounds awful, but in a weird way it feels like more of the same."

"How so?"

"Well, the whole reason I asked you about the medical examiner was to help move things along. So Walter could focus on his work again."

"And now everything's blown up even worse than before," I said.

She nodded, turning to me.

"The first time we spoke, do you remember how I said I couldn't believe she killed herself? Because she was so self-centered?"

I nodded.

"Well, it turns out I was right about that. And I know it's crazy, but I can't help thinking this murder investigation is like her parting shot. Like somehow, she arranged it so that her death would cause as much trouble as possible."

"You don't hold her responsible for her own murder, do you?" asked Dorothy.

"Of course not," said Eve. "It's just, she could be very . . .

erratic. The kind of person who'd do outrageous things on impulse."

"Such as?" asked Dorothy.

"One time she burned all of Walter's clothes. After a big fight. Just cleaned out his closet and lit a bonfire in their backyard. I had to order a whole new wardrobe for him."

"Ah," said Dorothy. "I see."

"But even *she* would have to draw the line at letting someone murder her. Obviously."

"So what do you think happened?" asked Dorothy. "She faked her own death and then someone took advantage, made it real? Maybe the person who helped her stage it?"

"I have no idea," Eve said simply.

"Did you notice anything strange the night she died?" Dorothy (nevertheless) persisted. "Last Wednesday?"

Eve shook her head. "I worked in my office pretty late that night. And then I went down to the kitchen and made a sandwich for myself. Around eight thirty. I took it up to my room, which I didn't leave till the next morning. Everything seemed normal when I woke up. It's so strange, looking back on it now. I went down and had some breakfast. The Shahs were there, all three of them. We talked about"—she gave Dorothy an embarrassed look—"well, *you*. And the election. . . . All that."

"Understandable," said Dorothy tersely.

"And then I came up here. Walter was already in the office next door, which was also normal. I got to work. It wasn't till a few hours later that I found out what happened, and by then the . . . the body had already been taken away."

"How *did* you find out?" asked Dorothy.

"It was Anne, actually. Anne Shah. She came up and asked me if I'd heard. I hadn't heard anything. I guess I'd been in my own world. I tend to get like that when I'm working."

"I can understand that." Dorothy hesitated delicately. "This may sound like a dramatic question, so I apologize in advance, but is there anyone here, in this house, who you think might have had something to do with Vivian's murder?"

"No-o."

We all heard the hesitation.

"What is it?" asked Dorothy. "Please don't hold back. You must realize we can hardly suspect *you*. If you hadn't asked for my help obtaining the toxicology findings, we'd be none the wiser that a murder happened."

And yet those findings would have come out at some point. By demanding the results as soon as possible, Eve Turner could have been trotting out one of the oldest tricks in the book: ye olde double bluff. I felt certain Dorothy appreciated this, but was doing everything she could to put the young woman at ease.

"At this point anything will help," continued Dorothy, "even an unfounded suspicion. We're not in a court of law or anything, this is all unofficial."

Eve took a deep breath and exhaled. "I'd look into her sister. Laura Duval. She's . . . an odd one."

"You're telling me!" I exclaimed, trying—perhaps desperately—to be friendly. "The day of the memorial service? I saw her in the main hall wearing this big black dress and veil. *Way* over the top."

"I didn't see her then," said Eve. "But I saw her later that day. After the memorial. After everyone had left. I went to Vivian's bedroom because Walter asked me to gather her personal effects and take them back to their regular house, here in Sacobago. I wasn't expecting anyone to be there so I opened the door without knocking. Laura was sitting at the vanity, holding up this big necklace to her throat that Vivian used to wear sometimes."

"I heard that Vivian had some family jewelry," said Dorothy. "But I'm not sure how valuable it was. Do you have any idea?"

Eve shook her head. "I'm not really into jewelry, I'm pretty clueless about that stuff. But that wasn't the odd part. I could tell she was annoyed I'd surprised her like that, and a little embarrassed. So I apologized and told her I'd come back later. And as I was leaving she waved her hand at me and said something like, 'No harm done, sugar.' Which is when I saw it, on her finger. Vivian's wedding ring. There's no mistaking it because she and Walter have the same ones, and they're very distinctive. It's the infinity symbol folded onto itself so the two loops become one double-banded loop. Hers has a diamond at the intersection point."

Eve looked from one to the other of us.

"She'd just stuck it on her own finger. As if it were hers now. And—I don't mean to sound jealous or anything, I promise you I'm not, but—I can't help noticing that every time she interacts with Walter, she flirts like crazy with him."

That's just the Blanche Dubois in her, I wanted to say. Was she really implying that Laura had killed her sister so she could have Walter Vogel for herself? Those eyes of his were purty and all, but come on. . . .

"Yes," said Dorothy thoughtfully, "That's interesting, thank you for sharing that. Well!" She rose from her chair. I did the same. "We've taken up more than enough of your valuable time. Thank you for answering our questions. Would you mind pointing us in the direction of Laura Duval's room?"

As it happened, Eve didn't mind at all. She even offered to take us there herself. I think she was happy to get rid of us.

CHAPTER 27

Eve was a fast walker—especially considering the heels she was wearing. We stayed on the second floor, crossing the Great Hall by way of the balcony that ran along the back of the building. It was more of a landing, really, much roomier than I'd realized from below. Rocking chairs, chaise lounges, and even a sofa had been placed there, overlooking the back of the property. But I wasn't going to be mesmerized by the view again. Instead, I made the mistake of looking up and nearly lost my footing. The glass roof was still a ways off, inducing a rush of vertigo that made me feel as though I might pitch over the railing and down onto the hard marble floor. (The popular conception of heights is that they're scary when a person looks down, but I've always found it to be much worse when I look up; try it sometime.) (Or actually, don't.)

Dorothy had been walking ahead of me, but somehow she sensed my discomfort, turning around.

"Are you all right?"

"I'm okay," I said. "This hall's just a little . . . high. What's on the third floor?"

Dorothy turned to Eve. "I think it's a gym, right?"

Eve nodded without stopping. "It has its own track and an Olympic-size pool. On the side we're crossing over to now is a greenhouse slash conservatory. You feel like you're outside with the glass roof over it."

"It's *very* strange being up there in winter," Dorothy assured me.

I didn't doubt her.

We turned down a long interior hallway. Eve gestured to the second door on the right, which had crime scene tape stretched across it in an X.

"That's Vivian's bedroom, obviously. I'd let you take a peek, but the police don't want anyone going in there and they locked it, anyway. Each of these bedrooms has a unique lock. It's one of the few things I like about the place."

She passed the next door. "That's Walter's room," she said, before stopping at the door after that. "And here's Laura. The room's actually identical to Vivian's, so it'll give you a good sense of the layout. Don't hesitate to let me know if I can help in any way. You know where to find me."

She nodded, departing the way she'd come. Dorothy raised her eyebrows at me as she held up her hand, rapping the door with two knuckles.

A syrupy-sweet voice rang out: "Come in!"

Officer Choi went first, doing a quick survey before stepping out again and nodding at us.

Like Eve's office, the wall opposite the door was made of glass—because every outside wall in this nightmare of a prism was made of glass. But a blackout shade the exact size of the wall had been lowered onto it, obliterating all the light except at the very edges.

With no artificial illumination other than a small lamp on a bedside table, it was gloomy at best in there, giving me flashbacks to my own childhood bedroom. Not that my childhood bedroom had a four-poster bed and matching vanity that looked to be from the Regency era. Or an en suite bathroom in one corner. Atop the dresser I saw an explosion of tubs and tubes, bottles and brushes. But my eye swept over these in favor of the dramatic tableau arranged on the bed.

Laura was lying horizontal in a gauzy, floor-length nightdress, her head propped up on several pillows. A moist towel had been draped over her forehead, on top of which she'd positioned the back of one hand like a Victorian lady, mid-swoon. She turned toward us languidly. Even in the half-light I could see how heavily made up she was: the swirls of foundation on her cheeks and chin.

"Hello," she said to me. "We met th'other day, didn't we?"

I informed her we had.

"This must be the neighbor you're staying with." She turned to Dorothy. "What's your name, sugar?"

Dorothy opened her eyes wide. I guessed it had been a while since anyone had asked her her name.

"I'm Dorothy," she said. "Dorothy Gibson."

"Hello, Dorothy. And what do you do?"

"You know, Laura, that's an excellent question. At the moment I'm trying to get to the bottom of things. To do all I can to support the investigation into your sister's death."

"Well, bless you for that," said Laura. "'Specially since I never liked getting to the bottom of *anythin'*. Sittin' pretty up top's more my style. Where the air is sweet and the view is nice 'n' clear."

Dorothy chuckled politely.

"Mind you, I always *knew* Veevo couldn't'a' killed herself." She turned to me. "Didn't I say as much, th'other day?"

She hadn't, but I nodded anyway.

"I'll do *anythin'* I can, of course. And you'll have to fuh-give me for not gettin' up. Please don't think I'm bein' rude. I'm jus' havin' one a'my headaches today."

"I'm sorry to hear that," said Dorothy. "Do you mind if we take off our coats?"

It had been chilly in Eve's office, but it was sweltering in here.

"Make yourself at home."

Dorothy laid her coat across the back of the tiny chair in front of the vanity. I put my kiwi-green number on top of hers.

"Do you mind if we take a quick look in your bathroom?" she asked. "A little birdie told me your room is laid out the same as your sister's."

"Sho is, sugar. Knock yuhselves out."

The bathroom was exactly as Walter Vogel had described it: a built-in tub at the far end of the room, in a little alcove. Leading up to it were a sink and toilet on one side, a shower stall on the other. No windows, no point of entry other than the door inside the bedroom. We came out almost immediately.

"You can set yourselves down there." Laura pointed to a dainty love seat to the left of the door, pushed up against the wall. It was big enough for two people, but only just, and as we sat down I was grateful we'd taken off our coats.

Dorothy leaned forward. "So I understand you arrived at the house on Wednesday a matter of hours before the, ah, tragic incident?"

"That's right."

"Well, that's interesting, because the day *before* that, on Tuesday, we ran into your sister at a liquor store in the neighborhood, and saw you waiting for her outside."

Remind me never to play a round of Texas Hold'em with Dorothy Gibson. The lady can bluff. Laura's body stiffened; I could see her willing herself back into her languid pose while she figured out what to say.

"Okay, ya got me," she admitted finally. "Truth is, Veevo called me a week earlier, *beggin'* me to come. Said it'd been too long, she could use the support. Now that wasn't something she *ever* said before. Either part. I could tell somethin' was off, y'know? So I came a day before I was supposed to. On Tuesday 'stead of Wednesday."

"Why?" asked Dorothy. "Were you trying to surprise her?"

She waved a hand in the air. "It wasn't as calculated as all that. I think I was just nervous, wanted to get there sooner than later. Anyway, I called her when I landed in Portland and she rushed to meet me there, said I couldn't come up yet, to this place. Said there was too much goin' on, I was gonna mess ever'thing up if I didn't come when I was supposed ta. That was also strange. The Veevo I knew played it fast and loose. *I* was always the particular one. I said we at least had to have lunch together, which became a liquid lunch pretty quick. Drinkin' heavily is a family tradition a'ours." She laughed huskily. "That's why we went to Betty's."

"I see," said Dorothy.

"Not sayin' much of anything to each other is also a family tradition, sad to say." Laura let out a lingering sigh. "We were so close as little girls. But then time goes by, and people change, don't they?" She shrugged—which was hard to do while fully reclining, but she managed it. "Didn't help she moved away first chance she got. Ran off to New York right after high school."

"To college?" asked Dorothy.

"Pshh." Laura took her hand off her forehead to flap it at Dorothy. "To the stage. She wanted to be a star."

"And you stayed closer to home?"

"That's right. But then I've always been a homebody. Plus, when our mama got sick, who was gonna take care a'her if not me? Our daddy died when we were little," she explained. "But don' you go thinkin' I resented her. We all have our path in life. And look where hers took her in the end." She let out another sigh. "Breaks my heart."

It was easy to pretend she didn't resent her sister, now that said sister was dead. I wondered. . . .

"Can't say I learned much a'anythin' that Tuesday. It's why I didn't mention it. Didn't see the point. She was stressed, no doubt about that. Worried 'bout Walter's career. 'Parently that presentation he's been puttin' on here wasn't goin' so well. Not that they needed the cash, but a thwarted man's a troubled man. They're not as used to bein' frustrated as we womenfolk."

Womenfolk? Was she going to slaughter a chicken before we were done?

"Veevo hustled me back to Portland on Tuesday afternoon. Put me up at a hotel for the night. Fancy one, too. Mint on the pilla 'n' ever'thing."

"I assume you arrived here the next day?"

Laura nodded. "Got a cab this time, Veevo had too much goin' on. Cost an arm and a leg. Least Veevo paid for it. She was always so thoughtful about money. But then, when your husband has a lot of it, you can afford to be, can't you?" she added cattily. "I've said it before and I'll say it again, my sister did well when she married Walter. I for one refuse to believe he had anything to do with her death. Nuh-uh. No way."

"I understand Vivian had a few family heirlooms of her own?" asked Dorothy. "Some jewelry and whatnot?"

Laura sat up eagerly, holding her forehead towel in place.

"She told you, didn't she? That secretary? That I was tryin' on Veevo's things? Well, I'm not ashamed to admit it. They were always meant for *both* a' us, mind you. We jus' figured she'd put 'em to better use in the big city than anything Mama or I'd get up to back home. We all have our own grievin' process. Made me feel closer to her, is all."

"I would never judge anyone for how they chose to grieve," said Dorothy.

"Wish you'd share that sentiment with *her*," said Laura. "Never could trust a woman named Eve," she muttered, sinking down a little. "Don't you tell anyone I said that," she added. "When you're a white lady who sounds like me, you gotta be careful sayin' anything bad about a person o'color. Can so easily come across the wrong way."

"I realize you didn't see them very often, but would you say that your sister and her husband had a good marriage?"

"*Absolutely*. I went to their weddin', of course. Such a beautiful event, you could really feel the love they had for each other. They'd both been married once before, y'know. Always knew that first husband a' Veevo's was no good. One of those finance crooks who never got the comeuppance he deserved. And *his* first wife, *well!* From what I hear she's a real hellion. They were worried she'd crash the weddin'."

"Really?" asked Dorothy. "So things didn't end well between them?"

"Ended about as bad as they could! 'Parently she called Walter up before the weddin', threatened to bring their son to the ceremony, force him to acknowledge the boy in front a' everyone. Poor boy, couldn't'a' been more'n a teenager at the time."

"They had a son together?" Dorothy sounded as surprised as I was to hear this. It was odd that Walter hadn't mentioned it.

Laura nodded. "Sure! Walter never talks about 'im, though. Or her. Likes to pretend they don't exist. Can't say I blame him. Y'know, I don' think she lives far from here? I were the police, I'd look into where she was last Wednesday night. Or that son a'hers. He's gotta be fully grown by now."

"I believe the police are looking into the possibility that someone could have entered the house from the outside," Dorothy said diplomatically. "But I'm wondering if anyone *inside* the house struck you as suspicious, or out of the ordinary? Especially that first day you got here?"

"Now let me think. . . . Well, y'know, there *was* something strange goin' on with the help."

"The help?" repeated Dorothy.

"That's right, the one with the messy hair?"

"You mean Paul."

"Yeah, that's the one. That Wednesday night, the night I arrived, Veevo and I, we were sittin' in her room having some wine." She slipped down to her previous horizontal position. "I was still tryin' to figure out what was going on with her, and she still wasn't givin' me a thing. Anyway, we were interrupted twice. First was when Walter said g'night. Such a sweet man. Second was a few minutes later. It was that Paul fella, and I couldn't hear what they were sayin' to each other because they were speakin' so low. But I could tell neither of 'em was happy. When he left I said to my sister, 'you not payin' him enough or something?' And she just laughed and said, 'I'm not paying him at all.' "

"*Real*-ly! Well, that's interesting," said Dorothy.

"I thought so too," said Laura. "And when I asked her how that worked, she just laughed and said she had a few tricks up her sleeve. But then Veevo always did. I loved her to pieces, but more often 'an not she was up to no good. Our mama used to call her Imp. That was her pet name for 'er. And it fit."

"Did you tell the police that when they questioned you?" asked Dorothy.

"Oh, I did'n' speak with the police," said Laura airily. "When they came by I was indisposed. Lucky you, you caught me at a better time. Nice intimate chat among friends is *much* more my speed, anyway."

"Well, so long as we're being intimate," said Dorothy slowly, "I wondered if I might be so bold as to ask whether you knew about the relationship between your sister's husband and Eve Turner?"

Laura looked from one to the other of us. She let loose a low and sultry laugh that brought to mind famous temptresses down the ages like Jezebel and Bathsheba. And Jessica Rabbit.

"I don' believe it for a second. *She* tell you that?"

"No, actually. *He* did."

Laura jerked into a sitting position once more, but this time the towel slid off her face.

"What?"

"He told us he and Vivian had an open relationship," explained Dorothy. "That they had an understanding about that sort of thing."

"It's a lie," she hissed. "A goddamned lie."

"Well, I wonder if maybe it's something she wasn't comfortable sharing with her sis—"

"*Absolutely* not. She was committed to him, they were—" She broke off, shaking her head as if to rid herself of the thought.

"It's a lie," she said again, tossing herself down on the mattress.

Dorothy and I looked at each other, unsure what to do. But Laura soon cleared this up for us.

"I'd like fuh you to leave now." She resettled the towel on her face. Now it was covering her eyes too.

"Of course," said Dorothy. "I'm sorry to have upset you, it's just—"

"Get out!" she thundered. "Now!"

For a moment we both sat there, too stunned to move. I grabbed our coats from the back of the chair and motioned Dorothy to make her exit. Following after her, I closed the door as gently as possible behind me.

Chapter 28

Dorothy was halfway down the hall by the time I let go of the handle. I hurried after her, trailing Officer Choi as we made our way to the "E" elevator.

"Well," I said, sidling up to her as she pressed the call button.

"Well," she agreed. "Do *you* have any idea what the hell is going on here?"

I shook my head.

She spread out her hands with a chuckle. "Nor do I! And I'm getting the sense I may not be helping here at all. Maybe Leila was right. She usually is."

The elevator dinged open and we got in. I didn't ask her where we were going, because it was obvious. We were leaving. What else do you do when someone screams at you to get out?

I had to physically restrain myself from gasping when we reached the ground floor. We were in the library—or Reading Room, to use its proper name—on the other side of the hall, the counterpart to the Reception Room. The two walls of this giant space that weren't glass were lined with books from floor to ceiling, and featured one of those wheeled ladders you can roll back and forth to reach the highest shelves. If I ever manage to buy my dream house, it will one hundred percent feature one of these ladders.

Unlike the Reception Room, the Reading Room was filled with furniture: armchairs, end tables, lamps, rugs. I even saw a few bean-bag chairs scattered here and there, and the buttercup shape of a papasan.

I wanted to stop, turn round and round, sing a song about how wonderful it was à la Belle in *Beauty and the Beast*. But Dorothy hadn't stopped, so I marched along with her through this marvellous room and out into the Great Hall . . . where the Shahs were waiting for us.

It was Anne who stepped forward.

"We were hoping we'd catch you. Do you think we could talk?"

The Recreation Room was next to the Reading Room. It was easily the biggest space I'd seen yet, taking up the same acreage as the kitchen *and* dining room across the hall. The four of us—Samir, Anne, Dorothy, and I—stepped into it, blinded for a moment by the drastic change in lighting. The ceiling was much lower here, dropped several feet to give it more of a den-like feel. And even though two of the walls were glass, they looked onto the eastern part of the sky, which by then (four o'clock on a December afternoon) was dark enough that it looked more like night than day.

A multitiered bar had been built into the wall opposite the door, and in the vast space between were little seating areas arranged for socializing: teeny-tiny cocktail tables that looked like pedestals missing their statuary with tall, giraffe-legged stools surrounding them; long leather couches in muted browns and reds, low coffee tables in front of them. On the northern end of the room, next to the elevator marked "N," was a pool table with a pendant light hanging over it, perfect for off-the-record interrogations by dirty cops who resorted to roughing up their suspects. Who knew? Maybe SI Locust could use it later.

It was a room built for a crowd, and yet there was no one in it except for Paul, who was standing behind the bar. It was a little like that bar scene in *The Shining*, actually, except that by "a little" I mean "a lot."

"What can I get you?" he asked.

An answer to what you and Vivian were arguing about the night she died? This was what I wanted to say. But instead I kept my mouth shut and let Dorothy order, which was a good thing because "gin martini" was a much more sensible reply—so much so, I ordered one myself.

The Shahs ordered glasses of Chablis, but I got the feeling they were being polite. Once we had our drinks, we sat on two leather sofas facing each other, far enough away from the bar that we didn't have to worry about Paul overhearing.

Samir Shah sat down last, on the very edge of his seat. He placed his glass on the table between us, next to his phone.

"I want you to know this isn't my idea, coming to you."

Anne rolled her eyes at him. "Thanks for that, dear."

He held up his hands. "Sorry. I just think this is a mistake."

"Well, now that you've released yourself from all responsibility, would it be okay with you if I talked?"

He gestured with the flat of his hand before picking up his wine and swigging it. (Dorothy and I hadn't wasted the opportunity to take a few swigs of our own by this time.)

Anne fingered her necklace, just as she had the day of the memorial. They were the same string of pearls, I noticed, but the Chanel suit was a different shade. How many Chanel suits did she own? As many as she wanted, I guessed.

"I heard you're helping out with the investigation."

"To the extent I can," said Dorothy.

"Well, I just think the world of you. I hope you know that. I could kick myself for not doing more for your campaign."

"We donated plenty," growled Samir. "You're stalling, Annie. Just get on with it."

She gave us an embarrassed smile. "He's right, I *am* stalling. Because I don't quite know how to put—"

"Then maybe you shouldn't—"

"Let me speak!" she shouted, surprising all of us, herself included.

She took a moment to collect herself, smoothing the buttons on the front of her jacket.

"I'm not sure if you're aware, but we'd been here for a week already when Vivian Davis died. We arrived on Wednesday, the twenty-third of November." She let out a tinkly socialite's laugh—but it was the tinkle of glass breaking. "It's easy to remember, because staying here has been like a prison sentence. I'm aware of every hour that's passed, grateful to have it behind me."

"I can't imagine how stressful this has been for you," murmured Dorothy.

"Thank you for that. As you probably know, my husband went to medical school with Walter Vogel, who'd reached out to him for funding. It had to do with an invention he's been developing in the field of dermatology. Based on his own experience with Dr. Vogel and what he'd heard through the professional grapevine, Samir didn't have high hopes for the product"—

Samir snorted.

"But he took the trip out here both as a favor to Walter and as a family trip for us with our son, Alex, who's sixteen."

Anne turned to me.

"The day of Vivian's memorial, you may have noticed a . . . strained dynamic between the two of us and Alex."

Samir snorted again. Anne side-eyed him a warning to keep quiet.

"I did," I admitted. "He seemed angry about something."

Anne nodded. "He was angry because he knew Samir and I

detested that woman. But when you asked about her, we pretended not to have much of an opinion."

"He called you hypocrites," I said, remembering easily.

"I think it was a combination of a child's simplistic idea of telling the truth, and the fact that he knew we were lying for *his* sake."

Beside her, Samir's leg began to shake uncontrollably.

"Almost as soon as we got here, you see, Alex started acting strangely. He's our only child, and I—I've always prided myself on how close we are. That probably sounds laughable to you. Or pathetic. But I try not to smother him, not to be one of *those* mothers. And he keeps his end of the bargain by not being one of *those* teenagers. We do pretty well that way." A smile rose to her lips at the memory of their normal state of affairs, despite her current predicament. "We actually *talk*, you know? I really mean it when I say he's my favorite person in the world."

Her husband put his hand over hers, leaving it there.

"But by that Saturday, three days after we arrived, he was . . . different. Withdrawn. Removed in a way he'd never been before. I told myself he was just bored. This first leg of the trip was always going to be the most trying for him, before we went to New York. But I knew even then. I knew it was something more serious. I kept asking him what was the matter and he kept putting me off. This went on for days." She looked to Samir, who nodded.

"Never been so frustrated with the kid," he said. "Which is really saying something for *me*, anyways. Didn't help I was getting the quack treatment from Dr. Demento all that time." He shook his head impatiently. "Walter was always pretty suss, even in med school. But I don't know what happened to him. The guy's a fraud. Makes Elizabeth Holmes look like Marie freakin' Curie."

"Back to *our son*," said Anne. "On Wednesday morning we took him to a diner. Breakfast has always been his favorite meal, and we made a point of lingering over it. Many pancakes later, he opened up."

"He's lucky to have two parents who care so much about him," observed Dorothy.

"Thank you, but I'm not sure 'lucky' is a word I'd use to describe him. Not anymore."

She unearthed a wadded-up tissue from her pocket and began dabbing at the corners of her eyes.

"I'm just going to say it, cuz I'm sure the suspense is killing you." Samir picked up his wife's hand. "That okay with you?"

She nodded.

He let go of her, running his hands through his spiky hair a few times.

"She assaulted him."

"Who?" asked Dorothy. "Who assaulted him?"

"Vivian Davis. She assaulted our son." He sat back, his eyes shining bright. "These weren't his words, of course. But that's what happened."

"She slipped inside his bedroom the third night we were here. Friday night." Anne was speaking more quietly now; I had to lean forward to hear her. "They"—she stopped to take another breath; this was obviously painful for her—"there was no intercourse. But they . . . there were other things they did together."

"You've seen him." Samir's leg was shaking again. "He's just a kid."

We sat in silence for a minute or two, because what do you say after such a revelation?

I'm not sure what I'd been expecting them to tell us. I'd known since the day of the memorial that something was up with them. But I never thought it was something like this.

I slugged down a good third of my gin martini, while across

from us Anne rested her hand on her husband's leg to stop it from shaking.

"I'm so sorry to hear about this," said Dorothy at last. "I can't imagine how difficult it must have been for you as parents to listen to your son recount all this."

Did you catch the careful wording there? I sure did. She wasn't assuming that what Alex had told them was the truth. Neither was I.

"What did you do?" asked Dorothy.

"We went straight to Vivian, of course," said Anne.

"And when was this?"

Anne hesitated, which was why I knew what she was going to say before she said it.

"Last Wednesday. The thirtieth of November."

Aka the last day of Vivian Davis's life. Not so good for the Shahs.

"And what did she say?"

"She was just as loony as her husband," said Samir. "Tried to claim our son had come on to *her*."

"She reversed the whole thing," said Anne. "She said he'd snuck into *her* bedroom and got into bed with her. It was *absurd*."

I could hear the outrage in her voice, could see it in the way her neck muscles were straining.

"She said she'd run into her bathroom until he left. She claimed nothing happened, which was why she'd been willing to laugh the whole thing off and hadn't said a word to us."

"Yeah right," scoffed Samir.

Anne blew her nose, emitting a muted, ladylike honk. "She said if we insisted on pursuing the issue, then she'd have to think about—pressing charges against him." She looked from one to the other of us. "His life would be ruined. Once an accusation like that gets made, it follows you around the rest of your life."

"You want to know what I think?" Samir didn't wait for an answer. "I think she did it as insurance. Knew her husband was a crook, wanted an easy way to get us to shut up about it."

I thought back to something Vivian's sister had said a few minutes earlier. How Vivian always had a few tricks up her sleeve. Was this one of her tricks? And if so, was it the one that had gotten her killed?

"When did all this happen?" asked Dorothy.

"On the afternoon of that day. Last Wednesday. We'd all eaten lunch together in the dining room. I asked her if Samir and I could speak to her and we went here, actually. No one comes here till later in the afternoon, so we were alone."

"Was it just her?" I asked. "Or was Walter with her too?"

"Just her," said Anne. "We have no idea if Walter knows anything about this."

Samir was snorting again.

"Weirdo sister of hers showed up right after," he said. "Two of them holed up together. Probably just an excuse to avoid us."

"Looking back, I wish we'd left the moment she told us those hideous lies," said Anne. "But the whole thing was like having an . . . an out-of-body experience. We needed time to think. About whether or not we should talk to Walter, or bring the police in on the spot, or document what little evidence we had before we left. That's why we stayed the night."

"Worst decision ever," said Samir.

"We were on autopilot at dinner with Walter, I don't even *know* what we talked about. And then of course we slept in Alex's bedroom," said Anne. "We couldn't leave him alone, couldn't take that chance. We laid out some sheets on the floor."

"Barely slept a wink," added Samir.

Dorothy stiffened ever so slightly, and I understood why. Parents weren't exactly the most reliable alibis for their children. And even if they *were* telling the truth, they'd just admitted to having been asleep at least some portion of the night. What was to have kept Alex from slipping out of his room and going to visit Vivian Davis while she was in her bath? I thought back to what Walter had said, about how devastating a sixteen-year-old boy might find this sort of rejection. . . .

Or maybe Samir, or Anne, or the two of them together had visited Vivian that night while their son slept peacefully. Maybe they'd tried to hash it out again and it had gone badly. Very badly. Parents had committed murder for the sake of their children's future before. We've all watched some version of that Texas cheerleader mom story at some point in our lives—it's inescapable.

And if a parent was willing to murder for the sake of a child's future, then why not the child himself? This meant Alex had two potential motives.

"The next morning, I woke up determined to bring matters to a head," said Anne. "So while Samir and Alex were packing, I went to Vivian's room."

Dorothy scooted forward in her seat. "You went to her room on Thursday morning?" she asked eagerly.

Anne nodded.

"What time?"

"Early," she said. "A little after seven. I knew she wouldn't be awake, she had terrible sleeping habits. But I didn't care. That's why I noticed right away that someone was moving around in the room. I hadn't been expecting to hear anything."

"What exactly did you hear?"

Anne paused. "It's hard to say. I'm afraid my memory's been affected by what I learned afterward. But I remember thinking it sounded like two people were fighting in there. Not that I heard shouts or anything like that, more like a . . . scuffling. A lot of commotion, if that makes sense."

"Did you hear *splashing* at all?" asked Dorothy.

Anne shook her head. "No," she said emphatically. "Definitely not."

"And this was at seven in the morning?"

Anne nodded. "It sounds terrible now, but I didn't care who was making noise, or what it meant. All I cared about was putting Vivian on notice that if she so much as said a word about our son, she'd have a legal battle on her hands. Samir and I had decided by then the best thing we could do was to take a strong stand against her. She was being a bully. And you have to stand up to a bully."

Samir scooted a few inches closer to her.

"So I knocked on the door. Loudly. I remember using the side of my fist. And whoever was in there froze. I knocked a number of times. Called out too. But no one responded."

"Did you try the door?" asked Dorothy.

"Yes, of course. It was locked."

That was interesting. The window for the time of death, you'll remember, was from nine the night before till three o'clock on Thursday morning. So at some point hours after Vivian had died, some person—or persons—had been in her room doing . . . what? Doctoring the crime scene? Looking for valuables that weren't there? Or something else we didn't know about?

"I wasn't about to break down the door. The last thing I wanted was to give her more ammunition against us. So I left, and we stayed for breakfast hoping we'd get a chance to speak to her. But then . . ." She looked helplessly at us. "We aren't fools," she said. "We know how this looks. When the police interviewed us this morning we didn't lie, but we also didn't tell them anything about this."

The tears were visible now—on the brink of overflowing.

"We have to tell them, don't we?"

"Well," said Dorothy slowly. "I would never counsel you to hold back anything from the police. If it makes it any easier, there's no question you'll have to tell them, because if you don't"—she looked from one to the other of them, smiling grimly—"I will."

"Unbelievable," muttered Samir through gritted teeth.

"I understand," said Anne. "It's what I expected you to say. It's what I *knew* you'd say. I think I just needed to hear it."

"Well"—I gestured to the doorway, which I happened to be facing—"there's no time like the present."

They turned. Special Investigator Locust had just entered the room, and—surprise!—he did *not* look happy.

Chapter 29

At some point between the morning and now, Locust had eaten something involving ketchup, as evidenced by the oblong, reddish stain running down the front of his shirt. He'd obviously tried to clean it, which had only succeeded in making the area wet and slightly see-through. I observed all this while he was covering the distance between the doorway of the Recreation Room and our two couches, sprinting as though he were competing in the final leg of a relay race.

He drew up to us, panting, pausing to adjust his tie so that it covered the stain as much as possible.

"What do you think you're doing here, Mrs. Gibson?"

"Hello, Officer Locust," replied Dorothy calmly. "It's nice to see you. I'm having a drink."

She gestured with her drink to Anne, who was mauling her pearls again, and Samir, who'd picked up his phone like a toddler reclaiming his binkie.

"I believe you've already met the Shahs."

SI Locust's nose screwed itself up, retreating as far as possible from the noxious presence of Dorothy Gibson.

"You're interfering in a police investigation. *My* police investigation."

By then DS Brooks had appeared in the doorway. He sauntered over, hands in his pockets, hanging back to observe the show.

"How am I interfering, exactly?" asked Dorothy.

"You can't go around asking everyone we've interviewed your own set of questions!"

"See now, that sounds like the same logic people tried using on same-sex marriage. The existence of one infringes the existence of the other. I didn't buy it then, and I'm not buying it now."

One of Dorothy Chase Gibson's more shining moments had been when she delivered a stirring speech on the floor of the Senate titled "Declaration of Conscience," in favor of marriage equality for all. This was many years before the U.S. Supreme Court got there, and a risky move at the time. What with having a gay son, she was significantly ahead of the issue compared to your average politician.

Locust shut his eyes. Now his nose looked pinched, harassed. "What?"

"I was making an analogy," explained Dorothy. "I reject your proposition that any questions *I* ask impinge on the questions *you've* already asked. Ih-hin fact, I think if anything, it's the opposite! Have you considered I might be helping you? That's certainly my goal here."

"I don't need your—"

"For example, given the conversation I've just had with the Shahs, I'm certain you're going to want to ask them a few more questions." She turned to Anne and Samir. "I promise I'll do everything I can to bring the truth out in the end. You have my word on that. Go ahead and tell these two detectives everything you've told me."

She rose, turning in my direction.

"Shall we?"

We made for the door. But SI Locust wasn't done with us.

"Mrs. Gibson. Mrs. Gibson! Turn around."

We stopped. When we turned, he was right there, looming over us.

"Let me be very clear." He raised his index finger, waggling it as he spoke. (Who did he think he was, Will Smith's mom from *The Fresh Prince of Bel-Air* opening sequence?) "I want you to stop asking questions. *Now.* This is not your investigation. This is *my* investigation. An investigation *you*, Mrs. Gibson, are very much a subject of. So contrary to your belief, you are *not* helping. You are interfering, and doing yourself no favors. I demand that you stop."

"I hear you," said Dorothy. "Loud and clear."

It was dark by the time we reached the woods behind the Crystal Palace. I even heard an owl hoot at one point. Dorothy didn't say a word, and I was fine with that. A quiet walk at night is actually one of my favorite pastimes. It's secretly the reason I love New York as much as I do, the city being the perfect place for solitary, nocturnal ramblings—in the right neighborhoods, of course. I tend not to walk alone in the country, as I can't help imagining the way older and wiser people will shake their heads upon discovering my decomposing corpse at the bottom of some lonely roadside ditch. But now I had Dorothy by my side, and—more importantly—a third lady armed and trained in various combat skills.

We entered Dorothy's house by way of the sitting room, in the rear of the building. A drinks cart stood to the side of the French windows. Dorothy made a beeline for it now.

"What do you say to another preprandial cocktail?" she asked, shrugging off her coat.

I'm not going to lie: that gin martini had gone to my head. I never should have finished it, but if I hadn't, then I probably wouldn't have taken Dorothy up on her offer.

"I love that you're a person who uses a word like *preprandial* in casual conversation," I told her as she poured various liquids into a metal tumbler.

"And I love that you're a person who would note my usage of a word like *preprandial*," she replied.

There was no question about it: we were both drunk.

"So what did you make of today?" she asked after she'd finished tumbling. She even had real martini glasses: the ones shaped like a shallow V whose contents you can't help spilling. Especially when you're already intoxicated.

"It's hard to say." I accepted the glass she offered me, pretending not to notice the liquid sloshing over the side. "It was interesting how often people contradicted one another, don't you think?"

"MMMM-hm. I *absolutely* agree."

"Like Walter claiming he and Vivian were in an open relationship, when her sister had no idea." I took my first sip. Dorothy's martini was about five times stronger than the one at the Crystal Palace: like drinking liquid fire. I put it down, determined not to pick it up again. "Here's another one for you. Dr. Shah said Walter was a fraud, and Eve said he was a genius. So which is it?"

"I've found over the years that the truth tends to lie in the middle," said Dorothy. "Somewhere between the extremes. That's my nugget of elder wisdom." She took a sip of her own, closing her eyes in satisfaction. "What was your sense of Walter Vogel?"

"I don't trust him," I said. "But then, I don't trust many people."

"No." She looked at me closely. "I don't think you do, do you?"

I may have been drunk, but not drunk enough to respond in kind. I'd like to reiterate that my trust and intimacy issues don't stem from a single event, or even a series of events. Each of us is a mysterious combination of our experiences, and any number of predispositions divorced from experience. I don't expect to be solving this mystery as it pertains to me anytime soon. Can you say any different for yourself? Truly?

"Also," I continued, moving *swiftly* along, "Laura claiming Vivian and Paul had a disagreement the night she died, what was that about? Either Laura's lying or Paul is, by omission, anyway. Because he didn't say a word about it."

"MMMM-hm, MMMM-hm."

"Not that I trust Laura very much. I still don't understand why she lied and said she got here Wednesday, when she actually got here Tuesday."

"*Very* strange, I agree."

"It's a good thing Peter mentioned having seen her."

"Yes, it's quite a thrill when my son proves useful." Dorothy took a much larger swig.

"And then, of course, there's that whole mess with the Shahs."

She opened her eyes wide. "Can you buh-*lieve* that?"

"I know!" I cried. "I *can't*, really, which is going to be a problem for them. I mean, I'm sure they're not lying about *something* happening, because why would they make that up? But maybe they figured Walter was going to say something anyway—"

"Which he did," put in Dorothy.

"Exactly. So maybe they figured it was better to get in front of it? With their version? Because it kind of gives them a pretty good motive, don't you think?"

"*Any* of the three of them, yes." Dorothy nodded her head slowly. "God knows parents have done some crazy stuff for the sake of their kids' college applications."

"So have the kids," I added. "Or maybe Alex really was infatuated. Maybe he couldn't handle being rejected. There's a chance he's tapped into that whole 'incel' thing online, it's pretty active."

(In case you're unaware: "incel" is short for "involuntary celibate," a subset of straight men who bond online over how they've been denied the sex they're owed, hence their decision to wage war on women for not giving them said sex. Fun!)

"Ugh, let's hope not," said Dorothy.

"It's not hard to picture Alex slipping out of bed while his parents were asleep."

"I wish we could narrow down the time," she said. "Nine till three is such a large window. Though if Anne Shah really heard someone in the bedroom early on Thursday, that would indicate it happened on the later side."

"Or maybe she was making that up because it happened hours earlier, when her son snuck off to see Vivian. And not to blame the victim or anything, but I could easily picture Vivian being awful to him. Taunting him from her bath, just straight up laughing about his feelings for her. Teenagers take everything out of proportion. He could've just—"

"Snapped," finished Dorothy.

I watched her take small sips from her glass as she reflected on this, and before I realized what I was doing I'd picked up my drink and taken a sip of my own. Huh, not nearly so bad as before. This was a sure sign I was getting *very* drunk, but I ignored it and took a bigger sip, swishing it around before swallowing.

"They honestly *all* have motives," I said. "Except maybe Paul. Although, don't you think you'd resent doing housework for one of your friends? I'm sorry, but he was way too cheerful. *And* nervous. There was something weird going on there."

"I agree," said Dorothy. "Especially if we're to believe he wasn't getting paid. Not that I do believe it, necessarily."

"Walter is the most obvious suspect, motive-wise."

"Spouses the world over want to murder each other daily," observed Dorothy dryly.

"And do," I added. "The motive would be related for Eve, I guess. I got the feeling she wasn't all that cool with the open relationship thing. Maybe she wanted Vivian out of the way."

"It's possible."

"But you told her she wasn't a suspect—"

"I was bluffing, of course."

"Okay good, because that's exactly what *she* might have been doing, right?"

"Yep. That toxicology report would have come out eventually. By forcing the issue, she made herself look innocent. Very useful, *if* she had something to do with it."

"Classic double bluff." I took another sip. "By the way, did you actually *see* her and Walter making out in the kitchen?"

"Not at all," said Dorothy. "But it was obvious there was something happening there."

"So when you asked Walter about his affair . . . ?"

"I took a shot."

"Well played."

We cheers-ed.

"The Shahs we already covered," I nattered on. "Combination of lust and loathing, though you could argue killing someone for reputation's sake has more to do with monetary gain, meaning the motive falls more squarely under lucre."

"Someone's been reading her P.D. James," observed Dorothy.

I nodded. "The Four Ls: Love, Lust, Loathing, and Lucre. And this case has them all."

"It certainly does."

"The interesting thing is that Laura's the only one with a proper lucre motive, even though it's not much of one. But those family heirlooms obviously meant something to her. And more often than not it *is* greed of some sort that's at the heart of these things."

"A*men* to that."

"Do you think it's possible she has a thing for her sister's husband?" I asked. "For Walter?"

"Anything is possible," replied Dorothy. "I try to remind myself of that as often as I can."

"Maybe that explains why she got so upset hearing about Walter's affair. I understand feeling angry on your sister's behalf, but didn't you think it was a bit much when she freaked out on us like that?"

"I did," said Dorothy. "You know, I can't help thinking motive is the way this case gets solved. Because it's a level playing field as to means and opportunity. Remarkably so."

"Any of them could have done it," I agreed.

"MMMM-hm. But the motives are all over the place. As we've been discussing. And some are stronger than others."

"So I guess that puts Walter Vogel and the Shahs at the forefront?" I hazarded.

"I suppose," she said doubtfully. "I just can't help feeling I'm *missing* something. Something staring me in the face." She threw up her hands, managing not to spill what little liquid was left in her glass. "To tell you the truth, I felt like I was stumbling around in the dark most of today. It's a familiar feeling for me, sad to say."

She knocked back her glass, draining it. When she spoke again, her voice was quieter, the brassy timbre it usually held gone soft, mellowed. "All I ever wanted to do was help people, you know. Make something good out of the tragedy of losing my husband. To be of *value* some way. I know no one believes me when I say that—"

"I believe you."

"Well, thank you for that." She sighed. "Sometimes I wish I had a magic wand."

"Don't we all?" I joked.

"No." She shook her head impatiently. "No, that's not what I mean. It's everyone *else* I'd give the magic to. So they knew I was telling the truth about wanting to help." She set down her empty glass. "Maybe then they'd let me."

Everyone goes on and on about how ambitious Dorothy Gibson is—because sexism/double standards, duh. And it's true; she *is* ambitious. Is there any greater ambition than wanting to make the world better? Ambition isn't inherently evil. . . .

I finished off my glass. The gin martini was officially delicious now.

"I think it might be worthwhile to look up Walter Vogel's first wife," said Dorothy a few minutes later. "And his son, if we can find him."

"But you told that detective, Locust—"

She pressed her lips together, her cheeks folding in on themselves along the fault lines of her wrinkles as she offered up her mischievous chipmunk smile. "I told him I heard him," she said. "Loud and clear. I never promised to do what he said. I'll have Leila look into it, do some research. *If* Leila's still talking to me. I think Laura said they live close by." She sprang up, the pile of gin she'd imbibed no match for her brisk constitution. "You know, I'm so glad you were able to come with me today. It was a real comfort, and a help. I mean that. We two work well together." She held her hand out for my glass. "A martini or two doesn't hurt either, eh?"

It wasn't quite six o'clock, but the night had come to an end. Dorothy invited me to eat some cold chicken Trudy had left in the refrigerator. I declined, pretending to have every intention of coming down later for a makeshift dinner. And then I stumbled my way upstairs, collapsing facedown on the log cabin quilt.

I passed out immediately.

CHAPTER 30

It was almost 11 p.m. when I woke up. The good news: I was not hungover. The bad news: I was still drunk.

Although *was* this bad news?

I found myself consumed with a hunger no amount of cold chicken could satisfy. After gargling some mouthwash and patting my cheeks a few times, I threw on Dorothy's kiwi-green coat and crept downstairs.

No one was around. The house was cloaked in darkness, and I couldn't help thinking that it was around this time that someone had snuck down an empty, silent hallway of the Crystal Palace and into Vivian Davis's bedroom. Then into her bathroom, their hands reaching out to a woman lying oblivious in her tub. . . .

I shook away this macabre tableau, lest it put me off my intended plan. I opened the front door, bracing myself against the elements. It was truly freezing outside, but the kiwi-green coat shielded me from the worst of it as I hurried down the front path, a gibbous moon lighting my way.

There was a small building on the winding drive that led up to the house, which you could call any number of things depending on your persuasion. An "ADU" if you were in real estate; a "guesthouse" or "cottage" if you were being optimistic about the possible uses for this puny structure; a "shack" if you were being more of a pessimist; a "gatehouse" if, like me, you've read far too many novels set in nineteenth century England; a "woodshed" if you've read *Cold Comfort Farm* by Stella Gibbons too many times (though I take issue with this; you cannot read *Cold Comfort Farm* too many times). I believe the official term for it was a "remote office." It was inside this edifice that Dorothy's security team based their operations. The building had its own working fireplace, which was as good a means of heating this tiny space as any other, and I was delighted to see smoke curling from its brick chimney as I left the driveway and traipsed down the narrow footpath leading to the rustic structure. In the summer, the leaves from the aspens on either side would have been brushing against me, but by turning sideways I was able to avoid their white-skinned branches—more silver than white in the moonlight spilling from above.

I didn't know for sure that the Bodyguard would be there. Or that he'd be alone. All I knew was that this was where the security officers tended to congregate when they weren't on active duty. Or perusing ill-fated debut novels by crotchety ghostwriters.

The door in front of me was letting in generous chinks of light not only from the bottom but from both sides and the top. It reminded me of the door in the larder back at the Crystal Palace, and the way the sunlight had seeped round the edges of the blackout shade in Laura Duval's bedroom. Despite the intensity of my focus on the Bodyguard, I found myself thinking about the way Laura tried to brush aside the weirdness of trying on her dead sister's jewelry. We like to idealize sisters (*Little Women* has ruined us), but the real thing is often much uglier.

I pounded my fist against the door, rattling it in its frame. I cannot tell you what I was thinking as I waited for an answer. I simply wanted to see him: to see his eyes, and skin—that glowy skin—to hear his voice. To smell him, and feel him, and yes, to taste him.

I was horny, goddamnit.

The door opened more quickly than I expected. Or maybe in my drunken state, I was a poor judge of the passage of time.

There he was, his magnificent frame backlit by the fireplace: luminous as any Greek or Norse or Egyptian deity (the pagans got it right; may as well make the gods you worship eye candy to boot).

"Ooh."

I leaned against the doorframe in what was intended to be a seductive pose, except that I missed the frame the first time and had to make a second go of it. Maybe he hadn't noticed?

"Toasty."

The fireplace wasn't so much heating the room as roasting it. I walked inside, closing the door behind me. Aside from the heat, it was surprisingly nice in there, with a kitchenette and a bathroom in one corner. The fireplace was on the wall opposite, two saggy couches on either side of it. Most of the floorspace was taken up by a long oval table, the kind you've seen in countless conference rooms, except this one had electronic devices littering its surface, most of which I couldn't identify. This plus the maps tacked onto the walls gave the space the flavor of a war room.

But I was there to make love, not war.

The Bodyguard was in one of his skin-tight T-shirts, Lord love him. His cheeks were flushed, and I could feel my own body reacting to the heat: those little pinpricks you get when your skin is still cold began tickling my upper thighs, the blood rushing to the skin's surface. I intended to be tickling my upper thighs a whole lot more in about thirty seconds, and shucked off my jacket, letting it fall to the floor.

"Let's fuck," I said.

If it's dawned on you that he hadn't yet said a word, let me assure you it had not dawned on me.

"Right here."

I gestured at the table, imagining him sweeping all those devices to the floor and lifting me onto it.

He bent down (unfortunately, he was facing me) and picked up my coat.

"You should go to bed."

When he offered me my coat I made no move to take it, so he draped it over my shoulder.

"Alone," he added.

"Come on, you know you want me. *Everybody* knows, apparently. No need to be so coy about it. I'm in the mood for some steamy love-shack sex. Looks like the steamy won't be a problem."

"You're drunk," he noted.

"Aw, come on, are you still mad I blew you off? I'm sorry about that, okay? Let's move on." I took a step toward him, the coat on my shoulder falling to the floor. "If we do, I can promise you another kind of blowing altogether."

I admit: it wasn't my best wordplay.

He picked up my coat for the second time. "That's not going to happen," he said firmly, though his firmness was belied by the gentle way he helped me on with my coat.

When was the last time someone helped me on with my coat who wasn't angling for a tip? Grade school, probably. God, that's depressing.

"Boo," I replied. "Hiss."

This at least got a smile.

"Are you okay to walk back to the house?"

"No," I said. "I think I'm going to need some help. A *lot* of help."

He sighed.

We walked single-file down the aspen-lined path to the main driveway, but after that he offered me his arm. I leaned on it. Heavily. Our progress was slow, the thinnest layer of ice having formed on the ground. We broke through this crust with each footstep, and I was reminded of the way Dorothy and I had crunched through the snow earlier that day. The Bodyguard's feet were so big, his boots so heavy, his footsteps were more like chomps than crunches.

"So why did you?" he asked after a while. "Blow me off?"

"It's what I do," I said. "Push people away. Even when they're super-duper, five-alarm-fire handsome."

He smiled again. "That seems like a strange thing to do, doesn't it?"

"Sure does."

I eyed him without moving my head, a live version of the "side-eye" emoji Rhonda likes to send me when I'm taking too long to get back to her on something. His smile deepened, his eyes going all crinkly—as they tended to do.

God, he was beautiful.

"So you're a weirdo," he said. "Is that what you're telling me?"

"Unfortunately, yes." I sighed theatrically, which isn't to say it was a fake sigh. Sometimes the emotions we put on display are perfectly real.

He opened the front door, stepping back to let me go ahead of him.

"Not so unfortunate for me." His smile widened, his gray eyes gleaming silver like the moon above us. "I've always had a thing for freaks."

CHAPTER 31

Did you think this was leading to a night of hot passion on the log-cabin quilt, as witnessed by the Andrew Wyeth painting?

So did I.

But alas, the Bodyguard ushered me into my bedroom, took off my coat and shoes, and then stopped at my pants. I watched dumbly as he moved about the room more stealthily than I would have thought possible for a man his size—closing the window I'd left cracked open, placing the wastepaper basket that lived beneath the child-size desk by the side of my bed. He even put my coat and shoes away in the closet.

"Were you in the military?"

He jumped a little when I said this. I'm guessing he thought I was passed out by then. Walking over to the bed, he kneeled down, putting his face level with mine.

I received a regulation salute.

"It's the neat-freak thing, isn't it? Hard to get out of your system."

"That and your posture." I turned on my side so as to face him fully, slipping one hand underneath my cheek. "Neither of which are qualities *I'd* want to get out of my system."

I could see his stubble up close, which was light, but still much darker than his tawny hair. When I reached out, he let me rub his jaw with the back of my hand—the way you might indulge a child who doesn't know any better.

His face was warm to the touch.

I let go, but before I could retract my hand, he turned it palm up and began massaging the underside of my knuckle joints at the base of my fingers. . . . It felt so good, I almost moaned—catching myself just in time.

"So do you think *she* got it out of her system?" he asked.

"Who? Dorothy?"

He nodded. "The whole P.I. thing."

"It's really more of a sleuth than a P.I. thing. Whodunit, rather than a noir."

"Gotcha."

When he finished with the first hand, he started on the second one without my having to ask. I could have let him do this for days. Years. Lifetimes.

"So I'll take that as a no then?" he asked.

"Hard no. I'm pretty sure she's just getting started."

He sighed. "I was afraid of that."

"Are you *sure* we can't have sex tonight?"

"Yeah, sorry."

When the massage was over he planted a kiss on my forehead (warm, dry, and squeaky clean: a freshly laundered kiss). He rose from his kneeling position. I took in a deep breath to get the maximum of sandalwood scent from off his body.

"There's always tomorrow, though," he said. "Night night."

Before I could think of anything witty to say, he'd closed the door behind him.

It had been a long time since I'd gotten drunk like that, and as I learned the next morning, my body was no longer able to process alcohol as easily as it used to. Youth really is wasted on the young, because I should have marveled at my ability when I was twenty-one to drink terrible wine all night, get two hours' sleep, and wake up in time for a 9 a.m. "Women and Cinema" class during which I didn't nap—not even when the professor dimmed the lights and showed us 1930s women's weepies. Fortunately, I'd had the presence of mind to set the alarm clock on my phone before venturing out in search of the Bodyguard. It went off at seven, and by seven thirty I managed to throw aside the log-cabin quilt and begin the process of making myself look presentable.

I probably don't need to tell you that I did no writing that morning. The problem with such self-imposed routines is that when you fail to do them, they feel defunct—as though your failure is final, permanent. So it was not just with a leaden stomach but a leaden heart that I trudged downstairs to the kitchen.

Thank God for small wonders: Officer Choi was on duty again, so I at least didn't have to endure the humiliation of eye contact with the Bodyguard before eating something.

"Good morning!" boomed Dorothy.

She was dressed like Dorothy Gibson again: in a pantsuit, her hair and makeup on point. How on earth had she been able to get up early enough to do this?

I shouldn't have been surprised. Dorothy was renowned for liking—and holding—her liquor. I looked away as she took a gloppy, heaping forkful of some steaming egg dish, forcing myself to pour out a small bowl of cornflakes with a splash of skim milk.

"Oh, dear. Was I a bad influence last night? You look a little green about the gills."

"I'm okay," I assured her. "I've always had a weak stomach."

"Would you like me to make you an omelette too? I find they're great for hangovers. Eggs are my specialty, you know."

Saying you're good at eggs is like saying you're good at working your iPhone. *Everyone* can make eggs. But instead of insulting her with this observation, I concentrated on keeping my cereal from rising up my throat.

"So I have good news. Leila found Minna Hawley—that's

Walter's first wife—and e-mailed her. She's already responded and said she's willing to talk to us today. I've also managed to make up with Joe after our standoff yesterday, and he's agreed to drive us there."

A response on my part was called for here, but I was still too focused on not retching.

"Listen, if you need to stay put, tend to your wounds, I *more* than understand."

"No," I said at last. "I want to go."

"Good! We'll get started after breakfast."

"Is Leila coming?"

"She'll be holding down the fort here. She would never admit it, but I think she's still a little put out by the way things played out yesterday. Besides . . ." Dorothy paused, suspending her fork in front of her mouth. (I saw a broccoli floret smothered in ketchup, *the horror*.) "This is our thing, right?"

I nodded as emphatically as I could.

A half hour later, the cornflakes had done wonders, as had a hillock of ibuprofen tablets. Tangent alert, but were you aware the original meaning of "euphoria" was the relief a sick person experiences when their pain goes away? Call me euphoric, then, as I slid into the Lincoln Town Car free of any major aches and pains. Officer Choi rode with us in the front passenger seat beside Officer Donnelly, which meant I was able to ride in the back with Dorothy.

"So where exactly are we headed?"

The sky was covered in iron-gray clouds that gave no clue as to where the sun might be hiding behind them. The air had that humid quality to it that foretells precipitation of some sort. If it hadn't been noticeably warmer today, I would have guessed it was going to snow again.

"Durham Cliffs," said Dorothy. "They live in a little town along the coast, about an hour south of here."

"They?"

"The mother and son live together. Minna and Robert Hawley. Nice, right? Two for the price of one."

"Was Leila able to find out anything about them?"

"Minna Hawley is fifty-one and works as an administrative assistant at a big hospital nearby. Looks like she's been doing that for twenty years, which is as old as her son is. Apparently he enrolled in a local community college after graduating from the local high school, but dropped out in the middle of his first year. That was a year and a half ago. Since then there's no record of him doing anything."

"When did she and Walter Vogel get divorced?" I asked.

"Good question. I had Leila cross-check the dates, and the divorce went through two months *before* Robert Hawley was born."

"So he divorced his pregnant wife a few months before she was about to have their baby?"

"Yep," said Dorothy. "But let's not jump to conclusions. We don't know the circumstances. Yet."

"Is that what you're hoping to learn from her? What kind of a husband Walter Vogel was?"

"Ye-es. Not just who he was as a husband, but a better sense of what kind of a person he is. That's what I find so frustrating. I was lying awake in bed last night, going over it all"—probably around the same time I was getting a hand-gasm from the Bodyguard—"and it struck me that I still don't really know *who* Vivian Davis was. In large part because her husband is such a mystery too. We've met Walter Vogel twice now, but he's a tough nut to crack."

I nodded. No doubt about that.

"It's what we were saying last night—all the accounts we've gotten of those two from the people around them don't add up. Were they devoted to each other, or not? Is Walter really a con man? If so, was Vivian his partner or another of his victims? If we could nail down *who* they are, the true nature of their relationship, I'm convinced it would go a long way toward solving this thing." She let out a mocking chuckle. "I'm not sure *why* I'm convinced of that, but I am! Am I making sense at all?"

"Yes," I assured her, sitting up a little. "It's like you'd expect witnesses to contradict each other over where they were, or who they were with, or what time it was when something happened. But there's almost none of that here. Everyone was in the house around the time we know Vivian was killed, and they all had access to her room. So none of that matters. It's all about motive. Like we were saying last night. And what lies behind motive? Character. It's character."

"Exactly," said Dorothy. "*That's* what we have to figure out."

I felt my phone buzz in my pocket. When I took it out, there was a text from Leila.

Pls don't let her do anything too crazy today. Security's job to keep her physically safe, but I'm counting on you to minimize any damage or blowback or other weirdness from all this Nancy Drew b.s.

Understood, I wrote back. And then, because I can't quite shake off the people-pleaser-y A+ student overachiever I used to be, **We're on the same team here.**

She responded with a thumbs-up.

I fell asleep soon afterward. This to me is the true kidney punch of drinking: the way it disturbs your sleep so that on top of feeling ill and malnourished, you're bone-tired. But sleep was exactly what I needed, as evidenced by the fact that I felt much better—almost back to normal—when I returned to consciousness.

To my horror, at some point during my nap I'd lurched away from my window as far as my belted-in body would allow, sprawling diagonally over not only my seat, but the unoccupied middle area. Dorothy had pressed herself into her corner to give me as much room as possible. It couldn't have been very comfortable for her, though.

She looked up from her phone, eyeing me coolly. "Good sleep?"

I could feel wetness in the corner of my mouth, and wiped it away before I could estimate how much drool had accumulated there. Good God. Collecting my limbs, I retreated to my side of the car with what little dignity I could muster.

"Perfect timing, actually." She slipped her phone into her front pants pocket. "We're minutes away. I've just been texting with Minna Hawley. She said to come right in."

I nodded, shoving the sunglasses I'd remembered this time onto my nose and pressing my face against the window. It was still cloudy, but the clouds had weakened, the sun's white beams pouring through the gauzy firmament as though God with a capital G were about to make an appearance.

We were already on top of the cliffs from which I supposed Durham Cliffs took its name, on a coastal road that afforded a sweeping view of the wild and rocky Maine coastline. Maine's beauty has always reminded me of Ireland's: bewitching and no-nonsense at the same time. Aside from the temperature of the water, it's impossible for me to imagine anyone lolling for hours on such narrow, uneven shingles. These are beaches made for existential contemplation, not semi-naked recreation. In other words: my kind of beaches. I was sorry I'd missed part of the show while sleeping, and made up for lost time by gluing my face to the glass like a dog or small child.

"Spectacular, isn't it?" murmured Dorothy.

"So I guess this is Down East?" I asked. I didn't know much about Maine, but I knew enough to know the coastal part of the state was referred to this way.

"Sort of. Down East is really farther north."

"How does that work?"

"Well, the term comes from ships sailing *downwind*, from Boston to the coast of Maine and Canada," she explained. "The farther north you go, the farther east you go, also. That's just the way God made this beautiful coastline."

I could hear the reverence in her voice, could feel the love of home and country.

"I sure do love this state," she added unnecessarily.

Eventually, and much to my disappointment, we moved away from the water—far enough that you could neither see nor hear the ocean anymore. Entering the residential outskirts of a small town, the car began inching down a street with houses that were all two stories high. There were no mansions here, but there was something equally precious to an American sensibility: an unbreakable chain of middle-class prosperity in the form of quarter-acre plots repeated over and over again, nary a weak link among them. Despite the New England-y ambiance, it reminded me of the street I'd grown up on. Of course, the lawns outside Phoenix were more parched, and the patios featured lots more faux-Navajo décor. But a suburb's a suburb, and I suspected the ratio of rebels to causes was as skewed in Durham Cliffs as it was in my hometown.

From the outside, there was nothing remarkable about where Minna and Robert Hawley lived. Their house had a peaked roof with a single gable: a triangle on top of a square, like a child's drawing of a house. Real icicles hung off the eaves, and a thin coat of snow covered the lawn, blade tips poking through like green confetti. The berries on the holly bushes lining the front path looked fake, they were so red—as though I'd get paint on my hands if I touched them. In the driveway sat one of those older, humpbacked Saabs, the bottom third of it covered in the random grit that mars every vehicle for the duration of winter on the East Coast.

If it seems as though we were staring at the house for quite some time before entering, your perception is correct. We sat gawking for a good quarter of an hour—with the heat on—while Officer Choi went in ahead of us to conduct a sweep. At long last she emerged from the house, waving us inside.

"Finally," grumbled Dorothy.

Chapter 32

We trudged up the front path, which featured ice patches here and there. Minna Hawley was waiting for us inside the front door, and it wasn't till we were stamping our shoes on the mat inside that my eyes had adjusted and I could get a good look at her.

Look: we all dry out in winter. (In fact, it's the dryness of artificially heated air that many believe accounts for the prevalence of illness in cold weather—not the coldness itself, but the fact that our mucous membranes dry out along with our skin, making us less adept at fending off infection.) But I have never seen a more *desiccated* human being than Minna Hawley. Whole swathes of her chin and forehead were flaking off; her swollen lips had deep, painful-looking cracks in them; and when she gave me her hand it felt as though I were grasping a cheese grater. (I just had to pause to spread some moisturizer on my hands. Much better.)

"Pleased to meet you," she said. Even her voice was dry, with a harsh, rasping quality to it. It was true that she was smiling, but her smile struck me as one of anticipation rather than welcome. In younger (and better hydrated) days, she must have been conventionally attractive. She had large blue eyes, and a petite, elfin face that came to a point at her chin. Somewhere along the way, however, the elf had turned into a witch.

My guess is that she cut her whitish-gray hair herself, because no professional would have consented to butcher it into its current state for any amount of money. It was short—anywhere from a scant few millimeters to an inch or two, the longer pieces flopping onto her forehead or curling at her neck, the shorter ones standing upright and waving wispily. I knew from the dossier Leila had worked up that she was fifty-one, but if I'd seen her on the street I would have guessed she was in her late sixties.

Her muumuu, or housecoat, with its high mandarin collar seemed to be an attempt to cover up the excessive thinness of her body. But there was no mistaking the way it hung off her meager frame. I wondered if she were sick.

"It's a pleasure to meet you, Ms. Hawley!"

Dorothy had shifted into high jovial mode.

"*Miss* Hawley."

"Oh! All right then. Pleasure to meet you, Miss Hawley!"

"When I got my divorce, I decided to treat it like an annulment. Not in a religious sense, but in a moral sense. I've become *un*married. Therefore, I choose to go by 'Miss.' "

So much for icebreakers.

"My son is in the living room. Wait for me there."

She pointed to a door on our right before turning abruptly and receding down the hallway.

Dorothy and I raised our eyebrows at each other while walking in the direction indicated: into a formal living room made less formal by wall-to-wall pink carpeting. A floral-patterned sofa set dominated the space: sofa, love seat, armchair, ottoman, all festooned with a generous ruffle at the bottom. The heat was blasting; it was almost intolerably stuffy. To our right was a bay window (I caught sight of Officer Donnelly stretching his legs, grinning at something on his phone), and to our left was a fireplace, its mantel taken up by half a dozen porcelain dolls in elaborate Victorian-style hoop skirts.

“Hey.” A man occupying the full width of the love seat waved at us without getting up. “I’m Bobby.”

His belly was large enough to be cradled between his legs, and I couldn’t help noticing the way his upper-arm flab waved along with his hand. (He was wearing short sleeves, which is what I would have done if I lived there; the thermostat had to be set to at least 80 degrees.) I looked for signs of resemblance to his father, and found none. In fact, I couldn’t imagine two people who looked *less* alike, though it was true the twenty-year-old’s hair—reddish-brown, like a fox’s or squirrel’s—was already thinning. Walter Vogel was brimming with energy, whereas Bobby Hawley seemed to be where energy went to die. Already I could tell his failure to get up and give us a proper greeting had nothing to do with rudeness or irritation. He simply wasn’t in the habit of exerting himself. Ever.

Point in fact: his teeth were noticeably brown, in addition to being noticeably crooked. Rarely have I seen such poorly maintained teeth on an American who had the means to care for them. I guessed he never brushed them or went to a dentist, which said a lot about him. But didn’t it say a lot about his mother, too?

“Well, hello there, Bobby!” boomed Dorothy. “What a lovely home you have!”

“Take a load off.” He pointed to the long sofa opposite the love seat. “Mommy’s just getting us something to eat.”

We sat on either end of the sofa. Our backs were to the bay window, which put us in position for a staring contest with the dolls above the fireplace. (Spoiler: the dolls won.) We’d only just settled ourselves when Minna Hawley came stomping in with a tea tray she dropped on the coffee table. There was a silver tea service on it—quite a beautiful one, actually—and a cake on a plate that was clearly one of those Duncan Hines or Betty Crocker numbers from a box: yellow on the inside, chocolate frosting on the outside. I knew it was yellow because a quarter of it was missing, and while I was certain it was delicious (it's impossible for such cakes *not* to be delicious), I was equally certain I wouldn't be eating it. The very air in that house felt poisoned—stale and sour, like curdled milk or rotten lettuce, despite the overpowering scent of lemony air freshener.

"Did someone just celebrate a birthday?" asked Dorothy.

"No," said Minna flatly. "Tea?" She hovered over the tray, looking from one to the other of us. "I'd offer you coffee, but we don't have any in the house because we hate it."

Dorothy told her a cup of tea would be "lovely," and I too accepted one out of politeness. Minna poured them in record time, and then spent several minutes fussing over a cup for Bobby that involved so much cream and sugar, I'm surprised she was able to fit any tea in there. She poured her own cup last, leaving it black.

"I want to thank you for sitting down with me tod—"

"I always knew this day would come." Our hostess leaned forward, the brown liquid in her cup slopping over the rim, dribbling onto her saucer. "I always knew we'd be called on to bear witness to the kind of person he *really* is."

"I take it you're aware of what happened to Vivian Davis, then?"

"We are." She put her cup down with a *clink*. "Good riddance too."

From the love seat Bobby snickered, spreading his legs a little wider.

"I wonder," said Dorothy neutrally, "if you could give us a sense of your history with your ex-husband."

"Happy to."

But she didn't look happy. Those eyes of hers were blazing with a fury so hot, I was surprised the rest of her face wasn't melting around them like that guy at the end of *Indiana Jones and the Last Crusade*—you know, the one who chose . . . *poorly*.

"Walter and I met in college. Harvard."

I tried to picture Minna Hawley as a fresh-faced eighteen-year-old on that stately campus.

I failed.

"Our freshman dorm rooms were next to each other. We started dating by the end of fall semester, and for the next four years we never parted. It was a campus joke, Walter and Minna, always an item. He was my first time." Her eyes flickered toward her son. "I don't have to censor myself around Bobby-boy. There are no secrets between us."

"You betcha, Mommy."

Say it with me: *Yikes!*

"Walter always wanted to be a doctor. He went straight to medical school after graduating. Harvard again. That was unusual. They don't let many undergraduates in, but he always tested well. That and a little bit of old-fashioned cheating. It's important you understand. He has no moral code. But then, we're living proof of that."

She gestured to her son, who let out a bubbly, mirthful noise.

"We moved a few hundred feet into some depressing post-grad residence. *I* went straight into slaving away for him. He got his degree."

"So you were together through all his medical training?" asked Dorothy.

"Yes," she said. "All *nine* years of it. Never mind he almost got kicked out of his program. Twice. Once in preclinical and again during his residency."

"Kicked out why?" asked Dorothy.

"He was caught cheating on an exam the first time," she said. "*Quite* a shock."

Bobby let out a different laugh this time, a sort of sidekick/henchman's *heh heh heh*.

"The second time, a colleague of his said he sexually harassed her. He claimed it didn't happen and I believed him, fool that I was. So did the disciplinary board. The bastard pulled the wool over everyone's eyes." She shook her head as though her brain were an Etch A Sketch and she was ridding it of the memory. "Thanks in no small part to my doing everything for him, down to *tying his own shoelaces* while he ate breakfast, he managed to squeak by. Got a job at a practice out here in the middle of nowhere. He was lucky to get anything." She smacked her lips by way of punctuation. "We were both thirty-one by then. And much to my delight, and my delight *alone*, I found out after we moved that I was pregnant."

Bobby gave us a flirty wave.

"We'd talked about having children. But I should've known he'd turn out to be one of those men who can't stand not being the center of attention. He didn't even stick around long enough for the baby to get here. I wasn't waiting on him hand and foot anymore, you see. That did *not* sit well with Walter Vogel."

"How 'bout some cake, Mommy?"

Minna cut off an enormous hunk of cake for her son—practically another quarter—and glared at us when we both declined. Out of principle, she cleaved the slimmest of slivers for herself. I couldn't help thinking of these two pieces as representations of the humans who would consume them. I guess you really are what you eat.

"Tell them about him calling you the c-word," said Bobby—or at least I think he did, because his mouth was full while he said it.

"Oh yes, a true red-banner moment. When I was eight months pregnant too. He was angry because I told him I'd be suing for child support. You can bet I got it in the end. Not that he ever paid on time. The man can't be trusted, plain and simple."

Bobby swallowed thickly. "Don't forget when he gave you the bruises."

His mother nodded. "Happened in this very room. Right by the window. I'm surprised the neighbors didn't call the police. He grabbed me by my arm so hard"—she lifted the arm in question—"I had bruises all up and down it."

I got the feeling that if she could have preserved these twenty-year-old bruises, she would have—that she would have preferred walking around with permanent visible proof of her ex-husband's infamy.

"Soon as I could leave Bobby with a babysitter, I got a job as a secretary to a bunch of doctors." She flattened her lips in an approximation of a smile; I worried the cracks in them would start bleeding. "Already had a decade's experience working for a doctor. Deathly dull. But it pays the bills."

There was a pause during which I couldn't help glancing at her son.

"Bobby's still figuring out his path in life," she said, intuiting the meaning of my glance. Her voice softened for the first time in our conversation. "Isn't that right, Bobby-boy?"

He nodded slowly, his expression growing serious. "I need to find my passion."

I was pretty sure his passion was cake, but I kept this thought to myself and nodded along with him.

"What sort of contact do you have with Walter now?" asked Dorothy.

Bobby let out a laugh so loud, I literally jumped in my seat. It was *meant* to be loud, of course: a mockery of the notion of contact with his father. Minna waited for him to finish with the indulgent air of a mother.

"Haven't seen him since the night he bruised me." She lifted her arm again. "Our lawyer speaks to his lawyer. Not once—not *once*, mind you—has he made an effort to reach out to Bobby."

Bobby crossed his arms over his chest, grinning broadly.

"Then I take it you never met Vivian Davis."

"Of course not," spat Minna.

"I heard there was talk about you coming to the wedding, er, uninvited. The two of you."

Minna's lip curled. "I would never subject my child to that filth. When I heard he was marrying again, I felt sorry for her. But then I looked her up online. I could see he'd finally met his match. Someone as obsessed with status as he is."

"*She* never had a kid," chirped Bobby. "Too self-absorbed."

It was obvious he was mimicking something his mother had said—most likely more than once. Even Minna looked a little ashamed to hear him parroting her now.

"How about another piece of cake, Bobby-boy?"

"Yes, please!" He handed over his plate.

"So other than online, you've never seen her? Even from afar?" pressed Dorothy.

There was a pause—a slight one, and yet it was unmistakable—before Minna answered.

"No. What are you trying to suggest? You may as well just say it."

"I'm not trying to suggest anything," replied Dorothy calmly. "If I were in your shoes, I'd find it hard not to at least drive by their place . . . if I happened to find myself in the neighborhood."

Minna hacked off a second wedge of cake, knocking it onto her son's plate.

"Good thing you aren't in my shoes then."

She handed the plate to Bobby, who was apparently feeling comfortable enough at this point to pick up the cake with both hands. I watched him wolf down half of it in one bite.

"I have to ask"—Dorothy let out a muted version of her joyous cackle in the attempt to keep things light—"Ih-hi hope you don't mind if I ask you what you both were doing last Wednesday night?"

"Don't mind at all. Unlike Walter, I have nothing to hide.

Neither of us do. Last Wednesday night we were where we always are. Here. At home. Together. Bobby and I watched some TV after dinner, and then we went to bed. Ten thirty. It's when we always go to bed."

Not the same bed, I hoped? I mean—it was a fair question at this point.

"What did you watch?" asked Dorothy.

"Dateline."

That sounded about right.

"Doesn't *Dateline* air on Fridays?"

Ooh, good catch, Dorothy.

"We record every episode so we can watch our favorites whenever we want. Didn't wake up till the next morning. Isn't that right, Bobby-boy?"

Bobby nodded, his mouth too full of cake to form any words.

The second piece was already gone.

Chapter 33

I took another look at the front of the house once we were back inside the Lincoln Town Car. The shutters needed to be repainted, and a drainpipe running along the right wall had popped out, the rusty metal bands meant to be holding it in place sticking straight out—a tetanus infection waiting to happen. And was that mold creeping out of the doorframe? Now that I was acquainted with the rot and decay on the inside, it was hard not to see it on the outside too.

Come to think of it, that Saab of theirs was ancient—at least twenty years old. I guessed it was the one Minna had been driving when Walter left her. I imagined her back then: a young wife moving into her pretty home in coastal Maine, which her handsome doctor husband had bought for the two of them, the man she'd known since she was eighteen. . . . But then it all went sideways, and her failure to move on—the way this failure had consumed not only her but the child she would raise in the shadow of her wasted hopes and dreams—struck me as a hideous, modern spin on Miss Havisham.

This is what happens when you read too much Dickens.

The click of a smartphone camera interrupted my thoughts.

"Don't mind me," said Dorothy. "Just getting a photo of their license plate. We can go now, Joe."

Officer Donnelly started up the car. I can't say I was sad to see the Hawleys' house slide out of view.

"Why'd you want to get their license plate?"

"I figure it can't hurt." Dorothy raised an eyebrow at me. "I don't believe for a second those two never took a ride over to Sacobago to check out what Walter Vogel and Vivian Davis were up to. In fact, I'm fairly certain they made a habit of it." She leaned forward. "Hey, Joe?"

Officer Donnelly cleared his throat. "Ma'am?"

"How long is the trip between here and the house?"

"Forty-eight minutes with no traffic," he answered promptly.

"Thanks, Joe." She sat back, turning to me. "An easy enough distance, wouldn't you say?"

"I would. . . ." I hesitated.

"What?"

"You don't really think they had anything to do with it, do you?"

She shrugged. "Who could tell with those two?"

"Agreed, they were a total nightmare. But that's just it. If they really *were* involved, they didn't do a very good job of hiding it."

"Given they seem to have devoted their lives to resenting Walter, and more recently, Vivian," said Dorothy drily, "I don't think hiding their feelings is an option. And by being forthright about it they get the benefit of reverse psychology."

"True," I conceded, "But what's the point? It's not like they'd get anything tangible out of killing Vivian Davis."

"Frankly, I think hate is an underrated motivation for *lots* of things. Walter Vogel has been the most obvious suspect from the start. So much so, it's hard to believe he would have killed his wife this way, unless he was stupid. And he definitely *isn't* stupid."

"You mean . . . you think they killed her to frame *him*? So that he'd go to jail for the rest of his life?"

"I admit it sounds far-fetched. But people *do* love the idea of 'locking up' their enemies, don't they?"

It had been mere weeks since the daily rallies in which such fantasies about the curtailing of Dorothy's liberty were routinely aired.

"How would they even have gotten in, though? We know there were cameras all over the place."

Dorothy shrugged again. "Even the best cameras can be avoided. And Walter told us he didn't turn on the alarm till he went upstairs for the night. Maybe they got inside the house earlier that day, and hid in one of the empty offices on the second floor or something. It's not as if the entire place was being used. It's enormous."

I tried imagining Bobby Hawley creeping about the Crystal Palace: nope. But when I pictured Minna Hawley flitting down empty hallways, slipping through doorways, a shiver ran down my spine. I imagined her creeping on all fours toward a clueless Vivian Davis lounging in her tub, feet propped up on the rim. . . . I could so easily see those calloused hands closing in on the silky-wet ankles . . . *yanking* with a savage ferocity.

"It's too bad we can't review the security footage," I said aloud. "Do you think the police still have it?"

A spark lit up Dorothy's eyes. She pitched her body forward, leaning into the front of the car again.

"Sarah, we do surveillance on the entrance to the property, don't we? When you come in off the parkway?"

Officer Choi turned in her seat. I hadn't seen her at close range before. She was older than I'd realized—not because I saw any of the typical signs of aging, but because there was a weariness to her expression, a bone-deep fatigue that no twentysomething could ever exhibit, no matter how sleep-deprived they might be. She was in her mid-to-late thirties, I guessed.

"We do, ma'am."

"How long do we keep them?"

"I believe we cache the footage for three months."

"Fantastic. Thanks." Dorothy drew back, but then she leaned forward again. "Sleep training not going so well, eh?"

She grimaced. "Not so well, ma'am."

"You'll get there." Dorothy patted her on the shoulder—a single pat, with just two fingers—a gesture so awkward, I had to turn my head and pretend to be fascinated by the doughnut and dry-cleaning shops outside the window.

"I'm assuming the security camera picks up any car coming in off the highway?" I asked. "Whether or not it's headed for your place or the Crystal Palace?"

"Correct. Meaning we'd be able to see if the Hawleys made an impromptu visit last Wednesday." She paused. "This way I don't have to ask Special Investigator Locust a thing."

It was just after one when we got back to Dorothy's place, stopping in front of the little footpath I'd stumbled down the night before on the way to my humiliating encounter.

"You go on up to the house, Sarah," said Dorothy. "Get a little rest if you can. Officer Peters is going to play back the footage for us inside the office; I've just been texting with him."

Huh? Texting with the Bodyguard?

Dorothy got out, walking around the back of the car. She tapped on my window with a fingernail.

"Are you coming?"

"Of course I am!" I cried. I was going to have to face him sooner or later.

By the time I got out of the car, Dorothy had walked down the path and was already knocking on the door of the remote office.

CHAPTER 34

Today the Bodyguard was wearing an olive-green shirt with a waffle pattern and a Henley neck. Two of his three chest buttons were undone, and the third was straining to join its friends.

I'd been too cowardly to make eye contact with him when I came in, which didn't stop me from getting a good whiff as he shut the door behind me: his usual sandalwood, but with a trace of sweat underneath that sweetened the deal—the same way a hint of gasoline livens up the leathery scent of a car. For me, anyway.

We sat around the conference table. You know, the one I'd wanted to drape my naked body across fifteen-or-so hours earlier. An oversize laptop stood open in a briefcase lined with foam. It looked like the kind of gadget Kiefer Sutherland might carry around in *24*. (Remember when everyone used to watch *24*? Weird.)

"I've got the footage all ready to go."

"Splendid," said Dorothy crisply. "One question before we start. I think I know the answer to this, but are there any other routes in or out of the Crystal Palace property, other than the road that leads to the parkway? A back path or something?"

The Bodyguard shook his head. "Nothing. It's all woods, impassable by vehicle. That's the only way in or out."

"All right." She rubbed her hands together in anticipation, wobbling her head from side to side. "Let's get down to business."

I am omitting the few vehicles that went to and from Dorothy's property, since they were immaterial to our investigation. We started with Wednesday morning, the last day of Vivian Davis's life. I have to say, the camera angle was excellent. Every car that entered or exited the Crystal Palace property passed through its field of vision, meaning we could see not only the license plate, but in the case of those leaving, the driver's face and anyone who might be sitting in the front passenger seat.

The first car that appeared was an SUV leaving the property at 8:04 a.m. Dr. Shah was driving, and his wife, Anne, was in the passenger seat. The way she was twisting toward the back, I had to assume their son was with them, though I couldn't see him.

"That must have been when they went to breakfast," I said. "For their long talk with Alex."

"MMMM-hm."

At 8:42 a.m. Vivian Davis appeared, the sight of her jolting me in my solar plexus. I'd spent so much time thinking about the woman, it was weird to see her—even just on a screen. She was driving a BMW convertible with the top down, and there was no mistaking that crest of salon-caliber hair, or that hoodie. When we'd met her at the liquor store, the hoodie had been down, but this time she'd put it over the back of her head, no doubt to preserve her perfect 'do in the wind.

"Didn't Walter say that Vivian always slept late?" I asked.

"He did indeed," said Dorothy.

So either she'd been lying to him, or he'd been lying to us.

Pretty interesting, either way.

It wasn't till 11:17 that we saw another car. This one was also leaving the Crystal Palace: a beat-up Honda I would have guessed was Paul's except I didn't have to because his face—or more accurately, his hair—was easily spotted through the windshield.

Oddly, he drove back onto the property a mere five minutes later, at 11:22.

"Supermarket run?" I guessed.

"Nope," said the Bodyguard, forcing me to look at him.

At least he was smiling at me.

His eyes were dancing, actually.

"What, then?" I demanded.

"Not telling," he replied airily. "You'll see."

Dorothy paused, looking curiously from one to the other of us. I stared at the screen as though my livelihood depended on it, which perhaps it did. If it had been possible to make a deal with the devil himself not to blush in this moment, I would have signed whatever scroll he put in front of me.

At 11:31 a.m., the Shahs returned in their SUV.

At 11:46 a.m., Paul left again in his Honda, only to return at 11:51.

"All right, what on earth is he doing?" asked Dorothy.

"Dealing drugs," replied the Bodyguard matter-of-factly. "Mainly weed. A little E."

"What?"

"It's low-level enough that we haven't flagged it," he explained. "If it doesn't pose a security risk to you, our policy is to look the other way. Otherwise things get"—his eyes flickered in my direction—"complicated. Quickly."

A new car appeared. This one was entering the property, and it was a Saab—an old one.

"Well, now *this* is interesting."

We paused the tape while Dorothy took out her phone to compare the license plate on the screen to the one she'd captured on her phone.

Perfect match.

"Enter the Hawleys," I said.

"Yep."

It was 1:44 p.m. when they drove onto the property. Unfortunately, we couldn't see who was driving, but when the car exited a mere four minutes later, there was only one person visible: the driver, Bobby Hawley.

Dorothy and I breathed in at the same time.

"Honestly," I said, "I'm surprised he knows how to drive."

She let out one of her juddering cackles.

"We're going to have to tell the police about this."

"Yes, we are." She grinned. "I'm going to enjoy that."

Just after 2:00 p.m., Vivian returned from whatever she'd been doing all day.

"We should ask Walter where she was," I said.

"We should. I'd be interested to see what he says."

Paul did two more of his drug runs in the 4:00 hour, and then at 5:37 p.m. Eve left in a tiny Volkswagen, returning a little after 8:30.

"Didn't she say she'd been working in her office all night?"

Dorothy nodded. "That's what Walter said too. He backed her up on that."

This video footage was turning out to be quite the gold mine of information.

That was it for Wednesday, but we fast-forwarded through the entire night to be sure. At 7:57 a.m. on Thursday, a flower delivery van drove onto the estate, leaving at 8:08 a.m. This at least lined up with Walter's account. And then, exactly three hours later at 11:08 a.m., a van labeled CUMBERLAND COUNTY MEDICAL EXAMINER rushed onto the property.

"I think we've seen enough," said Dorothy. "Thank you, Officer Peters."

"You know, you can call me Denny," he said. "Just please don't call me the Bodyguard."

I could hear the smile in his voice, but once again I refused to look.

"Well, in that case you can call me Dorothy." She smacked her palms on the table's surface, lifting herself out of her chair. "Well! Let's get going. We've got work to do."

"Where are we going, exactly?" I asked.

"First, I say we pop on over to the Crystal Palace, have a conversation with"—she held up her index finger—"Paul, about his extracurricular activities, and what Vivian may have thought of them."

"You're thinking that's what they could have been arguing about?"

Dorothy nodded. She raised her middle finger. "Then we speak to Eve about what she was up to that Wednesday night." Her ring finger joined the party. "And I'd like to have another chat with Walter Vogel." She widened her eyes comically. "About a *lot* of things."

I nodded back at her—a little wearily, I must admit. I for one would have loved to take off my shoes for a few minutes. I also wouldn't have been averse to grabbing a bite to eat. Maybe two bites. Now that my hangover was behind me, a few cornflakes and a slug of Minna Hawley's tea wasn't cutting it.

But I wasn't about to be shown up by a sixty-nine-year-old and her apparently endless reserves of energy.

CHAPTER 35

When we walked up to the main house, Officer Donnelly was standing next to the car wolfing down a ham sandwich I could smell from several feet away. (It smelled delicious.) The Bodyguard offered to drive us to the Crystal Palace himself, so that "Joe" could finish his lunch and "Sarah" wouldn't have to cut her break short. I took heart in the fact that he wasn't avoiding me—so much so that while getting in the car, I made eye contact with him and smiled pleasantly, the way a functional adult human might do. #fakeittillyoumakeit

When we got to the fork in the road, I looked for the camera I knew had to be there, nestled in the trees. But even then I couldn't see it, it was so well hidden.

The evergreens looked darker than before—nothing green about them. "Everblack" was more like it, their shadows thick and menacing. Looking back on this moment, I'm reminded of fairytales like *Snow White* and *The Wizard of Oz*, where the trees go sinister, their gnarled branches and knotted trunks turning into jagged claws and leering faces. The naïve heroine always seems to throw her arms up during these sequences in a laughable effort to protect herself. Fortunately, this story had no naïve heroine, so it was with our arms stuck firmly to our sides that we exited the woods and drew up to that silent, sinister cube, the Crystal Palace.

* * *

Our first hint that something was wrong had to do with the car parked out front. It was the humpbacked Saab we'd seen earlier in the day, and at this point I knew its license plate by heart, so there was no need to cross-check the number. What the hell were the Hawleys doing here? They must have left their house right after we did.

The second hint was the front door, which was wide open: a rectangular hole in the smooth glass façade. An unattended open door is an unsettling sight in any building, but it was particularly disturbing in this case—the imposing fortress rendered pregnable.

Dorothy drew in her breath. "What on earth?"

"Let me check it out"—Dorothy was already out of the car; the Bodyguard hadn't even come to a full stop, but he did now, cranking up the parking brake—"first."

I hurried after her. There was someone in the back of the Saab, and a few steps later I saw that it was Bobby Hawley. He had his head in his hands and he was rocking back and forth—the way a person might do while sobbing uncontrollably. Except he wasn't making a sound.

Dorothy and I exchanged a look, agreeing wordlessly to sidestep whatever this disaster might be for now, and head into the house.

That's when the screaming began.

I'm not sure why such screams are said to "curdle" one's blood. Isn't curdling the province of dairy products? "Piercing" is another word often used, but this sound was so loud, so intrusive, it didn't so much pierce the air as occupy every atom available to it: not just the space around me, but my body too—the inside of my nose, the cavity behind my eyes. I could feel it vibrating in my very bones. That scream felt like an assault, and I'm not ashamed to admit it terrified me.

We stood rooted to the ground, unable to move for as long as it lasted—which was probably only a few seconds, though it felt like an eternity. I remember noting in a dispassionate way how much of the whites of Dorothy's eyes I could see, how I had a much better sense of eyeball-in-socket than I would have preferred.

And then, as suddenly as it had started, it stopped. No trailing off. As if someone had flicked a switch.

The Bodyguard had caught up to us by then. "Stay back!" he commanded. "We don't know what's in there."

But Dorothy did not stay back; she made a break for the open door with a speed and agility I hadn't been expecting. Neither had the Bodyguard, by the look of slack-jawed horror on his face. But he recovered more quickly than I did, hurling himself through the rectangular hole in swift pursuit. I hesitated, having no desire to put myself in physical danger. But I also have a strong aversion to being left alone and out of the loop, and in a second (maybe two) this aversion won handily.

When I crossed the threshold, I had to pull up short to keep from bumping into Denny's upside-down triangle of a back. I peered around him, taking great gulps of air both from the impromptu aerobic activity, and the shocking nature of the scene playing out in front of me.

It felt exactly like that: a scene. Something from a play or a TV show. Have you ever witnessed a dramatic event in real life that you're used to seeing acted out on a stage or screen? A fistfight, say, or the immediate aftermath of a car accident? The only way you can process these incidents is by comparison to their fictional counterparts—as "theatrical" events that diverge from your expectations in interesting ways. (Punches land with a dull, anticlimactic thud, as opposed to the "smack" inserted by sound engineers; air bags release a white powder so fine, it hangs in the air like fairy dust.)

In the very center of the Great Hall, where three days earlier I'd seen Laura Duval dressed in mourning attire, lay the body of Walter Vogel, its limbs (already an "it," no longer a "he") splayed crookedly, as though some giant-size child had dropped a doll from the glass roof three stories above.

I'd been in the presence of a deceased person only once before, and on that occasion I'd been in close proximity to the body—which was why I was happy to keep my distance now. But even from that distance I was struck by how *in*human it was: a skin bag, lying discarded on the floor. A pile of debris whose only significance now was that someone would have to go through the (considerable) effort of gathering it up and disposing of it properly. I don't believe in the idea of a soul, or any of the various intangibles that religious- or spiritual-minded people like to spout. And yet it's impossible to ignore the fact that there *is* something about being human that has nothing to do with one's body—not a soul, per se, but life itself. This thing bore no resemblance to Walter Vogel. It was no longer a person, but a collection of physical matter.

Fluid was pooling with an alarming rapidity. I had a thought I've found hard to shake since—that our bodies hold any number of fluids, all of them poised to spill out any moment. That it's amazing we don't manifest our liquid state oftener than we do.

It was dark fluid—much darker than expected, practically black. But it wasn't the color so much as the smell that surprised me. Imagine biting your tongue, and the meaty taste of iron filling the bottom of your mouth; or maybe try burying your nose in a geranium and breathing in its metallic scent. If you menstruate, chances are you know precisely what I mean. Now multiply that by a thousand and you'll get some sense of what it was like to be in the presence of that much blood.

I'm lucky my stomach was empty, or I would have vomited, which happened to be what Anne Shah was doing—into one of the planters holding those giant ferns, though she managed to do so with dignity, kneeling in her pantyhose and yet another killer Chanel suit (a pink one this time). Above her, in the second-story gallery, Eve Turner was leaning against a column for support, one hand clamped over her mouth like the It Girl on a horror movie poster. I looked higher, to the third-story gallery, where Samir Shah was pulling his son by the hoodie in a vain attempt to drag him away. But Alex was enraptured by the bloody scene below. . . .

They looked like actors in an old-timey pantomime. Or cardboard figures in a diorama, who would disappear when turned sideways.

"We gotta call the police. And an ambulance, I guess."

The voice came from Paul Reston, on the other side of the hall. He looked almost comical clutching a bunch of carrots in one hand and a butcher knife in the other. When he stepped toward the body, a figure who'd been obscured by a column farther up the room scrabbled across the tiled floor, brushing past him. This figure came to rest at the pool's bloody shore, submerging one of her hands in the black goo and lifting it up.

The liquid coating her palm was a bright, almost gaudy shade of red—much lighter than the pool from which it came, but darker than the dry and bloodless lips she parted now. I crushed one ear against the Bodyguard's side, knowing what was about to happen, knowing this gesture would do little to drown out the sound I'd heard before. But where that banshee wail was concerned, every bit helped.

To be fair to Minna Hawley, it isn't every day a person gets to *literally* scream bloody murder.

CHAPTER 36

We spent the next six hours at the Crystal Palace. The medics who answered the 911 call shepherded us into the dining room, which was where we waited for the police to arrive.

This room was as oversize as every other on the first floor of the building. Two of its four walls were made of glass, of course, though the sky was still overcast, the swiftly sinking sun failing to assert its presence. The two interior walls featured wood paneling from the waist down, with an enormous work of abstract art looming above the paneling—I'm sure by some painter I should have recognized, but didn't. This piece stretched across both walls and all the way to the ceiling, an interconnecting series of muted, pastel-y colors that swirled this way and that like a massive screen saver, the louche cousin to an M.C. Escher drawing. It wasn't unpleasant, actually. Except if it was all you had to contemplate while wondering who among you had just killed a man.

You might think such a scene would be full of drama, and intrigue, and activity. But we'd all just seen—and smelled—the dead body of a person we knew: a human who'd been just as alive as we were, and not very long ago. This was weird. And sad. And scary. The predominant vibe as we waited was one of anxiety and awkwardness.

The table in the center of the room was long, absurdly so: a narrow rectangle we sat at in little clusters. The Shahs occupied the head, the invisible barrier that is the province of every family unit holding them together, keeping all outsiders at bay. Dorothy and I sat midway down the table, the Bodyguard standing nearby with his back to the wall, no doubt ready to spring into action should anyone make a sudden move and decide to commit Murder #3. Every few seconds he muttered something into his earpiece; I had to imagine he was in communication with his fellow security officers Choi and Donnelly, and possibly others. This was a bodyguard's nightmare, of course: his detail cloistered with an active killer, and I found myself offering frequent looks of sympathy, most of which lingered too long and became extended bouts of ogling since even now, even here, I had brain space left over to check him out. That tight thermal shirt had been an unfortunate choice for what was turning out to be a busy day. He was sweating visibly not just under his arms but at his chest, the perspiration glistening in the narrow hollow between his pecs—a bit of man cleavage I promised myself I'd ravish if ever I got the chance. Also, his jeans were bootcut, which I decided to mock him for at the earliest opportunity.

At the foot of the table sat Minna and Bobby Hawley. Bobby at least had come alive and was trying to ply his mother with a half-drunk bottle of Mountain Dew he must have brought in from the car. Minna sat slumped in her chair, insensible to her son—or seemingly so—staring with a blank expression at the painting on the wall. She'd wiped her bloody palms on her house-dress, I noticed. Its yellow paisley pattern was streaked with red now, making it uglier than it already was.

Eve Turner was standing about as far away as possible, in front of the elevator marked "W." She looked as though she were about to get on it, which I'm sure she would've done if she could have. Paul Reston, on the other hand, had latched on to us, which was ironic (in the faulty, Alanis Morissette way), as he was the one we'd come to see first. He sat directly on the table, legs swinging in a manic fashion.

"Oh man, oh man, I can't believe it, I just really can't believe it, you know? I was just washing the carrots—" He looked down at the bunch in his hand, realizing perhaps for the first time that he was still holding them. (The Bodyguard had relieved him of his butcher knife when we entered the room, slipping it somewhere in his waist area with an alacrity that impressed *and* alarmed me.) Paul laid the carrots on the table. He looked up at us, his train of thought not so much lost as derailed, lying sideways at the bottom of a ditch. "You just don't think anything like this is gonna happen to *you*, you know?"

"I do know," said Dorothy soothingly. "So what exactly *did* happen?"

"Well, I was in the kitchen, getting dinner started, and I was like"—he cocked his head, the way a dog would in a heartwarming family comedy—"what the heck was that? Haha. Sort of a crash, or a bang I guess? But I didn't go look cuz I was busy, figured if it was important I'd hear something else. And boy did I! 'Bout five, maybe ten minutes later. Loudest scream I ever heard. *That* got me running."

"That's when you went into the hall?" asked Dorothy.

He nodded in rhythm with his swinging legs.

"What did you see?"

"Those two."

He pointed at the Hawleys.

"Were they close to the body?" asked Dorothy.

"*She* was. She was standing right over it, bawling her head off. He was just inside the front door. I ran over to—it. Poor guy, he was dead, that was obvious. Someone'd pushed him from one of the upper floors, you could tell by the way he was splayed out."

"Do you think he could have jumped?" I asked.

"Not unless he slit his own throat too."

"Someone slit his throat? How terrible," said Dorothy. "I didn't realize that."

"Oh yeah, full-on Sicilian necktie. Brutal."

This accounted for all the blood pooling under the body. It also meant that Walter Vogel's murderer had to be one of the people still inside the house.

"Was his throat slit before or after the fall?" I asked.

Paul stuck his hands out on either side, the shrug emoji come to life. "No idea."

If it had happened after the fall, that put the Hawleys at the top of the suspect list—especially since Minna Hawley was the only one among us with visible bloodstains on her clothes. But maybe whoever had done this had stood behind Walter, attacked him with a knife or some other instrument, and then pushed him over the railing from one of the upper stories. I thought back to the way everyone had been arrayed on different floors. Given that at least five and as many as ten minutes had elapsed between the fall of the body and its discovery, that was more than enough time for the killer to race up or down as need be on one among the four elevators available. Clothes could have been changed, weapons concealed (or cleaned; I thought back to Paul standing there with his gleaming knife), appropriate expressions of horror fixed in place. Just as in Vivian's case, any of them could have done it.

Except Walter, of course.

A uniformed police officer entered the room. If I'd seen him on the street I would have guessed he was in high school. His acne was worse than Alex Shah's.

"Paul Reston?"

Paul hopped off the table. "That's my name, don't wear it out."

"The detectives want a word with you."

We all watched as Paul made his way to the door. It was a little like when one of your classmates in elementary school is called to the principal's office, except no one oohed and aahed, and one of us was a murderer.

"Are we going to be questioned one by one?" Dorothy asked the officer. "Is that the idea?"

"I think so."

"Do you have any sense of how long that's going to take?"

"Detective Locust said it would take as long as it's going to take."

I was surprised Locust hadn't graced us en masse with his presence yet, but the day was young.

Paul paused in the doorway to give us a little salute as though he were heading out to his execution, and then he left, the uniformed officer following him out.

The room was quieter now. I watched as Minna Hawley leaned forward in slow motion, lowering her forehead onto the table. This is actually one of my favorite ways to read, with a book cradled in my lap (I read the entire works of Jane Austen this way in middle school—in the school library's "Quiet Zone" during lunch), but she let her arms hang stiff and straight, swaying ever so slightly.

I realized that Bobby Hawley was watching me watch her, and more from embarrassment than anything else I smiled at him. He smiled back, lumbering out of his seat and shuffling over.

"Incoming," I muttered.

Dorothy had been texting. She put her phone facedown on the table, careful to avoid Paul's carrots. Bobby dragged a chair over. He sat down heavily.

"Your mother doesn't seem to be doing too well," observed Dorothy. "Do you think she might need medical attention? For the shock?"

He shrugged his shoulders. "She gets like this sometimes. It'll pass."

We exchanged a look while Bobby took a swig of Mountain Dew.

"How are *you* doing?" she asked. "And let me just say how sorry I am for your loss."

"Eh." He did that hand-swipe thing you usually see much older men do, especially if they're Italian and prone to saying *Fuhgeddaboutit!* "I don't care. He was an asshole."

"So what were you doing here?" I asked.

"Mommy wanted to see him. She got real upset after talking to you. Said she wanted t'give him a piece of her mind." He hesitated. "I think she just wanted to"—he glanced in her direction, but she was as catatonic as before—"rub it in his face. About how bad everything was going for him. You coming to see us gave her a good excuse."

"MMMM-hm," said Dorothy. "And what happened when you got here?"

"The door was open so we just walked through and . . ." Bobby swallowed thickly. "He was lying there. Like you saw. It must've just happened cuz there wasn't a lotta blood yet. Mommy ran up to him, but you could tell he was dead. Then she started screaming."

"Was anyone else there who you could see?" asked Dorothy.

"Just that funny-looking guy with the hair. The one who left. He was holding a knife, and at first I thought he did it, but there wasn't any blood on it. The knife, I mean. What is he, a chef or something?"

"Something like that," said Dorothy.

"There was another lady who started screaming too. Up high on the balcony, like she was screaming from the ceiling." He looked around. "She isn't here."

It was only then that I realized Laura was missing from the group.

"Long brown hair?" I asked.

"Yeah, real pretty. Didn't scream as long as Mommy did. Or

as loud. I saw her turn and leave, and then I . . . I had to leave too. I couldn't keep on listening to it."

"MMMM-hm. Well, I can certainly understand that."

"By the time I got back to the car she stopped. But then she started again."

That was the point at which we'd arrived.

"I see," said Dorothy.

I wondered what she did see. It was hard to take Bobby Hawley at face value. Was it really the sound of his mother screaming that had upset him? Or had his mother gotten into an argument with his father on one of the balconies, and had he witnessed her attack him? Push him? Was that what had sent him running for the car?

I took another look at Minna Hawley, her forehead still plastered to the table. She looked dead herself. Was this a woman who had simply discovered her ex-husband's corpse? Or was she in shock over what she'd done? (Or maybe what her son had done? I dismissed this thought immediately: impossible to imagine Bobby Hawley expending enough energy to kill a man—his father, no less.) It was pretty convenient that she'd managed to cover herself in blood while in full view of everyone, effectively obliterating any spatter that may have hit her earlier.

I hadn't forgotten the surveillance video, which proved that at least one of them could have been at the Crystal Palace the night Vivian Davis was killed. This appalling mother/son duo had been on or at least near the scene when both murders were committed. Surely that couldn't be a coincidence?

"I should get back to her," he muttered, getting up hastily.

There was no time to debrief, because as soon as Bobby Hawley had receded, Eve Turner approached, hovering over his empty chair.

"Do you mind if I join you?"

She had on pants for the first time in my experience of her:

form-fitting, made of a shimmery black material that made them look both utilitarian and fashionable. If we were friends, I would have asked her where she'd bought them.

Dorothy gestured for her to sit. She sank down slowly, in a controlled manner. Even now, her poise was perfect. Her hair was down today—the braids swept back in a loose ponytail that reached well past her shoulders.

"How are you doing?" asked Dorothy.

"I'm all right. You?"

"Same."

I expected Eve to ask how I was doing, if only from a baseline sense of politeness, but she didn't.

We all blinked at one another a few times.

"I guess I'm in shock," she said finally.

Was she, though? She was so calm, so collected: surely *this* was the way a cold-blooded murderer would behave? She'd been on the second floor when the body was discovered: the same floor as her office, as all the bedrooms. It would have been so easy for her to conceal a weapon there, change her clothes. Maybe that was why she was wearing pants now?

"Did you see it happen?" asked Dorothy. "I hope not, for your sake."

She shook her head. "I was working in my office. I didn't hear a thing till the first scream. There was no ignoring *that*."

Was she telling the truth? It was impossible to know. I thought back to the video footage we'd reviewed earlier that day—the three hours she'd been away from the property, during which time she said she'd been working in her office. Now that *was* a lie, no question about it.

I decided to test her.

"Where were you last Wednesday night?" I asked. "The night Vivian died? You were gone the whole first part of the evening."

Dorothy frowned at me. But I knew she wasn't actually displeased with my question, just taking the opportunity to cast herself as the good cop.

Eve eyed me coolly, smart enough not to deny what I'd said. She made a big show of turning to Dorothy and addressing her alone.

"I'm sorry I lied to you before. The truth is, I was embarrassed. I went to a hotel nearby, one that Walter and I visited whenever we were out here. You can check, I'll give you all the particulars." She held up her chin: a defiant gesture. "It's not like I used a fake name or anything."

"Walter didn't meet you, though, did he?" asked Dorothy.

She shook her head. "That never happened before. Even if he couldn't make it at the last minute, he'd always let me know. But he didn't answer any of my calls or texts. It's why I waited there so long. When I got back he said he'd misplaced his phone, lost track of time."

"That must have annoyed you."

She didn't respond.

"It would have annoyed me!"

"It annoyed me, sure. But then the next day, once Vivian was found. . . . None of it mattered. And now—"

Her face contorted, the agony breaking through, rupturing her self-possession.

"Now it *really* doesn't matter. Nothing does." Her voice shook, on the precipice of breaking. "Excuse me."

She hurried away, retreating to the corner near the elevator. I watched her take out her phone and pretend to read it.

So much for calm and collected.

"Well," said Dorothy in an undertone. "That wasn't *un*interesting."

"Not uninteresting at all," I agreed.

Had Walter Vogel been trying to end things with his secretary? Maybe she was more attached to him than we—or he—had realized. Could she have been obsessed enough to murder his wife, and then murder *him* when things didn't go her way? I went over that scene in the kitchen, when we'd walked in on what had obviously been an intimate moment between them. Had Walter been annoyed at being discovered, or was it the intimate moment *itself* that had angered him? Maybe he'd been trying to get rid of Eve Turner for a while. . . .

There was a commotion at the head of the table. Alex Shah jerked his chair back. The sound was atrocious, a nails-on-chalkboard screech. For this reason we were all watching when he hit his father square in the chest—not with his fist, just the flat of his hand, but still. It was hard enough that Samir's chair moved too.

"It's *not* my fault!" Alex cried out. "It's *yours*!"

Anne sprang up, placing herself between the two of them and imploring in furtive tones that they quiet down. Our eyes met across the room. I found myself staring into the face of a hunted animal—as melodramatic as that sounds. It's what I imagine it's like when you come across one of those deer that cross the road in this part of the world with such alarming frequency. I jerked my head away, watching peripherally as she placed both hands on her son's shoulders and begged him in hushed, tearful tones. Alex was looking at the ground, refusing to engage. His father sat hunched in his chair, staring at his hands.

It struck me that we'd neglected the Shahs since speaking to them yesterday. But if Vivian Davis was going to be an impediment to Alex's future, then Walter Vogel would have been one too. What had Samir and Alex been doing all the way on the third floor, anyway? I remembered the way Walter had cast aspersions on Alex in our interview with him; could his murder simply have been part two of a hastily concocted plot—by Alex, or his parents? Or all three of them?

Or maybe the person who hadn't seen fit to show her face was the most suspicious of all. What was Laura Duval doing, exactly, hiding up in her bedroom? And would she ever come out?

More to the point: would I ever stop asking questions? The more I thought about this case, the more questions I had. But I kept them to myself. Dorothy was on her phone again, and it's not like we could have spoken freely, anyway. So I continued to sit there, taking a break every now and then to gawk at the Bodyguard, the questions roiling like so much milk in my butter churn of a brain.

CHAPTER 37

The next time the door to the Great Hall opened, SI Locust entered the room.

We straightened up the way people do when an authority figure appears.

He stood inside the doorway, gazing down on us without looking at anyone in particular, and without speaking—as though he were waiting for us to quiet down, even though no one was making a sound. His nose was quivering: so slightly, it struck me as a nervous tic. I had a moment of sympathy for SI Locust. It couldn't have been good for his career that a second person had died on his watch—a murder that probably would have been prevented if he'd already figured out whodunit. Not that whoever had killed Vivian Davis had necessarily killed Walter Vogel, but there was no question the two deaths were related. Or that a murderer was on the loose.

After a minute or two he took a folded piece of paper from the inside pocket of his suit jacket. He unfolded it slowly, clearing his throat.

"You have been through a traumatic experience," he read off the paper. "First, I would like to extend my condolences and let you know we are here to help. This is our foremost goal."

He paused. While his contempt may not have been audible, it was unquestionably palpable.

"A grief and trauma counselor is on her way," he continued. "If any of you would like to speak with her"—he lifted his eyes to glance at Minna Hawley, who had at least raised her head by this point—"I would encourage you to do so."

Locust folded up the paper, returning it to his jacket pocket.

"We're going to speak with you one by one," he said. "About what you saw. And what you know. I'm going to insist you all stay in this room for the duration of these interviews, which we will conduct as quickly as possible. Please know that an officer is stationed outside this door, who you can call on if you need anything. Mr. Reston has already been interviewed, and has kindly agreed to prepare an early dinner so you all have something to eat."

So that was why Paul Reston had been questioned first. This was downright thoughtful of Locust. I was impressed. And a little surprised.

"Ms. Turner, you're up next. Come with me, please."

Eve took her time reaching the door. Once they'd left, Minna Hawley lay her head down on the table again, and the Shahs began whispering noisily among themselves. Dorothy turned to me.

"What do you say we go pay Paul Reston a visit in the kitchen?" she asked quietly. "Pose him a few questions?"

"You mean do exactly what Locust told us not to do?"

She nodded.

"Sounds good to me."

You may not know this, but Dorothy Gibson loves her food—*almost* as much as she loves her booze.

We could smell the pasta sauce while we were still in the hallway: that unique fragrance of a tomato's acidity being broken down over low heat, and mixing with the delicate pungency of onions, garlic, and unless I was mistaken, some red bell pepper. My stomach convulsed—violently, like one of those deluded girls in Salem. I still hadn't eaten anything since my sad little hangover breakfast.

"Now that smells goo-ood!" Dorothy turned her head, looking behind her. "Don't you agree, Denny?"

This was meant as a peace offering. The Bodyguard nodded. Curtly. He was less than pleased with our impromptu trip to the kitchen, and had made his displeasure known while we were exiting through the dining room's back door. I can't remember his exact words, but I'm pretty sure "insane" and "irresponsible" were both in there somewhere. This back door connected to the hallway we were walking down now—the one with the glass wall, which gave onto the garden.

We turned into the kitchen, where Paul was bent over a steaming copper pot so massive, I could have taken a hip bath in it. At the table sat the teenage police officer we'd seen before, who was doing something on his phone. Playing a video game, most likely.

"Hey there!" cried Dorothy.

Paul jumped—not very high, but a veritable jump, both feet leaving the ground. The police officer dropped his phone on the terra-cotta tiles with a clatter.

"I'm sorry!" she boomed. "Didn't mean to scare you!"

She let loose one of her hearty cackles, striding over and handing the junior officer his phone before he could pick it up himself. "We're going to ask Paul here a few questions. I'd *so* appreciate it if you stepped outside with my friend Denny. I promise it'll be fine."

Officer Clueless mumbled something or other before walking to the doorway as he was told. The Bodyguard and I exchanged a glance during which I conveyed a "what are you gonna do?" expression meant to relieve me of all responsibility for what was happening, and which he made clear he wasn't buying. Whatsoever. The two of them went into the hallway.

"That sauce smells fabulous." Dorothy sat down at the table, motioning Paul to join her. "What's your secret?"

"I use butter instead of olive oil." He grinned, plopping down opposite her while I slipped into the chair on her left. "You really don't want to know how much butter is in there."

"I'm sure I don't!"

She took a deep breath, her face going serious.

"Now, Paul, I know you just answered a bunch of questions from the police, but we have a few questions of our own, and we'd really appreciate it if you indulged us by answering them. Do you think you can do that?"

He nodded, his clown's wig of hair flapping along with him. "Yeah, yeah, sure. Course I can. Whatever I can do to help."

Dorothy looked at me.

"Would you like to do the honors?"

"Oh. Okay."

I hadn't been expecting this, but I recovered quickly, leaning forward in my chair and threading my hands together on top of the table as though we were commencing a business meeting.

"The thing is. . . ." I paused for effect. "We know your secret."

I admit: this was rather Regina George of me, but it had the desired effect. Paul's piggy eyes grew wide, and he was silent a few moments. (I could hear the murmurings of the Bodyguard and the police officer chatting in the hall—about what I have no idea. Sports teams, maybe? How fun it was to have been born in the '90s?)

"I just gotta put the pasta in, do you mind?"

We waited as he dumped four or five pounds' worth of dried spaghetti into the behemoth pot, which was now at a rolling boil. When he sat down again, he let out a heavy sigh.

"Oh man, ever since Viv died I knew it'd come out sooner or later, all the digging everyone's been doing. Police didn't ask diddly about it, though. Do they know?"

"Not that we're aware of," said Dorothy.

"I wouldn't even care if it was just me I had to worry about, but it's my hus"—he stopped himself—"my soon-to-be *ex*-husband who's the problem. We've got a kid," he explained. "Danny's nine, and my ex's a lot richer than I am. He's going for full custody and he'll use this against me, I know he will. You gotta understand." He looked from one to the other of us, both corners of his mouth drawn down in a beseeching manner I was sure he'd perfected for the stage. "Danny's the best thing in my life. I can't lose him. Do you think there's any chance we can keep the whole thing quiet, keep it out of the investigation?"

"Well," I said. "The thing is, there's video surveillance, they'll probably—"

"There's *video*? I knew Viv had some photos, but how the hell'd she get *video*?"

Dorothy and I exchanged a look without moving our heads, without even really looking at each other. We'd obviously stumbled onto something new without realizing it. I held up my hand—just an inch or two, but she understood, as I knew she would. This was my interrogation.

"I want you to walk us through the whole thing," I said. "From the beginning. Can you do that for us? Then we'll see what we can do."

He nodded his head miserably. "Yeah yeah, okay."

"Do you need a moment?" asked Dorothy.

It was too bad there wasn't a vending machine out in the hallway from which we could offer him a cold soda or his favorite pack of cigarettes.

"Nah, it's all pretty simple, anyway. I already told you how when Viv and I met, back in the day, we were still kids, right?

She was eighteen, but I was a high school dropout, still technically a minor. But I was so impatient, I had all these big plans to be an *ack-tor*"—he broke up the word with snooty emphasis—"the next Olivier or Irving or whatever." He shook his head. "Fast-forward four, five months and I'm making ends meet doing escort work for rich old gay dudes. Viv too. Not for gay dudes, obviously. But that's *really* how we met. Even though we both ended up doing that *Richard III* show together. I'm the one who convinced her to audition for it, actually. She never thought she'd get the part, but I knew she'd be a kickass Lady Anne. Anyways, everything I told you was true. We really *were* friends, even though we only saw each other every now and then. It's not like I hated her guts or anything. Not till. . . ."

"Till she made you take this job. It never made sense to me that you would do it willingly. It's far away, for one thing." I paused before taking another plunge. "Plus, the little detail you left out about not getting paid anything for it."

"Wow, you really *do* know everything, huh? Okay, yeah, so we hadn't talked in a while, and she just showed up at my place in Brooklyn a month or two ago, out of the blue. Not like that was crazy unusual or anything, but it was definitely random. I hadn't seen much of her since she married Walter and moved up here full time." He rubbed his fingers against the wood grain of the table. "At first she tried to pretend it was a friendly visit, but it didn't take long for her to get down to business. She told me she needed my help for a few weeks here. I was pretty taken aback. Like you said, it was *awkward*, and no way did I want to be her freaking *butler*, even for a few weeks. So I told her no, nice as I could. But she wouldn't take no for an answer. We went back and forth a few times . . . and that's when she got nasty."

He fidgeted in his seat, the legs of his chair scraping against the tiles.

"She had the photos in her purse. From our . . . exploits, I guess you could call them. Haha. Back in the day. She fanned them out on the table like we were in a Lifetime movie or something. It would've been funny if it weren't so mean. She said she had copies of all of 'em, and she'd send them to my ex if I didn't do what she wanted. She knew all about the custody battle, I'm not even sure how. But Viv was always a big gossip, she always had all the dirt."

"How did she have these photos?" asked Dorothy.

"Well, um, there were a few times we were involved in . . . group situations." I looked down at my hands, Puritan that I am. "You'd be surprised how often photography was involved, actually. Clients paid extra if they could have souvenirs. Less risky back then, before everything could be uploaded so easily. Except obviously not *totally* risk-free."

"MMMM-hm."

"But I still don't understand how there could be *video*. What, was she hiding a camcorder in the wall or something? What exactly did you see?"

"We don't need to get into that right now," I said smoothly. "The important point is that she was blackmailing you."

"I mean, that's making it sound *much* more dramatic than it was. But sure, I guess you could call it that."

He stared at us. We stared back. Suddenly his mouth fell open in a look of horror that also felt crafted for the stage.

"I obviously didn't kill her! Viv was a total bitch but I'd never *murder* her. Or anyone! I'm trying to make sure I can still be a part of my son's life, you really think I'd go around drowning people and pushing them off balconies?"

"I agree that would be very foolish," said Dorothy. "But what I still don't understand is why?"

"Why what?" asked Paul.

"Why did Vivian have to blackmail you? Why couldn't she just hire someone else?"

"Oh! That's easy enough. Cuz she was broke. They both were. She and Walter maxed out their credit cards renting out this place. She told me that. I mean, cat was pretty much out of the bag once she threatened me with those photos." He got up to give the pasta a stir. "This whole thing they were trying to do? Getting that Indian dude to float them a bunch of cash for Walter's skin thing? It was like their last chance; everything was riding on it. *Everything.*" He sat back down. "They needed to look like they were flush with cash, but without actually spending anything. Which was where I came in."

I remembered Samir Shah calling Walter a fraud, saying how no one should believe a word he or Vivian said. I'd thought he'd been exaggerating. But maybe he was right.

"So when you and Vivian were arguing the night she died," I said, "it was about this, I assume? I can't say I blame you."

He looked at me blankly. "What're you talking about? I never argued with her. Once I agreed to the job I just pretended everything was fine. Makes life a lot easier, I learned that a long time ago."

"According to her sister, Laura, you went up to her bedroom late on Wednesday night. She said the two of you stood in her doorway arguing about something, but she couldn't hear what."

"Sister Laura's lying then. That lady is a total weirdo anyway, I've barely seen her this whole time. She's always lying around in her room, forcing me to leave trays outside her door like this is a Four Seasons or something." He waved a flabby hand dismissively. "Probably just trying to get attention."

Given that she had been correct about Paul not being paid for his services, I was less willing to dismiss what Laura Duval had to say. But I let it go. I still had my final card to play.

"Well, I can see now why you had to keep up your side hustle as a drug dealer while you were here. Given you weren't being paid anything."

Despite the pudginess of his face, his lips were thin, and they grew flatter as he smirked at me. "Course you know about that too. Bet there's a camera somewhere on the road, isn't there?"

I nodded.

"Makes sense." He shrugged. "Thought I'd get a few weeks off from the hustle coming up here, but word gets around fast. These Mainers aren't kidding around. Struggling actor's gotta do what a struggling actor's gotta do, right?"

"You're not concerned about the effect that may have on your custody battle?" asked Dorothy.

He laughed. "Who do you think my supplier is? Told you my ex makes way more than I do."

Suddenly I felt bad for nine-year-old Danny. But it was also heartening to see two dads making such a mess of their child. Garbage parenting was no longer the sole province of heterosexual couples.

Dorothy stood up. I did too. "Well, Paul, I have to thank you for being so forthcoming with us. We really appreciate it."

He nodded uncertainly—no doubt wondering just how badly this interview had gone for him.

"By the way." Dorothy was halfway to the door. She turned around. "I'm curious. What role did *you* play? In *Richard III*?"

"Oh! Well, don't laugh, but—"

He stood up, a defiant gleam in his little, piggy eyes.

"Murderer Number 1."

Chapter 38

"Nice work in there," said Dorothy.

We were in the hallway again—on our way back to the dining room, the Bodyguard loping behind us.

"Thank you," I said. "So do you think he did it? It's a pretty good motive."

"The custody of a child hanging in the balance? I agree, it is. In fact, it might be the best motive we've come across."

"And you said this case will probably come down to motive in the end."

"I did," she agreed.

"Well, even if Vivian wasn't a great actor, she must've been a great acting coach," I said. "Because apparently Walter Vogel was lying to us all over the place when we talked to him. Those two are as big a mystery as they ever were."

Dorothy stopped walking.

I stopped too.

She turned to me.

"That's an interesting point," she said. "*Very* interesting."

I nodded, happy to have made what she considered to be an interesting point, though I had no idea *why* it was interesting. She stood there a while longer, staring over my shoulder into the middle distance.

The Bodyguard and I exchanged an infinitesimal shoulder shrug.

"I still don't see how it's *possible*," she murmured.

"Pardon?" I asked, though I'd heard her perfectly.

"Unless. . . ." Her eyes fluttered, her breath catching in her throat. Whatever she'd just thought of, it wasn't pleasant.

"Are you okay?"

She made a little shimmying motion, shaking herself out of her reverie. "I'm fine. Come on, let's go. With any luck we'll be back before Locust."

Alas, our luck was out. When we slipped back into the dining room, SI Locust was waiting for us with arms crossed, and nostrils arched. The others were all waiting too, their attitudes ranging from sympathetic (Anne Shah) to gleeful (Bobby Hawley).

"You were given specific instructions not to leave."

"Well, as you can see, we're safe," said Dorothy. "And since our safety is your number one priority, I imagine that must come as a relief."

"Yes, if only all of us could have an armed guard at all times." Locust looked pointedly at the Bodyguard, who did a muted version of that chest-jutting peacock thing men do when confronting other men, even now in this wokest of ages.

"It's a great privilege, I couldn't agree with you more," said Dorothy.

"Well, since you're up," he sneered, "you may as well come with me." He paused, looking in my direction. "Both of you."

It was impressive, I reflected as he swept out of the room, nose leading the way, how he managed to make this sound like a threat.

The homicide unit had been busy while we were all in the dining room. Technicians dressed in yellow Tyvek jumpsuits I'd associated up till then with NASCAR and nuclear spills were scurrying to and fro, carrying all sorts of heavy, intimidating-looking equipment. There was a buzz of activity in the air, enough to make the Great Hall feel occupied for the first time in my experience of it.

A circular curtain had been placed around the area where the body still lay—or so I assumed, since the curtain was blocking our view. The pool of blood was visible, though, peeking out under the curtain, which was raised an inch or two off the ground by little metal feet that reminded me of a bird's talons. I guessed they were a design feature meant to address this exact issue.

A woman in dress slacks and sensible shoes came out from behind the curtain, her dark hair in a bun placed high on her head like a ballerina's, except the bun was messy, the bottom half of it falling onto her neck. She was smiling before she even saw us, and from that and her bustling gait I could tell she had a naturally cheerful disposition. Such people irritate me less than you might think; it's false or opportunistic joviality I abhor, and usually when I come across people like this, I want to ask them what their secret is. Especially if they aren't idiots, which I was sure she was not because she also happened to be the medical examiner. I knew this because her white jacket said CUMBERLAND COUNTY MEDICAL EXAMINER & CORONER on it.

She froze when she saw us, her mouth falling open easily.

"Oh my God. You're Dorothy Gibson."

"La-hast time I checked!"

"I am just—" She put a hand on her chest, gulping for air. "I cannot believe I'm meeting you right now, it's such an honor—I mean, I *heard* you were involved in what was happening, I knew you were in the vicinity, *everyone* knows that by now"—

Out of the corner of my eye, I saw SI Locust take a step back and cross his arms. I was sure he expected someone to notice him (because men like him are used to being noticed): that Dorothy and this young woman were meant to pick up on his displeasure and stop talking of their own accord. But to my delight, they were so absorbed in each other, they ignored him completely.

"My name is Sheila, by the way."

"Hello, Sheila!"

"You have been—oh my God, I think I'm going to cry, this is so embarrassing—you have been an *inspiration* to me ever since I was a little girl. Right up to the election, which I *still* can't believe you lost. I was sure you would win."

"Well, thank you for that," said Dorothy. "It means a lot. So tell me, what exactly are you up to here?"

"I'm estimating the time of death!" She said this with the brightness and enthusiasm of a party hostess informing her guests where the refreshments are.

"MMMM-hm, MMMM-hm. But is there any question about it in this case?" asked Dorothy.

SI Locust's nose began to tremble. . . .

"We always do it no matter what. Standard operating procedure."

"I see, and how do you go about it? I'm so curious."

"Usually by taking temperature measurements of the body and its environment—the air around it, the water it's submerged in, whatever. Then you can estimate how long it's been, based on the temperature differential between the two. Also the extent to which rigor mortis has set in." She was really warming to her topic now. "Since that happens so quickly, it's important to observe the level of stiffness as soon as possible. Pretty much everything else happens at the lab."

"MMMM-hm."

Locust cleared his throat, but neither of them noticed.

"In this case there's also the blood pool and arterial spatter to give us an idea. Coagulation's another great time marker," she explained.

"Arterial spatter?" echoed Dorothy.

Sheila pointed upward. "On the third-floor balcony. Perforation of the victim's right carotid prior to the fall—*massive* perforation, practically a severing. Pretty surprising, given how dull the instrument was." Her hand flew up to her mouth. "I'm so sorry, I forget sometimes how heartless it can sound when I go all clinical like that. I guess it's because I'm nervous, this is my first solo eval, and then to meet *you*—"

"Yes, thank you, Dr. Hasan, we'll have a chat later about the multitude of ways in which the conversation I just witnessed was outrageously inappropriate." SI Locust flicked his wrist, looking down at his watch. "Assuming you're done gabbing, maybe you can see fit to get back to work? Unless you want this to be your first *and* last 'eval' out in the field?"

Sheila's face crumpled in on itself. She flashed one last humiliated look at her idol, before whisking herself away behind the curtain.

Dorothy's face did not crumple, but it contracted: her eyes narrowing, the corners of her mouth pinching the skin on both sides. "I don't think that was necessary."

"I don't care what you think is necessary," replied Locust. "You're not in charge. No matter how hard it is for others to believe."

He let loose a lopsided jeer: left nostril scrunched, right at full sail. And then, as I suspected he'd been itching to do for some time, he went there.

"You got close, Mrs. Gibson. But you couldn't seal the deal."

CHAPTER 39

SI Locust gestured for Dorothy to walk ahead of him, across the ant trail of technicians scurrying from one end of the Great Hall to the other, and into the Recreation Room. She executed one of her slow-motion swaggers in that direction and I followed—until someone tapped me lightly on the elbow.

I turned.

"We're actually going to be in the . . . I think it's called the Reception Room?" DS Brooks gave me a goofy grin. "I feel like *any* of these rooms could be called the Reception Room."

He had a point, but I was more occupied by the relief and consternation flooding me in equal parts: relief that I wouldn't have to sit in the same room as SI Locust for the next however many minutes, consternation that Dorothy would. Alone. I looked at her now.

"Yes, we're breaking up the dynamic duo." SI Locust looked as though he might peck at me with that enormous beak of his. "Don't worry, it won't be long. Somehow I think you'll both survive."

"It's fine," I said coldly.

And it really was. There was a good chance I'd be able to get much more out of Brooks than she would out of Locust—which is to say, *anything*. I guessed that Dorothy appreciated this point, based on her jaunty nod and half wave of farewell. In fact, I found myself locking eyes not with her but with the Bodyguard, who—surely I was flattering myself?—looked as though he would have preferred to follow me instead of Dorothy. . . . But of course, he had no choice in the matter.

We sat on the metal benches where I'd sat with the Shahs on the afternoon of Vivian's memorial. With only two people in it, the Reception Room felt like more of a cavern than ever. I felt the childish urge to yell "Echo!" and see how many times the word repeated itself.

"Okay, I'll just admit it."

DS Brooks was leaning forward, elbows on his knees, chin cupped in one hand. He was wearing cargo pants today. (Remember when cargo pants were a thing? Apparently DS Brooks did.)

"We have no idea what's going on."

I was pretty sure Locust's interview with Dorothy was not starting the same way over in the Recreation Room.

"How about I tell you everything we've found out. *Off* the record," I added, remembering Paul Reston and his custody woes. "And we go from there?"

"Peachy."

DS Brooks took no notes this time, I was happy to see. Anyway, by the end of my recitation he was nearly catatonic from all the information I'd given him.

"Wow. Just, wow."

He arched his back like a cat, rolling his neck a few times.

"I guess it's only fair I tell you everything we know that you don't. Not that there's much." He snickered at me. "You showed me yours, now I show you mine."

Ew. But I was too eager to hear what he had to say to call him out on this.

"It's true that Walter Vogel and Vivian Davis were hanging

on by a thread. Financially, that is. Basically they'd been in debt forever, getting deeper in the hole every year. Not that that's all that unusual. You'd be surprised how many people live that way, even the rich ones. They also had a bunch of investments go bad recently. They really *had* maxed out their credit cards—like a bunch of them. Staying at this place"—he waved an arm in the air—"pretty much finished off their savings, so I don't think it's too much of a stretch to say they had *a lot* riding on getting funding for Walter's invention. Far as we can make out it's legit, even though I have no idea *how* legit."

"So he wasn't making the whole thing up?"

Brooks shook his head. "Definitely not. The other interesting thing we learned about them was that they'd taken out several TROs on Minna Hawley before."

"TROs?"

"Sorry, temporary restraining orders."

"Ah."

Where had I heard about a temporary restraining order recently? I couldn't place it, but something—some instinct—told me it was important.

"Let's just say Minna Hawley definitely *had* visited Walter and Vivian before—at their permanent home here in town, at Walter's office in Portland, a few restaurants, a theater even. Like, a lot. So it doesn't surprise me she came here too. I would've been surprised if she *hadn't*. It's one of the reasons we did our own review of the surveillance footage on the exterior walls of this place. We were looking for her, and anything else suspicious."

He paused the way one does before imparting crucial information.

"And?"

"She never showed. We saw plenty of Walter and Vivian, and the others staying here. But nothing suspicious." He paused again. "With one exception."

"What?" I demanded impatiently.

"The camera on the southwestern side of the house stopped working."

"The one looking out on the garden?" I asked. "Off the kitchen?"

He nodded. "That's the one. Late in the morning on Sunday, the twenty-seventh of November—the Sunday before the Wednesday Vivian was killed—the camera goes out. Just goes black. We looked into it and the wire was actually *cut*. So there's no way it was an accident."

"Huh. That's interesting. It also means it couldn't have been a random person."

"Bingo. Maybe Minna Hawley was working with someone inside the house?" he suggested dubiously. "When they drove onto the estate on Wednesday, she could've snuck in through the door there. Then afterward, she could've left through the woods, had her son waiting somewhere to pick her up. He'd do anything she wanted, no questions asked. Kid's a loser."

"Why, though? I mean, it's obvious why Minna Hawley would want to kill them both, but who would agree to help her? She doesn't have much money, does she?"

"Actually, she *does*," said Brooks triumphantly. "Unlike her ex-husband, she made some pretty savvy investments. Well, one in particular. Put practically everything she could spare into Amazon. Super early on." He raised his eyebrows. "Smart move. She's actually pretty rich now."

I thought back to the Hawleys' house—its air of stagnation and decay. Why live like that if you didn't have to? But of course, that was the point; it was a choice. If Miss Havisham hadn't been capable of bettering her situation simply by lifting a finger and making it so, her way of life wouldn't have been nearly as tragic—or meaningful—as it was.

"But yeah, it's pretty hard to imagine any of these people helping some psycho-bitch commit a double murder," admitted Brooks.

I realize this is a controversial statement, but I think "bitch" is one of those words that can be used with impunity only by those who've been hurt or otherwise marginalized by it. Men who casually say "bitch" make me nervous. Especially when they're as likable as DS Brooks.

"The Shahs are loaded themselves. Big surprise, right? Paul Reston is a doofus, I just don't think he has it in him. And Eve Turner was in love with the guy. I don't see her killing him, even though I could totally see her killing the wife. What was it about him, anyway? Do you see it?" he asked with an urgency that surprised me. "Why is it all these women were so obsessed with him? He wasn't even that good-looking."

The male preoccupation with pulchritude—not only in the objects of their attraction, but in their rivals for attraction—never ceases to both amaze and bore me.

"He had a quality. But you haven't mentioned Laura Duval yet."

He pointed an index finger at me. "Gold star for you. I had to lay cash on anyone? It'd be her. She'd only just gotten here, and we barely know anything about her. We haven't even been able to interview her properly. Every time we try, she's got some excuse. Her latest one's the best yet. You know she's barely conscious up there?" He jabbed his finger at the ceiling. "Took some sort of a sedative after she saw the body."

"The second body," I clarified.

"Right. We had to get an EMT to check her out to make sure she's okay. 'Parently she is, just won't be coherent for a while."

He put his elbows on his knees again, covering his face with his fingers.

"This is all such a mess," he moaned. "This was supposed to be my big break, it's not like murders like this come around every day."

"I know," I said quietly, grateful I wasn't the only one crass or craven enough to view a murder—two murders—as an opportunity.

He dragged his fingers down his face, curling them into fists under his chin.

"If they hadn't brought in Locust, I might've been able to get somewhere. But he's got me on the tightest leash possible, and the guy doesn't know what the heck he's doing. Talk about a fragile ego, sheesh. You know I have an anxiety disorder?" he asked rhetorically. "Had to take a double dose of my meds this morning, basically woke up in the middle of a panic attack. I've got three kids under ten, my wife and I are barely holding it together on a normal day." He dug his fists into his eyes—so hard, I winced. "Can't say I blame the sister for taking some downers. Maybe I can borrow some." He looked up at me. "I'm joking. Mainly."

"You'll figure it out," I said weakly. I've never been very good at comforting others. Or myself, for that matter.

"We're gonna have to. And fast. Because unlike the first murder, this second one was done *super* quick. Think about it. Who slits a person's throat and then pushes them off a balcony onto a marble floor? It's cuckoo. They got lucky, too, cuz no one saw it happen. Which means any of them could've done it."

The broken, rag-doll body of Walter Vogel returned unbidden to my mind: all that blood pooling around it. . . .

"Impossible to keep track of everyone's movements with all these goddamned elevators," grumbled Brooks.

"So you know for sure he was attacked *before* he fell?"

"Oh yeah, no question. Blood's all over the third-floor balcony in the eastern corner. Weapon's there too. No fingerprints of course," he added glumly.

"That reminds me," I said. "The examiner mentioned the instrument was dull, especially for how deep of a cut it made. What *was* it?"

"Letter opener," he said.

I pictured the letter opener sitting so prominently on Eve Turner's desk.

"Eve Turner's?"

He nodded. "She confirmed it when we showed it to her."

"How do you slit someone's throat with a letter opener?" I wondered aloud. (Surely one of the more unlikely sentences I've uttered.)

"Well, it wasn't really *slit*, more of a straight puncture followed by a tearing of the—"

"Got it," I said hastily.

"Sorry. It's a nasty one, no question. Only good thing I can say about it is that it almost definitely had to have been done by a man."

"Really?"

"For sure. Walter wasn't big, but he was a fit guy, he could hold his own. I find it hard to believe a woman could've done that unless he was sleeping or something, but there's no question it happened out on the balcony while he was standing there. Perpetrator was facing him too. Whole bunch of blood spray that should be on the site that isn't there. We've got people looking for stained clothes, of course. You see anyone with blood on them?"

"No one other than Minna Hawley. But that was from later. At least, I think it was."

"Yeah, we're on that too," he said. "We *might* be able to differentiate if there were two separate points of contact. We'll see. She's the only woman out of the bunch I could see pulling it off. Although honestly? Most likely scenario is more than one person ganging up on him. One guy holds his arms down from behind, while the other does the deed."

I thought of Samir and Alex Shah standing on the third-floor balcony, staring down at the body. They were by far the closest to where the murder had taken place. I hadn't seen any blood on them, but maybe they'd peeled off an outer layer and stashed it somewhere. My mind went back to the dining room: Alex hitting his father, arguing with him about whose fault it was. I thought about when I first met Samir and noted how tall he was, how springy. It was easy to miss, but there was a great deal of strength coiled up in that string-bean body of his. He'd be a formidable opponent if he was ever on the attack. I told all this to Brooks.

"We're aware," he said grimly. "Samir Shah is our next interview, and it's gonna be a long one." He let out a sigh that lay halfway between exhaustion and exasperation. "I'll tell you this. Whoever did it is getting desperate."

DS Brooks waited till I was looking at him.

"And that's never a good thing where a killer's concerned."

CHAPTER 40

Dorothy was still in her interview with Locust when I got back to the dining room. I took out my phone for the first time in a while, alarmed to see a number of missed calls from Leila (I'd silenced it ages ago) and a string of unanswered texts:

WTF is happening??

D isn't answering

HELLO

losing my mind are you 2 OK??

There was a gap then, during which she presumably got an update from the Bodyguard or one of his colleagues.

Pls know I'm not joking when I say I will destroy your career if anything happens to her b/c of something you did, or encouraged her to do.

This HAS to end.

I MEAN IT.

I stared at this a minute or two and then exited my messages, clicking onto my web browser and landing on an article in The Cut about whether or not a runner's high is a real thing. I stared at the article, pretending to read it. What I should have been doing was interacting with the suspects still arrayed in the room. Poirot would have been getting them to talk, hence slip up, thereby incriminating themselves for purposes of his grand denouement. Miss Marple's brain was always whizzing and whirring while she sat there knitting so placidly. But it had been a long-ass day, and I was spent.

Dorothy's interview ended up going twice as long as mine. This was the first indication it had not gone swimmingly. The second was the dark and stormy look on Locust's face as he followed her into the dining room.

They entered just as Paul came through the back entrance holding a giant tureen of steaming pasta dressed in his homemade, buttery sauce.

"Ooh!" Dorothy rubbed her hands together in a caricature of anticipation. "I was just about to leave, but I've got to try a little—"

"*Now*, Mrs. Gibson."

"Oh, come now, Detective Locust! You're not going to let me have any of this delicious pasta Paul here worked so hard to make?"

"No."

"Weh-hell all right then!"

Dorothy caught my eye, jerking her head toward the door. I got up and booked it out of there as quickly as my depleted reserves of energy would allow. (I'm not going to lie: some pasta would have been nice.) Out in the Great Hall, as we were sidestepping a gurney being carried in by two techs, we heard the *click-click-click* of a camera behind the curtain—a real one, not just somebody's phone—interspersed by careful steps.

Sheila Hasan was hard at work.

Dorothy fell face forward onto my shoulder in the back seat, letting out a gasp somewhere between an exclamation and a laugh. I'd seen her make such exaggerated gestures before, but never with me. Normally I am not a fan of uninitiated physical contact, but I surprised myself by leaning into it now, even reciprocating a little.

"That bad, huh?" I asked.

"Terrible."

She lifted herself off me, settling into her seat as the Bodyguard started the engine. The sun had set, and then some. It was still early in the evening, but by the looks of the sky it could have been midnight.

"I've been banned, in no uncertain terms this time, from engaging in any further activity having to do with the case."

"Seriously?" I squawked, though this was hardly a surprise.

"He said he'd arrest me." She widened her eyes comically. "He would too. Can you imagine how much people would love that?"

I snorted.

"He told me nothing, naturally. And when I tried telling him what we found out, especially about the Hawleys, he wouldn't let me. Said he didn't want any evidence to be 'tainted,' which makes no sense because evidence can only be tainted by improper police conduct. I know I'm not a practicing lawyer, but he *does* realize I'm familiar with the law, doesn't he?"

"I'm not sure he understands that women can be lawyers, or familiar with the law."

"You're probably right."

"So what were you doing in there for so long?"

"Listening to him yell. And then listening to him whine. And then yell some more. And whine. And so on. The usual." She sighed. "What about you, how'd you fare? You at least got the good cop, I'm jealous."

"The Jeff to his Mutt," I said. "Or is it the other way around? I've never been able to figure that one out."

"Me neither," she admitted.

"Anyway, unlike his partner, Detective Brooks was *very* willing to listen. And share."

I told her about my interview.

"So it's worse than I thought," she said when I finished. "They have no idea what they're doing."

"None. But he gave me his cell number and said I should feel free to call it anytime."

"So I'm banned and you're enlisted. Well, at least one of us has an in." She let out a yawn. "I don't know about you, but I'm exhausted, it's been *quite* a day. I think the best thing to do would be to have a quick dinner, then turn in for the night. We can regroup in the morning."

I told her this sounded like an excellent plan. And then, for the rest of the short ride back to Dorothy's, I stared out the window. I could pretend I was observing the profound darkness of the woods at nighttime. Or the stars peeping through the branches. Or the dull gleam of the icy snow on the ground. But I saw none of this. I was simply avoiding eye contact with the Bodyguard. Because as tired as I was, I had every intention of making much, *much* more contact with him than I could with my eyes. And I wanted to save it up till I could gorge properly.

You might find this unseemly, given the events of the day: my proximity to death, and to whoever had brought about this death. But that's precisely why I was aroused. I was alive, goddamnit. And I wanted to be as alive as possible.

This time when I knocked on the door of the remote office, the Bodyguard answered so quickly, he must have heard me walking up. He'd run some sort of creamy product through his surfer hair, which gave it more texture than usual, and smelled vaguely—and deliciously—of . . . was it vanilla? No, not vanilla. Sugar cookies.

I would've taken a bite out of his hair, if it were possible.

He'd changed his shirt while Dorothy and I were eating dinner. This one had long sleeves and a collar, and wonder of wonders, it wasn't tight. The firelight was dancing behind him, his body glowing. For the hundredth (thousandth?) time, his beauty shocked me: a visceral sensation, and I do mean that literally because it hit me right in the viscera, a veritable blow to the heart/gut/kidneys, almost too much to handle.

I was old enough by then to appreciate what a gift it was to spend time with a person you *want* to have sex with, knowing you are almost definitely *going* to have sex with him, and soon. The expectation is the best part, of course, and I extended it now for as long as our combined libidos would allow. Gone was my exhaustion from the long, eventful day. Forget sleep; I could sleep when I was dead. Like Vivian and Walter.

"Not gonna lie," I remarked, slipping into one of the many folding chairs arrayed round the conference table, "I'm glad to see you changed out of those bootcut jeans of yours. You do realize it's not 2002 anymore?"

"Considering I was twelve in 2002, I'd say I'm aware."

"Oof, that hurts."

He shrugged his shoulders. (Such lovely shoulders.) "Sorry."

And yet it meant he was in his late twenties; not nearly as bad as I'd feared.

He sat down in the chair beside me—much closer than would have been appropriate if we weren't going to be ripping each other's clothes off shortly. We stared at each other without speaking, but it wasn't an awkward pause. We were simply taking each other in.

"And here I thought you were just a writer," he said finally. "Not an actual . . . it's sleuth, right?"

I nodded.

"Sleuth," he repeated. "The two of you make quite a pair."

"Well, the police aren't really cutting it, so someone's got to do it. Nature abhors a vacuum."

Ugh, why do I say stuff like this?

"You ever hear the theory that every saying has its opposite?" he asked. "Meaning they kind of cancel each other out?"

"Explain."

"Like, say, absence makes the heart grow fonder, and out of sight out of mind."

"I see. So what's the opposite of nature abhors a vacuum?"

He paused, a puckish smile twisting his mouth into something approaching a perfect circle. "Fools rush in where angels fear to tread."

"Hmph. Point taken. So is this little linguistic theory of yours something you trot out on a first or second date? It's pretty effective."

He laughed, forcing the air through his nose. (Such a beautiful nose.) "Maybe I would if I ever dated."

"That's at least one thing we have in common, then."

He'd folded his shirt cuffs back, displaying his manly forearms. It was a strange thing to fixate on, but he had perfect arm hair: dark, yet flecked with gold. Abundant, but not *too* abundant—

"Ahem."

He was looking down at me.

"You're staring at my arm."

"Well, it's a pretty nice arm." (Understatement of the century.) "So who do you think did it? Between us."

"Uh-uh." He shook his head. "You're not gonna get me to play that game. I don't know, and I don't *want* to know. And I really wish you and the senator would leave it to the professionals."

"Well, one of those professionals practically begged us to keep helping him."

"The little guy?"

"His name is Brooks and he's not *that* little," I retorted. Even though he was.

"Sorry to offend. I didn't realize you two were so close."

"You're not *jealous*, are you?"

We'd been inching closer to each other this whole time, and we were so close now, I could smell his breath, which was fresh and minty. Fortunately, mine was too; I'd gargled before leaving the house.

"He's like . . . the bridge troll from the *Three Billy Goats Gruff*," I said cruelly. "And you're the third billy goat. The strongest, biggest, beautifulest of them all."

He winced.

"What? You don't like goats or something?"

"It just seems like the only thing you like about me is the way I look. Makes me a little sad, is all."

"Aw, you're sad because everyone objectifies you? That must be so hard."

"I don't care about everyone. Just you."

Our feet touched. Shoe on shoe. But still.

"So you're admitting everyone objectifies you. Conceited much?"

His face was so close, I could see the individual hairs of his eyebrows, one of which was out of alignment. I reached up, smoothing it down with the others. His skin was warm. So was mine. . . .

"Stop talking," he said softly.

"And now you're trying to silence me."

But there was no chance of that. Our conversation may have come to an end, but it would be many hours before either of us fell silent.

Also? Turns out that sometimes, the expectation is nowhere near as good as the reality.

The more you know.

CHAPTER 41

It was nearly two in the morning when I slipped into my bed: weak-limbed, overcome by a physical exhaustion vastly preferable to the mental fatigue I was used to. I slept late the next day—late for anyone, not just early-bird me. Even before I opened my eyes, I could tell by the way the light was pushing against my eyelids in swirls of purple and red that it couldn't be early morning anymore. The swirls reminded me of that painting in the dining room of the Crystal Palace, and the events of the day before came rushing back to me the way they do when you're waking up, the world intruding on your first inkling of consciousness, marking the end of those precious few moments you get to exist independently of the events of your life. I was used to waking up in hotel rooms and remembering with a jolt that I'd become a ghostwriter with many meetings to attend and pages to write. That I was no longer a girl who loved—lived—to read, with two schoolteacher parents and a big sister I secretly admired. It was a much bigger jolt to realize on this morning that I was sleeping in Dorothy Gibson's house, up to my neck in a double homicide investigation as baffling to me after eight-and-a-half hours of sleep as it had been the day before.

I showered and dressed in a hurry, relieved that no one was

in the kitchen to watch me bolt two heaping bowlfuls of Grape-Nuts and three quarters of a carton of blueberries (gotta get those superfoods when you can). I carried my steaming mug of coffee to the library, pausing in the darkened hallway when I heard two voices on the other side of the door, raised in anger.

". . . because if I didn't tell you, I wouldn't be doing my job."

"Well, for the time being, Leila, consider it as falling outside your job description."

"So you don't want to know, for example, that '#Detective-Dotty' has been trending for hours with all sorts of awful jokes, including from people who are supposed to be our *friends*? Or that you-know-who's been retweeting insane conspiracy theories saying you killed them all?"

There was a long silence.

"Dorothy?"

"Sorry, I was just actively erasing what you said from my brain. I'm done now."

An even longer silence followed, during which I entered the room.

"She lives," said Leila without looking up.

Even if I hadn't known they were fighting, it would have been obvious from their strained expressions, the heightened color in both their faces.

"*There* you are!" Dorothy snapped her laptop shut. "Did you have a good sleep? I know I did!"

I nodded. Denny was standing on the far side of the room, in front of one of the bay windows, the sunlight streaming onto him sideways. (Did he *always* have to be lit like an ancient god/warrior?) He smiled at me, and I smiled back without thinking.

When I caught Leila smirking at us like the Wicked Witch of the West, I wished I *had* thought.

"You ate, I hope?" asked Dorothy.

I nodded.

"Good! Because I was just about to leave without you, and I was *really* hoping I wouldn't have to."

"But we have—"

"I'm rescheduling my morning," she interrupted Leila. "I already let Clara know, she's making all the necessary calls. Don't worry, I'll be back in time for the taping."

Leila shoved her tablet under her arm and stalked out of the room. She wasn't smirking anymore.

Dorothy watched her go a little sadly before turning back to me. "I was just explaining to Denny here that our investigation is almost over."

It was?

"And how I'm confident we won't be putting ourselves in harm's way with our little excursion this morning."

Excursion?

"I'm going to hold you to that, ma'am—Dorothy," he corrected himself.

"Please do," she said.

"Where are we going?" I asked her.

She gave me one of her demented, open-mouthed smiles, her green eyes sparkling.

"The morgue."

The headquarters of the Cumberland County Medical Examiner is not in Cumberland County; it's in Augusta, which is the capital of Maine, and a good hour north of Portland. But the county also rented space from a state medical college about twenty minutes away, on a campus that looked more like a business park where dreams went to die than a site of learning and exploration. The buildings were boxy and low to the ground, the greenery pretty much nonexistent. A man in blue scrubs stood beside one of those steel ashtrays you don't see too often anymore other than at airport terminals, grinding his cigarette into its sandy bowl with a grim determination. Even the sun was dimmer here, hiding behind a single cloud as though it were a pillow and the scene below it a horror movie full of jump scares.

Officer Choi had replaced Denny for this excursion, which I may as well admit was a relief. By the looks of her, her night had been much more eventful than the one Denny and I had shared, though nowhere near as fun.

"He still not sleeping?" I asked her.

"He's teething now," she said—in the way the hapless townsfolk used to speak in days of yore about the werewolf or swamp monster that terrorized them nightly. I did her the courtesy of keeping my shudder on the inside.

"Senator Gibson! Senator Gibson!"

Sheila Hasan waved to us from the back door of a building. Dorothy waved back, and together the three of us crossed a gravel path to reach her. She was wearing the same white lab coat, though today she had a sundress on underneath it. She must have been freezing; I'd learned on the ride over that Dorothy had reached out to her late the night before, and I guessed this sundress was the nicest thing she owned.

"Sheila, I want to thank you for taking time out of your busy schedule to help us," said Dorothy, grasping her hand.

"Are you kidding me? The honor's all mine. I felt so bad about how things ended yesterday." She opened the door behind her, waving us in. "I hope you don't mind me saying this, but that head policeman is a jerk."

"We-hee don't mind at all!"

Dorothy's laughter echoed in the long and narrow stairwell we found ourselves in now. Sheila led us down the first flight of stairs.

"The other one is super nice. Brooks. I've run into him a few times before. Not the most effective, but super nice."

"That sums him up pretty well," I snarked.

"I know it's not my job to worry about the investigation, but

I can't help feeling they need all the help they can get. I'm glad you called."

"Well, I appreciate you indulging my request." Dorothy sounded a little out of breath. Even though we were walking downstairs, Sheila was moving at a fast clip. We were already two or three stories down; how far into the bowels of the earth did this building go? "I'm just trying to figure out what's going on like everyone else."

"Of course you are, that's what you do. You help people. And to be honest? Even if this case was humming along, I would've done whatever you asked because in a weird way, I have you to thank for taking my career to the next level."

"Oh really? How so?"

"Well, I don't know if you know this, and maybe don't go crazy telling everyone, but the guy who did the on-site of Vivian Davis was put on leave."

"Nathan Islington?" Dorothy had plucked this name from when I'd relayed it to her in the car after Vivian's memorial, recounting my conversation with Eve Turner. He was the doctor Eve had been yelling at over the phone, the one who'd come to collect Vivian's body—just as Sheila had done the day before with Walter.

"God, you're just like my mom, somehow you manage to know everything!"

"I'll take that as a big compliment!"

"Please do! Well, once the CME had to step in—"

"The chief medical examiner?"

"That's right, once he stepped in—thanks to you—he took one look at the chart for Vivian Davis and was *totally* horrified at what a mess it was. Not that *I* was surprised. Nathan's always been sloppy, he cuts corners constantly. Didn't show any of his work for the time of death estimate, snapped a few blurry photos, called it a day. I've seen him do it dozens of times before, but for once he was called out on it."

"I see," said Dorothy.

"That's why I got to do the on-site yesterday. It was my first job out in the field, and it's all because of you!"

"Well, I'm sure that's not true," said Dorothy. "I'm sure you put in hours upon hours of hard work leading up to this moment."

"Now that's *exactly* what I would expect you to say!" Sheila beamed at her. "God, I love you."

I did my best not to get drenched by all the gushing while Sheila led us out of the stairwell on what must have been the fifth basement floor, down a dimly lit hallway. (Maybe *she* was the murderer?) I've come across this breathless reaction to Dorothy on the part of young women many times since then: enough that it doesn't surprise me anymore. I expected the twentysomething ladies to turn their noses up at her dorkily straightforward, second-wave feminism (third-wave, if I'm being generous). But she still counted for something. For a lot of things, apparently.

"Just so you know"—she paused to wave her ID in front of a door, a light above its handle turning green and emitting a *click*—"this is very much not allowed."

"I hope you're not doing anything you shouldn't?" asked Dorothy as we followed her inside.

"Well, you're not supposed to admit nonprofessionals and let them examine a dead body," she said airily, "but fortunately, there's *no one on Earth* who's more of a professional than you are." She was beaming; I think she may have been on the verge of tears. "So we're good. Really."

Dorothy let out a chuckle. "Well, thanks. I appreciate that."

And then I saw it, in the center of the room—a big, stainless-steel examination table with something on top of it—something I couldn't see because it was covered by a sheet.

I looked around the room, which was preferable to staring at the table. It wasn't what I had expected, which I suppose was a wall of drawers out of which you could pull so many bodies like cards in a card catalogue (RIP, card catalogues). It reminded me a little of my high school science lab, actually, with a black counter lining all three interior walls in a U shape, except for a doorway in the righthand wall that led to some interior office. Backless stools had been placed every three feet or so, about a dozen total. And while there weren't Bunsen burners at each station like in my high school lab, there *was* a drain in the middle of the tiled floor, which was a feature that never failed to go unnoticed by teenagers who'd been raised on horror movies like *The Texas Chainsaw Massacre*. I could just imagine the bodily juices dribbling down the sides of the table and onto the tiled floor, a lab tech sluicing them down the drain with a black hose—

"Are you all right?"

Dorothy was staring at me. So was Sheila.

"I'm fine," I lied.

"If you're not comfortable with this, I'm more than okay with you waiting outside."

She said this kindly, not angrily. And yet I shook my head at her as though we were in conflict.

"I'm fine," I said again, believing it a little more this time. "That's Vivian Davis under there, isn't it?"

Sheila nodded. "I got her all ready to go so we could be in and out of here." She hesitated. "If anyone saw you two, it would be really awkward. . . ."

"Of course," said Dorothy. "We'll make this quick."

"Okay, great!" She walked over to the table. Dorothy followed and so did I, keeping my eyes glued to Sheila's face. I refused to look down until I had to.

"So I'm just going to peel back the sheet from the head. That's all you need to see, right? The face?"

This was news to me, but Dorothy nodded briskly.

"Great." She sounded relieved. "The rest is *not* something I'd advise showing to the uninitiated, it's—" She cut herself off. "You know what? I'm going to shut up now."

Sheila folded back the sheet. It was too fast; I wasn't ready. Out of my peripheral vision I saw Dorothy nodding.

"MMMM-hm."

I looked down.

It was a woman with her eyes closed, and while I'm not going to say "she may have been asleep," it was nowhere near as horrible as I feared it was going to be. Her skin wasn't bloated; her features weren't distorted. I could see quite clearly what she looked like.

And therein lay the problem.

I looked up at Dorothy.

"I don't understand."

I meant this on two levels. First, because I'd never seen this woman before. She had blond hair like the woman in Betty's Liquor Mart, but it was much longer, nearly shoulder length, and the blond was mixed with a fair amount of gray. Her nose was crooked like a prize fighter's. Her high forehead was lined in a way the vixen who chatted us up never would have allowed. I couldn't see her body, but based on her head I guessed she was much larger than that other woman too.

The second reason for my confusion was that Dorothy obviously did not share it. She was beaming, her cheek-apples in high relief. I could see that something had been confirmed for her by viewing this strange woman lying here on this cold metal table. That this all made sense to her, somehow.

Well, it made no sense to me.

Because if this was the body of Vivian Davis, then who the hell was the woman we'd met at Betty's Liquor Mart?

CHAPTER 42

I never got a chance to ask Dorothy this question, because while the sheet was still turned down, the door to the room burst open.

In walked Special Investigator Locust.

He froze. We froze with him. It was a striking tableau, with the body between us, and despite my horror, I had to appreciate the undiluted nature of the situation. There was no denying what we were doing here, no way to hedge or prevaricate or otherwise mitigate the illicit nature of our presence. This was *bad*, and Locust was going to make us pay for it.

I kept expecting Dorothy to say something. But she said nothing. She kept perfectly still.

It was Locust who had to make the first move. I watched his eyes travel downward—from us to the body, where they stayed a good long while.

And then, the blood began dripping from his nose.

As soon as it happened, it felt inevitable. *Of course* Locust's nose was prone to bleeds. It was a nose that insisted on using all the tools at its disposal to communicate its complex emotions. The blood wasn't gushing, but it was definitely more than a trickle, and even though he whipped out a handkerchief as soon as he could, it dripped onto his shirt in the exact spot where I'd noticed the ketchup stain a few days earlier.

"God*damn*it," he muttered.

That was one mystery solved. Why had I ever thought SI Locust was a messy eater? He was probably one of those people who tucked a napkin into his collar at the start of each meal.

"Are you all right?" asked Dorothy.

"I'm fine," he snapped. "Not that I can say the same for you. My instructions were very clear, Mrs. Gibson—"

"You're right, they—"

"And *you.*" He whirled on Sheila, pointing with the hand that wasn't clamped over his nose. "Your career is going to be over before it started. If you think you're ever going to work as a medical examiner here or anywhere else in the contiguous United States of America, you have another thing coming."

I was tempted to ask why Alaska and Hawaii were still on the table, but there was no denying he held all the power here. Even with that stupendous nose of his covered, and his voice all high-pitched and whiny.

"Oh my God!" Sheila began to cry, and then, embarrassed by her tears, she turned around, facing the wall.

"I'd like to speak with you," said Dorothy sternly.

"Oho!" he cried out. (Really: "Oho!" Like he was a character in a Shakespeare play.) "What a surprise! The busybody wants to speak with me! Well, for once, I'd like to speak with you too."

"In private." She gestured to the door in the righthand wall. "It looks like there's a little office in there. Is that right, Sheila?"

Sheila nodded without looking. Officer Choi—who had been occupying a corner of the room in her covert way—went over and stuck her head in, scouting it out.

"We can do all our speaking back at the station," snarled Locust. "In an interrogation room."

"That isn't going to work for me."

Locust's hand dropped. His nose looked pinched and harassed as it regarded Dorothy incredulously.

"Why on earth do you think I would go along with anything you wanted to do right now?"

"Because I know everything."

Sheila's sobs cut off with a gasp.

"I know who did it, and how, and I'm going to tell you right now. But *not* at the station. If we go to the station, I tell you nothing. Are we good, Sarah?"

Officer Choi nodded. Dorothy walked over, turning around when she reached the door.

SI Locust released a grandiose sigh. "Fine. But she"—he whirled again; now he was pointing at me—"stays out."

Dorothy looked at me. I gave her a nod, and she gave me one back.

"Fine."

Locust walked slowly across the room, dabbing at his nose. By the time he reached the door, Dorothy had disappeared inside. He took a moment to scowl at me before closing the door behind him.

CHAPTER 43

They were in that office for over an hour. During that time, I got to know Sheila Hasan a little better. We pushed two stools together, leaning our elbows on the counter. It felt oddly like we were at a bar, though the key element was missing.

Sheila's immigrant parents had been determined that she be a doctor. Sheila, however, had grown up on a steady diet of murder mysteries and crime procedurals and decided early on that she wanted to be a, wait for it, detective. A medical examiner was the best compromise the three of them could come up with.

"But now that's all ruined, and I'm not going to be able to pay my rent, so I'm going to have to move back in with them after I finally convinced them to let me move out, which took literally three years since I'm not married!" she explained, bursting into tears again.

I was doing my best "there, there" (not a high bar) when the door to the office flew open and SI Locust came stalking out. He rushed for the door, flinging himself into the hallway without a word or glance in our direction.

Dorothy came sauntering out a few seconds later. She laid a hand on Sheila's shoulder.

"Don't worry about your job," she said. "He won't do anything."

She lifted her tear-stained face. "Really?"

"Really." Dorothy looked at me. "Come on, let's go. We've got a lot to do."

She didn't say a word to me on the way back to the car. Or once we got in and Officer Donnelly began driving. She stared out the window, her phone sitting unattended on her lap.

"So what happened in there?" I asked finally.

She turned to me, blinking. "I told him I'd hold a press conference and explain everything to the national media if he didn't do what I wanted. His nose started bleeding again," she added. "Poor man."

"What was it you wanted him to do?"

"To gather everyone at the Crystal Palace at three o'clock this afternoon."

"Will Colonel Mustard and Professor Plum be there too?"

She thrust her head back, letting loose a full-on Dorothy cackle.

"Thanks, I needed that! But in all seriousness, I want to do this right. That woman lying on that table deserves it. And I told him if he gives me that, I'll let him take all the credit. *All* of it. I've had more than enough of the spotlight by this point in my life, thank you very much."

She turned back to the window.

"Are you really not going to tell me?"

She turned to me with a pitiful look I resented immediately. "I'm not, if you don't mind. You see, I told him I wouldn't tell anyone. Even you." She let out a chuckle. "*Especially* you."

So now you have a problem breaking your word to him? I wanted to say. *Because I do mind. I mind a lot.*

"Of course," I said. "I don't mind at all."

She patted my hand. "I knew you wouldn't. Take it as a compliment, I think he's threatened by you."

"You didn't say anything about giving me a few clues, though, did you?"

She chuckled again. "I did not!"

I waited as she paused, thinking it over.

"You would do well"—she widened her eyes significantly—"to think about what *usually* happens to phones when they're submerged in water. I'd also take a closer look at Anne if I were you."

Given the violent nature of Walter's death, Anne Shah was one of the few people I'd assumed had to be innocent, even if her husband and/or son weren't. I imagined arterial blood spraying onto one of her immaculate Chanel suits. It was absurd, like something out of a Tarantino film.

"And that broken surveillance camera. That's key, as it turns out."

"But wasn't Vivian's phone found in the bedroom?" I asked. "It wasn't submerged—"

She held up one hand. "That's all I can say!"

Hmm. This did not clear things up for me. But I nodded as though these clues meant something.

"What about the medical examiner?" I asked. "The one who Sheila replaced?"

"Nathan Islington? I imagine he's already skipped town, if not the country. Locust is following up now—that was one of the more time-sensitive issues I asked him to address." She let out a chuckle. "One of a few tasks I gave him. They'll get Dr. Islington eventually, I have no doubt. He can't be all that intelligent of a person."

She returned to the window. I could sense that if I asked her more questions, I'd be making a nuisance of myself. I sat back, trying not to look as annoyed as I felt. Because if Dorothy had been able to figure it out, then I should have been too. There was nothing she knew that I didn't.

I checked the time on my phone. It was almost noon, which meant I had a little over three hours before we convened at the Crystal Palace. With any luck that would be enough time for me to work out the solution *and* throw together a Miss Scarlett cosplay outfit from my limited wardrobe.

Part Five
The Solution

CHAPTER 44

So I didn't dress up as Miss Scarlett. And I didn't figure out the solution on my own. Dorothy did dress up, though—not for her big drawing room "denouement," but because it was December 7th, the anniversary of Pearl Harbor. (I'd had no idea till Dorothy told me.) Upon returning to the house, she had a full face of makeup put on, and her hair blown out by a woman named Tina. We then traveled to Portland, working on the outline for her memoir all the way in the car, arriving at a depressing little studio where she taped a message that struck me as both wooden and corny, regarding the importance of this day in history and our present moment. For this recording she wore a pantsuit, of course: mustard yellow, but the spicy kind—more brown than yellow, with a texture to it. We'd come straight from the studio to the Crystal Palace, cutting it rather close.

It was as "Dorothy Gibson" then, arrayed in her full glory, that she stood before us at three that afternoon in the Reception Room, the same room where the memorial for Vivian Davis had been held four days earlier. There were folding chairs facing the rear wall—the one with the view, and if I hadn't known why we were here, I would have thought we were about to attend a small wedding. Dorothy was the officiant, of course, surveying the assembly gathered before her. Glowering from the front row was SI Locust: the father of the bride, who'd been forced to make his peace with this hasty arrangement, and who was eager for the ceremony to be over. Beside him sat DS Brooks, a sunny smile on his face. I suppose he was the father of the groom, happy for his son in that frank, uncomplicated, specifically male way he had about him, though in all honesty he struck me as the mother of the bride, thrilled that this day was upon her at last and the whole thing would be over in a few short hours—when her only remaining job would be picking up the pieces of her devastated partner.

Behind them sat Anne and Samir Shah. Anne was the bride's older sister, who'd gone through all this years ago and had her own husband to show for it. Not that she was looking triumphant in this moment. Both Shahs looked miserable: her skin had the pinched, drawn look of one who hadn't slept well for days, and Samir's leg was shaking harder than ever. If misery loves company, then theirs was some of the more fulfilled misery I'd ever encountered.

Behind them in the back row sat Minna and Bobby Hawley, though to be accurate I should say Minna sat while Bobby slouched. They were the weirdo relatives who couldn't be left off the guest list, despite the fact that no one wanted them there. Even so, I was heartened to see that Minna Hawley was doing much better than the day before, her blank stare replaced by a gimlet eye she was giving anyone who dared look her way.

On the other side of the gathering sat Eve Turner, very much on her own, legs and arms crossed. She'd paired a navy-blue shift with a chunky gold necklace, and it was easy to imagine her as a former girlfriend of the groom who'd been asked because she was still in their friend circle, meaning she felt obligated to come despite her conflicted feelings. Much less conflicted was Paul Reston, who looked happy to be sitting down for once. He was out of his chef (or chef-adjacent) outfit: in jeans now, his nylon rainbow jacket unzipped over a T-shirt. Paul was the best man, of course, and would give a bumbling, drunken speech later in the night. Beside him sat—here was a surprise—Dorothy's son, Peter, who she must have summoned for her big moment. We made eye contact, and he gave me a jaunty little wave with his pinkie. Every wedding has to have at least one crasher, I suppose. On his other side, I was less surprised to see Sheila Hasan: a bridesmaid or perhaps even a flower girl intent on performing her duties to perfection.

Standing behind us all was Leila. She was obviously the wedding planner, consulting her tablet while issuing hushed, last-minute instructions via wireless earbuds. (I suspected she was keeping herself busy so as not to make eye contact with Dorothy, or anyone else.) The only other person in the room was Denny, who I couldn't really place in the wedding milieu—but then, I couldn't place myself in it, either. He was standing where he'd stood the last time we'd all been here: beside the door that led to the Great Hall, across the room's wide expanse of concrete. I resisted the urge to stare at him and turned around, settling into my seat.

There were two people missing. One was Alex Shah, who was currently in a one-on-one therapy session upstairs with a crisis counselor. I knew this because Dorothy had confirmed as much when his parents came in, and I wondered if this weren't her way of separating the murderer from his protectors while she revealed what he'd done. Maybe they already knew; maybe that was why they looked so shattered. The other absentee was Laura Duval, which made her the bride, of course—especially since she'd be down any moment. Dorothy had gone up herself to request the honor of her presence. Fortunately, the sedatives had worn off, and she'd agreed to make an appearance.

"It's two minutes past three," snarled Locust. "Let's get this circus started."

I expected Dorothy to say we couldn't begin yet—that we had to wait for Laura because you had to have every single person (or at least every adult) present at the grand denouement, as anyone who's ever read a work of detective fiction knows.

"I hear you," said Dorothy brightly. "I don't much like waiting, either. Ms. Duval will have to catch up, I suppose."

DS Brooks held up his phone. I was close enough to see him select the video option inside his camera app and hit the red record button. "This is Detective Sergeant Daniel Brooks, and it is December seventh at three-oh-two—oop!—three-oh-*three* in the afternoon, at the Crystal Palace estate in Sacobago, Maine. Everyone present has been made aware that these proceedings are being recorded and may be used as evidence in a court of law." He trained the camera on Dorothy, nodding brightly. "Go ahead."

Dorothy cleared her throat, and when she spoke next it was as though she had procured an invisible microphone, her voice ringing out and filling the prodigious space. By then I'd grown used to her tendency to lend her every utterance an official air, which made for a jarring effect when she was engaged in the mundanities of living. (Just imagine Dorothy Gibson asking, "Is the dishwasher clean or dirty?")

"I want to thank you all for coming." She gestured to the glass wall behind her. "It was important that we all gather here, because everything that's happened could *only* have happened at the Crystal Palace. What I mean by that is, if Walter Vogel and Vivian Davis had chosen some other place to play host and hostess for a few weeks, they'd still be with us now. None of this would ever have happened."

She paused—not because she had to, but because we were hanging on her every word and the pause ensured we knew it. This was a power move, and it worked brilliantly. I guess you learn a thing or two being a public speaker for decades.

"There was always one aspect of this case that made no

sense. How could Vivian Davis have been drowned in a bathtub with no marks of any kind on her? At the very least, someone would have had to hold her down. There would have been a bruise, *something*. But then someone very clever and learned reminded me of a famous case from a hundred years ago, in which multiple women were drowned in their baths without any bruises or markings. And I stopped asking how it was possible for Vivian Davis to have been killed this way."

She glanced in my direction, flashing me an apologetic smile.

"That was a big mistake, as it turned out. I should have kept asking, because the answer, as is so often the case, is simple. People who drown without any marks on them don't drown in bathtubs. They drown in much larger bodies of water."

She turned around, facing the rear wall along with the rest of us. I glanced at Locust, who looked as though steam might issue from his ears at any moment. I hoped his nose didn't start bleeding again.

Dorothy spread her arms wide.

"The Crystal Palace property encompasses the end point of the Crystal River, where it empties into Crystal Lake to the southwest of the house." She faced us again. "As I was reminded recently, this has caused some issues in the past. Which wouldn't be the first time riparian rights have stirred up a whole heap of trouble in the great state of Maine, let me tell you!"

She chuckled. Alone.

"This time, however, the river's tendency to collect debris presented an opportunity rather than a problem."

She began pacing.

"Two Sundays ago, on the twenty-seventh of November, a woman named Paula Fitzgerald disappeared. She was a swim instructor, and apparently she and her husband were having marital problems. I'm sad to say that Paula succumbed to her personal demons, walking into the Crystal River somewhere upstream on that Sunday. Given her occupation, I'd say there's little chance she died by accident. My guess is she weighed her clothes down with stones, or something heavy."

Virginia Woolf's face floated before my mind's eye as it always does when someone brings up suicide by drowning—as much as I strive not to define an artist by her suicide. (Same issue with Sylvia Plath and gas ovens.)

"She drowned, at which point her body was pulled along by the river's strong downhill current, ending in Crystal Lake, where it was discovered by the people who were renting the property at the time." She stopped, luxuriating in another pause. "Walter Vogel and Vivian Davis."

"But what does that have to—"

Dorothy held up her hand, silencing Samir Shah.

"It will make sense," she said. "Soon. I promise."

She began pacing again.

"So what did Walter Vogel and Vivian Davis do when they saw this body? Did they think about this woman's friends and family? About their devastation? Their right to be told *immediately* what had happened? No. They thought only of themselves and what they might be able to get out of a corpse that had washed up on their shore. Especially since Paula Fitzgerald's phone was still on her, and—this is crucial—still working. She was a swim instructor, after all, so it was natural for her to have a sturdy, waterproof phone case. This meant they could send texts purporting to be her, buying themselves a few crucial days. They sent messages to Paula's husband telling him she was leaving, and to a friend or two saying she needed time away on her own. I imagine it was easy to imitate her; we all have text chains in our phones going back weeks, if not months. It's all right there for anyone to see."

Dorothy shook her head wonderingly. I could have done the same. I couldn't believe I'd been naïve enough to accept at face value what I'd heard on Nextdoor, of all places.

"It was Walter and Vivian who broke the security camera,

the same day they found the body. The camera's on the southwest side of the house, where a hyperbaric oxygen chamber sits. The perfect temperature-controlled spot to store a body for a few days. The decomposition would be kept to a minimum, and any smell would be contained. And then, three days later, late on the night of Wednesday the thirtieth of November, or more accurately, early on the morning of December first, when everyone was asleep, they carried the body the short distance from that chamber through the door on that side of the house, and up to the second floor. The elevator made that part of the job easier, but even so, I suspect that moving the body into the house was a lot more work than they realized. The sounds you heard"—Dorothy gestured to Anne—"early on that Thursday morning must have been their final preparations, placing the body where it needed to be found."

"So the body that was found in Vivian's bathroom wasn't actually Vivian?" asked Anne. "But how is that—"

"Possible?" interrupted Dorothy. "It's possible if you're friends with a medical examiner who's easily corrupted."

"Nathan Islington!" Sheila and Eve cried out simultaneously. (Someone owed someone a Coke.)

"Oh man, *that* guy's still rattling around?" Samir barked like a seal. "Nate the Late, we used to call him back in school. Cuz he never showed up to class on time. Dude was the *worst.*"

"It would seem so." Dorothy turned to Brooks and Locust. "Any luck on finding him, by the way?"

"You bet," said Brooks, "It's a pretty great story, actually. . . ." He trailed off, his partner having turned to him with a look of such seething fury, the little blood vessels lining the rim of Locust's nostrils looked to be in danger of bursting.

"Which I will *not* be telling," Brooks added.

"Dr. Islington has been apprehended," said SI Locust grimly. "He is in custody and currently under interrogation."

"Fantastic!" Dorothy beamed. "That's why the identification was never in question, or the time of death, which"—she nodded at Sheila Hasan—"was ascertained on-site, according to standard procedure. The examiner falsely recorded the time of death as happening hours earlier, when in fact the body was several days old by that point."

"So the woman at the morgue?" I asked. "She was—"

"Paula Fitzgerald." Dorothy nodded. "That's right."

"But then where is Vivian?"

"That's easy, sugar. I'm right here."

We all turned.

A woman was standing behind us. It was unclear how long she'd been in the room, since she'd already crossed that great expanse of concrete. Beside her stood Officer Choi, who must have escorted her from upstairs. This made sense, as judging by the woman's voice there was no question she was Laura Duval, whose arrival we'd been expecting. But the picture didn't match the sound, and in the same way people become dizzy when their brain and eyes tell them two different things, I became disoriented. Because even though I'd heard Laura Duval, it was not Laura Duval I was seeing now.

It was Vivian Davis.

Chapter 45

Well, she was an actress, after all.

I thought back to the two times I'd seen Laura: first, on the day of the memorial service in that black veil, and then the next day in her room, with the lights darkened and a towel on her head. She'd never allowed us to get a proper look at her, and for good reason. She'd been in costume the whole time.

How easy it must have been to slip a long brown wig over that sleek, blond pixie cut of hers. The big nose had obviously been fake, which I felt like an idiot for not realizing. But *Tootsie* and *Mrs. Doubtfire* notwithstanding, you simply don't expect people you meet to be wearing rubber prosthetics.

When we'd first met Vivian at Betty's Liquor Mart—where the lights had *also* been dim—she'd been wearing yoga pants and a hoodie, and while the lacy dress she wore now was nowhere near as sporty (it was downright vampy: burgundy red, off the shoulder), it was equally revealing of her fit/toned figure—a far cry from Laura's heavier frame. (I learned later she used padding.)

"I'm glad you finally joined us."

Dorothy waved her to the front of the room, not that Vivian needed the invitation. She floated past us: an actor assuming her mark, eager to play to her audience.

"If Paula Fitzgerald's phone had had a real pass code on it, we would've given up the whole crazy idea."

She faced us, her hands pressed together in front of her as though she were about to say "namaste." A beatific smile appeared on her face.

"It's strange a plot so big could hinge on something so small, but it's true. We weren't cryptographers or anything. If we hadn't been able to access her texts, the whole thing would've been too risky. But I entered one-two-three-four and it worked. First try." Her eyes took on a dreamy quality. "It was like the whole thing was meant to be. . . ."

Gone was the upspeak, the nasal whine I remembered from Betty's. That too had been an act. Her voice was deeper, richer, with no particular accent I could discern. Despite the content of her words, she had an attractive presence—magnetic, even.

"Now I wish we'd just left the body in the lake and called the police. That's what a normal person would have done. But we were never normal, Walter and I."

"You can say that again!"

Minna Hawley had half risen from her seat; Bobby rose with her, gently forcing her back down.

"I'm happy to." Vivian smiled warmly at her. "Walter and I agreed when we got married not to pretend to each other. We promised to be one hundred percent honest about who we were and what we wanted out of life. Which was a courtesy he never paid *you*."

Minna Hawley narrowed her eyes, waiting for the other shoe to drop.

"That must have been so hurtful. I can see that now, more than I ever could before. I'm sorry that happened to you."

Now we were *all* waiting for the other shoe to drop.

She turned to the Shahs. "We can't all be like *these* lovebirds. You two make me sick," she said—but genially; she was paying them a compliment. "I hope you realize you're the exception that proves the rule. You should've seen some of the stuff Paula Fitzgerald's husband wrote to her. He practically egged her on to suicide. I didn't mind pulling one over on him. Maybe that's awful, but it's the truth." She turned to Dorothy. "You're probably right about the stones in her coat pockets. She didn't have any coat on when we found her, so it must have fallen off after she drowned, which was why the current was able to take her so far. No question she drowned, there was frothy mucus all over her mouth. I had to clear it away because Walter was too squeamish." She laughed, a husky sound that matched her voice. "Men are such weaklings. We filed for the temporary restraining order online, in her name. And then I made a phone call to the police from her phone, pretending to be her, complaining about how abusive my husband was. I said I'd left him and wasn't coming back."

"How did you manage that?" asked Dorothy.

"She had a ton of videos uploaded to her Facebook account. I've always been a pretty good mimic, isn't that right, Paulie?"

"That's what I told them!" said Paul, who was the only person—besides Vivian—who seemed to be enjoying himself.

Dorothy turned to the two police officers. "What's the status of the Paula Fitzgerald case at the moment?"

"Her husband filed a missing person's report." Brooks consulted his notepad. "Four days ago. And I hate to say it, but that phone call and TRO application did the trick. File says she's likely hiding out from her husband." He looked up. "No follow-up as of yet."

"That's what happens when people lie and game the system," growled Locust. "Resources that are already spread too thin don't go to the right places."

"A*men* to that, Detective," said Dorothy.

"You have to understand," continued Vivian, "I really *was* devastated when you lost and that moron won. All Walter and I did was what everyone says they're going to do when their side loses. Leave the country, start over somewhere else. That's how we were—willing to do the things other people only talked about doing."

"Yes, well, it would be a whole lot more admirable if your go-get-'em spirit didn't involve the desecration of a body and criminal impersonation," said Dorothy dryly.

Vivian laughed her husky laugh again. "Touché, Senator. By the way, we used a wheelbarrow to move the body both times, it wasn't so bad. At first we weren't even going to bother bringing it upstairs, but then we figured someone in the house might notice if the examiner didn't go up to my room like he was supposed to. We just dumped it right inside the door." She turned to Anne Shah. "We were stripping off its clothes when you knocked. We were inches away, I've never been so startled in my life." She smiled at her wickedly. "Aren't you glad we didn't open up?"

Samir Shah turned sideways, shielding his wife from her. "I still don't understand why, though. *Why* go to all these lengths to pretend you died when you hadn't? What was the point?"

Dorothy gestured at Vivian with both hands: *the floor is yours.*

"The Kickstarter," she said simply. "It began as a joke. A way to let off steam, make fun of how much we all hated that awful man. But people were into it. More than I expected them to be. So Walter and I started brainstorming how we could make it bigger. How to make as much money out of it as we possibly could. Sure, we'd have to donate some of it, but it would be easy to pocket most of what we got. Especially since we were leaving the country anyway."

"How much has the Kickstarter brought in by this morning, Leila?" asked Dorothy.

Leila held up a finger while she pulled up the relevant website on her tablet.

"Three point eight million dollars. And *still* counting."

DS Brooks let out a low whistle.

"I always knew motive was the key to solving this thing," said Dorothy. "And as my colleague so astutely pointed out"—she gestured in my direction—"money is often at the bottom of these nefarious matters. The Kickstarter was the missing lucre motive staring me in the face. Because the only thing better than a jokey Kickstarter is a jokey Kickstarter created by someone who ends up killing herself over the very thing she was joking about."

I remembered Eve Turner telling us how it felt as though Vivian had arranged for her own murder. Little did we know how right she'd been.

"Especially with all the press you got from that photo you took with me," said Dorothy. "Another stroke of luck, eh?"

"It didn't hurt," admitted Vivian.

"You used me for publicity," said Dorothy. "In that way, I unknowingly helped your scheme."

Vivian nodded. "You couldn't buy that kind of publicity. Everything was humming along perfectly. Nathan had submitted the autopsy report, which meant we'd be able to collect the body and bury it as me. Whenever the toxicology report came out, he'd doctor that too, matching it to the drug in the sleeping pills I'd supposedly taken. All we had to do was wait around while the Kickstarter money poured in, then hightail it out of here a few weeks later for greener pastures. Well ahead of Inauguration Day."

"Any place in particular?" asked Dorothy.

"There was a short list. Brazil was always the frontrunner. Doesn't take too long to establish citizenship there based on residency. That, plus the beaches."

"But you were supposed to be dead by then," I said. "How were you going to travel on a dead person's passport?"

She cocked an eyebrow at me. "You're a smart cookie, but

you really overthink things. Do you know what happens when a person dies in Maine?"

I shook my head.

"A death certificate has to be filed with the Department of Health and Human Services—with the Office of Data, Research, and Vital Statistics, specifically. The person who does the filing is usually the funeral director, or in the case of people who don't have a funeral, the medical examiner handling the case. Can you guess who has two thumbs and opted not to have a funeral?" She poked herself in the chest. "Nate the Late was going to slow-boat that process too. Not that the Office of Data, Research, and Vital Statistics is known for its efficiency. Or the people who check your passport at customs. Sure, there was a chance they might recognize my name from all the press surrounding my supposed suicide, but fortunately, my legal name is very much *not* Vivian Davis."

"It's Joycelyn Duval," said Dorothy.

Vivian winced. "Don't remind me. It took about two seconds for the theater crowd to tell me I had to change it. Remember, Paulie?"

"Sure do," he piped up.

"My parents meant to name me Jocelyn, which is still an ugly name. They made a typo filling out the birth certificate. Because they were ignorant hicks. I haven't gone by Joycelyn in years, no way anyone was flagging my passport on the way to Rio."

"That was one of your few slip-ups, actually," said Dorothy. "When you were pretending to be your sister, Laura, you said you always called Vivian 'Veevo' growing up. But later, I learned that 'Vivian Davis' was your stage name, which you only started going by as an adult."

"Yeah, that was stupid," admitted Vivian. "Guess the apple doesn't fall as far from the tree as I'd like to pretend."

"I don't know, I think you were pretty clever about establishing Laura's identity. That phone call you took from Laura at Betty's Liquor Mart was certainly effective. I thought it was a little strange you took the call while you were in the middle of talking to us. Most people would have ignored it, but you wanted to establish your sister's existence early on, in a credible way. I assume it was Walter calling?"

Vivian nodded.

I marveled at the forethought of renaming his contact "Bitch Sister" in her phone and adding a cat photo to it. Ingenious in its simplicity.

"When we spoke to you in your bedroom, I thought it was curious you referenced Betty's by name, a store you'd been outside of only once. But, of course, as a long-time resident of Sacobago the name just slipped out." Dorothy paused. "I also thought it was . . . interesting when you told us how uncomfortable you were, casting aspersions on Ms. Turner. Due to her race and your Southern roots."

Out of the corner of my eye, I saw Eve Turner stiffen, her back growing straighter.

"Wow, you're good. Yeah, that was my sensibility for sure. You know, Laura *did* exist. My mama had a stillborn girl two years before me."

That "mama" was the first real evidence I'd heard of her Virginian roots.

"She named her Laura, and I grew up having it thrown in my face that I'd never be as good as Laura would've been, if she'd lived." Vivian sighed again. "I guess that's why I made her such a dumb bitch. The homebody to my busybody. The accent was a bit much, wasn't it?"

"It didn't help," said Dorothy. "I lived in the South for many years, you know. My own son has a Virginian accent. But a real one."

"Aw, shucks," drawled Peter.

Dorothy threw him a look of warning only a parent can give a child.

"The whole Laura thing was stupid. But I had to be *some-*

one once my body was carted away! Walter wanted me to leave when the body did, hide away in some hotel till it was over. But no way was I going to miss out on all the drama. You have to understand, it was still a joke at that point. It wasn't till later that things got . . . complicated." She sighed. "Even so, I stayed as far away from everyone as I could when I was Laura. Especially you, Paulie. You've seen the tricks of the trade, and we've known each other too long. I figured you'd see right through the disguise."

"Yes, I picked up on that the last time we spoke to Mr. Reston," said Dorothy. "I thought it was strange he hadn't seen you. And that even among those who *had* seen you, it had been sparingly at best. People talked about the way Laura and Vivian had been 'holed up' in Vivian's room that Wednesday night, but of course they were told that. They hadn't actually seen the two of you there."

"Right as usual," said Vivian. "It was easier after the body was taken away. I should never have come down during the memorial, but can you blame me? I defy anyone to pass up the opportunity to attend their own wake. Especially after a few too many gin and tonics alone in their bedroom. Again, we hadn't *killed* anyone, it was more fun than anything." She glanced at me. "Walter was so furious that I talked to you. But I told him you were the dreamy kind of smart who doesn't really put two and two together."

I was insulted, and yet I knew she was right. I had missed so much that had been staring me in the face. . . .

"Now I don't think that's fair." Dorothy came a step closer to me. "You're the one who put me on the right track when you reminded me that Vivian was an actor. I'd forgotten about that, and it was the perfect timing because we'd just been speaking to Paul Reston about *Richard III*." She turned to Vivian. "The big poofy widow's dress you were wearing the day of the memorial. It was from *Richard III*, wasn't it? Paul told us you never returned your costumes. You played the grieving widow, Lady Anne, who appears onstage in mourning."

So *that's* what Dorothy had meant by taking a closer look at "Anne." For the first time I was a little annoyed with her. Talk about a misleading clue!

"But much more importantly, there was the video footage we had access to—from the surveillance camera at the fork in the road, off the highway. You said you arrived here at the Crystal Palace the day Vivian died, on Wednesday. That a taxi from the airport brought you in. But when we reviewed the footage there was no taxi, no strange car bringing in a new guest. So how did you get here?"

Good God, how could I have missed that too?

"Also," Dorothy had begun pacing again, "when Walter talked about 'Laura' coming to visit, he made a big point of saying how she invited herself. But then you said it was Vivian who'd invited you. You did that on purpose, to deflect the focus away from Laura herself. Same idea with all the confusion over when you'd arrived, whether it was Tuesday or Wednesday. As long as we were focused on the inconsistencies in Laura Duval's statements, we were guaranteed to take Laura Duval's *existence* for granted."

"God," said Vivian. "The fact that you're not going to be our president in a few weeks' time is such a travesty. There is *nothing* more dangerous than a woman who gets stuff done." She smirked. "I should know."

"That's right," said Dorothy. "Because my involvement cut both ways, didn't it?"

Vivian nodded. "If you hadn't been around, we never would've gotten the publicity we did. But we *also* never would've had the rug pulled out from under us when the chief medical examiner took over the case. That's when everything fell apart."

"So . . . it was my fault then?" Eve Turner had her hand up

to her mouth, finishing lessons be damned. "When I asked you to go over Nathan Islington's head?"

Dorothy nodded gently. "It meant the toxicology report couldn't be doctored. All of a sudden, a suicide that had been tampered with after the fact became the subject of a homicide investigation."

"I . . ." Eve was trembling in the effort to hold back tears. "I was just trying to help him," she said quietly.

"I know you were." Vivian's voice was low, matching Eve's in volume. "I know you cared about him, and I hope you realize I'm not going to do the obvious thing here and hate you. None of this is your fault. *None.*"

Just as in the case of Minna Hawley, I waited for some sort of retraction, or at least a qualification. But apparently there wasn't any, apparently she was—

"If it's anyone's fault"—she swung from Eve Turner back to Dorothy—"it's yours."

And then she turned—gulp—to me.

"Yours too."

Huh?

Chapter 46

Allow me to repeat myself: *Huh?*

"You were the ones who told me my marriage with my husband was an open one. News to me! I couldn't help reacting at the time, but I worried later I might have given myself away, getting as upset as I did. No one cares *that* much about her dead sister's marriage."

"The thought occurred to me," admitted Dorothy.

"Our marriage was *not* open." Vivian looked at Eve Turner. "He lied to you. Just like he lied to me. And I know it sounds like a cliché, but it was the *lie* that hurt the most. If he'd sat me down and we'd discussed it openly and honestly, the way we always promised we'd be with each other, I probably would've been fine with it. I'm not a prude. Sex is sex. But he never said a word and I never suspected a thing, and it was all just so boring and sordid and not what I ever imagined my life to be."

"MMMM-hm, MMMM-hm."

"The real kicker was that he knew you'd tell me what he said. It's like he didn't want to bother telling me himself, so he just got someone else to do it for him. And I got the message. Loud and clear. Our marriage was over."

Her voice cracked. She paused, taking a moment to compose herself.

"If I were being generous to him, not that he deserves it, I'd note we were both freaking out at that point."

"Of course you were," said Dorothy. "You had a murder investigation on your hands all of a sudden. There was no question Walter was a lot more agitated the day after the memorial. He even slipped up once, referring to you in the present tense and almost spilling boiling water on me. Slip-ups like that are common when a loved one dies—it takes a while for our everyday parlance to catch up to our new situation. But it was his *reaction* that put me on my guard."

I thought back to that long interview we conducted with Walter in the kitchen. I remembered him telling us so solemnly he hadn't killed his wife, and how I assumed either he was telling the truth or he was a sociopath—how one of those things had to be true, but not the other. Yet again, I was wrong.

They were both true.

"It was a nightmare. At that point I really *did* have to stay in my room because what was I going to do if the police interviewed me? What would I say when they asked me to produce *ID*? At one point I suggested we just Thelma-and-Louise it, and I was only half joking. Because what's more romantic than Thelma-and-Louise'ing it with your husband, right? And that's the thing. As screwed as we were, I always assumed we were in it together."

"And to a certain extent you were," said Dorothy. "The day after the memorial, the two of you cast aspersions on pretty much every other person in the house. But never on each other."

"Well, if one of us got caught, we both got caught. I was pretty sure the second I heard about the chief medical examiner stepping in we were going down. It's just, I assumed we'd go down together. But I was wrong about that. Dead wrong." She paused, moving closer to Eve Turner. "For what it's worth, he really liked you."

"I think she's right," added Dorothy. "That must be why he stood you up at that hotel on Wednesday. He wanted you out of the way."

"Is *that* where he sent you?" Vivian laughed mirthlessly. "He said he sent you on an errand. Dorothy's right as usual, we had to prep the bedroom that afternoon. And the body. If you were around, you would've known something was up."

Eve nodded dumbly.

"Please don't think he was the love of your life," said Vivian, "I'm begging you. Please don't waste any more of your time mourning or whatever. He doesn't deserve it. Do you want to know how I did it?"

"Yes," said Dorothy, even though Vivian hadn't been speaking to her. "I think we all do."

Vivian nodded, pausing to regroup.

"I pretended not to mind about the affair. He didn't believe me at first, because he wasn't an idiot. But he *wanted* me to be okay with it, so it didn't take long for him to come around. He was desperate to free himself of the whole thing." She looked at Eve again. "He said he wanted to take you away. Somewhere far away and warm, same as he'd wanted to do with me. I said there was no reason both of us had to suffer. I told him I'd do what I could to shoulder the blame, say it had been my idea. That I'd found the body alone and he'd been in the dark like everyone else. Not very believable, but it was better than nothing, and at the very least he could say he'd been powerless to stop me. He didn't mind me playing the martyr, I think he expected it. Most men do. The only thing he didn't like was the blow to his ego at having to play the sidekick role."

Much to my surprise, I found myself commiserating with Walter Vogel.

"So in the end, he went for it. Like I knew he would. From there it wasn't too difficult to get him, well"—she smirked—"in the mood."

She nodded at Eve.

"You know how he was."

Eve looked away.

"I stole the letter opener from your desk. I'm sorry about that. I swear I wasn't trying to frame you. It's just, it was all so spur-of-the-moment, and I worried if I took the time to go all the way down to the kitchen for a proper weapon and all the way back up, I'd lose my nerve. I hate this stupid house with its stupid elevators. So I took the letter opener and then convinced him to go up to the third floor. I said I wanted to make love to him once more before I turned myself in. For old time's sake. We'd been intimate up there before.

"I realize how bad this sounds, but I'm glad I did it. Because it gave me such *clarity*. It wasn't till after I killed him that I realized how empty our life had been, how much more there is to the world. To *me*. And it was so easy. He had no idea what was happening till it already happened."

Her voice had gone dreamy, her eyes unfocused. . . .

"It slid right in. Like the pass code—like it was meant to be. There was one frozen moment when the blood was pouring out of him and he was still alive, and we looked at each other and he *knew*. That was enough for me. I'd done what I needed to do."

Her eyes cleared, her voice growing stronger.

"I pushed him over the railing like the trash he was." She turned to Dorothy. "Husbands have been killing their wives since the dawn of civilization. I think it's only fair that occasionally it work the other way around. Don't you?"

"No," said Dorothy firmly.

Vivian shrugged, turning back to the group. "All I had to do was wait till someone found him, which took a few minutes. Then I screamed my head off, adding to the general confusion, and headed back to my bedroom, where I hid my bloodstained clothes, took a bunch of sedatives." She turned to DS Brooks, who was still recording. "You'll find the clothes I wore under my mattress."

She turned back to Dorothy.

"But even as I was slipping into unconsciousness, I knew I wouldn't get away with it. That I wasn't *meant* to get away with it. It felt so inevitable when you walked into my room and said the time had come for me to confess. I'm so grateful for the opportunity. Thank you. All of you," she added, addressing her audience one last time.

It was as though she were wrapping up a TED talk. We stared at her, dumbstruck. At some point, the natural light in the room had dimmed to the point where the overhead lights had come on automatically, giving the space the exposed look of a theater after the house lights have been turned on. The performance was over, and yet we continued to stare . . . till an animal sound rang out: guttural, ferocious. Suddenly, Minna Hawley was running at Vivian like a lineman intent on sacking the quarterback.

Bobby caught her just in time, pinning her arms to her sides while she sobbed.

"Monster!" she shrieked.

"I am so sorry." Vivian was at a safe remove, but Brooks and Locust had gotten up during the commotion, and they remained standing now.

"I really hope you get some help," said Vivian. "I know therapy's been *so* helpful for me. I had a marathon session this morning, actually, on Skype. It did *wonders*, really helped give me the perspective I needed to do this." She glanced at Brooks and Locust, while Bobby led his sobbing mother back to her seat. "I'm sure my therapist will be in touch with you shortly. He told me he'd have to breach doctor-patient confidentiality, given what I disclosed."

"Which means this charade was completely unnecessary."

SI Locust jerked his head in Dorothy's direction. "I think we're done here, yes?"

"Almost," said Dorothy, "But first, I need Vivian to verify that what she said about Alex Shah was a lie."

Vivian threw up her hands. "Thank you for the reminder! Yes, I should have mentioned that, even though it has nothing to do with Paula Fitzgerald." She turned to the Shahs. "You probably already figured this out, but we couldn't have you suing, or badmouthing Walter to all your colleagues. We figured let's burn one bridge for the sake of building more in the future. So yes, I slipped into your son's bed. Nothing happened, of course. Unlike my husband, I was a faithful spouse, and I also happen not to be a pedophile. Poor kid, he developed a crush on me, I suppose. I should have seen it coming. I hope you can find it in your hearts to forgive me."

"Fuck. You."

Personally, I don't think Samir Shah could have put it any better.

"How could you?" hissed Anne.

"Get me away from that woman," sobbed Minna from her son's arms. "Get me away from her."

"Joycelyn Duval, you have the right to—"

"Before we all leave"—Dorothy held up a hand apologetically—"there's one more thing I'd like to share with you all."

SI Locust glowered at her, retracting the handcuffs he'd produced from his person.

"Paula Fitzgerald was the mother to Alton Fitzgerald, aged sixteen, and Mitzi Fitzgerald, aged thirteen. She volunteered at her local church each and every week, arranging the flowers for both Sunday services. She spent three years as the president of the PTA, which by all accounts nearly did her in, and was an avid lover of dogs, never having fewer than two at any one time. Every February she went to the Westminster Kennel Club show in Madison Square Garden. She hadn't missed it in eighteen years."

When on earth had Dorothy found the time to memorize this?

"When her mother, Rosie Kivlehan, was alive they talked every single day. Paula had been struggling with depression ever since she had her first child, which put a long-term strain on her marriage. She was also active in politics, an ardent supporter of our current president-elect, whose win she celebrated *qui-hite* vocally online!"

"You've got to be kidding me, you're going to stand there and fete a woman who would actually support that cretin?"

The anger Vivian had been so intent on containing spilled over now, distorting her features—though if anything was a distortion, I suspected it was the false composure she'd been displaying up till now.

"I certainly am," said Dorothy. "Because neither Paula nor her family deserved to have her bodily remains used as a prop for your selfish scheme. We'll never know what was going on in her head when she walked into that river, but her family has a right to know everything that happened to her afterward, and to bury and mourn her properly. They deserve that closure, and that is what they are going to get." She pressed her lips together. "I'm going to make sure of it."

Behind me, Leila cleared her throat. "Do all the good you can. . . ."

When I turned to look at her, I could see the tears in her eyes. She motioned for Dorothy to continue.

"For all the people you can," said Dorothy.

"In all the ways you can," continued Leila.

"As long as ever you can," finished Dorothy. "Yep. Exactly."

"Whatever." Vivian shrugged her shoulders. "Do you think they'll let me do a podcast from jail?"

SI Locust snapped the handcuffs on her, leading her out of the room.

CHAPTER 47

Once the police had left with their quarry, Dorothy explained to us how she'd told Locust the only way he'd get a full confession out of Vivian was if she had an audience.

"He was resistant to the idea, as you can imagine, but I knew she needed the drama of all this."

She swept her arm over the assembled group. By then the Shahs had hurried back to their son upstairs, and Paul Reston had left the building. No doubt he was eager for his extracurricular activities not to be remarked on by anyone in an official capacity.

"I still can't believe it." Sheila Hasan was shaking her head wonderingly. "The way she just stood there and laid it all out like that."

"I know what you mean," said Leila. "There was something so chilling about how . . . *woke* she was about the whole thing. The way she'd processed it all, you know?"

"You *do* realize that was all an act?" Eve Turner was clutching a tissue in her hand, but she hadn't used it yet. "She was just playing another role. She decided she was going to be evolved and empathetic, kind to everyone. Believe me, that was *not* what Vivian Davis was like." She paused. "Though I'm beginning to realize I have no idea what she was really like. I don't think any of us do."

"How many of us know the people in our lives?" asked Dorothy rhetorically. "Even the ones who are supposedly our nearest and dearest?"

This pronouncement put a pall over the room, interrupted only when Minna Hawley tried to get up and nearly fell over. She was back to looking half dead, and Bobby had to support her again, propping her on his shoulder. Dorothy sidled up to him.

"Your mother is going to need your help, Bobby. A lot of it. Do you think you're up to the task?"

Maybe I imagined this, but I swear his spine straightened a little as he replied: "I think so."

"Good." Dorothy gave his shoulder a pat.

We watched as the son helped his mother shuffle out of the room.

Sheila and Eve left soon thereafter, but not before Dorothy gave them her personal cell number and urged them to call her. "I'd like to help you however I can," she said. "You're both young, smart women who have so much to give to this world. And buh-*lieve* me, the world is going to need it!"

"Maybe the next four years won't actually be as bad as everyone thinks they're going to be?" said Sheila. "Maybe he'll surprise us. In a good way."

Dorothy grunted.

"From your lips to God's ears."

The only people left were in Dorothy's camp: Peter, Leila, Denny, Sarah, and of course, Dorothy and me. There was nothing stopping us from leaving . . . and yet, we didn't.

"Well, I know of a great place just down the road," said Peter brightly. "Nice little kitchen run by a woman named Trudy who I'm sure could rustle us up some grub and celebratory libations. Shall we all repair in that direction?"

"You know," said Dorothy as though she hadn't heard him, "there's one aspect of all this that still doesn't make sense."

"Just one?" asked Peter.

"How did Vivian know when to go to Betty's Liquor Mart to get that photo with me?"

She paused, looking from one to the other of us.

"Didn't she say it was another piece of luck?" I ventured.

"*I* said that. And she didn't contradict me. But as we were just discussing, we can't take everything Vivian Davis told us at face value. And given how important that photo was to their plan, I find it hard to believe she and Walter would have left it up to chance."

"Well, then why didn't you ask her?" asked Peter sharply.

"Because I already know what happened."

"You do?" asked Leila nervously.

"I sure do. It was someone close to me. Someone who was willing to sell information about where I was for the right price."

If the room had been quiet before, it was positively sepulchral now.

Leila put a hand to her chest. (She was still holding her tablet, so really, she put her tablet to her chest.) "I hope you don't think *I* did that?"

Dorothy eyed her coolly. "You know, for a while I did."

"I can't believe"—Leila broke off, the tears breaching her eyes. "I knew there was something going on, I *knew* it. The way you pulled away from me and went off with"—she thrust her chin in my direction—"*her.*"

"I'm sorry, Leila," said Dorothy. "*Of course* you had nothing to do with it. *Of course* I know that."

She held up a hand, which Leila clasped with her own. It struck me as a curiously masculine gesture of intimacy: the sort of thing you might see two Roman warriors do in their sandals and togas before heading off to battle. And yet it fit them perfectly.

"I've missed you," said Leila.

"I've missed you too," said Dorothy.

I'd like to remind you they were apart for essentially one day. Not even. Apparently Vivian Davis wasn't the only drama queen in the vicinity.

"The only thing I can say in my defense is that I wasn't willing to face the truth because I knew how hurtful it was going to be." She turned to her son. "How could you, Peter?"

He looked as if he were going to deny it . . . and then he just smirked at her.

"I asked you weeks ago for a little something to tide me over," he said. "And you said no. So I had to take matters into my own hands."

"Taking matters into your own hands would have been getting an actual *job* that pays you actual *money* by way of contributing an actual *product* or *service* to the world," spat out Dorothy. "I hate to say it, Peter, but you're nothing but a leech."

"Mother!" He was faux-shocked, but I couldn't help feeling there was real shock underneath it. The "faux" was a cover.

"You asked to go to that liquor store at that exact time. And then you didn't come in with us because you were coordinating with them over text, weren't you?"

He shrugged his shoulders.

"I hope you made sure the check cleared," said Dorothy acidly.

"Oh, I insisted on Venmo."

"And then a few days after that you called me up, repeating the lie you were fed about seeing Laura Duval and Vivian Davis together outside Betty's. Because of course you *couldn't* have seen them. You have no idea how far that set me back. I didn't question Laura's existence because I never imagined my *own son* would be actively working to mislead me. You even made me put you on speakerphone to spread the lie as far as possible. It makes me wonder if it was only a payout Walter and Vivian were dangling in front of you. I wouldn't be surprised if they were threatening to expose something they knew about you—"

He tried to interrupt her, but she held up her hand.

"I don't want to know!"

"Why didn't Vivian say anything about all this?" asked Leila wonderingly.

"Cuz she promised if I did what she asked, she'd leave me out of it," said Peter. "Guess she was good to her word." He turned back to his mother. "No one's *all* bad, y'know."

"I'm well aware of that," said Dorothy sadly. "Maybe more than most. And I'll tell you this, because it's the only comfort I can give you, cold as it may be. There's a difference between hurting people in your family and hurting complete strangers. Both are abhorrent, but when you graduate from the former to the latter? You know you've really hit rock bottom. Please, Peter, don't let that happen. I beg of you."

"I'm sorry," he said, and for once he sounded like he meant it. "It's just, I haven't been doing well and I—"

"Peter?" She rested a hand on his arm. "I'm tired. It's been an exhausting few days." She let out a dry little chuckle. "An exhausting few years, actually. You need to figure out your own problems. For yourself. I'm not going to help you."

"You're not?" he asked her incredulously.

"I'm really not. You know what I'm going to do instead?"

He shook his head.

"I'm going to go home, and get back to work. I suggest you do the same." Her hand fell off him, and she began moving toward the door. "See you around."

CHAPTER 48

I didn't follow Dorothy out the door, but everyone else did. Now the Reception Room was truly empty, and I stood looking out the window as Dorothy had done. The Crystal River was choppy as ever, its frothy current running along busily, though I couldn't help feeling there was something relentless about its never-ending motion. I imagined Paula Fitzgerald's body being carried along it on the way to Crystal Lake, borne by nothing more remarkable than gravity and currents. . . .

My phone buzzed. It was a text from Leila:

Where are you?

Sorry, I wrote back, **I just need to decompress a little, I'll grab an Uber back to D's in a bit.**

Were there even Ubers readily available in Sacobago, Maine? I had no idea.

Really? You sure?

Absolutely. See you soon.

It took about a minute for the ellipses on her end to produce a text. I could so easily picture them conferring in the Lincoln Town Car, wondering if I was having a breakdown or something.

Are you sure you're okay? D is asking.

She softened this with the emoji whose eyes are pointing upward, midroll. Back in 2003 (when people were just starting to use emoticons made of punctuation symbols), I made a solemn pact with myself that I would never use any sort of pictorial representation in my written communications. Otherwise, I would have sent her back the crying-laughing emoji, which was clearly the appropriate response.

Hundred percent, I wrote. **I'm actually taking down a bunch of notes & ideas, don't want to interrupt the flow while it's going strong.**

She took the hint, as I knew she would, and wrote nothing back. I stared out the window a few more minutes, but only because I wanted to give them enough time to leave. Then I made a pitstop in the bathroom out in the hallway—the one I'd been in when I overheard Eve Turner talking to Nathan Islington. If I hadn't gone to the bathroom then, would any of this have happened? Vivian and Walter would be packing their swimsuits for Rio, and I'd be ensconced on the fluffy couch with Dorothy, pinging ideas back and forth as though we were holding paddles instead of laptops.

I wished none of this had happened. Because Leila was right: Vivian Davis's "woke" explanation *had* been chilling. I wasn't a sociopath, and I couldn't really understand why she did what she did. But I could understand the way she'd felt. I'd felt that sort of anger before—at the world, for not being as inviting or interesting or helpful or *good* as it should have been. I may as well admit it: I *still* feel that sort of anger. It's a part of who I am.

I washed my face with hand soap. I clutched either side of the sink, looking at myself in the mirror the way people do in the movies. This got me nowhere.

There was nothing to be done other than to leave. So I exited the bathroom, stepping into the Great Hall for the last time.

* * *

He was waiting there for me. Like I knew he would be. Let me amend that: like I hoped he would be.

"Aren't you supposed to be guarding someone's body right now?"

"Don't be a jerk."

"Sorry."

"It's okay, I know you can't help it. Sarah went back with them." He paused. "I've got the rest of the night off."

I knew that if I wanted to, all I had to do was suggest we spend the night together and he would go for it. That if I wanted to, there was a good chance we'd spend many nights together—more than I'd spent with anyone. Which isn't saying much, for the record.

But it was saying something.

"You know no one really cares that we're . . . doing whatever it is we're doing, right? I know Leila can be a pain in the ass, but no one has a problem with it." He paused. "Except maybe you."

He waited for me to say something, but I didn't.

"You're not actually going back to the house, are you?"

I shook my head.

"And if I hadn't stayed here and come looking for you, you would've left without saying goodbye, right?"

I nodded.

"And you do realize I'm into you?"

"You bet I do."

"Har har. I meant that I like you. A lot."

"Well." I paused, deploying the same dry chuckle Dorothy had just used on Peter. "I like your face and body. A lot. But beyond that? I think we've got a little bit of a disconnect here."

"You're lying." He stepped closer to me. "You know you are."

"Do I? We barely know each other. Unless you're so shallow, all it takes is a few days and a roll in the hay to get to know you."

"A roll in the hay?"

I flushed.

"You know this almost never happens, right?" he asked.

"What?"

I knew what. But I needed him to say it.

"That you find a person you're attracted to, and who you want to be around, and that they feel the same way. Please don't deny it, you know that's what's happening here."

I didn't deny it.

He sighed—a manly sigh that made his chest swell.

"I should tell you, I know about your sister."

"How—"

"We have to do our due diligence, especially with anyone who's live-in. It's not like we can just google a person and call it a day. We run background checks, pay for access to police records—"

"I don't—"

"I know you don't want to talk about it. That's obvious. I just wanted you to know I'm aware of . . . what happened."

I nodded, refusing to look at him.

"You were only seventeen, right? That must have been—"

"Don't," I warned him. "There's no point."

He stared searchingly at me. "Aren't you tired of being alone all the time?"

"I'm not—"

"Yes, you are. I am too. I hate it."

He wasn't *so* perfect-looking, you know. That vein you sometimes see in people's foreheads was extremely pronounced in his, and I'd learned to use it as a sort of mood ring/barometer to determine how agitated—for good or bad—he might be. In this moment it was working overtime, practically pulsating.

"I know this is a dumb question, but . . . what do you even want out of life?"

"I want to write more books," I said. "Better books. Books that matter. And I want to become famous for it. So famous that people turn my name into a verb."

"Huh?"

"Like Bogart."

"Ah. Gotcha. Or MacGuyver."

I smiled. "Exactly."

"You know, you can still do all those things, and be in a relationship?"

My smile became pitying.

"Ohhh, I get it." He tried to give me a pitying smile back, but his was amateur hour compared to mine. "You're a coward."

"A realist," I retorted.

"Spoken like a coward," he retorted back. "Fine, go ahead and ruin your life if you want to."

Here's the thing: on the one hand he was right. I knew that. But on the other hand, he was wrong, because there was no question that going off with him would mean a dilution, a corruption of the purity I'd honed over two decades of adult life up to that point. An adult life I very much enjoyed, mind you, especially now that I was beginning to reap the fruits of all my effort and labor. How could I just toss it aside? I couldn't.

"You know," he continued, "I think you might be the stupidest smart person I've ever met."

"That's funny because I was just thinking the other day how you're the smartest stupid person I ever met."

"See? We're perfect for each other."

He shook his head, smiling sadly, and my stomach did a stop-drop-and-roll for what I knew was coming.

"Well, I hope you know you can get in touch with me whenever you want."

We both knew this would never happen.

"It's not hard. I'm around."

He walked out the front door. I heard a car engine turn on, and then fade away.

I made a deal with myself that if he returned, I'd go with him. But he had to try just *one more* time. It couldn't be me running after him or getting his contact information from Leila (who would be so smug about it, but who'd do it, I knew she would). So I stood there: in that awful mall atrium of a hall where I'd chatted with a murderer and then gawked at the corpse of her victim—stood there and waited like some tragic character in an Edith Wharton novel, except I didn't have the crowds of a European promenade or Grand Central Station or even a small municipal airport to surround me, and come to think of it, if those public places are heaven, then I'm pretty sure the Great Hall of the Crystal Palace is hell.

He didn't come. I pulled out my phone and requested an Uber, which was going to take 48 minutes to arrive, *good God.* (In the end it took over an hour.) And then I did what I claimed to be doing already: I started making notes, putting down ideas. Not for Dorothy's book, which would never get written (at least not by me—Rhonda would be so furious, I couldn't wait to tell her), but for this one. It was easy to do. I had a lifetime's experience of pouring my feelings into my work, after all.

And you know what? It *did* make me feel better. Forget the Great Hall; forget the silence; forget the Bodyguard. Scribbling away in my Notes app under that great glass ceiling was like coming home.

But now, the book is done. All the loose ends are tied up—except the one at which I find myself with no work to distract me. It's okay, though. Should I want it, another gig's around the corner. Rhonda's assured me I haven't made a *total* shambles of my career—far from it, if this book does half as well as we hope it does.

And there's always the chance another murder might come my way.

Acknowledgments

For five years, I spent many hours a week with my dear friend, Catherine Brobeck, honing my appreciation for the mystery genre overall, and for Agatha Christie in particular. Together, we made the podcast *All About Agatha*, a creative endeavor that led directly to this book. Catherine passed away at the end of 2021, and I miss her very much. The podcast continues, but it will never be the same, and without her, this book would not exist. Thank you, Catherine, for your intelligence, your passion, and your friendship.

Thank you also to Agatha Christie herself, as strange as it feels to write that—not only for the endless pleasure her novels have brought me as a reader, but for the inspiration they provided me in the crafting of this mystery. The world is a more intersting place for Agatha Christie.

My agent Abby Saul is a source of light and joy. Thank you, Abby, for always having my back, and for doing it with such grace.

I am so grateful to have found a home for the Ghostwriter with John Scognamiglio, and the whole team at Kensington Books. They have made me—and her!—feel so supported and appreciated. I can't wait to do it all over again.

Thank you to my friends, but in particular to the mystery-loving friends Catherine and I made along the way: Mark Aldridge, Jamie Bernthal-Hooker, Caroline Crampton, John Curran, Brad Friedman, John Goddard, Tina Hodgkinson, Michelle Kazmer, Tony Medawar, and Carla Valentine, among others. Thanks also to the *All About Agatha* listeners, especially those who reached out to me in the wake of Catherine's passing. Your correspondence is a delight—even when you're correcting my pronunciation of British proper nouns. (Long live Bovril. And hundreds and thousands, of coursee.)

Like Dame Agatha, the mystery authors Sophie Hannah and Alex Michaelides have helped me in a writerly way, by the example of their fabulous output. But they have also been good friends and confidantes. I'm so lucky to know them.

Catherine's mother, Linda Brobeck, shouldered co-hosting duties with me for the hardest podcast episode I ever produced. Together with Catherine's father Barry and her sister Elizabeth, Linda opened up her home on a beautiful June day in Minnesota to allow the many people Catherine touched to celebrate her. Thank you to the entire Brobeck family for providing this space, and to Linda for lending her artist's eye to the proceedings. It was an unforgettable experience.

Deborah Netburn is one of my very oldest friends, with whom I tread on ancient ground. She is also an ace reporter who wrote a beautiful article about the podcast I'll cherish forever. I feel so proud to have known her as long as I have.

Thank you to all my family: Donovans, Rousseaus, Blakers, Milches, Divolls, and in particular to my parents, Maureen and Daniel Donovan, who fostered my love of literature from the very beginning.

To my two daughters, Angelica and Maeve: what is there really to say? Thank you for existing, I suppose. Maeve is just learning to speak, but Angelica already enjoys a good mystery, and I look forward to reading many, many more stories with both of them. Sometimes I can't believe how fortunate I am to be their father.

And finally, to my husband, Adam Milch, who is my first reader, and my first everything. To say I love you feels like an understatement, and yet, it will have to do. I love you.